THE BLEEDING SEASON

GREG F. GIFUNE

JournalStone books may be ordered through booksellers or by contacting:
JournalStone
www.journalstone.com

ISBN: 978-1-947654-25-9 (sc)
ISBN: 978-1-947654-26-6 (ebook)

JournalStone rev. date: April 6, 2018
3rd Edition
Originally published by Delirium Books 2003
2nd Edition published by DarkFuse 2012

Library of Congress Control Number: 2018938508

Printed in the United States of America

Cover Design: Chuck Killorin
Interior Layout: Jess Landry

Proofread by Sean Leonard

This one's for everyone on the old crew, dead or alive. Here's to the memories, good and bad. And for Jimmy B., gone but never forgotten. See you on the other side. And finally, as always, for my wife Carol, with love.

ACKNOWLEDGMENTS

Thanks to Shane Staley, who first published *The Bleeding Season* back in 2003 through Delirium Books. He not only took a chance on a relatively new and not-yet-proven writer, he got behind this novel and helped make it the success both critically and commercially that it's been since its publication. *The Bleeding Season* put me on the map as a professional, has since been translated into other languages, hailed as a classic in the genre by many, made the rounds in Hollywood (twice, with the unfortunate conclusion by many that it was too difficult to adapt), and now enjoys something of a cult following wherever it's been published. None of that would've happened or even been possible without Shane Staley's belief, support, dedication, and expertise. Thank you, my friend, for everything.

Also, a big thank you to Chris Payne, Jess Landry, and everyone at JournalStone for giving *The Bleeding Season* new life and bringing out this special anniversary edition. I'm thrilled to see *The Bleeding Season* find a new home at JournalStone, and could not be more pleased to join your roster of authors.

Thank you also to my friends and colleagues Ron Malfi and Eric Shapiro for taking time from their busy schedules to pen a new introduction and afterword for this edition, and special thanks to Ron for setting the stage for this edition to happen in the first place.

And finally, thank you to my readers and fans all over the world for your continued support and enthusiasm.

AN INTRODUCTION
Ronald Malfi

My introduction to the work of Greg F. Gifune came around 2006 or so. He was one of two authors who'd recently signed to a brand-new independent (and ultimately doomed) "literary horror" book publisher whose name, in a show of goodwill, I shall keep out of this introduction. Greg's book, *A View from the Lake*, was the first (and only) novel published by this confused and schizophrenic little outfit, and despite the book's brilliance, the publisher still managed to bungle the release and drop the proverbial ball. Somehow, however, I managed to get a personalized copy of the book before the publisher shut its doors and the book went out of print. The other author who'd signed with this particular publisher was given his rights back, thus sparing him what could have been an even bigger headache in the long run. (That other author was, of course, me; the novel in question became my fourth published book, *Via Dolorosa*.)

Publishing woes aside, I tore through *A View from the Lake* and knew instantly upon closing the book that I had spent the better part of two afternoons in the presence of a true master. I suppose there was a fair amount of internet praise about Gifune back in 2006, but I was about as computer savvy as an ostrich back then (and am only slightly more so now). My exposure to the small presses was limited to the Xeroxed mailers I received on occasion from Delirium Books, advertising Ed Lee's *The Bighead* and titles of a similar ilk—mystifying and subversive tomes with grotesque yet beautiful artwork on the covers, accompanied by a quick, titillating elevator-pitch of a synopsis.

Hungry for more, I grabbed a copy of *Deep Night* from the public library. This was the Delirium Books trade paperback edition, over 500 pages, and I remember devouring that novel in a span of two or three days while seated in a wingback chair, framed in a panel of sunlight before a wall of windows that looked out onto the front yard. This was the first time I was confronted with the themes that I would come to associate with much of Greg's fiction—namely, the virtues and vices of male friendship, and, more inclusive, the darkness, like a rancid odor, that is borne on a wave of human despair.

There are some books that you enjoy so much, you cannot wait until the day winds down so you can crawl into bed, crack open that spine, and pick up where you left off. Sometimes you even think about that book during the day—you wonder what the characters are doing, wonder about what that night's reading will bring you, wonder just where the story is heading. Those are good books. With great books, you simply cannot wait for your regularly scheduled reading appointment, and instead make every possible attempt at working in a page here while waiting for the laundry to be done, a chapter here while getting the oil changed in the Toyota, a few pages here while standing in line at 7-Eleven with a carton of eggs under your arm.

That was how it was with me and *The Bleeding Season*. I read that book during one summer when I was trying to shed a few extra pounds. I'd enrolled in a local gym and worked my way over every bit of equipment in a cursory, assembly-line fashion, as if the more equipment I touched, the quicker those extra pounds would drop from my bones, regardless of how much time I actually spent using that equipment. (Admittedly, I have a very bipolar approach to diet and exercise: I'll either starve myself and run ten miles a day, or remain motionless on the couch while putting away a whole pepperoni pizza and a six-pack of Flying Dog. There is no middle ground.)

Much of *The Bleeding Season* was read in that gym, while humping along on a stationary bicycle. I became engrossed in the tale of three friends working through their grief and guilt at their friend's suicide in what I pictured to be a wintery New England fishing village. And when the three friends gathered together to hear the taped recording left behind by their deceased pal—a recording that is less a suicide note and more like a confession—the tension went up—I was hooked. I also forgot about the clock, and wound up pushing myself harder on that bike than I happened to realize at the time. (In a sense, Greg Gifune is, to this day, responsible for my athletic stature and six-pack abs, a photograph of which I made available to this publisher but who will no doubt refrain from including it herein, for fear it would overshadow Gifune's own smudgy, overused author photo. C'est la vie.)

I have an affinity for character-based horror stories that take place in quaint, suburban locales—a trope no doubt made popular by Stephen King with the publication of *Carrie* (1974) and *'Salem's Lot* (1975), and by the early films of Steven Spielberg. For me, this brings the horror home; it's something relatable and recognizable. In *The Bleeding Season*, the town of Potter's Cove is as eerily familiar as your own hometown.

Ostensibly, this is the story—on the outside, at least—of a group of friends who come to learn that their now-deceased friend was responsible for a series of heinous murders. Alan Chance is our narrator, and the most relatable of the crew; his grief over his friend's death is palpable, his marital woes strike a chord, and the increasingly stressful relationships with his childhood chums feels like a page from our own personal biographies. On top of all that, the poor bastard gets fired from his shitty job early in the novel. Desperate and—once his wife splits—all alone, he becomes the perfect vehicle for weeding out the truth of who their serial-killer buddy Bernard really was. And he learns the truth about himself and his friends in the process.

It's an interesting take on the serial killer subgenre (and I'm not even mentioning the demonic aspect of the murders at this point): where a town is held hostage by fear when the bodies of mutilated women begin to crop up, yet only Alan, Donald, and Rick realize that the killer—Bernard—is already dead. The fear isn't an external one, isn't what the citizens of Potter's Cove presume it to be; rather, it's internalized within Alan and his remaining friends, who find that coming to terms with who and what Bernard was might just bring about their own salvation. Or destruction.

It's a bold move—a thriller involving a series of murders that focuses instead on the spiritual war suddenly waged among the friends the murderer left behind. As explained in Bernard's recorded statement to his pals: "Be sober, be vigilant; because your adversary the devil, as a roaring lion, walketh about, seeking whom he may devour."

Alan's investigation takes him to some of the seedier places in and around town, including a warf-side bar populated by drug-fueled meatheads, and the home of an unabashed prostitute who helps Alan unlock some of those darker doors (a character who is complicit, ironically, in one of the more tender scenes in the novel...as well as one of the more horrifying). It gradually becomes clear that there was a method to Bernard's madness—that the killings of single mothers are an echo of the death of Bernard's own husbandless mother from his youth. But even that doesn't begin to scratch the surface of Bernard's perceived psychosis. Because, really, it isn't psychosis at all. It's something...darker.

Ah, but to delve any further would be to ruin the surprise. Were this an outroduction, I suppose we could talk about anything you'd like, spoilers be damned. But since this will most likely precede the novel itself, well, who am I to ruin a good story?

I will make one mention about the very end of the book, however, because it has prompted some discussion and, in a few cases, some consternation among Greg's readership. The conclusion can be interpreted in two distinctly different ways—either as a metaphor or in the literal sense. In preparation for writing this introduction, I re-read the book and discovered a depth—and a beauty—to the ending that I believe I missed when I originally read it back in 2006. Knowing Greg as well as I do now, and having read the majority of his published work, I am confident in saying that no onc takcaway is corrcct, and that, in a vcry Cifuncsquc fashion, the story is left to be interpreted by whatever it is the reader—you—brings to the reading of it. As is the case, I believe, with most good books.

I won't lie, kids. This is one dark story.

You're gonna love it.

—Ronald Malfi
March 23, 2018
Annapolis, Maryland

THE BLEEDING SEASON

"You tell yourself it is a bad dream. You tell yourself you have died—you, not the others—and have waked up in hell. But you know better. You know better. There is an end to dreams, and there is no end to this. And when people die they are dead—as who should know better than you?"

—Jim Thompson
The Getaway

WINTER

CHAPTER 1

I didn't know it then, but it was impossible to survive the darkest corners of his mind without first surviving the darkest corners of my own. I was headed for the same depths of Hell he had descended to, and though we passed through those flames for different reasons, our journeys are forever entwined. His story cannot be told without also telling mine, and maybe that's the way it should be. After all, Goodness is a state of grace.

Evil, is a state of mind.

***

There was a sudden intrusion to the darkness. A brief orange glimmer and the quiet hiss of a lit match faded quickly, leaving behind the scent of sulfur and a single burning ember like a dot on an otherwise murky horizon. I looked back at the silhouette on the bed, the cigarette dangling from her lips, fingers of smoke circling, caressing, and wondered if perhaps this time there was good reason to fear the dark.

Tired and still disoriented, I turned from her and attempted to focus the whirlwind of thoughts blurring my mind…I guess I thought we'd be friends forever. Even then, it still seemed that way, like we were all joined at the cosmic hip, like somehow our lives existed as extensions or offshoots of one another. Whether we wanted them to or not.

Originally there had been five of us. Tommy was killed early on in high school. We'd hopped off the bus, not paying any attention as we walked into the road. The woman who hit Tommy later claimed she hadn't seen the flashing lights and the stop sign on the side of the bus. One minute we were talking and laughing, the next there was a dull thud so unnatural that it didn't register until I saw Tommy fly into the air, suspended in space while the car rushed past, so close I thought for a split-second it had struck me too. And then I staggered back as the body twisted and turned like some gymnast in the throes of demonic possession, the car screeching to a halt in time for Tommy to land against the hood. The braking motion launched him back into midair, a human cannonball soaring soundlessly above the ground, finally cart-wheeling across asphalt, his head striking, neck bending at an impossible angle, body tumbling and flopping about as if boneless, set to the chorus of flesh slapping pavement.

Life support kept his body alive for two days following the incident, but I knew Tommy was dead the moment he came to rest along the side of the road. Those quiet eyes staring blankly at a curiously beautiful sky, a trickle of blood seeping free from somewhere above his blond hairline, the deep crimson just one more contrast painting a face even then frozen in a knowing smirk.

Tommy died the same way he'd lived, like nothing was worth taking too seriously, like maybe you had all the time in the world, or maybe, just around the corner, your time was up. Like in the end none of it really mattered anyway. Ironically, there had always been something undeniably spiritual about him, like he'd been told something the rest of us hadn't, and had then been sworn to secrecy.

Years later, even though life moved forward, as it always does, those visions—pictures of his face that day, of a casket draped in white carried to and placed before an altar of polished wood and sparkling gold—never left me.

I never mentioned to anyone that within days of Tommy's death I began to feel his presence all around me. Maybe it was survivor guilt; maybe it was Tommy saying goodbye the only way he could. Maybe it was all in my head. Regardless, Tommy's death served as a milestone in our lives. We went our separate ways for a while, like most people do once high school ends and real life begins.

Bernard joined the Marines, Donald went to college, Rick wound up in prison, and I married my high school sweetheart. But within a year Bernard was home from the Marines, having badly injured his knee in an ill-timed drop from a training platform, and had a job selling cars. Rick had served his time on an assault and battery conviction; Donald had dropped out of college, and I was still working the same low-paying security guard job I'd held since not long after graduation. What had been a bunch of inseparable high school kids had become a group of young men struggling with the past, the present, and whatever the future had planned. Through good, bad, and the often-indifferent detachment tedium breeds, we remained close.

When I married Toni, Donald was my best man and Bernard and Rick served as ushers. That was the closest the three of them ever got to another wedding. Although Rick lived with one of his girlfriends for a few years, he found it impossible to remain faithful, and the relationship eventually dissolved. The others remained bachelors. Marriage wasn't in the cards for Donald, and Bernard had never had much success with the opposite sex. He'd always been aloof when it came to his social life beyond our group, and although he often spoke of conquests we never actually saw any of them, and tended to write his stories off as just that. He lived at home with his mother until her death, and the bank had foreclosed on the property not long after. Bernard became detached and horribly depressed. He moved into the cellar apartment of his cousin's house in New Bedford, about half an hour away, and due to the distance and Bernard's increasingly dejected behavior, we began to see less and less of him.

Back in high school we had all purchased identical silver satin jackets and dubbed ourselves The Sultans, the only gang in Potter's Cove, Massachusetts, an otherwise quiet and unassuming working-class town nestled along the coast south of Boston. It was a joke, really, but it signified that we were one. Friends for life, always there for each other, the same blood brothers we'd become years before as kids, huddled in a tree house in Tommy's backyard, nicking our thumbs and sharing blood like in the B-Westerns.

Nineteen years out of high school I found myself standing in our bedroom holding that old Sultans jacket and wondering how we'd all managed to go so wrong.

Frustrated…marking time…

And now, we were only three.

I slipped the jacket back onto its plastic hangar, slid the closet door shut and moved to the window. My hands were trembling.

I never heard her get out of bed, only felt the sudden warmth of her as she embraced me from behind. Her voice filtered through those whispering in my head; distracted me from memories and the beginnings of a sunrise.

"Why did he do it?" I heard myself ask. "Why didn't he come to one of us?"

I replayed the moment the phone rang, jarring us from sleep, my startled and angry middle-of-the-night "Hello!" answered by Donald's voice—cracked, uncertain, vodka-slurred and void of the confidence that often bordered on arrogance in his tone. *Alan, I'm—Christ, I'm sorry to wake you, but—Alan, something terrible has happened.*

No longer worried she might see the tears in my eyes I looked at her and realized she was trying to comfort me, trying to be there for me, doing her best.

Her brown, doe-like eyes blinked, cleared. "You going to be okay?"

I touched her shoulder, so delicate beneath a plaid flannel nightshirt. Reminded of the nightmare Donald's phone call had interrupted—one horror replaced with another—I drew a deep breath and tried to sort my thoughts. Bernard was dead and the world hadn't even noticed. *We* hadn't even noticed. "I have to meet Donald and Rick in an hour."

She padded silently to the bed, plucked her cigarette from an ashtray on the nightstand and took a final drag before slipping her feet into a pair of slippers shaped like floppy-eared bunny rabbits.

I wanted to turn back to the window. I wanted to watch the sun come up, to wander into the living room, to slip the stereo headphones on and listen to The Mamas & The Papas sing about California and dreams and dancing in the streets while a thick and sloppy rain bled from gray skies. I wanted to forget the whole goddamn thing.

"You were having a nightmare," Toni said suddenly, as if she'd just remembered. "I was about to wake you when the phone rang."

I clenched shut my eyes. In those few short and blurred seconds before I'd escaped sleep and answered the phone, I'd already known Bernard was dead.

"He's been dead for five days." I focused on the slush sluicing along the window, rain becoming snow, night becoming day. "He didn't even leave a note."

"Come on," she said, gently taking my hand, "I'll make some coffee."

On our way down the hallway, Toni promised everything would be all right.

She lied.

CHAPTER 2

We stood near the tracks talking, the whistle from an approaching train blaring in the distance as an icy wind blew through the tall grass surrounding us. The snow had again become a light though slushy rain.

Nothing seemed real.

Donald flashed an annoyed look through bloodshot eyes. "Is there some point to being out here?"

"Privacy." Rick gazed through the grass, across the parking lot separating us from the diner, then considered his watch. "Besides, they don't open for a couple minutes anyway."

Fumbling through the pockets of his raincoat for cigarettes and a lighter, Donald rolled his eyes and sighed, his breath already converted to smoky plumes wafting about and tangling with ours like warring apparitions. "For Christ's sake, it's freezing out here."

"Don't be such a pussy, Donny." Rick puffed his chest up like a rooster and folded his arms across it. "So what did his cousin say, exactly?"

I stuffed my hands into the pockets of my leather jacket, shuffled my feet, and exchanged glances with Rick, who seemed unaffected by the weather. Our individuality was more evident at that moment somehow, and I found myself wondering how we had managed to stay so close despite our glaring differences.

Pieces of the whole, Tommy had said back in high school. Our original leader, long dead now, at some point replaced by Rick, the ultimate Alpha Male, always so happy to remind the rest of us how inadequate we were, how we were half the men we'd once been, yet always there to save us, to defend us if need be.

Donald struggled to light the cigarette against a mounting breeze. His eyes, saddled with heavy black bags, seemed more sunken than usual; his complexion more pallid, his frame thinner, bordering on emaciated. "I called him about ten o'clock." He finally got the cigarette going. "I'd had a few drinks and I didn't realize it was quite so late. I think I woke his cousin up, he sounded groggy when he answered. Bernard had called me a few times, left messages on my machine, but I hadn't had the chance to get back to him and I wanted to see how he was."

The train interrupted him, rushing past, its whistle deafening. We turned and watched the seemingly endless procession of boxcars until they had snaked off around a bend in the tracks. "Trash train," Rick announced, as if this common knowledge was something only he possessed.

Donald's wiry frame swayed with the wind as he smoothed his thinning hair with long, narrow fingers. "When I asked for Bernard," he continued, "his cousin didn't answer, and I thought for a moment maybe the line had gone dead. But then I could hear him breathing and I knew—I *knew* something was wrong. He finally said he was sorry and that Bernard had passed away. Those were the words he used, *passed away*."

"I still can't believe it." Rick shook his head, drawing attention to the blue bandana covering it and the small gold cross dangling from his ear. With his swarthy good looks and athletic, muscular build, he looked younger and better than Donald and I did, and he knew it. He'd stayed in shape playing various sports and lifting weights, still had all his hair, didn't smoke and rarely drank. Vanity, competition, sex with young women—those were Rick's vices, and his job as a bouncer at a local club gave him the opportunity to pursue all three.

"I asked what happened," Donald said flatly, smoking his cigarette with mechanical repetition. "He said he found Bernard Tuesday afternoon."

"Jesus," Rick sighed. "He was dead since then and we didn't even know."

Donald looked away. "When he didn't offer anything more, I asked again what had happened. That's when he said Bernard had hanged himself." I ignored the vision of a limp body suspended from rafters as it flashed across my mind's eye. I considered mentioning the nightmare I'd had, but decided against it. "It's state law that an autopsy be performed in all cases of unattended death," Donald explained. "Of course, Bernard's death was ruled a suicide, but apparently his cousin didn't have the funds to provide for funeral arrangements and Bernard was broke, so—"

"Why didn't this asshole call one of us?" Rick snapped. "Did you ask him that?"

Donald dropped his cigarette, crushed it beneath the sole of his shoe then hugged himself and shook his head in the negative. "I was in shock, I—I just wanted to get off the phone. I didn't want to hear anymore."

"So where is he?" I asked.

"The state covered the cost of his burial. Absolute minimum, I'm sure. His cousin said they have a section of one of the public cemeteries in the city for this kind of thing, and that's where Bernard was buried. He doesn't even have a headstone."

Rick put hands on hips and assumed an unintentional hero-like pose that would have been comical under different circumstances. "We'll take care of that down the road. I know a guy. Now, what about his things?"

"I don't imagine Bernard had much left." Donald motioned with his chin to the diner. The lights had come on. "Let's get out of the rain."

Normally the diner was hopping first thing in the morning, but since most of the clientele didn't work weekends, Saturdays got off to a slower start. But for two elderly and grizzled regulars already slumped on stools at the counter, swapping stories and sipping coffee, we were alone.

Donald and I slipped into a booth near the back while Rick grabbed a toothpick from a cup on the counter, rolled it into the corner of his mouth and chatted briefly with the waitress. He ambled down the aisle separating the rows of booths and joined us a moment later. "Ordered some coffees," he said, dropping across from me, next to Donald. "I worked last night, haven't been to bed yet, but I'm too wired to sleep now anyway. I say we take a ride to

New Bedford and have a talk with Bernard's cousin."

"Look, we don't know this guy at all," I said. "He might not want us around."

"Who gives a shit what he wants?"

Donald scrambled for his cigarettes. "What's the point?"

"I want to know what happened."

"For Christ's sake, I just told you what happened."

The waitress interrupted just in time, placed steaming mugs of coffee in front of us and asked if we planned to order breakfast. Through a forced smile I told her the coffee would be sufficient. Once she was out of earshot Rick leaned forward and zeroed in on me, forearms on the table between us. "What do you think?"

I warmed my hands on the side of the mug and gazed at the rain. "Bernard's gone, man. Doesn't make a damn bit of difference what we do."

Rick flopped back against the bench. "Fine, you guys do whatever you want. I'm going over there."

"Why?" Donald asked. "For what purpose, exactly?"

"One," Rick snapped, "I want to know where they buried him. Two, I want to know if he has any stuff left. Might be nice to have something of his, right? Like, remember when Tommy died and his mother sent us stuff?"

I did remember. Specifically, an illustration Tommy had made in elementary school his mother had given me not long after his death. I still had it tucked neatly away in my desk at home, and though I hadn't looked at it in years, the knowledge that it was there—some palpable piece of him, his history—was somehow comforting. I glanced at Donald, who was twisting a napkin in his hands as if it had done something to offend him. "We *do* need to know where he's buried."

"I don't even know where the house is," Donald said.

Rick threw back some coffee. "I do. We went out for lunch a couple weeks ago. I picked him up out in front."

"Was that the last time you saw him?" I asked. Rick gave a nod and looked away. An uncomfortable silence fell for what seemed an eternity, amplifying the sound of the rain. Flashes of the nightmare slithered through me, summoning a chill that began at the nape of my neck. "I hadn't seen him in about a month," I finally said.

"Me either." Donald threw the napkin aside. "I should've called him back sooner, I—"

"Don't do that to yourself, man." Rick cracked his knuckles with a loud pop, a nervous habit he'd possessed since childhood. "This ain't our fault. Bernard had some hard times—just like the rest of us—and he made a decision. That's it."

I sipped my coffee. "Why would he do it? Jesus, why would he—"

"Fucking cowardly if you ask me."

Donald glared at him. "No one asked."

"He didn't even have the balls to leave a note."

Donald crushed his cigarette in a small glass ashtray and slid it away with disgust. "Sometimes you are *such* an asshole. Do you think maybe we could mourn for a while before you start passing your usual lofty judgments? Don't we owe him that much?"

"We were his friends. We're like brothers. He should've come to us if it got that bad. He should've—"

"Did he call you in the two weeks since you saw him last? Did he? He called me. I know he called Alan, did he call you too, Rick? Did he?"

"I never called him back either," I admitted. "I kept meaning to but..."

Rick took a gulp of coffee and returned the mug to the table with a violent slam. "Fuck this. Things got tough and Bernard checked out. He took the easy way out, man, that's all I'm saying."

"The easy way," Donald said through a mock chuckle. "*Is* there such a thing?"

I reached across the table, grabbed Donald's pack of cigarettes and shook one free. I'd quit a few months prior, but now, recognizing a stressful and sorrowful time, the addiction was beckoning, calling to me once again. I rolled the cigarette between my fingers. "If we're going to do this let's get it the hell over with."

"You don't need that." Rick reached across the table, snatched the cigarette and crushed it in his hand. "Took you months to quit, why blow it now?"

Donald's jaw dropped. "Yeah, crush the whole pack, it's not like I have to pay for them or anything."

"Like I give a shit. Those things are killing us." Rick opened his hand, emptied the torn paper and loose tobacco onto the table then scrambled out of the booth. "Come on." He dug a wad of bills from his pocket, peeled off a few singles and tossed them over the mess he'd made. "We'll take my Jeep."

***

Rain drummed the roof, struggled with the squealing cadence of windshield wipers for attention.

The interior of Rick's Jeep Cherokee was neurotically immaculate, and since he didn't allow smoking, Donald, who was already fidgeting about in back, leaned forward and poked his head between the bucket seats. "What the hell is he doing in there?"

I squinted through the blurred window. "Looks like he's talking with the attendant."

"Christ, pay for the gas and get on with it." Donald sat back and crossed his legs, jeans squeaking against leather. "Sometimes, Alan, I could strangle the bastard."

"It's just Rick's way. You know he doesn't mean anything by it."

"Well I'm getting tired of Rick's way. God forbid he shows any emotion other than happiness or anger. Wouldn't be sufficiently butch, apparently."

I adjusted my position so I could look into the back. "That's Rick, always has been, always will be. He's as torn up over this as we are, he'll just never show it."

"Just like when Tommy died. The sonofabitch never shed a tear," Donald said in an almost absent tone. "It doesn't surprise me two of us ended up dead before we hit forty, only which two. I never thought I'd outlive any of you. Makes you wonder if life isn't arbitrary after all."

"Maybe you're just indestructible, you miserable prick."

Our eyes met, and somewhere behind the bloodshot roadmaps and dark circles I caught a glimpse of the past in Donald's expression, one of impish humor and biting exuberance, his trademark in years past, before the booze, before the darkness.

It seemed an inappropriate time for laughter, but we laughed anyway.

It faded quickly, absorbed by the din of a relentless rain.

***

The grating voice of a local sportscaster droned from the car stereo. The Bruins were struggling for a playoff spot and had lost the night before. Normally I would have been interested, but I focused instead on the hiss of tires against wet pavement and the fast-approaching cityscape of New Bedford.

"Fucking Bruins," Rick moaned. "You ask me, they need to goon it up, drop the gloves and throw some fists. All these fucking do-gooders are ruining the game."

I turned from the window long enough to glance at him and offer a quick nod, hopeful he would take my cue and be quiet before Donald let loose on him.

"It's even changed at the high school level," Rick said. "Shit, when we played we got the job done—and we played like fucking men. Remember the game against—"

"If I give you a dollar," Donald said from the back, "will you stop talking?"

Rick grinned. "You're just jealous because you never played."

"Yes, positively green with envy."

"Sure, make jokes, you know it's true."

"Can we talk about something else?" I said quickly.

Donald scoffed. "How about nothing at all?"

Rick tightened his grip on the wheel and decreased speed as we left the highway and veered along the Downtown New Bedford exit. "Same thing with football," he said. "I was one of the best players our school ever had, but you always made it out like it was no big deal. Guys like you always do, because you got no talent for it."

"Guys like me. Interesting."

"You know what I mean, don't go getting all politically correct on me."

Donald poked his head between the seats. "I'm glad you found such satisfaction in playing your games, Rick, really I am. But you're pushing forty, maybe it's time to focus on something a tad more adult."

"You're just bitter. All that fancy bullshit—books and classical music and all that poof-poof crap—none of it mattered in the long run. You can recite a poem some guy wrote a hundred fucking years ago, and you know all about plays and paintings and all that crap. So what? You ended up ditching college and living in Potter's Cove working a regular job just like the rest of us. At least I got—"

"Both of you just shut the fuck up, all right?"

Donald disappeared into the back and Rick looked at me with genuine surprise. I turned away but heard him mutter something unintelligible, and from the corner of my eye saw him shake his head.

We headed into the south end of the city, one of the rougher areas of New Bedford. Even in such weather, the streets seemed unusually empty, the city unnaturally quiet, as if in anticipation of our arrival.

"Nice neighborhood," I mumbled.

"Fucking shit-bin."

"As Melville said, '*Such dreary streets*,'" Donald offered quietly. "Such a historically significant city, such decent, diverse, hard-working people, yet still so dreary in some parts. I wonder what Herman would think of her now."

"Drugs, that's the goddamn problem," Rick said, turning onto a side street. "Drugs are ruining this country, and let me tell you—"

"Is there anything you *don't* have an opinion on?" Donald asked. "The city's been on the rise for quite some time now."

"I got your *rise* right here, swinging." The Jeep slowed and Rick pulled over into the only vacant space, a spot near the top of the block. The narrow street consisted of two-story tenements with tiny fenced-in yards and side driveways. Most were dilapidated and in various stages of disrepair, and even bathed in steady rain, strewn garbage and assorted filth defiantly clogged gutters and stained sidewalks. It seemed darker here; as if night had not yet fully released the city like it had the outskirts and beyond, as if the dreary streets Melville had written about in *Moby Dick* could still be conjured more than 150 years later. Rick pointed over my shoulder. "That's it."

The building stood on the corner, the front yard cordoned off by a rusted chain-link fence, the tiny section of grass beyond unkempt, cluttered with toys and other debris. I felt my stomach clench as I noticed a small window along the base of the tenement. Somewhere on the other side of that grimy pane of glass one of my best friends had lived out the final days of his life and eventually killed himself. My eyes shifted to the windows on the first floor. One facing the street was filled with light.

How could anyone continue to live there after what Bernard had done?

I tried to picture him walking this block, moving through the rickety gate and going inside. I tried to picture him alive here, but all I could see, all I could sense, was death.

"Let's go."

Rick's gruff tone snapped me back, and I was out of the Jeep and standing in the rain before I'd even thought about it. Donald, looking nauseous and pale, stepped out just as Rick rounded the front of the vehicle and set the alarm with a push of a button on his key chain. We all stood there a moment, watching the building like children staring down the local haunted house.

The next street over emptied into an enormous vacant and weed-infested lot, beyond which loomed one of the more infamous housing projects the city had to offer. I vaguely remembered cruising that project nearly two decades before while still in high school, searching for a quick pot buy before heading off to a party in nearby Westport.

This seemed like another life entirely, and maybe it was.

"Okay," I heard Donald say through a lengthy sigh. "Let me do the talking."

With Donald in the lead we moved through the gate and huddled near the front door. I could sense the ocean nearby, its smells and sounds and physical presence always evident, watching and whispering reminders that it was still the pulse of the city, and like an audacious child, it would not be ignored. Despite having lived my entire life within walking distance of the Atlantic Ocean, I was reminded how oddly uncomfortable it made me. Like the living thing it is, the sea, had always seemed ominous and threatening to me, a malevolent sentry eager to swallow me whole if only given the chance. The idea of drowning, of dying at sea was terrifying, and unlike most residents of southeastern Massachusetts, I was not an avid swimmer, only set foot on a boat if I absolutely had to, and wouldn't eat seafood with a gun to my head. The ocean had always been something I found fascinating but beautiful only in a fatalistic sense—much the way a tornado or a particularly violent storm could be beautiful—that by its very nature and power its magnificence was inherent. But it was also something I wanted to experience only from a comfortable and presumably safe distance. Living here meant that the ocean was always with you—always close—and even when you couldn't see or hear or smell it, you could *feel* it.

Why I was so focused on the ocean at that point I don't know, but death was on my mind, sharing space with the first sensations of fear. Beyond the door, somewhere in the bowels of this slowly decaying building, Bernard had died—*had been dead*—and no matter what was or wasn't said or done, we were too late.

Donald rapped on the door and the sound brought me back around. When no one answered, Rick gave it a try and seconds later we heard locks disengaging. I drew a deep breath and let it out slowly as the door swung partially open to reveal a tired-looking, slightly overweight woman. Her dark eyes narrowed a bit at the sight of us. From deep within the apartment behind her I heard a child's voice interspersed with sounds of a television. She stared at us questioningly.

"Hi there." Donald forced a smile. "Is Sammy in, by any chance?"

The woman nodded, held up a finger then closed the door.

"The bitch even speak English?" Rick mumbled.

Before Donald could argue with him or I could tell them both to knock it off the door opened a second time, this time fully, and a large man in a tank top and a pair of Dickeys stood before us. With thick and well-muscled arms covered in tattoos, a shock of dark bushy hair and more than a day's growth of beard, he was imposing and seemed anything but pleased with our presence on his steps. "Yeah?"

"I'm sorry to bother—"

"What do you want? I know you?"

From his expression I knew Rick felt challenged and planned to respond. He opened his mouth but Donald spoke before he had the chance. "I'm Donald LaCroix, I spoke with you late last night on the phone."

The man relaxed a bit. "Oh, you Bernard's friend?"

"Yes, we spoke last night."

"Right, right, okay."

Donald motioned to Rick and me. "Rick Brisco and Alan Chance."

He gave a quick nod, a genuine smile, and shook our hands in turn. "Bernard talked about you guys all the time, come on in out of the rain. Sorry, we don't get a whole lot of people coming to the door this time of morning, especially on a Saturday. Never know today, right?"

As he stepped back and let us pass, we all moved into a cramped and dim foyer. An adjacent hallway emptied into a well-lit kitchen near the rear of the building. To our immediate right was a modestly furnished den where two young girls sat in front of a console television eating cereal, and to the left was a closed door I knew without being told led to the basement.

Sammy closed the door, turned the deadbolt. "So what can I do for you guys?"

"I apologize for hanging up so abruptly last night," Donald said, "I was just—well—at any rate, we thought we'd stop by and see if there was anything we could do."

"Appreciate that," he said. "I wanted to call one of you guys but I didn't know your numbers or nothing, so I figured you'd get ahold of me eventually. There really ain't nothing left to be done." He looked into the den. His wife had joined the girls there, and all three seemed preoccupied with the TV. "Like I told you last night," he continued, "they buried him across town in one of the plots the state puts aside for people who can't pay. He ain't got no stone or nothing, but if you go to the office the cemetery workers can show you where he's at. I feel bad about it and all, I mean I wish I could've done more but you guys know how it is. I work two jobs, my old lady works; we got two kids, rent, the car. Money only goes so far every month and funerals are expensive."

"No," Donald said, "please don't think you have to explain any of this to us, we understand completely. I'm only sorry we couldn't have helped."

Sammy folded his arms and leaned against the wall. "To be honest, I figured the military would take care of everything. If a guy's a veteran and dies broke they cover the funeral and burial costs—all of it."

"Bernard was in the Marines for a year before he got hurt," I said.

"That was bullshit."

We all stood there silently, waiting for the other shoe to drop.

"Bernard lied," he finally said. "They got no record of him. He was never a Marine."

"How could that be?" I looked to the others for some sort of confirmation. "He joined up right after we graduated from high school."

"That's what he told you guys but it never really happened."

"So how'd he hurt his knee?" Rick asked. "He said he lost his balance on a training platform, wrecked his knee and that's why he got the early discharge."

"He went somewhere for a year," I said.

"Well it wasn't the Marines." Sammy shrugged. "It's nuts, I know. I was confused when they told me too. I mean, Bernard always claimed he'd been a Marine, and hey, I don't mean to disrespect the dead or nothing, but it just wasn't true—that simple. To be honest, we weren't all that close. You guys probably knew him a hell of a lot better than we did. Our family is so small, there ain't many of us left, and I felt bad for Bernard because he didn't really have anybody, no wife or girlfriend or nothing. It was kind of sad the way he always lived at home, you know? And when Aunt Linda died he was never the same. Bernard was a strange guy, kind of secretive, and lots of times I was never sure if he was telling the truth or not. He had problems, you guys know what I mean."

I suddenly wondered if we did.

"When he lost his job things got bad, and by the time the bank took the house he was a mess. Like I say, we weren't never that close, but he was family, and he was being put out on the street, what could I do? He asked if I'd put him up until he got back on his feet, so I let him move into the cellar." His eyes again shifted to the den before returning to us. "If I'd known what he was gonna do I never would've…I mean, what if one of my kids had found him, you know what I'm saying? Christ."

"Well," Donald said, "we just wanted to stop by to see if there was anything we could do."

"That's real nice of you guys, but it's over and done with and I just want to move on, you know?

The girls," he said softly, "they don't even know he died here. It's bad enough my old lady knows, still freaks her out. Me too, but what can you do?"

"Did Bernard leave anything behind?" Rick asked suddenly.

Sammy looked at him without bothering to mask his suspicion. "How do you mean? He didn't have no money if that's what you're asking. I already told you he was broke."

"Yeah, I heard you," Rick answered. "I didn't mean money, I was just wondering—"

"The only thing was his car, that old Buick he had, and a duffel bag he had his stuff in when he moved in. The car I sold to a guy at work. Didn't get much, it was a piece of shit, but it paid for the suit they buried him in anyway. The duffel bag I went through the day after he died but there wasn't no cash in it. Had all of two bucks in his wallet. I didn't charge him no rent or nothing, but we'd have him up for dinner when he was around, which wasn't that much. Still, he needed money for gas and shit, and toward the end he was totally broke. He hit me up a couple times, twenty here, ten there, but I ain't exactly a bank, right? I got bills." Sammy turned back to Donald, the pissing contest with Rick apparently over for the moment. "Why, you guys looking for something?"

"No," Donald said, "we just thought there might be some personal mementos he left behind. None of us have anything of Bernard's and sometimes it's nice to have—"

"I know what you mean." Sammy's eyes shifted between the three of us, lingered on Rick the longest then returned to Donald. "The duffel bag is still downstairs. I been meaning to run it over to the Salvation Army bin but I haven't had the chance. You guys can go through it if you want. Ain't nothing special, some clothes and stuff, that's about it, but if there's any of that shit you want—whatever—you know, you're welcome to it."

Even as he moved to the door I knew he didn't plan to simply go into the basement and retrieve the bag. Something in his eyes, in the way he sauntered to the door and hesitated, the knob in his hand, told me we'd be accompanying him into the cellar.

"Come on," he said, "it's down here."

The door opened and I forced a swallow. Donald glanced at me; he was on the verge of a major panic. I looked to Rick. He offered a quick wink and moved to the front of the line, but I could see through his cavalier routine, he was just as uncomfortable—if not more so—than Donald and I were. Yet like he so often did, Rick led the way, stepping through the doorway, old stairs creaking beneath his weight as he disappeared into darkness.

***

A musty odor filled my nostrils before I'd reached the bottom. Sammy flipped a switch from somewhere behind me, and the small section of basement Bernard had converted to a living area appeared. There was no fixture, only a single but powerful light bulb at the end of a thick wire dangling directly from the ceiling. Once we reached the bottom of the stairs I realized that the cellar had been divided into two separate areas. Directly in front of us another door stood closed, concealing what was undoubtedly the larger of the two areas.

Sammy was the last one down the stairs, but hesitated at the foot, bent forward and pointed to an old cot against the far cinderblock wall. "Bernard stayed there," he said, his voice distorted and unfamiliar as it bounced along the tomb-like cement cell. "We use the rest of the basement for storage."

At the head of the cot was a makeshift nightstand fashioned from a cranberry crate turned on end. The blankets he must have used were folded neatly at the foot, and as my eyes panned across the tiny cellar, I ignored the beams overhead and instead focused on the lone small window I had seen outside. The idea of living in these cramped and dingy quarters for any amount of time was nearly beyond belief, but nothing indicating the remnants of life resided there. It looked and felt and smelled like death, like a dungeon of sorts, a chamber where one might be sent to wither away and die, and that's exactly what Bernard had done. Yet I had no specific sense of him there, no trace of his or anyone else's presence, as if he'd never really been there at all, or perhaps it was this place itself that was void of even the echo of anything alive or vibrant.

Sammy pointed to a canvas bag propped against the wall next to the stairs. "That's his duffel there." He leaned further into the room without leaving the staircase and leveled a finger at a particular rafter perhaps a yard from where I was standing. "I found him right there."

Rick crossed the room in two strides and grabbed the duffel. Donald and I stayed where we were; it felt good to have a little elbow room. We'd been cramped from the moment we'd entered the house, and the claustrophobic feel had only worsened upon descending into the basement.

"He'd already been dead a while when I found him," Sammy added.

"You sure you want to go through that here?" I asked Rick.

"It's okay, I'll be upstairs. Come on up when you're done. Just make sure you shut the light off and lock the door behind you."

He left us, and I wished I could've joined him. There was something final about the way he closed the door behind him, and again, the nightmare I'd had began to play in my mind. I forced it away.

"Come on, man," I said to no one in particular, "let's get the hell out of here."

"What was that shit about the Marines?" Rick asked. "How could Bernard lie about being a Marine and us not know it?"

"Let's talk about this later, okay?"

"Don't go getting all spooky now."

"Bernard died here, man. Right fucking here. I want to leave, this place is creeping me out."

"I know it's freaky, but it's no different than standing in a hospital," he said. "People die in them all the time."

"I hate hospitals."

"My God," Donald whispered as if mesmerized. "What an awful place."

"Hurry the fuck up," I muttered.

Rick defiantly hoisted the duffel onto the cot, pulled it open and emptied the contents. Mostly dirty clothes tumbled free, wrinkled and old; many of them I remembered Bernard wearing at one point or another. I did my best to zero in on the contents of the bag, but noticed Donald gazing apprehensively at the rafters. His eyes brimmed with tears, so I pretended I hadn't seen him.

"Hey," Rick said, crouching over the items, "check this out, Alan."

My legs felt like they'd been filled with lead but I forced myself over to him. He held up an aged photograph that had been taken at my wedding. Rick, Donald, Bernard, and myself, together at the reception, smiling, holding up drinks or beer bottles, broad smiles spread across our faces. We looked so young. "I remember when that was taken," I said.

"Me too." Rick resumed rummaging through the pile.

The photograph trembled and I realized my hands were shaking again. "I remember that moment… that exact moment."

"He's got a bunch of them." Rick handed me a small stack and continued his search.

I rifled through them—six in all—four from my wedding and one of Tommy's high school yearbook picture, wallet-size. The sixth was of a woman I didn't recognize. I handed the rest to Donald. "Who is this?"

Rick glanced up and shrugged. "Dunno, some broad he knew I guess. A relative, maybe?"

There was something that told me she wasn't a relative. There was a casualness in the woman's posture and facial expression that signaled she might have been more to whoever took the picture. She had a medium complexion, thick auburn hair to her shoulders, and dark eyes. Her lips were curled into a combination smile/smirk, like an inside joke had been cracked just before the picture was snapped. The shot was from the waist up, and she wore a low cut shirt knotted just above her navel. Something.about her seemed overtly sexual. The smile was more than a friendly one, the glint in her eyes telling yet mysterious. The picture had been taken in what appeared to be a kitchenette of sorts; the woman leaned against a counter. The setting was not familiar. I showed the picture to Donald. "You know who she is?"

He took it and studied it a moment, then shook his head in the negative.

Rick found an old Walkman and a handful of cassettes amidst the clothing. "Anybody want these?"

"This is just *too* morbid," Donald sighed.

"Yeah, please, Rick. I'm begging you, man, let's roll." I felt like a buzzard picking through a carcass, gnawing scraps of meat from human bones.

He tossed the items aside and began stuffing everything back into the duffel when a small package fell free. We watched as it bounced soundlessly along the mattress, and as it came to rest, Rick scooped up a shopworn nylon appointment book and planner. After a quick inspection, he realized it was zipped shut, but as he opened it several papers and things fell free. "Jesus, it's stuffed."

"Probably left over from his job," I said.

Rick smiled and it struck me as obscene to do that here. But I saw that one of the things drawing his attention was a sports card in a plastic holder that had fallen free. He picked it up and looked at it a while. "It's his Bobby Orr rookie," he said. "I'm surprised douche bag upstairs didn't snag it and sell it. He must've missed it."

Rick stuffed the miscellaneous papers back into the planner and zipped it shut, but his eyes remained locked on the card. For the first time there was something in Rick's eyes beyond the usual. "Hey, you guys mind if I keep this?" Before I could answer Donald dropped a hand on Rick's shoulder and said, "I'm sure Bernard would've wanted you to have it." Rick held his smile and gave a slow nod.

"Definitely," I agreed. "Now please, let's go, all right?"

Rick stuffed the card in his jacket and Donald hung onto the photographs. It was then that I realized I had nothing, so I grabbed the planner, tucked it under my arm and explained I'd just as soon go through it later.

In a way, leaving that cellar was like saying goodbye to Bernard for the first time. Since it was something none of us had been given the opportunity to do except in dreams, we stood quietly at the foot of the stairs, finally able to take it all in, even the rafter he'd been found hanging from. Now that we understood its finality, for the first time it seemed like it was truly over, like Bernard really was dead and gone, and the time for quiet mourning and contemplation, fond memories and moving on had arrived.

In our own ways, we made our peace with that horrible little cellar, then headed back up the stairs. But like the tangible entity it often is, darkness followed.

It was far from finished with us.

CHAPTER 3

Nobody said much on the way back to Potter's Cove, and that was probably best. The rain continued to pour from dark skies while the three of us, together yet apart, retreated into ourselves for the ride. I considered bringing up the lie Bernard had told about being a Marine but there seemed little point, and along with the nightmare, I pushed it away and remembered happier times instead.

Before I knew it, we were back in the diner parking lot.

Rick parked but left the engine running and the wipers going. "I gotta get home and get some sleep."

"Me too," Donald said softly.

I believed Rick but knew Donald would first stop at a bar or package store and hide out with a bottle for a while. Had he leveled with me I'd have joined him, but since he didn't I tucked the planner inside my jacket and prepared for the sprint to my car. "I'll call you guys," I said absently.

"Why do you suppose he stayed in the basement?"

Rick glanced at me, then away, just before I looked over the seat at Donald. "What do you mean?"

"Why didn't he stay upstairs?" Donald stared at me as if I knew the answer and had refused to share it with him. "Why would you have your own cousin sleep in that terrible little space when you could just as easily put him up on the couch?"

"I don't know," I said. "Maybe it was just easier to—"

"Why? Why would you do that?"

"Donald, I don't know."

"I didn't like that fucker," Rick said.

"You don't like anybody," I reminded him.

He shook his head, the earring dancing as if alive. "Nah, there was something about him, something not right. Almost like the whole thing with Bernard scared him."

"Well shit, finding someone hanging in your basement is frightening stuff," I said.

"I don't mean like that. It was like he was scared having Bernard living there, so he put him down in the cellar, out of the way."

"Why would he be afraid of Bernard? No one was afraid of Bernard."

"What about this business with the Marines?" Donald asked suddenly. "Why would Bernard lie about such a thing? It makes no sense, I can't figure it out."

Neither could I, but I was relatively certain we wouldn't solve it right then and there. I rubbed my eyes, a vague headache had settled behind them. "Listen, we all need some rest."

"Yeah, I haven't slept since yesterday afternoon and I have to work tonight," Rick sighed. "Let's hook up in a couple days and have dinner or something."

"Sounds good." I looked into the back. "You going to be okay, Donald?"

His eyes darkened and I wasn't sure if I'd unintentionally struck a nerve or if there was something he wanted to tell me but for whatever reason couldn't. "Of course."

"Drive carefully," Rick said. "Nasty out there."

"See you guys soon." I pushed open the door and darted into the rain.

***

A coastal town south of Boston, Potter's Cove had once been a prosperous mill town, but as with the rest of its storied past, the economic affluence the town had once enjoyed was now little more than a vague memory.

Main Street housed an array of inexpensive eateries, independently owned shops and a number of empty storefronts. Several enormous buildings sat boarded up along the northern part of town—reminders of a former status only the elderly could recall with clarity. A clothing manufacturer and a national department store giant employed more than five hundred residents, but Potter's Cove was mostly comprised of working-class folks who had no choice but to seek employment elsewhere.

I drove across town, turned onto the main drag and parked behind a local pizza joint. Once out of the car, I hesitated and looked out at the train tracks and water beyond—*the* cove, as it were. I watched a pair of ducks glide along the surface, oblivious to the rain, and was suddenly confronted with the memory of my mother. Before her death several years prior, we'd stood together on that very spot countless times, feeding the ducks and talking quietly about whatever came to mind.

I thought of her often in winter.

I climbed the battered staircase at the rear of the building and slipped into the apartment. The building itself was a two-story zoned for both commercial and residential occupants. One half of the first floor housed the most popular pizza place in town; the other had sat vacant for more than three years. Our apartment constituted the entire second floor, and while it was safe and passably comfortable, we'd lived there for more than a decade. It was our first apartment. Twelve years later we still hadn't moved into our second, and unless we hit the lottery the idea of ever having an actual house was, at best, a wild fantasy.

The apartment was dark but for a lamp on an end table in the den. I put Bernard's planner on the coffee table, shook rainwater from my jacket, hung it in the closet and went looking for Toni.

I found her in the kitchen standing at the sink, staring through the double windows overlooking the fire escape. I wasn't certain she knew I was there, so I moved deeper into the room, my weight causing the floor to creak. Shadows wrestled with the sparse bright patches filtering through the windows, cloaking her profile in alternate bands of light and dark. She still hadn't turned to look at me, but I could tell from her expression that she knew I was there. Her eyes blinked slowly, gazed at the row of clay pots on the fire escape.

"In a few weeks it'll be spring," she said, wiping her hands with a dishrag.

"Can't come fast enough."

"For me either." She draped the folded towel over the faucet. "I'm going to plant some herbs this year. Parsley maybe. It's been so long I can't even remember what it's like to have a yard…an actual garden, but…"

As her voice trailed off into silence I went to the cupboard, grabbed a mug and poured myself some coffee from what was left in the pot. "I can't believe you're giving me shit today. I do the best I can, Toni."

She finally turned from the window and leaned back against the sink. "That wasn't a slam." Suddenly she was wide-eyed and innocent. "Not everything is, you know."

I sipped my coffee. Lukewarm piss. "Think I'll take a shower."

"Do you want breakfast?" she asked. "I have to run to the store but we have some eggs."

I glanced at my watch. It was only a little after eleven but seemed much later. "No, I'm all set. I just want to get clean and sit down, go through some of Bernard's things I brought home."

"Everything all right?"

"We've got some questions, but I suppose that's always the case when someone takes their own life." I reached around her and poured the coffee into the sink, then put the mug on the counter. She smelled vaguely of coconut and some other soap-induced scent I couldn't quite put my finger on. "You're not surprised he did it, are you?"

She recognized it as more statement than question but responded with a subtle nod anyway. "I'm sorry he did it," she said softly, "but not surprised."

"Why not?"

"Sometimes life is harsh. Not everyone's cut out for it."

"You never really liked Bernard much."

"I didn't know him that well."

I studied her eyes. "You're an awful liar."

She left the counter and strolled to the table. "Let's not do this, okay?"

"You knew him for years too."

"And I'm sorry he died, Alan." She snatched her purse from one of the kitchen chairs, slung it over her shoulder and faced me. "But you asked me if I was surprised. No, I'm not. Bernard was a strange guy. He lived at home with his mother until she died, he never had a girlfriend or any sort of relationship I know of with a woman—a man or anything else for that matter. He sold cars for a living without ever seeming to realize he was a walking caricature of a used car salesman, and while he could be sweet and was never anything but nice to me we both know he had a penchant for stretching the truth and being evasive. There was something inherently creepy about him, Alan."

She was right and I could think of nothing to say in his defense.

"He was also very sad," she continued. "You could see it in his eyes, if you bothered to look for it."

"Right," I said, glaring at her now. "If only I'd bothered." The nightmare had crept back into my mind and I was weakening against its resolve. I'd always had nightmares—even as an adult—but nothing like this, nothing that refused to let go even once I was fully awake. My hands were shaking again and I felt for a moment like I might collapse. I gripped the counter as casually as I could and felt my weight shift against it. Toni stood staring at me with those big brown eyes, the natural curves of her figure concealed beneath a baggy cotton sweat suit.

"You're finding an argument behind every word I say." She moved closer long enough to give me a peck on the cheek. "Take a nice hot shower and try to get some rest. I'll be back in a bit, okay?"

Before I could agree or disagree, go along or scream for help, she was gone.

***

I'd washed my face and thrown on jeans and a sweater but hadn't bathed before I left to meet Rick and Donald, so the hot water pulsing from the showerhead felt great. Wrapped in curtains of steam, I threw back my head and let the water cascade across my face and shoulders, savoring the quiet time, the peace.

It was short-lived.

The nightmare was back, replaying in my mind, and this time I allowed it to come, lost in the hypnotic warmth and resonance of surging water.

The ticking of that damn clock is driving me insane. It's one of those fancy desk clocks, the kind with a sketch of the double globes on it; you know the type. It's at least ten feet from the bed but in the small room it overpowers everything else, even the faint traces of traffic in the streets below and the occasional sounds trickling in from beyond the confines of my bedroom. A headache has settled behind my eyes and is making me nauseous. That damn ticking only makes it worse, as if the clock is counting off the gongs throbbing through my temples. I move my arm from across my forehead, my eyes focus on the low ceiling overhead and a hint of him at the edge of my peripheral vision. Folding my arms over my chest like a corpse, I draw a deep breath and slide shut my eyes.

Returning to the darkness is easier somehow. I hear the floor shift as he moves deeper into the room, hesitating just inside the doorway. He is looking at me now—I can feel it—waiting to be acknowledged. My mouth is bone dry and I know sitting up will only make my headache worse, but I do it anyway. With one quick heave I swing my feet around and settle into a sitting position on the edge of the bed. I rub my temples, look at him, then look away. He just stands there staring at me with those sad eyes. He looks…not sick exactly, but…he doesn't look like himself. Pale. He looks pale and pasty, like he hasn't slept in a very long time. I finally ask him what he's doing there. He smiles, and it's the saddest goddamn smile I've ever seen, and says he came to say goodbye, that they allowed him a few minutes to come and say goodbye. It's only Bernard… why am I so frightened? Because he's no longer alive, or because I sense he's not alone? I clear my throat, reach for a small cup of water on the nightstand and take a quick sip. I nod to Bernard and tell him I'm sorry about what happened. I try to explain just how sorry I am but he smiles that sad smile again and holds up a hand like…like he's telling me there's no need for explanations.

I know the others are nearby, and just the thought of them stirs a terror in me the depth of which I have never before experienced. Tangible, choking fear, the kind I don't want to explore because I know it is bigger and stronger and deadlier than I can ever be. Like some monster in a box. If I let it out, it's over. I keep talking, babbling now in the hopes that maybe this will quell my terror.

Again, Bernard holds up a hand, so this time I stop talking. I notice his hand is dirty, the nails a bit too long and caked with soil. He tells me he came to say goodbye and that he has to go. He kind of sighs and leans against the doorframe, like he might fall over if he doesn't. I just stand there stupidly by the bed, watching him, not sure what to think. Then…they come. They just file into the room from behind him.

My palms are sweating and my heart is thudding so hard I can hear it smashing against my chest. This is my bedroom and I don't want them here, I don't know any of them, they—they don't look familiar to me at all. There are four of them; three men and one woman, and they all just walk in like they belong here.

Bernard tells me it's okay but I'm so frightened. They scare me, these... people. They scare me because I know what they are. They never say a word, they just stand there staring at me with their black eyes, and Bernard never explains, but I know, I—I just know what they are and why they're there. Bernard smiles again, but this time his lips crack and crumble like hardened clay, leaking blood and saliva and dirt in one hideous string of drool as his eyes turn cold like the others. I hear a scream but it dies quickly, strangled to silence before I realize it's my own.

I turned the shower off and braced my hands against the porcelain, head bowed, body dripping as the drain gurgled and swallowed. My heart was racing but I felt that if I could just lie down for a while I'd sleep for days. As the last of the water and soapsuds vanished down the drain, I forced open my eyes and pulled back the curtain. The mirror was fogged over and sheets of heavy steam filled the bathroom. Rain hammered the lone window, shook the casing.

Through the mist the full-length mirror on the back of the door revealed my reflection. My hair seemed thinner every day. I needed a shave but liked the way my five o'clock shadow looked. It better defined my chin and brought out the light blue in my eyes. I continued to study myself as curls of steam rose gently toward the ceiling. Funny how age sneaks up on you, I thought. Gradually, softly—like any good seduction—it had a hold of you before you even realized it. I wasn't yet forty—was three years away from it, in fact—but felt decidedly older most days. Somewhere within the reflection staring back was the man I'd once been, a man who'd never imagined he could be so tired, so worn down. Not at thirty-seven, anyway.

And yet sometimes it seemed like that man was a total stranger, a detached and isolated character in someone else's story; someone I barely recognized.

I stood there dripping until the mirror fogged completely over, then I stepped from the shower and snatched a towel from the counter. My headache had subsided but my muscles ached. I dried myself then tossed the towel over my shoulder, opened the door and stepped into the cool bedroom air. I rolled onto the bed, stretched out and nestled deeper against my pillow as my eyes slid shut. The nightmare had receded, and darkness took me quickly.

My eyes popped open. My back was tight and my stomach was in mid-growl. Had I fallen asleep? If I had, something had jolted me awake in a less than normal manner. I lay there a moment, listening, eyes staring at the faded ceiling and numerous hairline cracks traversing the plaster.

The weather had grown worse from the sounds. Wind whipped angrily outside, rattled the windows. My eyes immediately darted to the source of the sound, and although I recognized the cause it bothered me nonetheless.

Another sound crept in from the den, only this time I wasn't certain wind had been the culprit. I remained perfectly still and strained to listen, but all I heard was the wind and rain. "Hello?"

I wondered if Toni had locked the door on her way out. She usually did, why would this time be any different? Yet something didn't seem right. I didn't *feel* alone. Slowly, I pushed myself up into a sitting position and slid down to the foot of the bed. "Toni?" I called. "Toni, are you home?"

I sat quietly for a few seconds. Although I heard no other noises, the relaxation portion of my day had clearly come and gone. I stood up, reached for the towel I'd brought with me and wrapped it around my waist. The bedroom door was slightly ajar, just enough to reveal a sliver of the den beyond, and as I moved silently across the carpeted floor, I suddenly realized what was wrong.

Due to the weather it was much darker than normal, and Toni had left lights on in the den and kitchen. Lights I didn't remember shutting off before getting into the shower. "Hello?" A chill caused my body to visibly shudder.

And then the phone rang.

I nearly jumped out of my skin, staggered back and scrambled around the end of the bed to the phone on the nightstand. The receiver was in my hand and pressed to my ear before it could ring a second time.

"Alan," a voice on the other end sobbed. "Alan, I—"

"Donald?"

"Alan, I'm…"

"What's wrong?" I stared at the door. "Where are you?"

"I'm home," he said, voice cracking. "I'm sorry, I've been drinking."

"It's okay. Listen, let me call you back in—"

"I wanted to say something today, I wanted to, but—"

"Listen—"

"I couldn't do it, I just—Alan, I'm having nightmares."

I nodded into the phone. "It'll be all right. I've—"

"You've had it too, haven't you?"

Something in his tone caught my attention, shifted it from the darkened den to the sound of his voice. "*It*?"

"The nightmare you can't get out of your mind, that won't leave you alone."

I could hear him crying, sobbing openly, and I knew he was not only drunk but utterly terrified. "I've had *a* nightmare."

"Did Bernard say goodbye to you in it? Were those things with him?"

My grip tightened on the phone and my legs trembled so violently I thought I might collapse. "How—How the hell do you know that?"

"I'm scared, Alan. Christ, I'm so fucking scared."

"*How* did you know that?"

"They never said anything but I knew—I know—just like you, I know what it was all about. They were taking him to Hell. There's more to this than we know. Why were they taking him to Hell, Alan? Why would they take Bernard to—"

"Answer me, goddamn it! How did you know?"

Donald gagged and coughed. "Because that's the only difference between our nightmares," he said in a near whisper. "In mine, Bernard told me he'd been to see you first."

***

I sped through the streets of town ignoring the black clouds perched overhead, the rain, and a level of darkness generally reserved for the dead of night. My mind raced, my palms were moist with perspiration, and I felt an odd detachment, as if I were more a passive observer of the reality surrounding me than an active participant in it.

Donald's cottage was less than two miles from our apartment and located in a small settlement of mostly summer cabins nestled into a heavily wooded bluff overlooking the largest stretch of beach in town. I turned onto the dirt road and followed it through the forest. In summer, this corner of Potter's Cove was bustling with campers and summer people, the cottages occupied, yards cluttered with lawn furniture and barbecues, people young and old following the dirt paths down to the beach while music played from boom boxes and car radios. But the summer season was still a couple months away, and as the area only housed a handful of year-round residents, most cottages were boarded up and abandoned. A seasonal ghost town of sorts, in dismal weather and at this time of year, it seemed a fitting location for recalling the past and exorcising the demons found there.

I pulled up in front of Donald's cottage. His old Volkswagen was parked in a narrow side driveway, and faint light bled through the sheer curtains in the front windows.

The front door was open, so I gave a quick knock and let myself in, stepping directly into the living room. It was modestly furnished and somewhat disheveled, and it hadn't occurred to me until that moment just how long it had been since I'd visited Donald at home. Magazines and paperbacks were strewn about, overflowing ashtrays, crumpled cigarette packs and empty vodka bottles littered most available coffee or end table space, and although the small kitchen at the rear of the cottage was clean, other than for the refrigerator, it was obviously seldom used. The bathroom and bedroom constituted the remaining area. Both were quiet and dark.

A television in the corner was on but muted, which explained the sparse light, and in a recliner on the opposite side of the room Donald had collapsed in a drunken heap, an ashtray balanced precariously on his knee, an empty bottle of vodka on the floor just beyond his dangling hand. His other hand still clutched the phone, which had since gone from dial tone to an annoying buzz. I pulled it free and hung it up. His eyelids fluttered a bit, then I noticed the cigarette he'd apparently been smoking when he'd nodded off had burned well into the filter and was still smoldering on the lip of the ashtray. "Christ," I sighed, butting it out, "one of these days you're going to burn this place down with you in it."

His eyes opened, and he struggled to raise his head. "Alan."

"You all right, man?"

Dry, chapped lips parted slowly. "I don't know," he said groggily. "Are you?"

I crouched next to the recliner. "How could we have the same dream?"

His eyes rolled about for a moment, then he blinked rapidly and seemed to focus somewhat. "I never believed in an afterlife, Alan, you know that. I…I never believed in any of it. You did but not me, not me…but…but this—I don't…I don't understand what's happening." He tried to sit up and nearly passed out. He wouldn't be conscious much longer. His bottom lip quivered. "I don't even quite know why but I…I'm frightened."

"So am I." I looked at the near-hysteria in his bloodshot eyes and wondered if mine looked the same. "It'll be all right. There's a reasonable explanation, we just have to find it."

"You didn't have to come over, I—I shouldn't have called you like that, I…I'm sorry I—"

"Take it easy, man, it's all right." Past experience with Donald's binges told me he'd only have limited memory of all this anyway.

He struggled to smile, but the alcohol and exhaustion took him, leaving him slumped forward in deep sleep.

I grabbed an old afghan from the back of the couch and gently covered him with it, then went to the phone and dialed our apartment. Toni answered on the second ring.

"It's me."

"Where are you?"

"I had to come over to Donald's for a minute."

"Is everything all right?"

"He had a little too much to drink, just wanted to make sure he was okay."

"Something new." When I offered no response, she said, "I thought you'd be here when I got back from the store."

"So did I." An old black and white movie flickering from the TV set distracted me. "I'll be home in a few minutes, all right? Just heading out now."

I quickly tidied up the living room and brought the ashtrays into the kitchen. As I emptied them into the wastebasket, I noticed the stack of pictures Rick had found in Bernard's duffel bag fanned out across the counter. They looked as if they'd been frantically shuffled through several times. The photograph of the woman none of us knew was on top. I don't know why, but I tucked it into my jacket pocket and returned to the living room.

Though Donald was out cold he was breathing normally. Even in alcohol-induced sleep his face bore an emotional torment that never fully left his expression, but he looked about as peaceful as he was likely to get.

Satisfied he'd be all right, I quietly headed for the door.

***

The aroma of roasting chicken wafted about the apartment, reminding me I hadn't eaten since the day before, and that, coupled with a lack of sleep and the events of the day thus far, had left me in a less than jovial mood.

While Toni prepared a salad to go with dinner, I took up position at the kitchen table and explained the situation as best I could. Donald and I had somehow shared a nightmare, and even before we realized we'd had the same dream, it had taunted us both as much while we'd been awake as it had in the throes of sleep. She listened patiently, refraining from comment until I'd finished. For what seemed an eternity, she sliced a cucumber and added it to the bed of lettuce, nibbling her bottom lip throughout, a signal I had come to recognize meant she did in fact have a response but was thinking it through before voicing it. Eventually, she looked over at me, brow knit. "Alan, when Dad died I had that dream about him, remember? And a few days later when I spoke to my mother I found out she'd dreamt about him too."

"This is different," I insisted. "You both had dreams—but you didn't have the *same* dream."

"Honey, neither did you and Donald."

"I'm telling you—"

"Listen," she said, "in my dream my father came to me, talked with me and told me everything would be all right. The dream Mom had was essentially the same. He came to her, they talked, he promised he was fine and everything was going to be okay. It's the same with you and Donald. You were both close to Bernard, you both dreamed of him in very similar ways, as if he were contacting you. It's not an uncommon occurrence at all. People dream of loved ones after they die all the time, particularly soon after death."

"This isn't the same thing, this—"

"Have you spoken to Rick about it?"

"No, not about this specifically, but I doubt—"

"Maybe the dreams people have—yours included—really are those who have died making contact. Was it really my father who came to me in that dream? I'd like to think so—it's comforting—and I believe in an afterlife, so assuming that's true, why would a visitation through dreams be outside the realm of possibility? It wouldn't." She smiled. "Maybe that was the only way Bernard could say goodbye."

"Fine. Then if that's true why couldn't we have had the same dream?"

"Essentially, you did."

"Not *essentially*."

Toni smiled. "Alan, first of all Donald's account is unreliable because of his condition. When someone drinks the way he does you can't—"

"It's not like I told him about my dream and in some drunken stupor he claimed to have had the same one. I never even brought it up. Donald told me about the nightmare first—and before I said anything he already knew I'd had the same one."

"Okay, then what did he say when he described the nightmare? What were his exact words?"

I stared at her, already aware of the direction in which her questions were headed, and suddenly skeptical of my own certainty. "He mentioned a few particulars that sounded exactly the same as my dream," I said, "but I didn't question him on every little detail."

"Well, there you go." She raised her hands, palms up, then let them fall and slap against the outside of her thighs. "You both had a dream where Bernard came to visit you. In both, he wasn't alone. In both, he had come to say goodbye, and in Donald's he said he had gone to see you. Is that the size of it or did I leave something out from what you've told me?"

"No," I sighed, "that's it."

"Just like lots of other people, you had similar dreams. *Similar*, Alan, not identical—and I'm not saying that isn't sometimes a little unsettling in itself—but there's nothing unique or even unusual about it." She returned to the counter to fuss with the salad. "Besides, when you two discussed this Donald was blasted out of his mind. Add to that the fact that you're exhausted and haven't slept or eaten and the two of you are still dealing with the shock and stress and emotional turmoil of the death of someone you loved, and you've got a situation that would almost certainly blur your sense of what's real—or more importantly, *accurate*—and what isn't."

"You're—yeah, I guess you're right. It's just..." I shook my head both in confusion and in the hopes of clearing it a bit. "Neither of us had a good feeling about it. It wasn't like a nice, reassuring dream. This was a nightmare."

"Well if one of your best friends was dead in it, of course it's a nightmare, sweetie."

"That's not what I mean." I was wringing my hands without even realizing it; my palms had again begun to perspire. "There was a darkness to it, a sense of—I know this sounds silly, but—a sense of *evil* to it. It was like Bernard was going to Hell."

Toni covered the salad with plastic foil and slid it into the refrigerator. "Honey, Bernard committed suicide, and it was a total shock to you guys. What's worse, he didn't even leave a note explaining or maybe shedding some light on why he did it. It's a horrible and hideous and painful thing." She looked at me, compassion in her eyes. "You probably feel some guilt—which is wrong but inevitable—and you have confusion and anger and God knows how many other emotions all boiling to the surface at once. What happened *is* a dark and evil thing, and you're dealing with it, working through it, trying to make sense of it. That's all, Alan—and that's enough—but that's all."

Something similar to a smile twitched across my lips. "Not bad."

"Can't work for a shrink for ten years and not learn a couple things." She grinned, but it left her quickly. "Death is a huge factor in a lot of the cases Gene sees."

Toni worked as a secretary for a psychiatrist in town with a private practice, and had learned quite a bit about human nature in her tenure there. Unlike my rent-a-cop gig, which I loathed, she had a job she genuinely enjoyed, where she got along with and was respected by her boss. Still, if there had ever been a person who should have continued their education beyond high school, it was Toni. She'd always had tremendous interest in psychology, and though I'd encouraged her to take some courses over the years, she never had. Whatever small bit of extra money we had always went directly into the "house fund," a savings account she'd set up right after our honeymoon. It grew at such an anemic rate we were consistently three or four hundred years away from ever owning a home, but she never closed it out or lost faith. In many ways it reminded me of our marriage, and why, despite our failings, she remained with me.

Certainly her physical beauty had lured me originally, and although we were the same age she looked considerably younger than I did and had maintained not only her figure but a good deal of the vibrancy of her teenage years. Still, her visceral advantages aside, it was the genuine connection between us that kept our relationship afloat. I knew better than anyone that I had not become the provider she'd expected—that I was trapped in the same lowly security guard job I'd held since right after high school—and that after twelve years of marriage odds were I probably wouldn't ever do anything else. For Toni, that was a realization she had accepted and learned to deal with long before I had, and at the end of the proverbial day, she'd chosen to stay.

It was something neither of us had ever voiced, but we were both somewhat disappointed in each other, in the often-monotonous routine our lives had become and in the robotic patterns we executed day in and day out. But there was comfort here, safety, trust, and there was something to be said for those things. Familiarity and reliability had replaced the passion that weakened after the first few years of marriage, and instead of panting lovers we were steady companions, friends, sound and dependable roommates who now and then made love, as if mistakenly.

"Not everyone can handle death," I heard her say. "Most can't. But it touches us all."

That was true, of course, but I'd come to believe Death had his favorites. In my thirty-seven years, Death had not only visited my life far too frequently, it had been there from the very start, as if gleefully lying in wait for the carnage to begin, when my father, a mason, was killed in a construction accident only weeks after I was born. While still in high school, Tommy had been struck by a negligent driver and killed right before my eyes. Toni's parents had both died while still in their fifties, her father from a sudden heart attack and her mother from the same only a year later. My mother had suffered a series of strokes and died in my arms not long after. And now Bernard had taken Death's hand and stepped off the edge as well. It all seemed so pointless—*arbitrary*, as Donald had called it—yet I had to believe that somewhere a cogent reason, a plan of sorts, *did* exist amidst the mayhem.

"Look, dinner's not going to be ready for a while yet," Toni said. "Why don't you go lay down and get some rest?"

I stood up, took her by the waist and pulled her close. Her arms found my shoulders and she looked up at me with a smile, but I could feel the tension in her body rise. I was willing to at least entertain what she'd said as fact—I was exhausted and my judgment probably was fogged—but I still couldn't shake the fear. "I just have a strange feeling about all this."

"You're probably worried about Donald," she said, stroking my neck with warm fingers.

"Well, that too." I held her tight. "I love you."

"I love you, too." After another quick kiss, she removed my hands and flashed a *behave yourself* smile. "Now go take a nap."

***

This time my sleep was dreamless. I barely remembered crawling onto the couch, but that's where I was when Toni woke me more than an hour later. I emerged from the dark gradually, like a diver rising toward the surface in a slow and steady glide through murky water. For the first time in recent memory I slipped away from sleep as if unnoticed, instead of being jolted then torn from its grip. Still, it felt foreign to come up out of sleep without feeling the warmth of Toni's body against my own. In those few seconds before I truly understood where I was, I reached out blindly for her but caught only air and a quick glimpse of her as she moved away, back toward the kitchen.

I lay there a moment, eyes again closed. Toni had turned the stereo on and was playing a CD; tranquil piano tunes tinkled softly from nearby speakers. A steady wind and periodic bursts of rain spraying the windows distracted me from the concert, but it was the sudden vision of Bernard—his face gawking at me as if pasted to the inside of my eyelids—that forced me into a sitting position. I drew a slow breath, released it, and pawed at my eyes.

We ate at the kitchen table; small talk interspersed with the occasional clang of silverware against plates, the muted sound of chewing and the seemingly endless downpour drenching the world outside. The meal was delicious, the conversation somewhat guarded. We were both reluctant to pursue the topics we'd discussed earlier, though I'm sure for different reasons. Toni was able to stay removed from it all—and no doubt found it easier that way—while I felt too connected, more level-headed than before, perhaps, but still unable to evade the fear, despite her solutions and explanations. Something was happening, or was about to happen, or perhaps had already happened, but something was going on; there was more to the nightmares and unshakable sensations of dread than Toni was willing to consider or I was able to realize. Of that much, I was certain.

After dinner Toni curled up on the couch with a novel and I went off to the bedroom with Bernard's planner and the photograph of the woman I had taken from Donald's apartment. Sitting on the foot of the bed, I went through the planner, searching the scribbles and notes for anything unusual, anything that might stand out. I found nothing out of the ordinary, and other than the photograph, nothing that would raise even remote suspicion. I slipped the picture inside the planner, zipped it shut and put it on my nightstand.

"Was that Bernard's?"

I saw Toni in the doorway. She'd changed into her bunny slippers and a pair of satin pajamas. The light from a lamp on the nightstand cast her in a subtle yellow glow. "Yeah."

She looked beyond me to the window. "Is this rain ever going to stop?"

I'd always loved rain, found it more peaceful than depressing. "I hope not."

"You're so weird." She smiled, revealing great teeth.

"Yeah, but you love me."

She shrugged. "You're okay."

I laughed, and it felt wonderful. Like the nightmares, it was disruptive, but in a positive way. A dull and uninteresting life suddenly interrupted by death, suicide, bad dreams, or nothing more than simple heartfelt laughter, existence seemed so easily jarred, so amazingly fragile. I watched her there in the doorway, beautiful and alive, and wondered if I was losing my mind. "Come here."

Her smile drifted away. "We're both tired, Alan."

My heart sank, as it always did, and I could only hope my expression hadn't betrayed me. "Awful early to sleep."

"You need to rest."

"I need..." My voice faded into oblivion.

Toni moved across the room with a purposeful stride, crossed to the other side of the bed and turned down the blankets. "Come on, let's snuggle a while."

It felt nice beneath the covers, our bodies cuddled together, arms and legs and fingers and toes touching; her cheek nestled against me in the curve where neck meets shoulder, her breath a warm and steady pulse on my chest. With the wind and rain raging so near, we lay still, silent and undisturbed in the serene eye of the storm. Like lovers.

Dim, but not wholly dark, the room was still awake too, shadows and phantom lights gliding along its walls and ceiling, writhing ghosts slinking from hiding places, beckoning night.

Toni shifted and let out a soft mewling sound. I slid my hand from her back to her shoulder, then down across her breast. She tensed immediately. "Alan, don't ruin it."

I stroked her hair instead, brushing renegade strands back and away from her forehead, my eyes closed, welcoming memories of the night my mother died.

We'd been in this same bed, in this same room, probably in this same position, until I'd slipped down between her breasts, nuzzling and kissing them, in need of that warmth. But when I took one of her nipples between my lips, Toni pushed me away. "Stop," she'd whispered, as if someone might hear. "For God's sake—*now*?" What had never occurred to her, what she'd never understood, was that at that moment, that exact and spontaneous moment, I needed to feel strong and masculine and sexual and alive. For her, making love was somehow inappropriate just hours after the death of my mother. For me, it was an essential expression of enduring love, *our* love, the love that would survive and define and support and protect us both.

Our sex life had not been the same since. Now, more often than not, Toni was disinterested, preferring to snuggle, as if anything more was distasteful, a destroyer of an otherwise wonderful moment. And when we did make love, it was almost always as studied as the other routines we'd come to know so well. Where the sexually charged woman I'd married had gone, I couldn't say. She wasn't talking. And I'd stopped asking long ago.

She sat up a bit, looking back at me with an angelic glow. "Tomorrow morning we'll do something, okay? But tonight let's just—"

I pulled her close, nibbled her neck. As her head fell back against the pillow she slammed shut her eyes, and I knew I'd lost her. Had never really had her, I suppose. I kissed her gently, without passion, and felt her body relax.

"When did we become these people?" I asked.

She gazed at me with what could only be devotion, stroked the dark hair in the center of my chest and whispered, "Go to sleep, my love."

And when I did, Bernard was waiting for me.

CHAPTER 4

The shrieking whistle from the morning train slithering through the back of town awakened me with a start, as it did most Sundays. Only a few dozen yards from our apartment, the tracks squealed as the first train of the week transporting garbage from Cape Cod made its usual pass between seven and eight o'clock, giving the whistle a precautionary blow as it moved parallel to the street. It rumbled by, throttling the entire apartment in the process. Glassware and place settings rattled behind cupboard doors, and as I rolled from bed and planted my feet against the floor, I found it impossible to hide my amusement. The fact that most of the trains along this particular route only transported trash seemed darkly apropos. Even things generally associated with romance and intrigue were reduced to inelegant terms when crossing my path, as if indicative of the dismal nightmares haunting me.

The pizza place downstairs didn't open for another couple hours, so none of the smells that normally invaded the apartment (no matter what we did to try and cover them) had seeped up through the floor yet. I sat there groggily for a moment, noticed it was still overcast and cloudy but the rain had stopped and the apartment was quiet. I looked back over my shoulder; the bed was empty, Toni's spot a clump of wrinkled sheets.

Apparently, I'd slept through the night without incident, but I still felt worn out, as if perhaps I'd spent the night doing something else. Like lugging cement blocks. Or digging ditches.

The phone rang just as I made my way out of the bathroom, and Toni arrived holding the cordless a moment later. "It's Nino," she said, rolling her eyes.

I took the handset and sat on the bed. "Nino, what's up?"

"Al," my supervisor's harried voice answered, "listen, man, I got a scheduling problem, need some help."

In all the years I'd worked for Battalia Security, Nino Battalia, the owner's brother and my direct supervisor, never called me at home for any other reason. "Okay." I sighed, glanced at Toni, who stood at the foot of the bed, hands on hips and head cocked. "I'm listening."

"Craig called in sick, he won't be in tonight."

"The new kid?"

"Yeah, you know how these newbies can be. Says he's sick—got a flu or some shit—I don't give a rat's ass what he got, you see what I'm saying? But the thing is, he's covering Bantam Motors. I can't piss them off, Al, that's a nice account."

I recognized the name as a car dealership in the south end of New Bedford, only blocks from where Bernard had killed himself. "First of all, that's not the greatest neighborhood," I said. "Second, that's a nightshift gig."

"Yes to both, but—"

"Come on, Nino. Jesus, I don't do nights anymore, and I don't do shit details. I'm senior guy. Besides, I just woke up. I would've stayed up and slept this afternoon if I knew you needed me tonight. I spend Sundays with my wife, dump it on somebody else."

I could hear a big glass of Alka-Seltzer fizzing; Nino drank it like most people drank Pepsi. "Al, you think I called you first? I hit everybody on the roster, man, can't nobody fill the shift. You're the only one I ever been able to count on. You know that. Just cover this shift for me and you can take Monday off. I'll toss a couple bucks extra in your check this week too, Okay?"

"How much?"

"How's twenty sound?"

"Like it's not enough. Fifty, and I want cash."

"Forty."

"Fine," I said. "I'll do it. Is this armed?"

"Nope, leave the piece home. Strictly stick on this one."

"Good. You on tonight?"

"Yeah, I'm working dispatch. I won't be around on supervisor rounds though, so youse can all relax." Nino gave a hearty laugh, which was interrupted by gulping sounds as he downed the Alka-Seltzer. "You need directions?"

"Nah, I know where it is. Report time?"

"In at eleven, out by seven."

"Am I sitting in my car all night or what?"

"Nope, inside. They got a nice desk for you and everything."

Toni crouched before me and rubbed my thigh. With the heat in my groin rising, I said, "Okay. I'll radio in tonight when I get settled."

Her hand slipped beneath my underwear, and her fingers curled around my scrotum.

Nino was still babbling, thanking me when I hung up and tossed the phone aside. Toni already had my briefs down around my ankles. I watched her pull them off entirely, and spread my legs wider as my erection grew, reaching for her. One hand moved from the back of my calf to the inside of my thigh, the other gripped and slid me into her mouth. I moaned and held her head as I pumped slowly, timing my subtle thrusts with her motion.

I stroked her hair and leaned forward, draping myself over her and pumping harder as she increased the pressure and tightened her lips. "Jesus," I gasped, but the words caught in my throat as she released me, still kneeling and just visible over the edge of the bed.

She laughed in a way that struck me as nearly dutiful, then flopped next to me on the bed, the mattress bouncing. My heart racing, I wrapped my arms around her and pulled her over on top of me, but she pushed away and stood up.

"What's wrong?" I asked. "What is it?"

"Nothing," she said, straightening her pajamas.

I reached for my underwear and pulled them on over my dying erection. "This is fucking ridiculous, *what* is the problem?"

Toni shook her head. "It's never enough for you, is it?"

"Never enough? Are you serious? When was the last time we made love?"

"That *was* your dick in my mouth just now, wasn't it?"

We stood staring at each other for what seemed a long time. "You know what I mean."

She arched an eyebrow, folded her arms across her chest. "Do I?"

"Well, if you don't then we really *are* in a world of shit, Toni."

"Is this where I'm supposed to pretend to have some clue as to what the hell you're talking about?"

"We don't make love anymore," I said, glaring at her now. "You take care of me, service me the way a hooker services a john, for Christ's sake. No passion, nothing real or heartfelt, just efficient, emotionless and robotic sexual acts."

"A *hooker*—that's a nice thing to say to me." Her lips trembled. "Asshole."

"Look, I'm sorry." I reached out and put my hands around her waist. She felt so small, so easily breakable. "It's just—I don't understand what's happening to us."

"Neither do I."

"It's like everything's broken, all confused and doesn't make sense anymore."

"Don't be so melodramatic."

The heat that had risen within me was gone, leaving behind a void, a feeling of nothingness. "You act like it doesn't matter," I said.

She looked away and mumbled something, but the phone rang, interrupting us again.

I snatched it from the bed angrily. "What?"

"Hey man, it's me, Rick."

"Let me call you back."

"We need to talk. There's some weird shit going on."

"Fucking *now* what?"

"We were wrong about Bernard," he said, his tone nervous. "He did leave a note."

I felt my heart drop, but it was only my knees as I sank back down onto the bed. "What are you talking about?"

"He left a suicide note, just not in the usual way." Rick cleared his throat. "I was going through my mail from yesterday and—I know this sounds fucked up but—there was something from Bernard. He left a note, man. He just didn't leave it down in that basement. He sent it to me."

CHAPTER 5

The sky had turned an odd shade of gray.

I parked next to an empty basketball court surrounded by chain link fence and hurried across the street, hesitating once I'd reached the dead front lawn of the apartment building. I noticed Donald's car and Rick's Jeep parked nearby. Although this was the poorest neighborhood in Potter's Cove, it was normally a vibrant part of town, but the area was quiet, the streets still. Two old men talking at the base of the front steps shuffled their feet against the raw wind and ignored me as I moved onto the landing and into the relative warmth of the foyer.

A door to my right opened with a loud squeak to reveal an emaciated black woman with a sallow face. I visited Rick often, and despite the high turnover rate, I recognized many of the tenants on sight. But this woman was definitely new; I hadn't seen her before. Dressed in a bathrobe and slippers, her sunken eyes blinked at me slowly, like a cat. "You here about the plumbing?" she asked.

"No, ma'am."

"You here about the plumbing?" a high-pitched voice echoed.

I glanced down to see a small boy peeking at me from behind the woman's frail legs. I offered a restrained smile and winked at the boy, who immediately hid behind his mother. The woman sighed, stepped back into her apartment and closed the door.

A battered staircase eventually led to Rick's third-floor apartment. I hesitated to listen for a moment then knocked lightly.

Rick answered quickly, his expression tense as he stepped away from the door and ushered me in. The apartment itself was small, decorated modestly and bore the clutter of a man used to living alone. Beyond the main den were a kitchen and a hallway that led to the bedroom. Since his former girlfriend moved out, the apartment had taken on an impersonal, somewhat transient feel. The only items that revealed Rick's specific presence was one wall covered with framed photographs and newspaper articles chronicling his high school athletic career, and a table beneath showcasing several trophies and faded ribbons. It was a shrine that had always seemed to me nothing more than a constant unpleasant reminder of distant glory and opportunities lost. Most teenagers with the athletic prowess Rick had possessed went on to college with full scholarships. Some eventually made it to the professional ranks. Instead, Rick went to prison after nearly beating a man to death during a brawl over a parking space at a local restaurant. Even though several witnesses testified that the man had swung first, many also testified that Rick had continued to beat the man long after he had clearly lost consciousness. The brutality of his retaliation, along with the massive medical injuries the man sustained, gave the judge ample reason to make an example of Rick. And that's exactly what he did, sentencing him to twelve months in Walpole State Prison, a maximum-security institution that housed some of the worst criminals in Massachusetts. He served the full term, and that year behind bars effectively destroyed any chance at college or a career as a professional athlete. It also changed him forever. Rick had always possessed a volatile, violent temper, but the time served made him harsher, and in many ways potentially even more violent. Memories of visiting him in that horrible place blinked through my mind. "Aren't you usually asleep this time of day?" I asked casually.

"Yup." He tried to appear unconcerned. "You want something to drink? I got Cokes in the fridge."

"I'm good. What's this shit about a note?"

A toilet flushed and a moment later Donald appeared from the hallway looking horribly hung-over. He gave a less than enthusiastic wave and lowered himself onto a worn couch. "The plot thickens."

I wondered if he remembered I'd been at his cottage the day before. "I'm listening."

Rick sat on the arm of the couch, grabbed a padded manila envelope from the cushion and tossed it to me. "That came in the mail yesterday. I didn't check my mail until this morning."

I caught the package; it was nearly weightless. Rick's name and address had been written across the front in black marker, and a label advertising a private mailbox and mailing service served as the return address. "*Mailbox Universe*? That's here in town. If Bernard's been dead almost a week why did you just get this yesterday?"

"Listen to the tape."

"Bernard must have left them instructions not to mail the package until a specific date," Donald said. "You can pay them to do that."

I nodded. "But why wait so long?" When no one answered I reached inside the torn opening and pulled out an unmarked cassette tape. I felt nothing else, so I peered inside the envelope. It was empty. "What's this?"

"His note," Rick said.

"He recorded it?"

"He must've used that Walkman we found in his duffel," Rick said. "I remember seeing a *Record* button on it."

I moved to a chair, sat down and put the envelope aside. "You already listened to it?"

"Rick has, I haven't." Donald sighed. "I didn't want to have to do this twice."

"There was nothing else in the envelope and the cassette's unmarked," Rick told me. "I didn't know what the hell it was until I listened to it."

I stared at the cassette, entranced and repelled at once.

"When I heard Bernard's voice I almost shit myself," he said, drawing my attention to his slowly flushing face. "When I heard what he had to say, I think I actually did."

Rick took the tape from my hand, walked it over to a stereo in the corner and dropped it into the cassette player. Multicolored lights on the equalizer came to life, rising then falling quickly, accompanied by a loud and steady hiss. The lights continued to dance as the hiss became breathing, and finally, the sound of Bernard's voice.

"If you're listening to this…if you're listening to this then it means I really did it."

He sounded different than I'd remembered, not just because on tape everyone's natural tone is somewhat altered, but because he sounded hollow, like he was speaking to us from the bottom of a stone well. I sat forward, hands together.

"Rick, I sent this to you first because it seemed like the right thing to do. I know you'll listen to it, and I know you'll make the right decision and share this with Donald and Alan. No offense, guys, but if I sent the tape to either of you I'm not sure you'd tell Rick or even each other. But I know you'll do the right thing, Rick, you're the chief. You're warlord."

My eyes met Donald's, then Rick's. The warlord was the leader, the head Sultan who ran our pseudo gang. When Tommy was killed Rick had become warlord—a term we'd used somewhat jokingly, and one I hadn't thought about in years, but it summoned the past in vivid terms, and I was relatively certain that had been Bernard's intention. Although toward the end he'd become a shell of what he'd once been, Bernard spent most of his adult life in sales, and like any good salesperson he'd been skilled at speaking to people and eliciting from them the responses he needed or wanted, a flair for manipulation, in terms less kind.

"I had the people at the mailbox place hold off and mail the package on a specific date," he continued, his voice eerie and laced with a faint echo. "I figured by the time you got this and listened to it you'd know I was...gone. I'm sure you all have questions and confusion and you're probably pissed with me for doing it, but...believe me when I tell you, guys, it was the best thing. Rick, you probably think I'm a pussy—a coward, right? That's what you're saying, anyway, but deep down, you know that's not true. And Donald, you're just sad and bitter about it, while Alan, I'll bet you're all withdrawn and introspective, like always. We've known each other too long, fellas, too long.

"But it's funny how even after all these years you find yourself wondering just how well you really know anyone. Hell, we've all been tight since we were kids—been through a lot together—but we still have secrets, don't we? All of us. None of us are ever exactly, precisely what we claim to be, are we? We're one way with some people, another way with other people, maybe another way still when we're all alone. That's what it boils down to, fellas. At night, when you're lying there in bed looking at the ceiling, remembering the day, thinking back through things you did and what lies ahead, when it's just you and whatever god you pray to in the dark...that's when all the masks are peeled away and it's just you. Just you, and whoever...or *what*ever you are."

There was a garbled sound, and then the hiss returned.

"Is that it?" I asked.

Rick shook his head in the negative and held his hand up like a traffic cop signaling cars to stop. More breathing followed a series of clicking sounds; Bernard had stopped recording then begun again. When he resumed speaking his voice sounded the same as before: distant and almost artificial.

"You guys ever wonder why we were friends? I mean *really* wonder. The last few weeks I've spent a lot of time thinking, going back through the past, remembering good times and bad—all of it—as much of it as I can, anyway. When I was a little kid, maybe five or six, my mother told me that in this life we're lucky if we have one or two true friends, people we can really count on and who stand by us through thick and thin. That's if we're *lucky*." Bernard gave a quiet sarcastic laugh. "Isn't it strange the way we stuck together all these years? All of us are from working-class families, all of us townies but...but that's where it ends, really, wouldn't you say? Even in school it made people wonder. Guys like us—so different, one from the other—might've been friends when we were little but surely once high school hit we'd go our separate ways and settle into the appropriate cliques. But we didn't. In a lot of ways we got closer, didn't we? In a sense, anyway. Rick the jock, Donald the bookworm honor student, Alan the rebel without a cause, Tommy the all-things-to-all-people charismatic leader...and then, me. The joke, the dork." Bernard's voice cracked, a clicking sound followed; then silence.

I glanced at the windows on the far wall. A light snow had begun to fall. It seemed too late in the season for more snow, but just like Bernard's distorted voice speaking to us as if from the beyond, there it was.

"Christ," Donald said softly, "how much more of this is there?"

"He sounds like he's in a tomb," I heard myself say.

"I think he recorded it down in that basement," Rick said as the hiss on the tape gave way to another loud click. "That's why he sounds so far away, those cement walls are distorting his voice."

Bernard continued, calmer now, "I'm not stupid, I know how

people saw me. Except for you guys, anyway. We were all well practiced at that, disregarding each other's faults, no matter how hideous. There's always been a bond, a common ground between us. Rick, you and me were only children; we both knew what it was like, the pros and cons of being the only one. No pressure there, huh?" Heavy breathing, a rustling sound. "And Donald, good old Donny. You and me, we know what it is to be different, don't we? We know what it's like to be left out, made fun of…terrorized. Isolation, that's what we know, isn't it Donny? Self-imposed or not, isolation's an old friend, too."

I glanced at them quickly while their names were mentioned. Neither made eye contact.

"Alan, we knew what it was like not to have a father around," Bernard said next. "How it was to grow up with a single mother, what it is to love and be close to your mother and all the shit people give you for that. Momma's boys, you and me…and proud of it, right?" He laughed lightly, and this time it sounded somewhat genuine. "And then I think about Tommy and I wonder…I wonder what it was we shared. It took me a long time, going over it again and again…and then it came to me. Tommy was like all of us in one way or another. If you took the best parts of each one of us and put them together into a single person, you had Tommy."

Donald, who was staring at the floor, nodded slightly. Rick had turned his back on us and was standing in front of the window, gazing out at the snow. But he knew Bernard was right too—Tommy had been the best of us.

"I always felt bad for you, Alan, because you were there when it happened. After he died a day didn't go by when I didn't think about staying after school that day, and how if I hadn't, I'd have been with you guys. Maybe I would've been the first one off the bus that day. Maybe I'd have been lying in the street instead of him. Would've made more sense…"

My throat cinched and I struggled to control my emotion. I had been two steps behind Tommy that day, and the same thoughts had crossed my mind ever since. How easily it could've been me instead. How perhaps it should have been.

"But the one thing we all shared, the one thing we all knew," Bernard said through a lengthy sigh, "was pain. We all know pain, don't we fellas, and the rage that comes with it. Yeah, we know rage, too. We know the rage of never amounting to what we should have, could have been. Falling short, that's been our specialty."

Donald pushed himself to his feet and began to pace, arms folded across his narrow chest.

"Rick, you could've been a pro football player. It's all you talked about from the time we were little, and you had it, you had it, man. But the rage got you. You almost beat that poor bastard to death over a parking space. For what, to impress some fucking girl you were dating at the time? The guy was in a coma for three days, for Christ's sake. A *coma*, Rick. For a parking space. I remember going to visit you in prison. We'd all pile into the car and make the drive to Walpole, everybody dead quiet—God, those were the longest trips because nobody said a word the whole way up and the whole way back. And when I went away one of the things I was running from was having to go see you in that fucking hole. You were always so strong—so much stronger than I was—I couldn't stand seeing you broken, locked away in that place.

"And look at you now, man. Fifteen minutes of rage in a parking lot and your whole life went to shit. Is that fair? Is it? Is that fucking fair?" Bernard hesitated, apparently cognizant that the volume of his voice had increased considerably. When he continued, his tone had returned to one softer and more controlled. "Are you happy, Rick? Life turn out the way you hoped? A bouncer at a nightclub, alone, still chasing chicks like a high school kid, hanging around your apartment staring at those old trophies. Jesus Christ, man, a far cry from the NFL, huh?"

Donald looked at me through bloodshot eyes. "This is absurd, why—"

"Be quiet," Rick snapped, his back still facing us.

"I don't think any of us need to hear this kind of—"

"Shut the fuck up and listen, Donny." Rick turned slowly, looked at us over his shoulder with dark eyes. "We've never had to hear anything so much."

"And then there's Donald," Bernard said flatly. "The king of underachievement. Fucking royalty in that department, huh, Donny?"

The nearly gleeful tone in Bernard's voice surprised me. I'd never known him to revel in someone else's pain, particularly if that someone was a friend. Donald's expression had shifted from discomfort to near-frenzy. He glared at me, and I tried to convey a look that told him it was all right, that everything would be okay.

"I always wondered who you thought you were punishing," Bernard went on, his lifeless voice cutting the silence. "You're the smartest guy I've ever known, Donny, and one of the most unhappy.

Remember when we were kids and you'd talk about moving away when we grew up? You used to talk about going to Paris and Berlin and London—all these places that seemed so impossibly far away back then. You wanted to teach, remember? You had it all planned out. A teaching job in some little European village, where it was quiet and you could sit and read and be at peace, that's the dream you talked about. The dream you should've realized but never did, because the demons got in the way, then the booze fucked everything up. But we all know the booze wasn't the real problem, don't we, Donny?"

Donald's eyes had grown moist. "He has no right," he whispered, "no right to do this to us."

"Imagine a good Catholic boy turning up faggot."

"Jesus," I groaned.

The pain on Donald's face was nearly tangible. He'd heard the slurs and hatred for years, just never from Bernard.

"You are what you are, Donny," Bernard said. "You just couldn't seem to go with it, to be what you are and be okay with it. Eventually, it'll probably kill you. Nobody to love but that goddamn bottle, hiding from yourself and from all the shit everyone always gave you. So you hit a bar now and then, find someone to share a few hours with—maybe a weekend—then it's back to work at that office, wasting away and typing up someone else's thoughts, not even able to make the ten-minute drive home without stopping at the package store first. *That's* how bad it is, Donny. Most people would give anything for your brains, and you tossed them aside like garbage. You met a guy once, some secret lover you had, but it didn't work out like you thought, like you hoped, like you needed it to. You were in love, you told me so, but he was just experimenting, right? Just pretending, just drunk, just *anything* but queer. And you were still hurt when you got to college. You brought your bottle with you when it all went to shit, and you couldn't shake it, couldn't cope, so you walked away from school like some whipped puppy and you've been pining for him ever since, living like some goddamn drunken monk or something. I always thought you were better than all that,

I always thought you'd be the one who'd make it out, who'd really be something. We all knew what the deal was, man, you never had to make any big announcements, and when you did you weren't telling us anything we didn't already know. We accepted you, man. Shit, even Rick did. For all the crap he talks and all the arguing between you two, he always stood up for you. Besides, you're not so different from the rest of us, not really. Not when you get right down to the bare fucking bone. You're lonely...and angry. Rage, man, always the rage. Always there to remind us how unfair life is, how when we open our arms it kicks us in the teeth every fucking time."

The tape clicked, and Bernard's voice was silenced.

Donald sank slowly back onto the couch like a deflating balloon, and Rick braced himself against the window casing, his eyes still trained on the falling flakes of snow.

"Turn it off," Donald said softly. "You don't have to listen, Alan."

But I didn't turn it off, and neither did anyone else. Instead, another click signaled the monologue was about to continue. I settled deeper into the chair, felt my bowels quiver and the beginnings of perspiration seep through my palms.

"Alan," Bernard said fondly, "you didn't think I'd forget about you, did you? How could I, you and I were friends first, remember? Do you, do you remember the first day we met? I do. We were seven, and it was just a few days before Halloween. My mother and I had just moved into the neighborhood and I didn't know anyone. I was playing on the front lawn in a new costume I'd gotten—a tiger costume—do you remember? Great costume, man, head to toe, built-in feet, the works. I was playing, and you were riding your bike. You stopped to say hello, and I was surprised how friendly you were, how you just talked to me and seemed to want to be my friend. You never even mentioned my glasses, or how thick they were, or how skinny I was, how much shorter I was than most kids our age—none of it. You just told me your name and pointed up the street at your house and said that's where you lived. Then you told me my costume was cool and you had to be a ghost again for the second year in a row because your mom couldn't afford a good costume. Plus, she'd cut up a perfectly good sheet making the eyeholes so there was nothing left to do with it except leave it a costume or shred it for rags."

I was stunned that he had remembered such detail. I looked to the floor, my memories of that afternoon as clear and bright as the day it happened.

"Then the two Berringer twins showed up on their bikes, came to a screeching stop right in front of the driveway, like they came out of nowhere, scared the hell out of me. And I knew by the look on your face that they were trouble. Those little motherfuckers, Christ I hated them, terrorizing the whole neighborhood, always picking on kids younger than them. They were thirteen; we were seven. Jackie and Johnny Berringer. Cocksuckers. I remember you told me to go in my house, but I didn't get it and just stood there. Then they started making fun of me, calling me all kinds of names because I had that costume on. I was so scared, and I kept hoping my mother would hear them and come outside, but she never did. You told me to go inside again, then the twins got off their bikes and started pushing you, telling you to mind your own business and that I was a baby for dressing like that. Do you remember, Alan?"

I felt myself nod, as if somehow he could see me.

"Jackie grabbed me and pushed me down," Bernard said, his voice shaking. "I started to cry—shit, I *was* a baby then and they were a lot older than us but...but then all of a sudden you went wild and started attacking them." Bernard's tone changed and it suddenly sounded like he was stifling laughter.

"You weren't a hell of a lot bigger than I was physically, and... Christ, they wailed the piss out of you that day, right there in my front yard. But you just kept getting up. They'd hit you and down you'd go; lip all busted up, nose bleeding. But you kept getting up, and you'd come back swinging. I tried to help but they pushed me down again and tore my costume and...I was crying and screaming for my mother, and you were lying in the driveway all bloody but on your way back for more...then the Berringer twins took off. I guess they were afraid my mother would hear all the screaming. They didn't know yet that she drank too much and usually slept in the afternoons. I never forgot that, Alan. You didn't even know me, but you defended me because you knew those two little sick fuckers were going to beat somebody up, and you didn't want it to be me. Nobody had ever done anything like that for me. Nobody."

At only seven, I'd seen some cruelty and brutality in the world, but not much, and nothing quite like what I witnessed that day. Bernard was so innocent, so small and weak and trusting. A little boy in a special tiger costume his mother had made, playing in his yard, minding his own business, the new kid in town totally unaware what the local bullies had in store for him. Welcome to the neighborhood. And even years later, I was still unable to understand what joy the Berringer twins derived from stopping and terrorizing a little boy who had done nothing to provoke them, a boy they didn't even know. And yet, the concept that they had so quickly determined Bernard was somehow less human, less important and thereby expendable was both repugnant and curious.

Bernard's voice interrupted my thoughts. "The next day you introduced me to Tommy and Rick and Donald," he said, "and we spent the day playing in the tree house in Tommy's yard. If it hadn't been for you, Alan, I don't know if I'd have had any friends at all. Probably not."

I wanted to let the emotion go, but I kept it bound and under control. He was letting me off the hook for some reason, praising me while he'd torn the others to shreds, and fond reminiscence had again given way to morbid uneasiness and confusion.

"I probably should've just mentioned that day," Bernard continued, "and let you tell the story, Alan. You were always so good at telling stories. As long as I can remember all you ever wanted to do was write."

When he mentioned my writing I knew I'd been wrong. He wasn't going to spare me after all.

"You were always scribbling in those little notebooks you used to carry around. Man, some of those stories were really good. You had a natural talent for it, no question about it. My favorite was the one you wrote—oh, I want to say it was around fourth, fifth grade, somewhere in there—about the jet and the UFO. Remember that one? The UFO stopped time and altered it or something and took everyone onboard away then replaced them, only they didn't remember any of it. Then they realized there was twenty minutes no one could account for, the exact amount of time radio communication had been cut off—shit, that was so good. Just like on *The Twilight Zone* or an episode of *The Outer Limits* on TV. All that talent at such a young age, what a shame that just like Rick and Donald you threw it away."

"Fuck this," Donald said suddenly. "Shut it off."

"Let it go," I said.

Neither of us moved.

"What the hell happened, Alan?" Bernard asked in a nearly tender tone. "You were going to be Steinbeck, man. What was it all the teachers said? If only that Chance kid would show up for school and stay out of trouble and study and use his talents...yeah, if only. But you knew better—and you really did." Brief, ironic laughter. "You were so cool back then, God I idolized you. It was like you knew who you were and what you wanted and how your life would be, and you didn't need all the bullshit at school and all the stupid social crap. You always walked your own path, man, and I respected the hell out of you for that.

"I never would've guessed you'd fucking blow it by getting married instead. Christ, man, you were going to New York, you were going to write and live in Greenwich Village and hang with artists and date hippie chicks and write great novels and be the coolest guy since Kerouac or James Dean or... Tell me, man, was Toni worth it? Was she? She's a great gal—I always liked her—but like I said before, when you're lying in bed at night, alone with God, and you ask yourself that question—and you know you do—what answer echoes through your mind?

"Toni's a small town girl. Always was, always will be. She wasn't cut out for all that. She was thinking more along the lines of a nice little house with the picket fence, the two-point-five kids, the dog and a Volvo in the driveway. Nothing wrong with that, but it was never you, was it, Alan? You gave up all you wanted because you knew she could never be a part of the world you'd envisioned and dreamed of creating for yourself your entire fucking life." Bernard's volume had increased again, and he stopped and drew a series of deep breaths before continuing. "The only way you two could be together was for you to give up what you wanted and stay here. Get a job, make a life. *A life*? In Potter's Cove? Fuck, good luck. How's that security guard position working out? Making more than minimum wage yet? Never did get that house, or the babies or the picket fence or the Volvo. Shit, you didn't even get the dog, so what the hell was the point? Do you resent Toni now, all these years later? Every time you look in the mirror and see you're another year older, a few pounds heavier, a bit more miserable than the year before. Every time you put that uniform on and spend the shift wondering *what if* instead of doing one of the few things that made you happy, that made you who you were, do you resent her then? And does she resent you, too, Alan? She never realized you really weren't that good at anything *but* writing, did she? Bet she realizes it now. Bet she realizes she should've picked someone else to spend her life with. But it's the way it is, and it's easier than tearing it down and starting over, right?

"Do you ever go through your old stories? Shit, do you even still have them? Do you ever think about what might have been?"

As he paused I could almost see him smiling, lying on the cot in that basement, the recorder in hand, just inches from his lips.

"Why is he doing this?" Donald asked. "*Why*? What the hell did he do that was so wonderful with his goddamn life? What right does he have to—"

"And what about me?" Bernard said, as if in response. "Yeah, what about me. Christ, we're all a bunch of stereotypes and we don't even realize it. But you know what? Most people are, fellas.

Most of us have no idea how fucked up we really are, much less those around us, and even given the chance, we're not sure we want to know. You know, the day Tommy was killed I saw him coming down the staircase at school. He was headed for the exit and the bus, and I was going the other way. We saw each other and smiled then I gave him a playful punch in the arm and told him I'd see him later. Well, I didn't see him later. The next fucking time I saw him he was in a casket. What I'd really wanted to do when I saw him was just smile, maybe even give him a hug, tell him thank you for being my friend. But, hey, *men* don't do shit like that. So here's a punch in the arm instead and a too cool 'See ya later' mumble. Bunch of goddamn hypocrites, all of us. Hell, I'm as guilty as the rest of you—some might say more so—but I never had the potential you guys did. I couldn't play sports; I wasn't tough or good-looking or highly intelligent or talented. All I could do was talk. Always been a decent talker; that's why sales worked out for me for so long. It was a safe place to hide for a while...but the truth always catches up to us, fellas. None of us can hold out forever. Eventually truth finds all of us and forces us into the light, whether we want to be there or not. Reality's a bitch, ain't it? Scary shit, man.

"Almost as scary as being ignored. Not that you guys would know anything about that, you've all spent your lives scratching and clawing at the edge of the cliffs you're hanging off of to make certain of that. That's what the rebel routine with you was all about, Alan, and it was even one of the reasons why you stepped in and tried to defend me from the Berringer twins that day. Even taking a beating was somehow preferable to being ignored. But, Christ, I'd have given my balls to be ignored just once. To be left the fuck alone by bullies and kids giving me a hard time and girls laughing at me for this or that. Not you guys, though. Our lives may be complete dog shit, but please God, just don't let us be ignored. Anything but that.

"Rick, that's why you still dress like a high school kid and go to the gym and try to act like you're eighteen instead of thirty-eight. Donald, it's why you drink yourself into oblivion, and Alan, it's why you stay with Toni and endure. Without all of the window dressing you'd all just fade away, and that's what terrifies you. I know, because I did it. I faded; I took the fall just to see what was down in that pit, and guess what, fellas? There is something down there in the dark.

"You know what else I realized? The dark's not so bad. As a matter of fact, I like it." His breathing rate became a bit heavier. "It's where I belong, it's safer here for me."

Donald pulled his cigarettes from his shirt pocket and stabbed one between his lips without lighting it. "What the hell is he babbling about?"

I shrugged and stared at the tape deck, waiting for Bernard to continue.

"But every road comes to an end," he said, "and mine's almost there. I tried, man, I really fucking did, but the shit was already decided—preordained, you know what I mean? Think real hard—try to remember, and you will."

Rick turned from the window, faced us, his mouth set firmly shut, jaw working as he ground his teeth.

"The point is," Bernard went on, "I'm not the harmless little loser-boy you thought I was. Outside of our group I never had a social life really. Girls never paid any attention to me, and when they did it was to laugh at me or give me one of those looks to let me know there was no chance in hell they'd ever have anything to do with me. The friendships and bonds I had with you guys only went so far... but when you went off and did your own thing, well, so did I. I stopped running from the rage, man. I faced it, grabbed it; used it.

"Quick confession...I was never in the Marines, but I did take off not long after graduation, I mean, I had to do something, right? You all had shit going on and I had nothing—no life, no plans, no girlfriend-soon-to-be-wife, not even a jail cell to sit in and pass the time."

"Sonofabitch," Rick muttered.

"My mother's lifestyle had started to catch up to her and her health wasn't the best. All that booze was starting to rot through her system, but she was still relatively young and I knew that I'd probably spend years caring for her, so I started to set things up a few months before graduation. I decided on the Marines because I knew it would blow everybody's mind. Who'd ever think scrawny little Bernard with the coke-bottle glasses could be a Marine? I told everyone that's where I was headed, but what I really did was save almost every dime I earned at work after school. I remember the last night I spent in Potter's Cove. It was a while after graduation, and Rick, you were already serving your sentence, had been for a few months, but Donny and Alan, you guys took me out to dinner at Brannigan's, remember? We had steaks and potatoes and beer and...Christ, we laughed our asses off that night. For a couple hours life was almost fucking bearable. It was quite a sendoff, only the next morning when you guys drove me to the bus station, I wasn't headed for boot camp."

I saw Donald shake his head, draw on the still unlit cigarette and run his hands through his hair. "This is madness."

"It was a new beginning, though. I went away to begin what I was finally able to admit was my destiny." Bernard was quiet for a time, but the tape kept rolling. "See, we all have the rage, fellas, but so few of us ever figure out what to do with it, how to love it and nurture it—like a loyal pet. I went to New York City, got a room and lived there until my money ran out. Less than a year later I was back in Potter's Cove telling you how I'd fallen off a training platform and wrecked my knee. Well I did hurt my knee but it wasn't from any training platform. I fell chasing somebody, if you want the truth. People run really fast when they're afraid. When they're terrified.

"New York was incredible. I had no idea how perfect a setting it was for me to begin my journey, but within a few days it was so obvious. A human zoo, that's how I saw it, with me as the warden. See, here's what I figured out down in the dark, fellas...the power I'd lacked my whole life was right there in front of me all along. When you step back and separate yourself from the herd it changes everything. That's when I figured out I could do whatever I wanted. And that's when I changed the world around me from a zoo to a slaughterhouse."

I felt my heart sink and I looked quickly to Rick, who was staring back at me with an *I-told-you-so* scowl.

"What the fuck is that supposed to mean?" I asked.

"Think back through the years, fellas," Bernard continued. "Think about the things deep inside you can't remember, don't want to remember. Think about all the times things with me just didn't add up, how things seemed just a bit off, just a little strange. Then think about how you reacted, how you dismissed it the same way you choose to ignore an unusual sound in the middle of the night. Ever do that? Have you ever been lying in bed, darkness all around, when suddenly there's an odd sound? You know you weren't dreaming; you know you heard it for sure and you know it's not commonplace. You know it's an intrusive sound, a sound that doesn't belong there, and even though it makes no sense, even though it might be an intruder or God knows what, you roll over and forget it...but have you ever wondered what you'd find if you didn't?

"I'm so tired," he said through a heavy sigh. "I'm so tired, fellas. I had it under control for a long time—or I thought I did—but it got away from me. I couldn't concentrate on my job, I knew my mother was dying, I...I knew without her my life would spiral down into nothingness. The only way the mortgage could be paid was through her savings and the disability checks she got every month. Without that income, even when I was working, I couldn't maintain the house and I knew I'd lose it. I couldn't hang on anymore, I...things were all confused. I couldn't think anymore, I...I just couldn't think clearly, you know? Too many goddamn voices at once, and...

"I couldn't do my job, lost that, then when Mom died and they took the house, I...Christ, how that woman suffered. For what? For what!"

He screamed the same phrase three times more, the volume and savagery of his voice such that it distorted through the large speakers and became indecipherable. I felt a chill burst through me. Bernard sounded completely, hopelessly insane.

"God abandoned me." The tremor in his voice indicated he was struggling to hold back tears. "I knew when I moved in here with Sammy my time was over. I did my thing, I made my mark...and I'm not afraid, not anymore. Face your fear, that's what people always say, and you'll conquer it. It's true. It's true. I faced my fear... then I *became* it. The things you see are beyond belief, but they're real.

"I'll miss you guys," he said a moment later. "I'm not who you thought I was—*what* you thought I was—but I'm still Bernard, man, still a loyal Sultan, still one of you, and I always will be. We'll always be together no matter what. I just wish that could've been enough, but ask yourself this—was it enough for you? I wish I could've told you the truth about me, about the things I've done, but if you're honest with yourselves and you stop and think long and hard, you'll realize the answers are right there and have been all along."

Donald struggled to his feet. "He's insane."

"I like the idea of dying in winter," Bernard's voice interrupted. "It's barren and cold and still and it's the perfect time for me to step away, now that my destiny has been fulfilled and I've done all I can to assure my place in the afterlife, in the realm of darkness where I belong, where I was born to be.

"When the seasons change and the world begins to warm and thaw out from the chill of winter, you'll better understand what I'm talking about. You'll see firsthand the fruit of my labor. Rancid fruit to be sure but fruit just the same, fellas. Like in the days of old when they'd *bleed* the illness, the darkness, the wickedness from a person, I've shown you the way by bleeding the world, man, by letting it flow in the fucking streets. It's why as much as I'd like to I can't slit my wrists. Yeah," he said in a quietly gleeful tone, "I *need* it where I'm going...down beyond the dirt...beyond the Earth. And just like here, where I'm going, you might just have to follow. But I have to go now. It's time."

The tape was quiet but we could still hear Bernard breathing. Eventually he spoke, but this time his voice was void of emotion, a detached monotone that could have been anyone. "*Be sober, be vigilant; because your adversary the devil, as a roaring lion, walketh about, seeking whom he may devour.*"

No one moved until the tape reached the end and the player clicked and stopped with a loud, eerie finality. We sat in stunned silence until Rick removed the cassette and tossed it back to me. I caught it and returned it to the envelope it had been mailed in, no longer wanting to touch it.

"Well, that was fun," Donald said. "Think it's available on CD?"

Rick stomped about, hands on hips. "Yeah, good, make jokes, asshole."

I cleared my throat and rose slowly to my feet. "We need to sort this out."

Rick whirled around, faced me. "You know what he was saying the same as I do."

I nodded. "We also know Bernard had problems."

"No one in their right mind hangs themselves," Donald added quickly. "And besides, you can hear him at the end of the tape, he's clearly disturbed."

"Doesn't make him a liar." Rick arched an eyebrow. "Does it?"

"Not necessarily, no."

"He was saying, without actually saying it, that…" I shook my head in disbelief, still hopeful none of this was happening. "He was claiming he'd killed people."

"Thank you, Inspector Poirot, what would we do without you?" Donald rolled his eyes and took another mock draw on his still unlit cigarette. "Look, this is Bernard we're talking about, *Bernard*, for Christ's sake. He wouldn't hurt a fly. He had some problems, yes, we all agree on that. He had a habit of stretching the truth from time to time, but he didn't—this is absurd—Bernard wasn't some—"

"Did you hear that shit at the end of the tape?" Rick asked. "That's a quote from the Bible."

Donald shrugged. "I assumed as much. So what?"

"This is bad shit." He looked to me, eyes imploring support. "Alan, this ain't Bernard making up some story, and you know it. We all know it. This is a suicide note; remember that. Pretty stupid time for pipe dreams, no?"

Rick had a point. The end was a time for truth, confession and hopefully redemption, not further deceit. But were Bernard insane, would he have even known the difference?

"He said when the seasons change we'd understand," I finally replied.

"Spring is still a few weeks off," Donald mumbled.

"This might explain our nightmares," I said.

Donald looked at me, his face failing to conceal the fear. "The… nightmares."

Pacing near the window, Rick came to an abrupt halt, mouth open and eyes wide. "What nightmares?"

I exchanged glances with Donald then said, "We've had similar dreams where—well—where Bernard—"

"Says goodbye," Rick said, finishing the sentence before I could. "There's people—or something *like* people—with him."

"Christ." Donald's hands were trembling so badly that the cigarette in his fingers snapped in half. "There's no way this is happening, this can't be real."

Rick moved closer. "Not making fucking jokes now, are ya?" He looked at me, what little color he still had in his face draining away as I confirmed his question with a quick nod. "And in the dream, do you know why they're there, these people?"

I nodded again, feeling dead inside. "To take him—"

"To Hell."

We turned in unison to Donald. He was shaking violently, still trying to occupy his hands with the frayed cigarette filter. "Why would they want to do that?" he said in a loud whisper. "Why would they want to take Bernard to Hell?"

"Because he wasn't lying," Rick answered. "Because everything he said on that tape is true, and when the seasons change we'll understand."

"Maybe we should turn this tape over to the police," Donald suggested.

Rick scoffed. "And tell them what? Hi, we think our friend—you know, the one who just offed himself in his cousin's cellar—killed some people. Here, listen to this tape, he sounds completely out of his fucking mind on it, and doesn't mention anything specific, but we thought we should turn it over to you guys."

"Why the hell not?"

"Because we'll look like fucking loons ourselves if we do that." Rick resumed his pacing.

"Besides, what if this shit is true? What if Bernard really did do something? I don't want to get involved in all that, I don't want the cops fucking snooping around my life and me just because we were friends. Who knows what kind of fucked up shit we might bring down on ourselves if we get involved?"

Donald seemed to think about what Rick had said for a moment, then turned his focus to me. "Alan, what do you think?"

"I think at this point we don't know what that tape means," I said. "It could be a confessional to murders and it could be nothing but the delusional ramblings of a mentally ill man at the end of the road, just hours away from taking his life. Either way, I think it needs to stay with us for now."

"I agree," Rick said. "Definitely."

"And if something should happen," I continued, "and in the following months we learn there is something to all this, then we can decide what to do from there. I just think going to the cops now is a bit premature. Besides, I'm not even certain what we're dealing with here is—I don't know if the cops could help."

"I'll hang onto the tape," Rick said, "put it away somewhere safe."

Donald's fight to regain control of himself had worked, at least for the moment, and he appeared more levelheaded, less shaken. "Granted, our dreams are strange," he said. "The fact that they're so similar and seem to have meaning beyond the norm is a bit unnerving, and that, coupled with the things Bernard said on the tape, is frightening, but we can't lose control here. We have to maintain our own sanity and try to approach this in a logical, unemotional manner."

"You do what you want," Rick said. "But I'm gonna keep my eyes open. This is some bad shit—you mark my words—and I bet we don't know the half of it."

I checked my watch. "I gotta go, I'm working tonight." I headed for the door, then hesitated and looked back at them. "And that shit Bernard said about Toni isn't true. He was always jealous of what we have. If I had it to do again I'd marry her in a heartbeat. She's the best thing that ever happened to me."

Donald grimaced. "You don't have to—"

"The *best* thing that ever happened to me."

Rick had resumed his position at the window. "Snow's starting to accumulate," he said absently. "One last kick in the balls from winter. Motherfucker never dies quietly."

Few things do.

CHAPTER 6

Located near the water, across from a long-abandoned and decaying factory, the car dealership occupied a large lot between an auto parts superstore and a Chinese restaurant along the tail end of a boulevard less than a mile from the state highway. My shift was eleven at night until seven in the morning, when the owner showed and opened for business. Once an hour or so, I was to take a quick stroll around the property, but mostly the shift would be spent at a salesman's desk positioned in the front window, which despite the periodic snow squalls gave me a perfect view of the entire lot as well as most of the street beyond. It wasn't an armed detail, which was good, because I'd never been comfortable strapping on a gun for the money I made. I carried a baton and a handheld company two-way, and usually passed the time either reading a paperback or listening to a portable radio I always brought with me. If anything happened, I was only there to put a call in to the police so they could handle it. I was a babysitter in costume, dressed like I was something more, something official, keeping an eye on a bunch of used cars no one would want anyway.

The vacant factory, only one of many that littered the city—mementos of an age when the textile industry had sustained it—the same as in Potter's Cove—loomed beyond the shadows of the lot across the street, the enormous rotting structure blocking much of the moon, the remaining portion masked by spitting bursts of snow.

Because I knew my supervisor wouldn't be around, I'd brought a six-pack with me. The beer relaxed me, and I hoped it might help me forget all that had happened and much of what Bernard had said on that tape. But even alcohol failed to rid me of the continuous stream of thoughts exploding through my mind, because just like the nightmares, we'd all experienced the tape. Now it was just a matter of deciphering it, and the potential danger therein was different than anything we'd encountered to that point. Different than a dream or a feeling, this was more than real; it was palpable. But were the things he'd hinted at on the tape just more of his stories, more dramatics, or had he spoken the truth down in that cellar?

Think back through the years, fellas. Think about all the times things with me just didn't add up, how things seemed just a bit off, just a little strange.

I dug a beer from a small cooler at the bottom of the gym bag I brought with me on each job, cracked it open and took a pull.

I wish I could've told you the truth about me, about the things I've done, but if you're honest with yourselves and you stop and think long and hard, you'll realize the answers are right there and have been all along.

Visions of Toni came to me then. She'd been asleep when I left for the shift, curled up and warm in bed. She always looked so beautiful and peaceful when she slept, like she hadn't a care in the world, and this time had been no exception. When I'd returned home from Rick's I told her about the tape but left out most of the specifics and downplayed the confessional aspect. She dismissed it as Bernard just being Bernard right to the end and was more concerned with how I was doing. We cuddled in the recliner and watched TV until she went to bed, then I sat with her and ran my fingers through her hair the way she liked until she'd drifted off to sleep. Sitting there on the edge of the bed, I wondered if perhaps part of what Bernard had said was true.

Bet she realizes she should've picked someone else to spend her life with.

Maybe that's why our lovemaking hadn't been the same in eons. Maybe she loved me but was no longer in love with me—hadn't been in years. Maybe she was afraid she'd become pregnant and the idea of bringing a child into a marriage such as ours was beyond what even she was prepared to endure. Maybe she was getting it somewhere else. Maybe it was as simple as that. Maybe it wasn't. Maybe we adored each other and simply had problems like any other couple. Maybe as long as we knew the other would always be there, it didn't really matter.

I killed the beer and tossed the empty into the gym bag.

Think back through the years, fellas...

***

But for certain specific episodes of importance or particular impact, the years prior to our teens were vague at best. Life in Potter's Cove was largely uneventful, and things rarely changed. It was a time when a distinction still existed between "school" clothes and "play" clothes, a time before VCRs or video games or cable television, before personal computers, the Internet and e-mail, cell phones and beepers and microwave ovens, and a time when the handheld (wireless) calculator was about as exciting as technology was liable to get. It was a time when kids spent most of their time playing outside, rarely watched what the seven television channels (nine or ten if you counted UHF and had the appropriate antenna) had to offer, and a period that produced the last generation to grow up in a world not quite so jaded and not yet consumed with technology. It was the beginning of the end of an era of innocence to be sure.

In the summer of 1975 we were all in the process of making the awkward transition into our teenage years. At thirteen, we were no longer considered little children per se, but were still far from adulthood, trapped instead for that and a handful of years to come at some unidentifiable point in between.

The year before, President Nixon had resigned, and Patty Hearst had been kidnapped. In January, men who seemed to be on television constantly at hearings none of us paid much attention to—John N. Mitchell, H.R. Haldeman, and John D. Erlichman—were found guilty of the Watergate cover-up and sentenced to jail time ranging from thirty months to eight years. In April, the Vietnam War finally ended as the city of Saigon surrendered and the remaining Americans were evacuated.

Between Vietnam and Watergate, times had changed—even at thirteen you could sense it—both had damaged us as people somehow, and things didn't feel the same. People had begun to view the world differently, with less trust and higher cynicism. The damage was done, and good, bad or indifferent, the country would never be the same again.

But that summer there were more important things to most thirteen-year-old boys. The Red Sox were tearing it up (and would go on to the World Series, only to lose to Cincinnati in a heartbreaking game-seven). Bernard's mother had taken us to the R-rated films *One Flew Over the Cuckoo's Nest* and *Dog Day Afternoon*, but when *Jaws* hit the theaters it immediately became the coolest and scariest thing any of us had ever been allowed to see. Even in summer hotspots like Potter's Cove and all throughout Cape Cod, people stayed out of the water in record numbers, constantly on the lookout for killer sharks, seeing fins behind every wave.

Later that year President Ford would survive two assassination attempts in less than seventeen days, then go on to lose to Jimmy Carter in the 1976 election.

But the summer prior, the summer of 1975, marked the first real memory I had that signaled there was something a bit different about Bernard.

Of the group, Bernard had the youngest mother, and although all our parents knew one another, none of them socialized or could be described as friends. She was the only one who didn't work. She had injured her back and received disability checks from the government, though she always looked fine to us. She drank a lot and rarely left the house during the day, but despite her problems, she was a very attractive woman, and considered by us to be a "cool" mom. Bernard slept at one of our houses almost every weekend, as his mother "entertained" various men she met at the local taverns she frequented and preferred to be alone with her beaus. This was common knowledge, but something none of us ever talked about, as Bernard seemed fine with it and only became embarrassed or upset if someone outside our group made a comment.

Of course, between her looks and behavior (which included sunbathing in their backyard in a bikini during the summer months) she quickly became a focal point for much of our hormone-crazed pubescent lust, but it was always kept quiet if Bernard was around. Still, he knew we were all drooling over his mother, but he seemed too preoccupied with every other female in town to notice. An interest in women was still relatively new to all of us, and Rick was the only one who'd had sex, having lost his virginity just weeks after his thirteenth birthday to a fifteen-year-old high school cheerleader the rest of us could only dream about even talking to.

Tommy had a more mature attitude than the rest of us did, and tended to hold back a bit, staying on the fringe of our mania like any sound leader. Yet we knew he easily could have found a girl to "do it" with had he wanted to. He was so good-looking it was unfair, yet he seemed to never use it to his advantage, as if somehow he were unaware of it. Donald was still at a point where he pretended (largely for the benefit of the rest of us) that girls were of sexual interest to him, and Bernard and I pulled up the proverbial rear, spending most waking hours thinking about girls but rarely getting anywhere near them.

The following September we'd enter high school, and within months I'd have my leather-jacket-wearing rebel routine down and my first real girlfriend. But that summer I was still a gangly and awkward kid with a twenty-four-hour erection—*a hard-on with feet*, my older brother Kenny had labeled me. He was five years older than I was, which had made him old enough to understand what had happened to our father, to miss him, and it devastated him. By the time I entered high school he had already graduated and enlisted in the Navy. He'd always seemed wholly uncomfortable in the role of big brother, much less surrogate father figure, so he kept his distance, and although it never seemed malicious or deliberate, I saw him just often enough to miss him, and frequently felt like an only child. He left home and joined the Navy at the end of that summer of 1975 and never looked back. From that point forward my memories of my brother consisted mostly of postcards he'd send from points all over the globe, and the one or two times a year I'd actually see him, when he'd blow into town for a day or two then head right back out on a ship to some distant locale.

A lot happened that summer—a lot changed, and memories were abundant—but on this night, sitting amidst the pale glow of security nightlights in that drab used car dealership, sipping beer and thinking back, I focused on one particular afternoon.

***

We moved through the forest purposefully, striding quickly

along the path until we reached an incline and finally a large clearing more than fifty yards in. Perhaps fifteen feet high and set on a circular cement platform stood an old stone fireplace. In years past, when this particular stretch of state forest had been a popular camping area, the fireplace had been a necessary intrusion to the natural setting that kept fires set by the hordes of campers who descended on the area each summer safely contained. But due to the continued growth of residential lots being sold and built upon, along with the emergence a few years prior of a more modern campground on the other side of town, this patch of woods had been all but forgotten. Here, the forest had been thinned out considerably, and the new house lots were slowly closing in, but the appeal for us was that you could still reach this relatively private area quickly, in less than five minutes in fact, from the center of town.

Once we'd reached the fireplace I stopped, surveyed the surrounding area for witnesses then gave Bernard the go-ahead nod.

He crouched down in front of the fireplace, removed several round stones blocking the front then reached his hand inside up to the elbow. It returned holding a magazine concealed in clear plastic. My heart skipped a beat—it was true. Bernard hadn't been making it up.

"Holy shit," I mumbled, "is that it?"

Bernard scrambled away from the fireplace and plunked down onto a bed of pine needles, eyes blinking rapidly behind thick lenses of glass. "Check it out."

I sat next to him. The sides of the plastic bag were blurred from condensation and dirt. "How long has it been in there?"

"Couple days." Bernard laid the bag across his lap and set to opening it as if handling fine china. "I didn't want to risk leaving it at home. If my mother finds this she'll freak out."

Bernard had claimed he'd come into possession of a certain magazine, one that supposedly made *Playboy* look like a comic book in comparison. He had not mentioned this magazine to anyone but me, or so he claimed, but you could never be totally sure with Bernard. His lies were never malicious, but they were often plentiful, and it left even close friends like me off guard at times as to when he was or wasn't telling the absolute truth. I'd been very leery when he'd first mentioned it that morning—a magazine so intense he couldn't keep it at home, couldn't tell anyone but his closest friends about because it was so bad—the whole thing reeked of a Bernard story. But, here we were.

I looked around, abruptly aware of how quiet the forest was but for the occasional cackle of a bird or the windy echo of a car speeding past on the nearby highway.

"Okay, we gotta go easy with it because it's not in the greatest shape." Bernard carefully removed what appeared to be a very old magazine from the plastic sleeve. On the cover was a black and white photograph of a blonde woman tied to a wooden chair. She wore a bra, panties, garter belt, stockings and high heels, and some sort of leather harness similar to a horse's bit had been attached to her mouth. At first glance she looked like a typical model on one of the true crime or detective magazines we'd managed to get a hold of in the past, magazines featuring scantily clad women and headlines like *Knife-Wielding Sex Fiend Tortures Bubbly Blondes!* (or some equally lurid blurb), and yet, even initially it seemed different somehow. The look in this woman's eyes didn't look posed or phony like the models I'd seen before. She looked genuinely terrified. My eyes shifted quickly to the words in bold red letters above her picture: BITCHES IN HEAT. The cover was cracked in several places, faded with age and dog-eared, and I couldn't find a price listed anywhere. It had something of an amateur look to it, not a nice slick and glossy cover, like most magazines I'd seen in stores or on the newsstands.

"You're not gonna fucking believe this." Bernard laughed, sounding more guttural than gleeful. "It's from the '60s, I guess, and it's *illegal.*"

"Where'd you get it?"

"Chuckie DiNunzio."

"Figures."

"I was gonna buy another *Penthouse* or something, but I asked if he had any other stuff, you know, better stuff where the girls were doing shit instead of just laying there. *Porno.*"

"Yeah, dip-shit, I know what it's called."

Bernard gave a wide grin. "Anyway, Chuckie said he had some underground stuff that used to belong to his old man. He said there was a big stack of them buried under a bunch of crap down in his basement, so he took me down there and let me go through them. Man, I was freaking out, thinking Chuckie's old man might show up, but Chuckie said the magazines had been down there so long his old man probably didn't even remember they were there. Anyway, I went through them real quick and picked one out. I didn't even know what was in it until I got a chance to sit down by myself and check it out, and then—*ohhh, baby*!"

I elbowed him lightly and laughed. "You're such a fucking goof, Bernard, I swear to God."

He laughed too, but quickly grew serious. "Hey, Chuckie says if they catch you with stuff this bad you're screwed royal."

I shrugged. "Chuckie DiNunzio's a moron."

"It was more expensive than the other ones, too," Bernard said as if he hadn't heard me. "Twenty bucks."

"*Twenty bucks*? Where the hell you get that much cash?"

"Lifted it out of my mother's purse."

"She's gonna miss that much, you fucking idiot."

"She already asked if I took it," he said through a smile. "I just said no and she believed me."

I shook my head. "You're nuts, man."

"Hey, don't tell anybody about the magazine, okay? Chuckie said if it got back to him that I told anybody where I got it him and DJ would kill me."

Chuckie DiNunzio was a squat kid who wore wayfarer sunglasses and his hair slicked straight back. From his skinny ties to his straight-legged Levi corduroys, Chuckie was a neighborhood legend that came from a family of convicts and seemed destined to follow. A year older than we were, he'd run the neighborhood's version of a black market for as long as we could remember. Whatever you needed, Chuckie either had it or could get it. If he came up empty his best friend and sidekick DJ Jablonski went to work on it. DJ, who was borderline retarded but physically enormous and the only sixteen-year-old still in junior high school, also provided Chuckie with the muscle he needed when deals went bad or "customers" got out of line. Chuckie dealt mostly in cigarettes, *Playboy* and *Penthouse* magazines, beer, pocket and hunting knives—even concert tickets once we hit high school. If you wanted it but couldn't get it, Chuckie DiNunzio was the man to see.

This, however, seemed over the top even for Chuckie.

"I ain't gonna say shit to anybody," I mumbled.

Bernard carefully peeled back the cover to reveal a group of pictures segmented into various panels across the page. All were black and white and continued in a series that had begun on the front cover. The same woman was bound to the chair, the photographs tight shots; the background dark and without depth, as if they had been shot in front of a ceiling-to-floor black sheet. My eyes moved slowly, taking in one picture after another, each worse than the one before it. A fat shirtless man in a leather mask had joined the woman, and stood next to a table on which several odd devices and instruments of torture had been scattered. The first series of pictures consisted of the man hovering over the woman threateningly then progressed to a row where he was holding her chin up and slapping her repeatedly across the face.

"That's fucked up," I said. This magazine was already having the opposite effect on me that others had. A naked woman was one thing, but this was dark and grotesque and not even remotely sexy.

"Oh," Bernard said breathlessly, "wait."

He turned the page and although something told me not to, I looked anyway.

The man had cut the woman's bra off and let it fall to the floor. In the remaining series he was touching her while she screamed and attempted to squirm away. The last photograph on the page showed the man standing next to the table, an odd metallic device with a long and thin rubber hose dangling from it in one hand, his other pointing a reprimanding finger at the still bound and terrified woman.

"What the hell is that?" I gulped so hard it hurt.

Bernard looked at me and smiled, his small chest rising and falling faster than before, a band of bright sunshine reflecting off his eyeglasses. "You know what an enema is?"

I did, but it took me a few seconds to remember the exact mechanics of it. "Jesus," I finally said, "he's not gonna do that, is he?"

Bernard nodded rapidly, his face flushed, but not from the sun. He turned the page.

"She looks all scared at first," he said, slowly returning his gaze to the magazine, "but then once it starts she likes it, see?"

"Oh, man, that's fucking nasty!" Afraid I might be sick, I struggled to my feet and brushed the pine needles from the seat of my pants. "Why the hell would I want to see something like that?"

"She likes it," he said again. "Look, on the last page he unties her from the chair and she—"

"You're fucking deranged, dude," I said, forcing a cavalier laugh.

Something changed in his expression, and he gave a subtle shrug. "Nice tits, though, huh?"

I nodded. "Yeah, I guess."

"You *guess*?"

"Well, fuck, man, she's probably older than my grandmother by now."

He closed the magazine and slid it back into the bag. "You think Julie Henderson's tits are that nice?"

"They're not as big as those," I said, relieved to see he was putting the magazine away. "But much nicer, not even close."

Julie Henderson was 19 and gorgeous, the older sister of Brian Henderson, one of our classmates. Everything alive and male lusted after her, and we were no exception. To make matters worse, Julie jogged through town in late afternoon wearing short-shorts and a skimpy top almost daily, so of course it was not unusual for us to stop whatever we were doing and make sure to be on the street to see her pass by. From this simple event, which usually took all of fifteen seconds, countless discussions arose regarding all things Julie—most typically locker room in nature, of course—which only further fanned the fires of our sexual fantasies.

Bernard crawled across the fireplace and stuffed the plastic bag deep inside before replacing the loose stones. He stood up and hopped down next to me. "You know she runs right by here, right?"

I hadn't known that but didn't want to appear ignorant of her route. "Yeah, sure."

"Sometimes I hide behind the fireplace and watch when she goes by."

"Yeah, okay, perv-boy."

"Sorry I'm not a fag like you."

"Shut up, asshole." I pushed him playfully, and not with much force. "Yeah, I'm a fag just because I don't hide in the woods and beat-off watching some girl run by."

Bernard staggered a bit, laughed then straightened his eyeglasses. "You watch her just like everybody else does."

"Yeah but not out here. I mean, if I'm outside and—"

"*If*? Oh, yeah—right!"

"Fine, so I make sure I'm outside when she runs by." We were both laughing now, and although I felt better, the pictures in that magazine kept appearing in my mind. "I look and I smile and she ignores me like always and jogs right by. Then I go inside and that's it. I don't fucking wait out in the woods and hide like some jack-off."

Bernard looked at me like the thoughts occupying his mind were more important than returning my put-down with one of his own. "You know," he said softly, "if you wanted to do something with her...this would be a good place to do it."

"Yeah, I'm sure Julie can't wait to come out here and fuck you, Bernard. She's probably home right now, all playing with herself and shit just thinking about it."

I expected him to laugh, but he didn't. "Maybe she wouldn't want to at first."

"Try ever. Shit, if you were the last guy on the planet she'd probably go lesbo."

"I'm being serious, dick-weed. She's going away to college in September, you know."

"So?"

"So, if we're gonna do something with her it has to be before the end of the summer."

"Bernard, listen to me. Julie Henderson would never do anything with you. Get a clue, dude, she probably doesn't even know who you are."

He walked toward the path leading out of the forest, then stopped and looked back at me. "I was talking to Rick about it."

"About Julie Henderson?"

"Yeah. He said it would be funny if we waited out here one day, then when she ran by one of us could stop her and start talking to her." He was smiling again, like he might be kidding. "Then one of us could sneak up behind her and pull her shorts down real fast. She'd be all embarrassed and stuff, but we'd get to see her."

I moved closer and a shaft of sunlight cut the trees, causing me to squint. "Rick said that?"

Bernard nodded. "See, that way if she got all mad we could just take off running like it was a big joke...but if she doesn't get mad, then we could try something else and see what happens."

"*Rick* said all this?"

"Yeah."

Another Bernard lie. "Bullshit."

"We're going over to his house in a couple minutes," he reminded me. "Ask him."

"You guys could get in major trouble doing something like that, man. Seriously."

"She wouldn't tell." Bernard's eyes narrowed. "They never tell."

Something in his tone caused my stomach muscles to clench. "What's that supposed to mean?"

"Girls usually don't tell when stuff like that happens to them," he said.

"How the hell would you know?"

"Saw a show about it on TV. That's what they said."

"Whatever. I wouldn't do anything like that anyway," I told him, still not certain he was serious.

"You wouldn't want to make it with Julie Henderson?"

"Of course I would, but...but, Jesus, I'd want her to want it too. If she doesn't then it's assault, dude—*rape*—that's what it is."

"So what?"

"So I don't want to fucking rape her, what's wrong with you?"

"But if she never told on you, and no one knew...then would you?"

"She'd know," I answered. "*I'd* know."

"*She'd* know," he said mockingly, holding his chest like he was dying and repeating in a high-pitched voice, "*I'd* know! *I'd* know!"

"You asshole." I laughed and threw a fake punch at him. "I thought you were serious."

"Maybe I am."

"Yeah, and maybe you aren't," I said as we turned and headed out of the forest.

"Besides, being a huge homo, you wouldn't know what to do with a girl anyway."

"Okay, gay-boy, whatever."

Our laughter echoed through the trees. As we followed the path on our way from the forest, we continued to insult each other with homophobic phrases and endlessly creative uses for profanity, as most teenage boys are wont to do.

In that regard, my memory of that afternoon seemed in no way out of the ordinary. Confronting Julie Henderson in the forest never came up in conversation again, and I dismissed it as nothing more than Bernard's wishful thinking.

But I now found myself questioning what until that point had seemed a harmless discussion between two boys huddled over an old porno rag. Had Bernard simply been trying to work through his own sexual awakenings, confusion and desire like the rest of us, talking typical teen male bravado and pretending to be something he wasn't? Or had it been a signal I'd missed—a warning that something else existed in him even then? Something dark... diseased...deadly.

She wouldn't tell. They never tell.

I hadn't thought about that afternoon in a very long time, yet the images that remained most vivid were also the most disturbing, even after all these years.

Glancing at the desk, I noticed three more empty beer bottles sitting in a neat row. I scooped them up, tossed them into the gym bag then propped my feet up and tried to get as comfortable as one can in a hard plastic chair.

A misting rain had replaced the snow. The night had grown darker it seemed.

My belly warmed with brew but my mind still reeling, I closed my eyes and searched for more memories, more clues.

***

It was just after two in the morning when I saw her.

A thick fog had rolled in off the water, making visibility a few feet at best. The street was quiet, I hadn't seen another living soul or even a car pass in more than an hour, and I was digging through my gym bag for another beer when I noticed movement from the corner of my eye.

I stood up and looked more closely at the fog, a small lamp and a night security bulb over the interior showroom provided the only nearby light. Two powerful beams on the roof sliced a canal through the fog, illuminating portions of the lot and the rows of cars. At the very edge of the property was a woman—a woman just standing there—thin arms dangling at her sides, vines of slow-moving fog curling about her, cradling her with ghost-like fingers.

I returned the unopened beer to my gym bag and moved around the side of the desk, never taking my eyes from her. Slowly, I slid closer to the showroom window. She was looking right at me, everything but her eyes masked in night and mist.

And while gazing into those eyes, it came to me. She looked like the woman with the little boy at Rick's apartment building. *You here about the plumbing?*

She looked exactly like her, from what I could remember. I moved so close to the window that I was able to place a hand against it. Had to just be some hooker out wandering the streets in the middle of the night, I told myself. In that neighborhood—even at that time of night—it wouldn't be unusual. But the woman looked sickly, and New Bedford was miles from Potter's Cove. It seemed wildly far-fetched, and yet, deep down, I knew it was the same woman.

And from the way she was staring at me, she recognized me too.

Curiosity won out over fear, and I made my way to the door. I unlocked a series of deadbolts on the front entrance, the sound of them disengaging unsettling somehow in the otherwise quiet night.

The woman was still there, arms now folded across her sunken chest.

The weight of the nightstick on my hip reminded me of its presence as I pushed the door open and stepped into the fog. The air was brisk, a bit cooler than it should have been, and the fog seemed to dissipate somewhat. The steady thud of my heart echoed in my ears. I slowly, casually dropped a hand to the nightstick, felt my fingers wrap around the handle and tighten.

I'd either had more to drink than I realized, or the recent events combined with an overall lack of sleep and the recurring Bernard nightmare had finally taken their toll. *Or*, I told myself, *all of this is actually happening.*

"Ma'am," I said through a hard swallow, "you all right?"

The woman gave no discernable response.

"Are you okay? Do you—you need some help, ma'am?"

Without saying a word, the woman let her arms drop back to her sides and left them dangling there, swaying as if broken and no longer of any use to her. But something in those eyes changed. They seemed to be imploring me, beckoning me.

My legs shuddered and I broke eye contact long enough to glance quickly across the front lot. I needed to know she was alone. The lot and street beyond were empty and still. My eyes returned to the woman in the fog.

"Can't be the same woman," I mumbled. "Can't be." I clutched the nightstick at my side but left it in my belt. "You live around here?"

Again, no response.

"You lost, lady?"

The woman turned away and drifted off.

I stood there, frightened, despising my weakness. "Are you lost?" I asked again, louder this time.

The woman continued on and slipped away into the fog, one final glimpse of her visible through the rolling clouds before they swallowed her completely as she reached the other side of the street.

With a deep breath, I held the nightstick tight and started across the lot after her.

CHAPTER 7

The fog thickened and embraced me from every direction, a giant specter with no beginning, middle or end. I moved to the outskirts of the lot, aware that the dealership was well behind me now and that from somewhere back there the two showroom roof lights were cutting the darkness and fog. Yet, what little light I could discern seemed to be coming from a solitary streetlight just across the width of road separating my position from the beginnings of the abandoned factory. I hesitated, waited for my eyes to adjust, and listened. There was no sign of the woman, and although the normal din of the city was still evident in the distance, it was quiet here, and but for the slow rolling fog, utterly still.

I held my ground for a moment and listened to the argument raging in my mind, wanting to forget all this and return to the relative safety of the dealership, but knowing I wouldn't, knowing I couldn't. I slid the nightstick free but kept it down against my leg as I stepped from the curb and crossed the street.

The fog parted, and I continued on to the far curb and what had once been the factory driveway. An old security and information hut sat boarded up and slowly dying a few feet from the beginning of the property, a long section of heavy though rusted chain still run across the lot entrance to prevent trespassers from driving too close to the abandoned building beyond. I pulled my flashlight from my belt, flicked it on and gave a slow sweep of the area. The beam was powerful but did little other than illuminate the fog, so I switched it off, returned it to my belt and allowed the streetlight to guide me.

Once I'd reached the chain I crouched and walked under it. The dark, ominous carcass of the factory stood before me, most of the long vertical windows blown out, the few panes still intact covered with the impenetrable filth of years of neglect. Decades before, those same myopic windowpanes had been blurred instead with sweat, while shadows, faceless and vague, submitted in silence. But I was certain those ghosts were long since exorcised. Something else was haunting this place now.

Or perhaps, only haunting me.

The thin layer of snow still blanketing the area had begun to melt, trickling and dripping from the factory to the pavement below. The windows on the first floor were boarded shut, but the large front doors had rotted and mostly fallen away, setting the mouth of the building in an eternal yawn.

I leaned closer to the opening. A partially rotted wooden plank that looked like it had fallen from above and landed there ages ago was wedged diagonally across the doorway. From within the enormous vacant structure I heard the echo of dripping water followed by a faint scratching sound. I reached again for my flashlight, aimed the beam at the plank and darkness beyond. Squatting at one end of the plank was an enormously plump rat. Making odd grunting noises, it sat back on its hind legs, reared up and bared its teeth.

Startled, I took a step back but kept the beam trained on him. The light reflected off his eyes, causing them to glow, two red orbs cutting the night. The standoff continued until finally, after a few contemplative sniffs, the rat turned, waddled to the end of the plank, and dropped down into darkness.

The acids in my stomach churned and I belched, tasted beer. Despite the chill in the air perspiration had beaded along my forehead, and my mind began to clear a bit. *What the fuck am I doing?* I looked back over my shoulder. The fog was so thick the dealership across the street was completely concealed by it, though the rooftop lights were just barely visible above the haze.

Something moved behind me.

I spun back around toward the factory, the flashlight in one hand, my nightstick in the other, both leveled in front of me and sweeping across the doorway in unison. Just beyond the rotted plank, partially shrouded in darkness, stood the woman.

Our eyes met and I offered a subtle nod.

She took a few steps deeper into the building then looked back at me.

I felt myself moving forward, swinging a leg over the plank and climbing through the doorway as if I no longer had complete control over myself. The flashlight flickered and extinguished. The darkness mixed with a soft cool breeze, the fear welling up in me in a single frantic rush as I shook the flashlight. The beam returned, casting a pool of light ahead of me, but by the time my eyes had adjusted I realized the woman was gone.

I stepped over a small pile of rubble and garbage and did my best to ignore the array of gut-wrenching smells. I swept the light about, searching for her, but found only a graffiti-covered wall and floors thick with debris. Scratching and then a scurrying sound I recognized as more rats momentarily distracted me, so I swung the light around.

Down a long and narrow hallway to my right, I saw a glint of light but no sign of the woman.

I carefully crossed the room, following the light at the end of the hallway. It led to another room, smaller and in even worse shape. I stopped in what was left of the doorway and saw a single candle burning on the floor, garbage strewn from one corner of the room to the next. The horrible stench of human waste filled the stale air.

The flashlight shook in my hand. I shut it off, returned it to my belt and gripped my nightstick with both hands. As I moved into the room, the flickering candlelight lapped the walls, casting shadows like thrashing demons. The woman was kneeling on the floor in the center of the room, holding something and rocking slowly. A dirty syringe, a spent book of matches and a blackened spoon lay scattered nearby. My eyes shifted; she was holding a boy in her arms—the same little boy who had hidden behind her leg at Rick's apartment building—but now the boy was lifeless. Cradled, arms and legs dangling, his head lolled to the side, rested in the crook of the woman's elbow, mouth open, small, swollen tongue protruding, eyes wide but seeing nothing—long dead.

Sinking deeper into madness, I shortened the distance between us. The woman's head turned to reveal a face tormented and dirty, eyes bloodshot and terrified, cheeks hollow, dark skin pockmarked.

She glared at me like I was to blame, slowly rocked her dead son in sickly thin, needle-ravaged arms, and whimpered softly.

"You here about the plumbing?"

"No, ma'am," I answered.

She looked away, eyes gliding to the far wall as if she'd seen something else, something more. Lips moving silently, she continued to rock the boy in her arms.

My eyes darted about the room, following the edges of light provided by the candle to the far wall, where drawn in either red paint or blood were odd symbols that looked almost like hieroglyphics, hastily smeared about. What was once the door to the room had been suspended between two small stacks of chipped cinderblocks, forming what appeared to be a makeshift altar of some kind. Something lay beneath it in a heap on the floor, dark and unmoving, but I couldn't make out what it was.

The woman moved, diverting my attention back to her. She laid the boy on the filthy floor gently and with great care, then began to pull at the belt holding her robe closed. Bony fingers worked furiously until the belt was undone or torn loose, and the robe had fallen open. She slid one hand beneath the boy's head, pulled it closer and leaned over him. A single small and emaciated brown breast fell free, the nipple elongated and raw.

She held the boy close, guided her nipple to his lips and pumped the loose skin along her breast, lips again moving rapidly but silently.

"Lady," I managed, "Christ—lady, let me—let me get you and the boy out of here."

She looked up at me. "You here about the plumbing?"

"No, I'm not here about the goddamn plumbing!"

Her eyes rolled back in her head as if she'd lost all control of them, and her body bucked, throttled by phantom hands.

I stood frozen as a small appendage emerged directly from the cracked skin along her nipple. At first I thought it was a long hair.

But then it moved.

Another matching thing broke through the skin, moved in time with the other along the boy's lips, as if searching for purchase. The woman's hand tightened around her breast, and as her nipple burst the shelled back of what appeared to be some sort of beetle or cockroach squirmed free, followed by another and another. As they bled from her onto the boy's mouth, forcing their way between his lips and disappearing between them, I realized the hair-like substance had been an antenna. The insects continued to gush from her in impossible numbers, overflowing in the boy's mouth like renegade parts of a single clicking, pulsating mass.

I reached blindly for the wall behind me, doubled over and somehow managed to choke back the vomit gurgling at the base of my throat. I staggered back, steadied myself against the wall, and looked at her.

She was still kneeling next to the boy, but no longer holding him.

The insects were gone. Her eyes, now unnaturally wide, began to bleed.

"What…what's happening to me?" I asked.

She lunged for me with inhuman speed and clamped her hands onto my forearm. Her grip was painful and possessed greater strength than she appeared to have, and the moment her flesh made contact with mine, I felt a surge of energy explode through me like an electrical shock. My body jerked to rigid attention, and as my head fell back I heard the sound of my nightstick bouncing along the concrete floor.

Horrible flashes of unspeakable carnage flickered through my mind like an old 16mm film. Faces, such hideous, boil-covered, bloody grinning faces; growls and guttural laughter; fire; the screams of nameless beings engulfed in plumes of brilliant orange flame and blood. Teeth—fangs—ripping at slabs of human meat, what had once been people hanging upside down and gutted like cattle. Depravity—depravity like I had never seen—and all of it gushing through me in a single violent stream, disintegrating into a shimmer and a wisp of fog, trailing away from my vision like a spiral of cigarette smoke snaking toward a ceiling.

But there was no ceiling, only dark sky and thick fog.

I was outside again, standing in the middle of the street between the factory and the car dealership. My nightstick was on the ground at my feet, but the flashlight was on and clutched firmly in my left hand. Heart racing, I crouched down, retrieved my baton and bolted for the dealership.

Consumed by the fog, I struggled to maintain my bearings, running as hard and as fast as I could despite the burning in my lungs and the ache in my legs. And although I could not see it, I knew the evil was still there, still with me. There, in the fog, chasing, circling me, calling to me in low, tortured growls.

CHAPTER 8

Three days. Three days of confusion and disbelief, of vague memory and flashes of terror. Three days of lying in bed, staring at the ceiling, wondering if it was night or day beyond shades pulled shut, of drug-induced sleep, of groggy submission even when I was somewhere near consciousness. Three days of trying to convince myself I had not gone utterly insane.

The owner of the dealership had gone to work that morning to find me gone without explanation, the door unlocked and the desk where I'd been stationed littered with a pile of spent beer bottles. Nino had tried several times to contact me via the two-way but I hadn't responded. I'd left the dealership and driven back to Potter's Cove, parked out in front of Rick's apartment building and waited for him to come home from the club.

At about four o'clock he pulled in and I met him on the street. Concerned, he invited me in but I declined, and asked him instead about the young black woman and her son who lived in the first-floor apartment when you first walked in.

That apartment was empty, Rick told me. Had been for months since the last tenant, a single middle-aged man, had moved out. Then she was a squatter and had broken in and was staying there without anyone's knowledge, I'd insisted, because I'd seen her the other day. She'd spoken to me the other day. Her *son* had spoken to me the other day.

Near total emotional collapse, I explained what had happened, and it was then that Rick insisted I let him drive me home. I agreed, but only after he promised he'd find out what was going on in that apartment.

I vaguely remember Toni thanking Rick before putting me to bed, then laying there, exhausted and spent, straining to hear their voices in the kitchen until I'd drifted off into something similar to sleep. At some later point she appeared with a prescription from her boss, pills that would relax me and help me sleep, she promised. Trust her, she'd said, and I did.

Now, three blurred days later, I found myself parked across the street from Battalia Security's home office, a small storefront space on Acushnet Avenue, one of the main drags in New Bedford. I sat in the car and watched the place until I felt ready to wade into what I knew would be an unpleasant situation at best.

A pair of tiny bells over the door signaled my entrance. I moved to the front desk where Marge, the receptionist, secretary, and occasional dispatcher, sat, headset in place, long acrylic fingernails tapping a keyboard. She saw me and offered a tentative smile. "Hey, Al."

"Hey."

"How you doin', hon?" she asked quietly. "You okay?"

I nodded. "Nino in?"

She cocked her head toward his office at the end of a small hallway behind her, the door closed. "He's waiting for you, go ahead in."

***

Nino, stressed out of his mind as usual, glanced up from an enormous pile of paperwork as I entered his office. He tendered a gaslock smile and motioned to a chair in front of his desk. "Have a seat."

I closed the door behind me, stepped over to his desk but stayed on my feet. "Nino, listen, I'm sorry about all this, I—"

Nino held his hands up, tossed a pen onto his desk and sat back in his leather swivel a bit. "I know you are, Al, I know you are." Again, he motioned to the chair. "Sit."

I moved to the chair and lowered myself into it, feeling like a child summoned to the principal's office. "Nino, there's no excuse for what happened, and I'm sorry, sincerely I am. I give you my word nothing like that will ever happen again. Ever."

His eyes darted about, looking anywhere but directly at me. He leaned back further in his chair and nervously stroked his mustache with stubby fingers. "You been with us a long time," he finally said. "You're the best employee we got. The best we ever had."

"I got fifteen years in here, Nino," I reminded him.

"I know you do. You're senior guy by like ten years, for Christ's sake." He again smiled briefly through obvious discomfort. "And besides all that, you—well, shit, you become a friend, you know what I'm saying?"

"I just—I'm having some problems at the moment, but—"

"Yeah, I hear ya." He straightened the chair, pushed away from the desk and stood up. A squat and bulbous man with a penchant for flashy jewelry, ill-fitting slacks and imitation silk shirts, on this day he had worn a sweat suit and tennis shoes, signaling he didn't plan to stay at the office long once our meeting was concluded. "Here's the thing, though. I talked to Petey last night, and I did what I could, but my brother's the boss, Al, you know how it is. I got say, but he's got final say."

"Look—"

"He thinks the world of you too, man, you know that." Nino waddled over to a water cooler in the corner, found the cup dispenser empty and grabbed a nearby coffee mug instead. "But shit, Al, you walked on a job."

"I know. I fucked up bad."

Nino sniffed the coffee-stained mug, then slid it under the nozzle and filled it with water. Watching the bubbles rise in the plastic bottle, he said, "Thing is, we lost the account."

"Christ, Nino, I'm sorry."

"I did everything I could." The mug now full, Nino returned to his desk and plopped into his swivel. From his middle desk drawer he pulled a package of two Alka-Seltzer tablets, tore them open and dropped them into the mug. "I'm sorry, we gotta let you go."

"Come on, Nino," I said, standing again. "I fucked up, but I got years in here."

"You walked on a job! You fucking walked away in the middle of the night and left the place unlocked!" He grabbed the mug and killed the contents in one frantic gulp. "Then, if that ain't bad enough, the guy finds beers all over the place!" He slammed the mug on the desk and it split from the force into two even halves. He glanced down, realized he was only holding a handle, and fired it at the wall. "Drinking on the fucking job happens now and then, you don't think I know that? But you clean the shit up, for Christ's sake! What kinda fucking moron leaves them lying around? What are you, freakin' *stunadz*? Petey had to get involved personally; you see what I'm saying? Petey don't like to have to get involved personally. He had to talk to the guy and calm his ass down. Shit, Al, he mighta sued us. He still might."

"If you can just give me a week or two," I said. "Just a week or two to get my shit together. A leave—give me a leave. No pay, just some time off so I can straighten things out."

"Come on, man, don't go making this more of a bitch than it already is," Nino said. "Me and Petey talked it over, and we decided even with the shit that happened we'll give you a good recommendation, okay?" He grabbed an envelope from one of the stacks on his desk. "Now, here's the money we owe ya from your last check, plus your vacation pay. I slipped a month of base pay in there, too. Take the money and run, Al."

I grabbed the envelope, stuffed it into my jacket and dropped my badge and employee ID card in front of him. I'd clipped the two-way to my belt earlier, just in case, and with a tug pulled it free and tossed it onto the desk with the other items.

Nino extended his hand across the desk.

After a moment, I accepted it.

***

It was a little after noon by the time I got back to town. Rick and Donald were waiting for me at the base of the staircase leading to my apartment. Decked out in a black leather jacket, heavy sweatshirt, jeans and a baseball cap worn backwards, Rick stood watching me with concern in his eyes. Donald, in a suit and tie, gave an awkward half-wave and a nervous smile. I didn't need to say anything; they knew I'd been fired.

"Motherfuckers," Rick mumbled.

I shrugged. "I had it coming, man. Can't walk on a job."

"Are you all right?" Donald asked.

"I'll live."

Rick scratched his five o'clock shadow then turned to face a gentle but crisp breeze blowing in off the water. "One of the part-time door guys is leaving next week," he said a moment later. "Already gave his notice. I can get you in at the club if you want."

"Thanks, but I need some time. I got to pull myself together."

Rick nodded; eyes trained on the still water, the slowly gliding ducks. "You didn't tell them about…you know."

"Yeah, I told Nino the reason I freaked out was because I'm being haunted by the ghosts of a little boy and his mother." I shook my head and turned into the breeze myself. "Not to mention the pink elephants under my bed and the flying elves that live in my fucking carpet."

"I called the landlord, told him one of my buddies thought he saw someone in the vacant apartment the other day. He sent someone from his office down and they checked it out. The door was locked; the place was totally secure. No signs of forced entry or any signs at all that anyone had been in there since the last tenant."

"I know what I saw, Rick."

He looked at me. "I was there. I went in with the guy. No one's been in that apartment."

"I know what I saw."

"I'm just telling you what—"

"No—horseshit—you're riding the fence. You're either with me on this or you're not."

"You're sure it was the same lady and kid?"

My whole body trembled. "Yeah, I'm positive." But the truth was, I could no longer be positive about anything. The truth was, I was terrified I'd lost my mind.

"All right, all right," Donald said, "everyone just calm down."

Rick turned and strutted toward his Jeep. "Come on."

"Where are we going?"

"Donny's on his lunch hour," he answered without looking back. "Let's go get something to eat and talk this through."

Five minutes later we parked a couple streets over, about half a block away from a Vietnamese guy selling hotdogs and cola from a vendor pushcart.

He and Donald both ordered hotdogs. I ordered a Coke. Lunch in hand we drifted a few feet away to the entrance to one of the parks in town. The sky was cloudless for the first time in recent memory, and the sun was strong and warming despite the chilly temperature in the air, a teaser now that spring was only days away. Although the area was heavily traveled, it afforded enough privacy for us to quietly continue our conversation.

"Let's cut to the chase," I said. "You guys don't believe me, that's the bottom line."

Donald bit into his lunch, chewed for a moment before responding. "No one said that, Alan. But you have to admit there's quite a difference between nightmares—dreams—we all shared and the things you've described. The dream aspect is strange, no doubt about it, but at the end of the day, all we've experienced are dreams. You're talking about things taking place while you're awake."

"All I know is that whoever this woman is, whoever this kid is, they're connected to Bernard somehow." I sipped my cola then dropped the rest of it into a nearby trash bin. "They're obviously trying to contact me. They're trying to tell me something."

Rick and Donald exchanged glances, but neither said a word.

"You know what? Fuck both you guys."

"You said you were drinking that night," Donald said. "Could that have had something to do with what happened?"

I faced him. "Oh, I don't really think you want to go there, do you?"

"Now, look, I'm just saying—"

"What? What are you *just saying*, Donald?"

Tension hung in the air like a shroud.

Rick took a bite of hotdog, grimaced, and looked at it as if to be certain he was, in fact, holding something edible. "You told me there was all kinds of weird shit in the factory," he eventually managed.

"Yeah, shit painted on the wall and what looked like an altar." I ran my hands through my hair. "The place is fucked up, I..." *I can't even remember the worst of what happened there*, is what I wanted to say, but couldn't. "It's just fucked up in there. You don't believe me, go look for yourselves."

Donald forced down the rest of his hotdog. "Stop being so confrontational. We never said we didn't believe you."

I looked to Rick. "So, what do we do?"

The frustration and anxiety etched across his face was disquieting. I was used to Rick having a temper, but I hadn't seen him struggle with this kind of fear and uncertainty since the day of his prison sentencing years before. "I don't know what the fuck's going on anymore. Dreams and thoughts and all kinds of dark shit racing through my mind, I—I don't know what's happening here, but there's gotta be something to it. It's like nothing seems real anymore. It's all fucking hazy and—"

"Incomplete," I said.

"Agreed." Donald lit a cigarette and looked at the ground. "It's the same for me. I feel like I should be able to remember certain things but I can't, I try but sometimes nothing makes any goddamn sense."

"I think no matter what," Rick said, "we stick together. We stick together and we look out for each other, like always. We go off on our own or start fighting between ourselves and we're fucked."

I nodded, welcoming them to my madness, grateful to no longer be drowning in it alone.

Rick spit out a bite of hotdog and fired the rest back in the direction of the vendor. "Jesus, these are fucking disgusting."

The vendor watched the remains of the hotdog roll along the pavement with a quizzical look.

"Take it easy," Donald said, "don't make a scene."

"Goddamn things *crunch*, for Christ's sake." He motioned to the vendor and increased the volume of his voice. "Peanuts crunch, motherfucker, not hotdogs. Fuckin' slant. What the hell you doing selling American food anyway? Ass-bags come to this country and—"

"Scoop up all the good jobs like selling hotdogs on street corners and picking produce for pennies a day. Bastards." Donald flicked his cigarette away and took Rick by the elbow. "Come on, you have to drive me back to work."

Rick jerked his arm free and started toward the vendor with a slow but threatening gait. "You looking at something, you fucking cocksucker?"

"I cannot tolerate it when he behaves like this," Donald said. "Goddamn child."

"Come on, man," I said, stepping between him and the vendor, who had already begun to move to another corner. "Don't take it out on him, let's just get the hell out of here."

Rick glared at me, looking like he might literally explode if he didn't hit something, and for a second, I thought that something might be me, but he spun around, stormed back to the Jeep and punched that instead.

***

The ride to Donald's office building was quiet and uncomfortable. After some brief and standard good-byes, Rick and I continued on to my apartment. He parked near the railroad tracks and we sat there without speaking for quite a while.

"I shouldn't have freaked out like that back there," he eventually said. "I just get—you know, shit builds up and—"

"Whatever," I said. "Don't worry about it."

"Maybe we're all going a little nuts."

"Maybe."

There was anger in his eyes, a defiance of fear. "What the hell's happening?"

"I don't know. But I think you were right when you said that whatever it is, it's some bad shit. And we don't know the half of it."

"You think we ever will?"

"Yeah," I said. "Whether we want to or not."

CHAPTER 9

I blinked open my eyes, escaped one darkness for another. What little I was able to discern of our bedroom slowly blended into focus. The shade was pulled but enough moonlight bled through to partially illuminate the far wall. I couldn't be sure how long I'd been out, but it felt late. I'd taken another one of those damn pills and slipped into dreamless sleep, and though I was now fully awake, I knew the aftereffects of the tranquilizer would linger for quite some time. The blankets were off and kicked down around my feet. On Toni's side of the bed they'd been neatly turned back and were still tucked in at the side. In the darkness beyond, the bedroom door stood slightly ajar, a faint light visible along the gap between its edge and the doorframe. I pawed at my eyes, the lids still heavy, and let loose a lengthy yawn.

Somewhere outside a siren blared before fading to silence. It was replaced by the distant sound of Toni's voice. I lay still and listened. She was on the kitchen phone, talking just above a whisper, the floor creaking occasionally as she walked. I couldn't make out any of what she was saying, but her tone was somber.

I focused on my feet, there at the edge of the bed. They looked so pale in the dark, so white and bloodless, as if they'd been carved from ivory.

One day I'll be nude and stretched out just like this, I thought, but instead of being in bed I'll be slapped atop a cold metal table. Someone I don't know and have probably never met will hover over me, preparing my body, desecrating it, draining the blood, replacing it with something else, something foreign and unnatural; something that once introduced will render me subhuman. The idea that my body would one day be transformed and treated, protected from decay so that it could lay sealed away beneath the ground—no longer a living organism, more an unseen ornament, a perverse version of what it had once been—seemed both hideous and fascinating. What would it be like? Would I know or even care when it was happening to me?

I wondered if other people looked at their bodies and thought about the same things.

My eyes shifted to the nightstand, and the dark lamp, the leather Bible draped in rosary beads, and the clock radio that resided there. I wondered when each item had been manufactured, and realized that regardless, unless purposely destroyed, in all likelihood each would be here in one form or another long after I'd gone.

The events of the last few days flashed through my mind in rapid succession. As the progression slowed, my memories focused on Rick strutting about and screaming at that poor hotdog vendor like some testosterone-gone-wild teenager. We were very different, Rick and I, and though I found certain aspects of his personality appalling, there were also those I envied. I didn't possess the discipline to hit the gym five days a week, to run three miles a day; I didn't share his fascination with keeping the body beautiful, his compulsive desire to stay forever young. I'd never longed for immortality. But for Rick, life and age were no different than any of the other games he'd mastered. In his mind they were opponents, and Rick played to win.

Some days it seemed nothing more than a desire to turn back time and erase the year he'd spent in prison, to freeze the clock and live instead as the person he'd been in the days before it all went bad. He never discussed his time behind bars, and I'd always respected that. In many ways, I had a healthy dose of guilty admiration for Rick. He was capable of things I was not, yet it often seemed he did things in order to prove to himself what was already glaringly apparent to everyone else. At eighteen, I wouldn't have survived a week in a maximum-security prison, and in my late thirties I didn't have the balls, confidence or even the inclination to go white water rafting or skydiving or mountain climbing the way he occasionally did. I couldn't remember what it was like to have a girl on my arm I didn't plan to spend more than a few hours with, or how it felt to make love to more than one person in the same week. That sort of lonely and vacuous freedom was a memory so distant, I questioned whether it had ever been a genuine facet of my life at all. Still, as Bernard had so cruelly said on the tape, Rick had never imagined his life would be spent as a bouncer at a local nightclub. Now, those things that had always given him the edge were necessary tools for survival. Younger, stronger men would soon be bucking for his job, if they weren't already, and eventually, one of them would show him the curb. Then, all the rugged good looks, pumped muscles, independence and tough-guy-swagger in the world wouldn't save him. As incomprehensible as it seemed, Rick would one day be old and unable to rely on his physical prowess, forced to admit he was just as frightened and uncertain as everyone else, and in the end, just another lost soul trying to find his way.

Perhaps that had been the source of his anger, his rage at how life had turned out and a fear of what lie ahead. But the violence in Rick had been there as long as I'd known him. Was the constant pressure of living up to the Superman image he'd created to blame, or were there specific incidents hidden somewhere in the past that better explained it?

That day in the forest with Bernard came to mind. *Had* something happened out there? Had Bernard done something to Julie Henderson in those woods? Had Rick helped him? Would Rick do something like that—could he have done something like that even then, even at thirteen? I closed my eyes, tried to remember back through the years. As far as I knew, Julie had gone off to college that September, but she'd been a lot older than we were and I'd hardly known her. I couldn't recall seeing her around town after that summer, and my friendship with her brother had waned so I'd no longer been privy to even casual information on Julie's life. But had something happened, it would've been big news in Potter's Cove. Everyone would've known about it, charges would've been pressed, assuming she'd told anyone.

They never tell.

I ran my hands through my hair and focused on the ceiling.

Things I'd been certain of no longer seemed absolute. Was Bernard right about a lot more on that tape than any of us wanted to admit? Were any of us what we seemed? Was I just an asshole for thinking Rick capable of such a thing or naïve for never before realizing Bernard was?

I tried to picture in my mind what Rick was doing at that very moment, but my thoughts drifted to Donald instead.

In many ways I'd always felt closer to Donald than I did to Rick, but like Bernard, he could be terribly aloof at times. The difference was that unlike the occasional mystery associated with Bernard, there was never anything along those lines evident in Donald's behavior. When he distanced himself I'd always believed it had more to do with a desire for basic privacy than it did with anything suspect. In fact, he was the absolute antithesis of Rick in that he was the most nonviolent person I'd ever known. I couldn't remember a single instance when Donald had raised a hand in anger against anyone. His mind had always been his weapon. A weapon he'd used often, until Tommy died. None of us had been quite the same since his death, but Donald shut down for more than a year after the incident, and any child-like essence or shred of wide-eyed wonderment that had still resided in him was instantaneously snuffed out.

I remembered walking the beach with him the day of Tommy's funeral. We walked the same stretch of deserted sand again and again, only speaking occasionally, and even then only in clipped phrases. On one pass, Donald spotted a rotting grapefruit resting in the tall grass along the edge of the beach. He picked it up and held it out for me with an awkward expression somewhere between tears and rage. I looked at him questioningly. "Just take it," he'd said quietly, his voice barely perceptible. "Nothing should ever go to waste."

Although it was rotten garbage, although it already had gone to waste, I took it anyway, carried it with me until we'd left the beach and returned home. Only when Donald had gone and I knew he wouldn't see did I throw the grapefruit away, and even then I'd felt guilty for having done so, because he'd been right. Nothing should ever go to waste. Not a grapefruit, not a teenage boy.

Donald had gone on to college as planned, but his heart was no longer in it, and his excitement and hopes for the future became memories; dreams unfulfilled, dead and buried along with Tommy. He began to drink more, and I suspected his problem had been festering for a number of years now, though only recently had it clearly gotten away from him.

Like Rick he hadn't had many serious relationships, but unlike Rick, he was not promiscuous. Unless he was with us, he was usually alone. I had only heard him mention a couple of people over the years, and those were more casual acquaintances—occasional dates or friends—not meaningful partners.

As Bernard said on the tape, there had been someone in high school, but that had apparently ended badly and only deepened Donald's cynicism and depression. He'd been hiding, in a sense, ever since. Even in a room full of people he seemed hopelessly alone, more purposely detached than shunned, as if he and he alone understood how futile and senseless existence could be.

Donald had thrown away a lot, but the list included neither his wit nor his sense of compassion. Though he'd tempered his humor over the years, it remained an enormous part of who he was, as did his genuine concern for others. He was a deeply complex man, and as well as I knew him, some days I wondered if he'd always be there on the other end of the phone, the other side of the door. Like Rick, and to a degree, like me, he was a survivor to be sure, but a survivor in spite of his actions, not because of them.

But maybe Donald wasn't exempt either. Did he know something else about what was happening? Did he share some secret with Bernard like perhaps Rick did? Could it have been to blame for his downward spiral escalating in recent months?

I sat up and slowly swung my feet around onto the floor. A brief dizzy spell replaced my shameless paranoia. I closed my eyes; saw the faces of the young boy and his mother glaring at me.

My eyes opened. The room had stopped spinning.

I had thought about the others, suspected and betrayed them in thought, but what about myself? Was there something *I* knew, something *I* shared with Bernard in all this without realizing it?

Before I could further search my mind I heard the kitchen phone returned to its cradle, followed by the sound of Toni padding toward the bedroom.

As the door opened she balked but quickly regained her composure. "I thought you'd be asleep," she said through a meager smile. "You startled me."

"Just woke up. Those pills knock me out."

"That's why Gene prescribed them. It's an anti-anxiety," she told me. "He said they'd help you sleep."

"He's right." I rubbed at the stiffness along the back of my neck. "What time is it?"

"A little after ten."

"At night, right?"

"Yes, sweetie, at night." Toni strode to the window, raised the shade.

I glanced at the moonlight, then back at her. I could almost feel her discomfort. "Look, I'm sorry about the job."

"You can always get another job."

"I had it coming, but Nino only fired me because Petey made him. After a few weeks he'll be begging me to come back. Where are they going to find anyone as reliable and loyal as me? Besides, I got that nice check, that'll help hold us over for a while."

Toni moved toward me with an air of caution I'd never seen her display, and sat next to me on the bed. "We need to talk, Alan."

"Isn't that what we're doing?"

"I mean about what happened the other night."

I nodded. She'd been smoking heavily; I could smell it on her. "Look, I told you everything that happened as best as—"

"I spoke with Gene about all this, and—"

"What? Why did you do that without talking to me first?"

"Honey, he's a psychiatrist, this is what he does."

I stood up, legs shaky. "It's none of his fucking business. Jesus Christ, Toni, why does Gene have to know every goddamn tidbit of what happens in our personal lives? You work for him, it's not like he's a member of the family—I don't even consider him a friend."

"Well, I do." Her hair, thick but styled short, was mussed. She combed a renegade strand away from tired, mascara-smudged eyes. "He's concerned about you, Alan, and so am I."

I stood there clad only in a pair of boxers, not certain what to do with myself. "I freaked out, okay? I'm fine."

"I don't think—"

"That's it, end of story."

She looked at the floor. "I'm afraid, Alan."

"So am I."

"I'm afraid of *you*."

I felt emotion well up at the base of my throat. "For Christ's sake, baby, come on." I sunk to my knees, put my hands in hers. "You know I'd never do anything to hurt you."

Trembling, her eyes brimmed with tears. "The other night was—I mean, I've never seen you like that it—you were babbling and insisting all these crazy things had happened and I couldn't calm you down or talk to you. You had a total collapse, a—a *breakdown*. That's not normal, Alan. It's not *healthy*."

"I'm okay," I told her. "I promise you, I'm okay."

She removed one hand from mine and wiped her eyes. "Gene feels it could be extremely beneficial for you to go in and discuss what happened that night."

"Who are you talking to, some patient?" I pulled my hands free and stood up. "Gene. What the hell's he know about it? Is that who you were on the phone with just now?"

"Yes, we—"

"Getting awful cozy with that fuck, aren't you?"

Her face dropped, the tears still staining flushed cheeks. "What the hell is that supposed to mean?"

I moved to the window. "Tell him to mind his own fucking business."

"I went to him for help, Alan."

"Well, stop going to him for help. Leave him the hell out of it." I grabbed either side of the window casing as a means of occupying my hands so I wouldn't put them through the wall. "I'm not some nut who needs a psychiatrist. I'm not one of his fucking whacked-out patients."

"I never said you were any of those things," she answered softly. "I just thought it might be a good idea to go and talk with him about it, that's all."

"About *what*, exactly?" I pushed away from the window, turned back to her. "About what? What should we cover first, my nightmares? That maybe Bernard was some sort of deranged psychopath and had been for years? That maybe all the clues were right there in front of us all that time and for some unknown reason we chose to ignore them? That maybe no one—motherfucking *no one*—including myself are who or what I thought they were? That I'm seeing people who aren't fucking there? Dead women and little boys in the dark—that's a good one. Or how about that I know even more things happened in that factory—bad—evil things that I—I don't want to remember, Toni, I—Christ almighty, they'll lock me up, I…"

What began as choking sobs quickly evolved into violent, uncontrollable weeping. Without a word she opened her arms, and I went to her quickly. We held each other, arms and tears entwined for what seemed a very long time.

I held her face in my hands, looked into her eyes. "I need to handle this on my own. I know it seems crazy but something is happening, and it's not in my mind. It's real. I'm not insane."

"I never said you were. But you're having problems, you—"

"It'll be all right. I need to find the truth now. I can't ignore it anymore, it—it won't let me, do you understand?"

She tried to smile as she touched my cheek, and for the first time I realized she was wearing only a long T-shirt and a pair of panties. The dark tint of her nipples showed through the thin fabric, erect and pressed against it as if trying to escape. She looked so helpless and afraid in the moonlight, as if her safety and sanity hinged solely on me, and perhaps it did. "I love you," I told her. "No matter what, I always love you."

Soft hands caressed my thighs, warm breath tickled my neck, and moments later Toni blended into focus above me. Soulful eyes blinked slowly, cradling history—our history—as her tongue flicked across my cheek, slid into my ear. My arms wrapped around her, fingers kneading firm buttocks, slinking gradually across her back and onto her shoulders. I felt myself harden between her legs, parting a soft tuft of hair there as she moved to meet me, raising her hips, arching her back, drawing me deeper. She slithered closer, her body moving like a python as she straightened her spine and lay on top of me, eyes holding mine as if fearful she might lose me in the dark.

***

When it was over she was by my side, her heart beating against me, warm fingers gently tracing the contours of my chest as we lay quietly in each other's arms, winded and wet. It was the first time we'd made love in quite some time. I couldn't help but wonder if it was because she feared it might be the last.

Everything trickled through my mind like falling rain: the cellar, the photograph of the woman none of us could identify, the tape, the nightmares, the hauntings, the abandoned factory. The madness.

"Bernard wasn't what we thought he was," I said softly. Toni snuggled closer but said nothing. knew she still didn't believe me, but then, I'm not sure anyone did.

Until winter melted away, became spring, and the first body was found.

SPRING

CHAPTER 10

Near the end of Main Street, the train tracks curved off into a wooded area where the shrubbery and grass grew wild and tall. The track was laid on a raised hill of dirt topped with crushed stone that tunneled through the otherwise natural setting, snaking along for as far as the eye could see. Following the tracks had been a popular pastime since our preteen years, and later, while in high school, the particular section near the end of Main Street, the section right before it disappeared into the overgrown landscape, became a meeting place. Though on foot it was accessible within moments from the street, the uneven and wild terrain discouraged most adults, including the cops, and as a result kids recognized it as a good hangout spot. We were no exception, and often congregated there to smoke cigarettes, a joint, maybe drink a beer or two, or sometimes to take a walk with a girlfriend.

Beyond the bend of one section of track was a low field that could be reached by a narrow dirt road carved through the forest on the far end. The ground there was disturbed on a regular basis and hastily packed back into place. The grass grew only in sparse patches, and a tiny rundown shed sat at one corner. Everyone knew it housed some tools and things—nothing of interest—and except for Mr. McIntyre, Potter's Cove's only animal control person, no one ever went down there.

That afternoon we'd decided to skip the latter portion of the school day. Bernard was depressed; his dog Curly had died the night before. Bernard had found him behind the picnic table in his backyard just that morning. Apparently the dog had been hit by a car and had somehow managed to get to the yard, where it collapsed behind the table and died. Mr. McIntyre had taken Curly away in a large, heavy duty plastic garbage bag, and since we all knew the town used this field as a burial ground for animals, we knew where to find his final resting place.

"How come you didn't just bury him in your yard?" I asked.

Bernard was sitting on the slope of hill between the tracks and the field below, a long piece of grass between his lips swaying with the wind. "I wanted to," he said softly, "but he was so big Mom said we couldn't dig up the yard like that even for Curly. She tried to hand me some line about how McIntyre would give him a good burial and all that—yeah, right." His eyes, still trained on the field, narrowed. "That must be where he put him," he said, pointing to a small patch of freshly turned earth in the distance. "You can tell that was just dug up. That must be where Curly is."

I felt bad for Bernard. I'd lost my cat a few years before, and I knew even though we were fifteen and at a stage where maintaining our level of cool was paramount, he was in a lot of pain. He'd had Curly since he'd been a toddler, and we'd all known and loved the dog too. "What kind of asshole hits a dog and keeps going?" I said, standing behind him while doing my best to look anywhere but at the field.

"I should've got him in before I went to bed," he mumbled. "It must've happened in the middle of the night. He was probably across the street digging through Mrs. Petrillo's garbage like he used to." Bernard chuckled. "Fucking dog always ate her garbage. He was probably on his way home when he got hit."

"Still, the fucker should've stopped."

"Maybe he did. It was late, and I found Curly in the backyard. He probably crawled back there and it was dark and shit and whoever hit him probably couldn't find him, figured he was all right and ran off. I don't know. Maybe it was just some prick who mowed him down and kept going, never gave it a fucking thought." He pulled the piece of grass from his mouth, studied the small chewed section a moment then looked up at me. "Curly didn't move as fast as he used to, he was old. Maybe he tried to make it but didn't. He was bleeding out of his ears, and Mr. McIntyre said that was probably because he got hit in the head by the car."

I stood there, unsure of what to say.

"I'm gonna miss that fucking dog, man."

"Me too," I said. "Curly was cool."

Bernard turned back to the field. "Thanks for taking off school with me."

"No prob." I kicked a stone from the slope. It bounced, clicked along the tracks. "You going to that party over at Michele Brannon's house tonight?"

"Nah."

"Might get your mind off shit."

The blade of grass was back between his lips, bouncing again with the breeze. "You ever seen anything dead, Al?"

I shrugged. "I guess so, yeah."

"Have you?"

"My cat Doc died."

"I remember. He got cancer."

"Yeah. Doctor Halstrom said he couldn't do anything to save him, he had this big tumor."

"So he killed him for you."

"He put him to sleep."

"Yeah, he killed him."

"I didn't want Doc to suffer, man. He was real sick."

"Did you see him do it or did you leave before?"

I walked around near the tracks, not wanting to think about such things. "We left the room before he actually did it. Doc was out of it though; he didn't know what was happening. My mom let me take him when it was over, and we buried him in the yard."

"I remember," Bernard said. "It's fucked up, seeing something that's dead."

"Yeah."

"Especially something you knew when it was alive." Bernard nodded, as if agreeing with himself. "Like, if you see something that's dead on the side of the road or something—something you never knew or gave a shit about or even saw when it was alive and walking around—it doesn't really mean anything. It's gross and all and you might think it's sad or whatever, maybe even kind of interesting in a way, but it's just dead. This dead...*thing*. But when you knew it before, when you're used to seeing it alive and then it's dead it—it's fucked up."

"You ever seen a dead person?" I asked.

He nodded. "Been to a couple wakes."

"I saw my grandmother after she was dead," I told him. "She looked so weird in the casket, all powdery-faced and everything—shit, didn't even look like her, not really."

"Because it wasn't her," Bernard said. "Not anymore."

"Everybody kept saying how good she looked—how peaceful she looked—and I was just a kid and even I knew it was a crock of shit. She looked awful, man. She looked fucking dead, that's what she looked."

"What do you think they look like out there?" Bernard motioned to the field with his chin. "What do you think it looks like under all that dirt and dead grass?"

"Probably mostly bones."

Bernard plucked the blade of grass from his mouth and tossed it in the direction of the field below. The breeze caught it, and it spiraled and danced away, riding the wind. He pulled his glasses off, wiped the thick lenses with his shirttail then replaced them. "Worst thing is, we're all gonna end up the same way. No matter what you do in your life—or what you don't do—no matter where you go or who you are, everybody croaks; everybody ends up dead and buried. Unless they torch you, spread your ashes all over. My mother had a cousin they did that to, sprinkled his ashes on the ocean."

"Guess it won't matter once you're dead."

"Guess not," he agreed. "But still, it's fucked up. We live our whole life knowing sooner or later, we're going in the ground. One day's gonna be the last."

"Nobody, nothing lives forever, Bernard."

He nodded absently. "We should though."

"Why?"

"Because it's cruel not to. It's like, from the minute you're born, you start getting older, right? So it's like, you're kind of dying right from the minute you're born. What's the point of life if it just ends and you're gone and the world keeps going like you were never even there? Yesterday Curly was playing in the yard, chewing his tennis ball, having his dinner, drinking out of the toilet—being a dog. Then *bang*, gone. Just like that. Like he was never here at all."

"That's why we have memories," I told him.

"Memories aren't worth shit."

I hopped off the tracks and sat down next to him. A cool breeze blew through the distant trees and across the field. The sky had turned ashen; a storm was brewing, rolling in off the ocean. We sat quietly, listened to our thoughts.

"You believe in God, Al?" Bernard asked.

"Sure, don't you?"

"Yeah. You ever wonder about Him?"

"Like what He looks like and shit?"

"No, like why He does what He does."

"Yeah, sometimes."

"I wonder why God hates me."

"Bernard, God doesn't hate anybody. He's God."

Bernard drew his knees up close, rested his chin on them and wrapped his arms around his legs. "You believe in the Devil?"

"I don't know, man. I guess so."

"If there's a God there has to be a Devil too."

"Okay."

"Well, it's true. Everything has an opposite, right?"

"Sure."

"Sometimes I get so fucking pissed, man, I just want to go crazy, you know?" Bernard looked at me and shook his head, as if the words bothered him more than they ever could me. "I want to say fuck it and just smash everything, smash everybody because none of it matters anyway. You do what you do and the world keeps going, nothing stops. If it mattered—if there was a point, it would—it would stop. It'd stop and take fucking notice. But it doesn't."

I put a hand on his shoulder, gave it a squeeze then shook him gently, playfully, and let him go. "Everybody feels like that sometimes, dude, don't worry about it."

Bernard's eyes blinked slowly, slightly distorted behind thick glasses. "I'm *not* worried," he said. "One of these days I'm gonna snap, Al, and when that happens somebody's gonna get hurt."

Normally I would've teased him for making such a statement, but I let it pass and remained quiet, like I believed him.

"Hurt bad," he muttered.

Just Bernard being Bernard. Couldn't fight a lick, intimidated no one. Talking tough but never able to back it up. He was angry and frustrated and missed his dog, so I let him be. I let him be whatever he said he was.

"You ever think that maybe God's just fucking with us?"

"He definitely has a twisted sense of humor." I laughed dutifully.

"I'm serious."

"Life sucks sometimes, that's just how it is."

"I think I like the Devil better."

"You shouldn't say shit like that, man."

"Well, it's true."

"No, it's not."

Bernard shrugged. "At least with him you know where you stand."

"Oh yeah?" I elbowed him, doing my best to lighten the mood. "You been talking to him lately?"

"Sometimes I think I hear him talking to me."

"Shut up!" I chased away a chill with another forced laugh. "Fucking whacko."

Bernard offered a glimmer of a smile and pushed himself to his feet. "It's gonna storm."

I stood up, brushed the dirt from the seat of my pants.

"You think when you die you get to see other people who died first?" he asked.

"I think you do, yeah."

"How about animals?"

"Sure. God made them the same as people, why wouldn't they have a soul too?"

Bernard thought about what I'd said for a moment, his eyes again focused on the fresh dirt in the field. "I think you're right."

"I'll bet you anything Curly's running around in Heaven right now, knocking over garbage cans and eating everybody's trash."

"Maybe we got it all backwards," he said softly. "Maybe none of us really start living…until we're dead."

Thunder rumbled in the distance.

"Come on," I said. "Let's get out of here."

As we left, a gentle rain began to fall.

I couldn't remember the last time I'd ventured to that part of the tracks, and now, all these years later, I sat in my car across the street from the animal burial ground and watched the goings on up to and beyond the yellow police tape. On the seat next to me was the newspaper from the evening before, the headline of which described the grisly discovery a town worker had made in the early morning hours. A body—nude, mutilated and partially decomposed—had been left amidst the field containing the bones of generations of animals in a shallow grave that had given way with the change of season. The worker had noticed something he could not immediately identify protruding from the earth, and upon closer inspection, realized it was the foot and calf of a human being. The article and subsequent television reports revealed that the body was that of a young woman who had been dead for a number of weeks, but her identity had not yet been established. State police investigators, who were scouring the field and surrounding areas, had joined the local police force, and a flood of media people had converged on Potter's Cove to cover the event.

There had only been three murders in town in the last two decades. A teenager had shot his former best friend with his father's handgun. A woman who had endured years of physical abuse took a hammer to her husband's head one night after he'd passed out drunk, and a man known by police to be a drug dealer had been executed gangland style in an alley downtown. Those had been the most infamous killings Potter's Cove had ever seen, until now, and those cases were cut and dry, easy to close. This was different.

And it was only the beginning.

Although the body had already been removed, a throng of people still filled the surrounding streets, milling about behind the police tape like fans huddled near a stage door awaiting a glimpse of a rock star. At the far end of one group, standing near the curb, arms folded and brow knit, stood Donald. In the past two weeks I hadn't seen much of him or Rick, had only spoken to them on the phone a few times, in fact, as being apart was somehow easier for the time being.

Even though a few capsules remained on the anti-anxiety prescription, I'd stopped taking the pills several days before, and my head felt clearer, my senses sharper. Toni had retreated into a distant mode, and I honestly couldn't blame her, as I'd not even attempted to look for work and had refused to discuss counseling or anything that had happened that night. Lately, I'd spent most of my waking hours thinking, remembering; searching my mind for anything that might lead me in the right direction. And I spent a lot of time driving aimlessly around town, as if hoping to find answers on the side of the road. Now I wondered how many times in the last few weeks I'd driven within a few dozen yards of where the body had been found. Cruel, really, the irony.

The frequency of the recurring nightmare had decreased somewhat, but the dark thoughts and strobe-like memory flashes of the night in the abandoned factory continued to haunt me with vicious consistency. I got out of the car, leaned against the side of the hood and stared at Donald until he noticed me. He was dressed for work, in a suit, but his tie was undone and hung loosely, giving him an unusually tousled look. The moment he saw me he walked across the street to my car.

"How are you?" he asked.

"How are *you*?"

It was a clear and pleasant day, but not terribly sunny. Donald removed his sunglasses long enough to paw at the dark bags under his eyes, then replaced them, concealing himself behind black lenses. "I got up, shaved, took a shower, got dressed for work as usual then called in sick and came here instead. I don't even know why, exactly."

"Sure you do."

He joined me against the side of the car, pulled cigarettes and a lighter from his shirt pocket. "They haven't released much about the victim yet."

"Only that it's a young woman."

He rolled a cigarette into the corner of his mouth, left it there and returned the pack to his pocket. "Yes." Cupping the flame, he lit the cigarette then snapped shut the lighter, his actions emphasized. "And that she's been dead for weeks."

"Are you still having the nightmare?" I asked.

His nod was barely detectable. "You?"

"Not as often as before."

"Heard from Rick?" he asked.

"Not in a while."

"He wants to get together at Brannigan's later this afternoon. Four o'clock."

I wished I could see his eyes. "I'll be there."

He took a few drags before he spoke again, the smoke slowly releasing through his nostrils. "Things are going to get worse, Alan."

"Of course they are," I said. "We're damned."

Face expressionless, he flicked his cigarette away. "Think so?"

"Don't you?"

Without answering, Donald gave my arm a reassuring pat, moved back across the street and faded into the crowd.

CHAPTER 11

I drove down Main Street, left the festivities behind and turned onto Sycamore Way, a quiet tree-lined street that acted as a kind of palisade between Potter's Cove's largely commercially zoned working-class downtown and the beginnings of the middle and upper-class, exclusively residential neighborhoods to the north. The buildings on either side of the street were original town structures—historical landmarks all—restored but constructed in colonial times not long after the town itself was founded. Only a few were residences, the rest housed the town's historical society, an art center and several small medical and law offices. Unlike the area I lived in, this part of town was clean and manicured and quaint. Here, Potter's Cove was still more a small town than the burgeoning city it had become in the less affluent districts.

At the end of Sycamore I turned right onto Bridge Street and followed it slowly, reducing my speed to a creeping roll. Like everything else, the street had changed over time. Some new inexpensive homes had been built where small sections of woods had once resided, and many of the houses had been renovated, but for the most part it looked basically the same as it had years before when I'd grown up here. Bridge Street, named for the small wooden bridge built above a stream that cut across the very end of the road, was still a relatively poor neighborhood abutting the beginnings of more exclusive parts of town. The last outpost, the last street where houses weren't quite as big, where cars weren't quite as new and where people weren't quite as well dressed; even after all these years, good, bad, or indifferent, Bridge Street summoned true feelings of *home*. Yet at the same time I felt strangely uncomfortable here as well. Familiarity, in this case, did not exclusively breed warmth and solace. I studied first the stretch of sidewalk where my mother had taught me to ride a bicycle, then the ancient stone wall where I'd had many a crash and where years later my friends and I congregated and spent hours talking, smoking cigarettes and hanging out. Despite these and a wealth of other landmarks that invoked fond childhood reminiscences, this hallowed ground also brought forth a great sense of uneasiness in me. Good and bad, even here, even amidst the perceived simplicity of the past, had melded into a single enigmatic entity.

Blinking away phantoms, I pulled over in front of our old house. I lived less than two miles away, but seldom returned here. Bridge Street was out of the way, a place people only went to if that was their destination, and it was rarely mine.

The house, a small single-story set back from the road, had sat in the middle of a dirt lot when I'd lived there, but the dirt had been replaced by a lawn years ago, and instead of cracked and weathered shingles, the house now sported relatively new vinyl siding. Still, beyond the aesthetics, it basically looked the same. My old bedroom window was now dressed with lacey curtains, and I wondered who lived there these days. We had never owned the house, and after my mother's death the landlord sold the property to another family. Since that time ownership had changed hands again, but I knew nothing of the current tenants. In fact, as far as I knew none of the families who had resided on Bridge Street at the time of my childhood were still there. Even smaller-town America had become transient it seemed, the days of families occupying homes for generations relegated to a nostalgic quaintness of yesteryear.

Hesitant to leave the false sense of security the car provided, I turned off the engine and looked to my left, further down the street toward the squat two-story house Bernard and his mother had lived in. Of all the houses on the street, it was the only one unoccupied, and since Bernard's mother had died less than a year before, the only one still closely tied to the past. A modest two-story badly in need of a paint job, the windows were dark, the front yard unkempt and the driveway empty. Taken over by the bank, it had apparently sat unsold, empty and sealed shut since, and was well on its way to becoming the neighborhood eyesore. If it remained vacant much longer, the kids in the area would undoubtedly dub it the local haunted house—if they hadn't already—never realizing just how near the truth they might be.

In her later years, Bernard's mother had lost much of her beauty to the ravages of cancer. In and out of the hospital for months, eventually the doctors had admitted there was nothing else they could do for her, and she was sent home to die. Less than a month later, in the upstairs bedroom just to the right of the staircase, that's precisely what she did. Bernard later told me he had been in the room when she died, that he'd held her hand and watched her take her final breath. I knew all too well what it was like to see that happen. My mother had died in my arms, gray skin stretched across a face I barely recognized, eyes sunken but open, awaiting things only dying eyes could comprehend. To watch your physical creator, the human being from whom you came, the literal flesh and blood vessel responsible for your conception and birth, wither and die, was something beyond explanation. Like soldiers who have survived the horrors of combat, you'd either experienced it or you hadn't. You either understood what it was like, what it meant to be infected to your core by such things, or you didn't.

She went quietly, he'd said desperately, as if determined to convince me. *I don't think she could even feel the pain anymore, she—she went quietly.* His voice murmured to me from the past, sounding the same as it had through the phone line that morning. I'd told him how sorry I was, and that I understood what he was going through.

I know, he'd said. *That's why I told you first.*

The squeak of the car door echoed along the pavement as I stepped from the Pontiac. I made my way slowly along the sidewalk, waiting to cross until I was in front of Bernard's old house.

Memories ricocheted about—mostly blurs—but large chunks of the past remained elusive. Particularly those portions of the past tied directly to this street, this neighborhood, and this house. I had always assumed those uneventful periods in life simply faded and all but vanished over time because they held nothing of particular importance, but now I felt differently. As I approached the waist-high fence surrounding the backyard, it seemed a better bet that those things just beyond the grasp of memory had been forgotten deliberately, and not because they were unimportant, but because they held within them things too unpleasant to confront. Even now.

I felt the aged wood against my hand, pushed open the gate and stepped through into the side yard. The lawn was dead, a victim of winter, the parched brown grass accompanied by occasional patches of bare dirt scattered about like a sprinkling of landmines. As I moved deeper onto the property an unseen bird shrieked more warning than welcome from its perch somewhere within the half circle of lofty trees just beyond the fence in the backyard.

Several windows on the side and rear of the house had been broken or cracked by thrown stones, and someone had written *Eat Me* in spray paint along the back door. On the cement patio off the rear entrance sat the same lawn furniture that had been there the last time I had visited, days after his mother had died and only a month or two before the bank had seized the house. The white plastic table and chairs had faded and cracked in places, and one of the chair legs had been broken clean off and tossed aside. Next to a weather and time ravaged chaise lounge, several large garbage bags had been left in a neat row along the back of the house. Each bag had been filled to capacity, and I tried to imagine what they contained. The day Bernard lost the house he'd been served with a warrant and had been unable to retrieve many of his personal items still trapped within. I pictured workers gathering items—*his* items, his mother's items—and stuffingtheminto those garbage bags.

Two entire lifetimes seemingly reduced to a neglected shell of a building, some broken furniture and a row of trash bags, as if nothing else remained of either of them.

I looked up at the back of the house and the darkness on the other side of the smudged windowpanes on the second floor. The sensation of someone watching me from just beyond the swathe of shadows rattled my already frayed nerves. "Bernard," I whispered. "Are you here?"

The trees, stirred by a momentary breeze, answered for him.

Small windows along the foundation of the house reminded me of the cellar in New Bedford where he had hanged himself. But this was his home, a place of history, so what had Bernard conjured here, in this house where he'd once claimed the Devil sometimes spoke to him? What demons had he summoned and brought to life here? And why? Why had he done it in the first place? Why had he listened when evil beckoned—even if it had come from within him—why had he chosen to embrace it?

I moved to the edge of the patio and crouched down; eyes fixed on the old chaise lounge, its canvas backing tattered and soiled. What had I seen and experienced here, incidents my mind had relegated to hazy spirits that haunted me from the shadows even now? How had they blinded me, stolen my vision and left a void where their memory should have existed instead? Or had I given it away, buried the knowledge so deeply myself that it no longer seemed real?

If thine eye offends thee, pluck it out.

Just as a lie told countless times in one's own mind eventually becomes memory rather than fantasy, blurring the line between that which was imagined and that which actually took place, could the same be true of real experiences? If one pretended a literal occurrence never happened with enough passion and over a sufficient amount of time, did it eventually cease to exist in the conscious mind? Did it too blur the lines between the imaginary and the actual? Even as I reached for the decaying chaise lounge, I knew the answer to those questions was yes.

On particularly warm and sunny days the chaise lounge was always moved to the center of the backyard, where Bernard's mother could lay out and sunbathe, the house blocking any view from the road and the trees in back forming a barrier between her and the houses beyond. How many times had I seen her stretched out under the summer sun, skin browned and glistening with tanning lotion, head back, eyes closed, chin tilted toward the sky, soft blonde hair contrasting with the gaudy flowery pattern on the padded pillow of the chaise lounge, Jackie-O sunglasses and a fluffy white beach towel resting next to a portable radio on the grass, playing disco tunes always a bit louder than necessary? How many times had I watched her breasts, barely contained in a bright bikini top, rise and fall, her legs outstretched, toes pointed like a prone ballerina while the sun caught the gold bracelet adorning her ankle? How many times had I touched myself and thought of her—my friend's *mother*, for Christ's sake—*how many times?*

In those years before she'd become sick she was beautiful, but not like everyone else's mom. Linda was different. She was still a parent, but younger, sexier, more like us than other adults. She'd possessed an impish quality, with expressive light blue eyes, a tiny nose and thin though shapely lips, dyed blonde hair that she kept relatively short in length but that was thick and always a bit wild, as if she'd not quite had the time to style it properly, and a deep, bawdy laugh that sounded implausibly obscene coming from such an otherwise delicate woman. So delicate, in fact, that she often seemed practiced, studied in the ways of carrying oneself in an unquestionably female, unmistakably sexual, undeniably alluring manner. In a boring town like Potter's Cove, she was the most glamorous being any of us had ever laid eyes on. A misplaced movie starlet banished with her bastard son to the ends of the Earth, sentenced to a life of boredom and loneliness in a place where but for those who ridiculed her, the only attention a woman like Linda Moore was paid was at local bars after dark. I'd once heard my mother talking on the telephone with a friend about her, about how she had gone from her native New Bedford to New York City, where she had become involved with some shady characters. Underworld types who liked to have a woman like Linda on their arms and in their beds. But there had been a murder, so the story went, a mob hit where she had been caught in the middle of a bad situation and fled. She had returned home pregnant, with a drinking problem and a bad reputation, and ended up in Potter's Cove. Most felt her stay would be temporary, that a party girl without a party would quickly tire of life outside the fast lane and eventually return to it. And in a sense, she did, albeit a small town version. Under more typical circumstances, she was the kind of girl who left the area and went on to bigger things in more sensational locales. But instead she'd become a scandalous woman the older townies spoke about softly, sometimes in outright whispers, hands raised to cover their mouths and eyes cast askance; a woman most grown men and teenage boys alike fantasized about, and a woman Bernard worshipped.

I stood up and stepped back, away from the house, and again watched the upstairs windows for a time. The sense that someone was watching me surfaced a second time, though I had the impression whoever or whatever it was had now moved to some point behind me—perhaps the trees just beyond the fence. I ignored the feeling and without looking back walked slowly around to the side of the house from which I'd come. As I closed the gate I glanced at the backyard, gradually lifting my eyes to the still gently swaying trees.

Satisfied that no one was there, I crossed to the front of the house. The front door, a door we had always been told to knock on once and then feel free to enter through, drew my attention. It was an odd thing, to simply knock once then walk into someone else's home, not to mention a practice foreign to me and in direct opposition to the more formal rules of etiquette my mother had taught and insisted I adhere to. But it was Linda's rule. And that was another thing. Calling an adult, particularly a friend's mother, by their first name was not done and considered disrespectful. But again, it was Linda's rule. So, when visiting, I'd knock once on the front door then enter, and whenever in her company I'd address her simply as *Linda*, just like everyone else.

The countless times I had walked in and caught Bernard's mother in some state of undress trickled through my mind, images of flirting ghosts and sneering demons blurring one into the next to form a single spectral whirlwind. So often when I stopped by she just happened to be scantily or sexily clad, or was changing or had just stepped out of the shower, a skimpy towel somehow managing to cover all the right spots, though just barely, except for those occasions when it slipped or fell completely away to reveal a quick flash of nipple, buttock or pubic hair as she nonchalantly climbed the stairs or pranced into her bedroom. In those days, I'd often wondered if she did the same thing when Bernard's other friends came to the house.

Bernard's in his room, sugar. Go on up and see him.

All these years later, I had no doubt that she had.

***

I stared at the house, called on all the recollections and mysteries it held within its slowly dying walls, summoned them from its bowels to the light of day, to the sidewalk where I now stood. And like the slow rise of blood from an exceptionally deep wound, they came. Slow and seeping at first, and then, as I held the wound open wider still, it gushed, this blood of memories and secrets, leaking from the windows, dripping across the walls, bubbling from cracks in the foundation, frothing and swelling free like waves crashing shoreline, determined to knock me over and drag me under.

And down I went.

The house opened before me like a parting curtain, a yawning mouth vomiting forth the past like the repellent *thing* that it was.

Knock once and enter.

Just beyond the front door, the staircase at the head of the small entranceway came into focus, the living room to the left, a small closet to the right, the smell of cigarettes, booze, and Linda's perfume in the air as always. Barely audible sounds of the television in the other room turned down low lingered in my ear even when the stairs began to creak as I climbed them, shifting with each hesitant step.

The door opening—no—*already open* on the bedroom just to the right of the stairs. Linda's room, where the bed sat against the back wall, mismatched nightstands on either side of the headboard cluttered with overflowing ashtrays and empty liquor bottles, garments stuffed into plastic clothesbaskets and strewn about the room as if thrown or dropped there, an ironing board against one wall, a dressing table with mirror and closet against another. Lipsticks and makeup, small bottles of polish and colognes and body sprays, tins of soap and powder rattling, clicking one against the other until it all faded to black.

***

The house watched me now, offering nothing.

While I glared back, the ghosts led my thoughts to the cemetery instead. I hadn't been there in quite some time, even in my mind. Bernard's mother and my parents had been buried in the same one, and while I often felt guilty for not tending more consistent attention to my mother's so-called final resting place, I knew she would have understood. "It's only our bodies there anyway," she'd once assured me, eyes blinking tranquilly, telling me everything, and nothing at all. "I'll be in Heaven with Daddy by then."

She'd always referred to my father as "Daddy," as if sweetening his moniker might make his absence more tolerable, the void somehow more human once assigned an innocent and childlike title. But he remained a stranger to me, a character in other peoples' stories, a smiling and gentle-looking man in faded photographs, a name chiseled into granite. At least I'd had that much; Bernard knew virtually nothing about his father, though I'd never been quite sure which experience was preferable. His mother had rarely spoken about the subject, and it wasn't until I'd become an adult that her reasons began to make sense. Although Bernard and I never discussed it and I had no way to know for sure, I believed Linda had never told him who his father was because she hadn't been certain herself.

Visions of the cemetery scurried about, reached for me, revealed Linda sitting atop her headstone, laughing while Bernard crouched before her, digging furiously with fingers raw and bleeding, flinging soil across the flowers decorating her grave.

The demons were at play but the house fell silent.

For now, the ghosts had stopped talking.

CHAPTER 12

In a matter of weeks the public beach would be packed with tourists and locals alike, though for now, but for the steady toll of waves lapping the shore and the occasional cackle of a soaring gull, the area remained quiet. I seldom went to the beach during the summer season, preferring instead to come in the quiet months when it was an entirely different experience. Although I harbored a rather primitive fear of the ocean, I'd been coming to this beach since childhood, and it had figured into many seminal points during my life. I remembered coming here the day Rick was released from prison, in fact, just one of numerous memories of this place, so despite my inherent uneasiness, I also found an ironic sense of comfort in the waves, in the majestic and familiar power of it all.

I drove carefully along the dirt lot, my old car throttled by purposely uneven terrain designed to prevent people from speeding, and parked near a row of stump-like wooden posts connected with heavy rope that separated the sand from the parking lot. Mine was the only car in the lot, but further down the beach, near a stone jetty that stabbed quite a distance into the ocean, I noticed a young woman in a windbreaker playing with a black lab. I wondered if she knew about the body that had been found.

On the seat next to me was a hardback composition notebook I'd picked up a few days earlier. I had begun to transfer my thoughts, memories and dreams to paper in the hopes of perhaps better sorting through them, and decided to consult my notes one more time before making a definite move. The nightmare still haunted me, but not as frequently, and thankfully, there had been no more hallucinations or visions—no more women, no more little boys—only a continued sense of dread and the persistent flicker of memories both recent and distant I found impossible to shake.

I flipped open the notebook, eyed my latest list of options and drew a line through the first, *Nightmares*, then the second, *Hauntings*. My pen hesitated at the third, *Abandoned Factory*, then the fourth, *Photograph of Mystery Woman*. I skipped over both, moved to the fifth, *Memories and Questions*. Beneath that I'd written down the most disturbing or curious memories that had come to me of late and followed them with questions.

So many goddamn questions.

Of course the discovery of the young woman's body changed everything. I had no choice but to continue to force myself to remember the darkest corners of the past, but if I ever hoped to know who Bernard had really been, simple memory would not be enough. To fill in the blank spaces, to know for sure what he had done, and what he hadn't, I'd need to reconstruct a history of sorts. Bernard's history.

Somewhere in the distance the black lab barked. I looked up, saw the woman throw a tennis ball. The dog bolted after it along the sand, retrieved it then gleefully galloped back to her. It suddenly occurred to me that had I been so inclined, it would have been ridiculously easy to step from my car, walk across the deserted beach and slaughter this woman. Strobe-like flashes of her covered in blood blinked across my eyes, vanishing quickly. Similar thoughts had almost certainly coursed through Bernard's mind as well, but allowing even the faint beginnings of the evil he had called upon and held so close to seep into my own head was wildly unsettling. I pushed it all away and focused on the woman instead. She crouched down, took the lab's head in her hands and kissed his nose. The dog licked her face, his tail wagging. We were so vulnerable, all of us so ripe for the picking without even realizing it, and there wasn't a fucking thing we could do about it. I closed the notebook, tossed it into the backseat.

The day had slipped away. It was nearly four o'clock.

***

Brannigan's was surprisingly busy for a late afternoon on a weekday. One of the older establishments in town, over the years it had undergone a series of incarnations and varied themes but had essentially remained a sports pub with an attached dining area. It had been a townie watering hole for years, a place to go and have some beers, shoot some pool or play pinball, order a pizza or a wide range of appetizers from the menu and eat them right at the bar or in the darkened booths that lined the back wall, and a place where, for the most part, everyone knew one another. But just like those who had come before us, and those who followed, the older we got the less we frequented the bar and opted for the dining area instead. Although I still occasionally stopped in for a beer or two, the bar always had and always would pander to a predominantly younger crowd, and the farther I crept into my thirties the less tolerance I had for the language, music, fashion, and overall attitude of those ten years or so my junior.

I entered through the side door, which led directly to the dining room. It took several seconds for my eyes to adjust to the dim lighting, as both the dining area and bar were always annoyingly darker than seemed necessary, but after scanning the room I could locate neither Donald nor Rick.

"Hi, Alan."

I turned, saw a waitress fly by, a large tray of entrees balanced on her shoulder. "Hey, how's it going?" I muttered, unable to remember her name but recognizing her as a local I'd gone to high school with and who had worked there for years. I wasn't sure she even heard my response, as she'd already slipped between the tables and been absorbed into the noise, so I followed the wall to an archway with double swinging half-doors and moved into the bar. It was packed. All three of the pool tables were in use, and against one wall people were huddled around the pinball machines, the bells and electronic noises barely audible over the strains of a Stevie Ray Vaughn tune playing on the jukebox. The televisions mounted above either corner of the bar normally featured sporting events, but both were tuned to newscasts, neither of which could be heard.

As I walked slowly through the crowd it became apparent that nearly everyone was discussing the discovery of the dead body.

At the far end of the room, I found Rick and Donald sitting in the last of a row of booths. It was even darker there in the corner, a candle in the center of the table and encased in tinted glass providing minimal flickering light.

I slid in next to Donald, who was absently playing with a thin red straw floating in his drink. He stopped long enough to acknowledge me with a slight nod. Across from us, Rick sat clutching a bottle of cola with both hands, his expression darker than usual. "Heard the latest?"

"I haven't seen the news since this morning," I told him. "They found a body, it's a woman, and she's been dead for weeks. That's all I know."

Donald spoke without looking at me. "They've identified her."

"Twenty-two years old, single mother from New Bedford," Rick said. "Been missing almost two months."

I looked back across the room, hoping to locate a waitress. The throng of patrons reminded me of the days in our early twenties when we'd come here, so full of life, young and strong and together, still so certain we were indestructible. All the time in the world, we'd thought then. Downing drinks, smoking cigarettes and eating whatever the hell we pleased without giving any of it another thought. Until that moment I hadn't realized just how much I missed feeling like that, so enthusiastically *alive.*

"Remember when we used to come here before I got married?" I asked.

Rick stared at me like I'd spoken Mandarin, but Donald allowed the slightest quiver of a smile and nodded. "Can you believe we actually once found this place fun?"

I caught the attention of a waitress near the bar. When she got to us I ordered a beer then turned back to the table. "Those were good days," I said. "Weren't they?"

"Are you asking?" Donald gazed into what was left of his drink. "Or only hopeful?"

"A little of both."

"Missing your youth, Alan?"

"Almost."

"Don't worry, we're not old yet," he said softly. "We're just not young anymore."

Rick leaned forward. "I hate to interrupt you two and your stroll down memory-fucking-lane over here, but we got some important shit to talk about."

"So talk," I said. "You're the one who called the meeting."

Rick's eyes swept across me, sized me up. He opened his mouth to say something but the waitress appeared with my beer and asked if he and Donald wanted anything else. Donald ordered another vodka and tonic. "All set, sweetie, thanks," Rick said.

The waitress hesitated just long enough to give him a flirtatious smile then vanished.

"We need to decide what to do," Donald said.

"Do?" I looked at him, then at Rick. "What's there to do?"

Eventually Donald said, "Could Bernard have really done this? Could he have *killed* that girl?"

My immediate inclination was to tell him to keep his voice down, but the din in the bar was such that I could just barely hear him myself. "We don't know for sure that he did, but—"

"Yes we do," Rick said. "Don't be an idiot."

I sighed. "Look, all I'm saying is—"

"I just can't seem to get my mind around this," Donald interrupted.

Rick cracked his knuckles and fired Donald a cross look. "Donny thinks we should turn the tape over to the cops."

"I said we should consider it."

"All that's going to do is drag us right into the middle of this," I said.

Donald looked at me with glazed eyes. "We're already right in the middle of this." He threw back the remainder of his drink just as the waitress appeared with a refill. Once she'd gone, he lit a cigarette and continued. "Look, we're in possession of potential evidence here. We need to do the right thing, and the right thing, it seems to me, is to at least consider turning the tape over to the authorities."

"No," Rick snapped. "Fuck that."

I took a gulp of beer, ran the cold bottle across my forehead. "I don't know if it's a good idea to give it to the police. Rick has a point, with all the news coverage this thing is getting, why draw attention to ourselves?"

"We haven't done anything wrong," Donald said. "What *is* it with you two? The entire area is in a panic. People think a killer is on the loose in Potter's Cove, and if what Bernard said was true, it won't end here. More bodies will be found. We're going to have something on our hands here the likes of which this town has never seen."

"And eventually it'll pass." Rick pushed his cola aside, put his hands flat on the table between us and again leaned in close. "What's done is done, Donny. That tape's not gonna bring anybody back to life, it's not gonna prove a goddamn thing, and turning it over to the cops isn't gonna do anything except get our names in the paper. I tried to make this crystal fucking clear before. I'm an ex-con. I don't need the cops up my ass, snooping around my personal life. I want nothing to do with any of this, you hear me? Nothing. I got no doubt Bernard told the truth on that tape, that he did this shit for real. But it's over. It's not like he can kill again and we can do something to stop it—that'd be different—he's dead and buried. There won't be no more victims."

"Fine, what if I turn it over to them? I'll say it came to me and—"

"No chance."

"Look, this isn't just your decision. This involves all three of us."

Rick shook his head. "I'm making the final call."

"This is absurd." Donald gave me a pleading look. "Alan, for Christ's sake, help me out here."

"Sorry, man," I said. "I'm with Rick on this one."

His eyes searched mine. "Tell me why."

"Because in the overall scheme of things, the tape doesn't mean shit."

Rick and Donald exchanged glances. "What's that mean?"

"We all know there's more to this than meets the eye," I said. "The only way to get to the bottom of it, the only way we'll ever know for sure who Bernard was and what he did is to go back to the beginning." I powered down the rest of my beer, belched under my breath and explained my plan to construct a history of Bernard's activities.

Donald drew on his cigarette, expression thoughtful. "I understand your desire to put all of this into some semblance of order, Alan, sincerely I do. But..."

"But what?"

"Aren't things bad enough? The deeper we delve into this the higher the odds that we'll begin to open doors that are almost certainly better left closed."

"We might find even worse things," Rick added. "Things we don't want to know."

"Yeah." I nodded at him through the graceful trails of smoke weaving between us. "We just might."

"Then what's the point?" Rick shrugged. "We can just keep our mouths shut, lay low and wait until the storm passes, you see what I mean?"

"Are you afraid of what we might find, Rick?"

His features hardened. "I'm not the one who freaked out and saw shit that wasn't there, now was I?"

I set the empty beer bottle on the table and pushed it closer to the edge, ignoring the desire to smash it over his head. "You do what you want. I'm going to get to the truth."

"A young woman was butchered and left in a shallow grave in a field the town uses to bury dead animals," Donald said flatly. "Bernard almost certainly did it to her and who knows how many others, and the entire time we never even suspected he was a psychopath. *That's* the truth, Alan. How much more do we need to know?"

Rick gave an enthusiastic nod. "Finally making some goddamn sense, Donny."

A sudden cheer from a group of young men at one of the pinball machines startled us, and we turned in unison to look. "High score!" one of them yelled.

Donald rolled his eyes. "Notify the networks."

I laughed lightly without really thinking about it. Odd, how laughter could defy the darkness of nearly any situation. But it was out of place here, and dissipated quickly. "Are you sure we never suspected what Bernard was doing?" I let the words hang between us for a few seconds. "Or did we just ignore it, not pay particular attention? Maybe that's the problem. Maybe there's so much in the past we can't remember or don't want to remember that what really terrifies us is what we might find out about ourselves."

Rick stabbed a finger at me. "Listen, when you had your problem with the shit you were seeing, who was there to help you out? When you were outside my apartment all freaked out and in the middle of a total fucking breakdown, who was there to get you home?"

"You were, and I appreciate it. What's your point?"

"Yes, Bernard wasn't who we thought he was. Yes, bad shit happened and people died. But there's a limit to how much of this heebie-jeebies bullshit I can deal with. *That's* my fucking point, okay?"

"You said yourself something more was happening here," I reminded him. "Didn't you have the nightmares too? Didn't you have the dark thoughts, the fear, just like Donald and I had? That is what you said, wasn't it?"

"I don't know anything anymore."

"Oh, so now that a body shows up and all this becomes something real, all bets are off? Time to go hide under the bed, is that it?"

"What the fuck are you trying to prove, Alan? That shit goes bump in the night? That maybe there's stuff at work here that we never asked to know about and don't want any part of anyway?" He looked to Donald for support but got none. "Remember on the tape when Bernard talked about waking up in the middle of the night and hearing something, a sound that's not supposed to be there? Remember how he said we usually just roll back over and go to sleep? Well, I say that's the smart move here, okay? I say we just roll over, go back to sleep and wait for morning."

"You do what you want," I said again. "But I'm telling you that whatever it is out there in the dark making those noises isn't going to just go away, Rick. Bernard was connected to it, and we were connected to Bernard. Bernard's gone, but it's still here."

Donald tilted his glass, slid some ice cubes into his mouth and crunched them. "And what would *it* be, precisely?"

"I don't know yet," I answered. "But I'm going to find out."

"Could be a Pandora's Box."

"This goes back years," I told them. "Things happened in the neighborhood, in that house, and later, when we were all adults. Dark things. And somehow they all tie together."

Rick leaned back against the booth, pulled his money clip from his pocket and fired some bills onto the table. "Tell you what, you decide to start making some fucking sense, you let me know."

"Evil."

The word froze him. "What?"

"You heard me."

He swallowed so hard I saw his throat bob. "What about evil?"

"I think Bernard conjured it. I think he was responsible for it."

"Yeah, real magical bastard, Bernard," he snorted. "I wish you could sit over here so you could hear yourself saying this shit. You sound like a fucking mental case."

"Stop it, Rick," Donald said suddenly.

"Well, for Christ's sake—"

"Just stop it." Donald rubbed his eyes. "Don't do that to him."

Rick waved his hands, dismissing us. "Whatever."

"I'm hearing those noises in the night and I'm going to go see what they are," I said. "Now are you coming with me or are you going back to sleep? We're either in this together or we're not. In or out, Rick? What's it going to be?"

Anger, maybe something more, simmered in his eyes. "I'm in. okay, you fuck? I'm in."

I looked to Donald. He answered with a slow nod.

"I'll be in touch." With the solemn faces of the dead still congregated in my mind, I slid from the booth and crossed the bar.

CHAPTER 13

The days were becoming longer, the nights shorter. In winter, night fell prior to six p.m., but with spring came a more gradual darkness that allowed daylight to linger. With my newfound anxiety, I welcomed the change, and had spent the early evening in the bedroom, sitting on a stool in the closet doorway rummaging through a storage box filled with old stories I'd written years before. It was only when reading became more difficult that I glanced at a window and realized the sun had finally gone down. Still, I continued to paw through the stacks of stories, there in the near dark, and although silly and often juvenile both technically and in content, the old tales seemed irrefutable evidence of whom I had once been, and that a dream had existed within me, a dream that in many ways had defined me. Or maybe still did.

The feeling that I had been joined by someone else in the room crept along my spine as Bernard's taped voice played back in my mind. *Do you ever go through your old stories? Shit, do you even still have them? Do you ever think about what might have been?*

My eyes searched the room. Nothing.

The slam of a door nearly sent my heart out through my mouth, and I sprang from the stool so quickly I lost my balance. After staggering about I regained my footing and looked to the bedroom doorway. Toni stood there with a baffled expression.

"Are you all right?" It was all she ever asked anymore, and I couldn't blame her.

I nodded, drew a deep breath and struck a casual pose.

"Did you get the message I left on the answering machine?"

"Yeah." I glanced at my watch. "I didn't realize you'd be so late."

"Hadn't planned to be, I was just going to work late for a bit, but then Martha called and asked if I wanted to get a bite to eat. I hadn't seen her in a few weeks so I figured, why not? Didn't think you'd mind."

Martha had always been exclusively Toni's friend, not mine. We hadn't gotten along since high school and probably never would, so we kept our distance. When Toni felt the need to socialize with her, she did so alone. "How *is* Martha?"

Apparently assuming it to be a rhetorical question, Toni offered no reply. I moved to the nightstand and turned on a lamp, but she remained in the doorway, just beyond its reach, a small purse dangling from one hand and the other at her side. Her skirt suit looked somewhat disheveled but I told myself that was normal since she'd been wearing it all day. "So you had to work late, huh?"

"I figured a little OT couldn't hurt. I was behind this week anyway, had tons of paperwork to do, and Gene didn't mind, so—"

"No, I bet he didn't."

I expected her to defend herself, or maybe to fight back. Instead, she said, "I saw the news earlier. Do they know anything else yet?"

"They've identified the woman, that's all. Single mother from New Bedford."

"Awful," she said. "Just awful."

"That it is."

She made eye contact with me for the first time since she'd appeared in the doorway. "Do you really think Bernard had something to do with this?"

"Yes." I sat at the foot of the bed. "And I don't think it's going to end here."

"Then you have to go to the police. You have to tell them what you know."

"I don't have any proof. Not yet, anyway."

She shook her head, placed a hand above her eyes. "This is beyond belief."

I allowed a slight smile. "Tell me about it."

"What about the tape he sent to Rick? Did it—"

"I need to ask you about that," I interrupted. "I know you've spoken to Gene about all this, but I need to know if you mentioned the tape to him."

"What I spoke to Gene about was the night you had those... *problems.* I never mentioned the tape or anything else we've discussed."

"It's very important that you tell me the truth about this."

She stood perfectly still in the doorway. "I just did."

I gave a reserved nod.

"Don't you think you should turn the tape over to the police?"

"We decided against it."

"Why don't you want them to have it? I don't understand."

"Rick doesn't want us involved in this any more than we already are."

"But—"

"And neither do I. Besides, we already put it to a vote."

"A vote? You still behave as if you're ten-year-olds playing in a tree fort, for God's sake. This is a very serious situation, Alan."

"I don't need you to tell me what it is." I let the words loiter awhile. "What I do need is for you to promise me that you won't tell anyone else about the tape. Not Gene, not Martha, not anyone." I could only hope the look on my face left no doubt as to how serious I was.

She stared at me for a time before she finally complied. "All right. I promise."

"We're going to handle this on our own, Rick and Donald and me. We're going to get to the bottom of this shit pile one way or another."

Toni wrestled with a frown. "But you just said you didn't want to be involved."

"We don't want to involve or be involved with the police."

"Sounds like something a criminal might say."

I let it go. "We need to do this on our own, that's all."

"And what makes you think you're equipped to do that?"

"Don't worry about it."

Anger brewed just beneath the controlled exterior she was trying so furiously to sustain. "Right, what was I thinking? Not like it's any of my business or anything."

"A few weeks ago, I was crazy. Now a body turns up and all of a sudden—"

"I never said you were crazy, Alan. It's just—I mean, how could Bernard have done this? I just can't fathom it. A man we've known for so many years, someone who was there at our wedding, who we had in our home, had conversations with and socialized with and ate with and laughed with and shared so much with, how could... Someone we trusted, for God's sake. How could he have been slaughtering people at the same time? How could he be both of those things? Do you honestly believe he did this?"

I looked away. "I don't know."

Toni stepped into the room and noticed the box of manuscripts in the closet doorway. "Your old stories," she said with a fondness that surprised me.

"Yeah, I was going through them before. Silly, I know."

"No it isn't. You should've never given up on your writing. You had such potential."

"Can't pay the rent with potential."

"You should start again."

"It's the strangest thing." I went to the closet and crouched next to the storage box. "Half the time I can't remember what I was thinking ten minutes ago, but when I went through these stories I could remember exactly what I was feeling when I wrote every one of them, exactly what was going on in my life when I'd written them, and even what I was thinking when I'd written certain sentences." I looked back over my shoulder at her. "Isn't that something?"

She nodded and let her free hand rest on my shoulder. I studied it, so slender and delicate, the hand of a partner, a nursemaid, a lover, a friend, a vulnerable girl and a strong woman, victim and protector, predator and prey all residing beneath that soft skin, so many sides to the same being bound by a single soul. I turned away, packed the papers back into the box and slid the entire thing into the rear of the closet where I'd found it. By the time I'd closed the closet door and turned back in Toni's direction she'd tossed her purse onto the bed and begun to undress.

"Look," I said in the gravest tone I could muster, "we have to keep this tape business and any suspicions we have about Bernard quiet and strictly between us, all right?"

"You already said that." She draped her suit jacket over the foot of the bed and unbuttoned her blouse. "I heard you the first time."

"I just need to be sure—"

"I *heard* you the first time, Alan." She glared at me with a level of belligerence I'd never seen her express. Then, like a slowly receding tide, her small body began to relax, her shoulders drooped a bit and she turned away, slipped out of her blouse and let it fall to the floor. "Am I supposed to swear on a stack of Bibles or something?"

"I just want you to understand how import—"

"Wait, I know! A lie detector test." She turned and glared at me again. "You could hook me up to a lie detector, how's that sound?"

I felt impervious to her jokes, if that's what they were, and wondered if she felt the same. Once she realized I had no intention of answering her she aimed her death stare elsewhere, kicked off her pumps and busied herself with the zipper on the back of her skirt. She peeled the skirt down beyond her hips, wiggled it off the rest of the way until it slid down into a heap at her ankles, then she stepped away and hitched her thumbs into the back of her pantyhose.

The smells from the pizzeria downstairs were suddenly unbearable, or perhaps they had been all along and I'd only just then noticed them. Regardless, I went to the window and opened it wider in the hopes that fresh sea air might overpower the reek of pizza dough, canned tomato sauce and fried meats. Outside, the darkness continued to gain power, to deepen and develop and take shape.

Toni's nude form reflected in the window drew my attention. An odd feeling washed over me and although I did my best to shake free, it hung tight. It was as if everyone I had ever known that had died was watching us. Flashes of them—each and every one—appeared in my mind then faded as I stood there, pretending to watch the night but really watching Toni reflected in the upper pane as she carried her dirty clothes to a small hamper in the corner and silently dropped them in.

Behind her, blurred figures, faceless and vague, appeared in the glass as if they were passing, pushing through the wall gradually, reaching for her. I closed my eyes and held them shut until I was certain the feeling and visions had retreated to wherever they'd come from, then turned and saw Toni slipping into a lightweight robe. Oblivious, she grabbed two towels from her bureau, headed for the bathroom and mumbled, "I'm going to take a shower."

"It's not about love, is it?" It wasn't a question, and she knew it, because she stopped and looked back at me. The anger had escaped, replaced by sorrow. "This *thing* that's going on with you and Gene. It's not about love."

Her expression was one that might follow a round of violent tears or uncontrollable wailing, only none of that had happened. At least not in front of me it hadn't. She simply looked at me with sadness so overwhelming no amount of tears could ever sufficiently convey its depth. And there in the lamplight, with night in full swing, Toni looked like she had aged for the first time since I'd known her. The tiny lines around her eyes and along the sides of her mouth seemed more evident, as if she'd somehow brought them to life just then. She was tired just like I was, exhausted and drained and doing what we all did: Getting out of bed every morning and doing the best she could, trying her best not to scream or cry or explode in violence and rage or cut her wrists or throw herself in front of a bus or just drop out and allow the streets and shadows to swallow her whole. She was doing what was necessary for survival and sanity, but survival was a tough business, and not at all what life was solely meant to be about.

I closed my eyes again, this time because the pain on her face was hurting me too. "Or am I wrong again?" I asked.

"Yes," she managed, "you're wrong."

"Then it *is* about love?"

"It's about friendship, support, listening. It's about helping me when I need it."

"You're having an affair with him."

"I can't believe you'd ask me such a thing."

"It wasn't a question."

She sighed. "I'm going to take a shower."

"Toni," I said, hopeful it hadn't sounded quite as desperate as it felt, "good, bad or indifferent, I need to know that something in my life is real, that *something* is what it appears to be, do you understand?"

"Yes, I do. I do understand what you mean. I understand exactly what you mean. And do you know why? Would you like to know why I understand so well, Alan?" She waited a moment then said, "Because I need that too."

A breeze blew in off the cove, sent the curtains fluttering while sirens blared from the street below. A fire engine rushed by, followed by an ambulance. It wasn't warm enough yet for the windows to be open so wide at night, so I took my cue and closed it, hoping perhaps to shut out the rest of the world along with the clamor of Main Street after dark. I hesitated at the window, refused to look into the glass for fear of what might be looking back. Everything suddenly seemed so goddamn futile.

"Just tell me it's not about love," I said so softly I wasn't sure she'd even heard me.

"Why do you always assume we need different things?"

"Just tell me."

"It's not about love."

My throat then stomach clenched, and I thought I'd be sick, but the feeling passed more quickly than I'd imagined it might. The circumstances didn't seem to require conflict, screaming or tears or any of the drama these things normally entailed. Rather, a quiet, nearly calm sense of irrepressible grief, an immediate mourning of sorts, assumed control. Bernard was a butcher. My wife was fucking someone else. The world had ruptured, shattered into millions of pieces. And none of it had made a sound.

"You're always so infuriatingly alone," she said. "Even when I'm standing right next to you."

I resisted the urge to reach out and touch her, to hold her in my arms and to tell her everything would be all right. Instead, I shrugged, unsure of what to do.

Toni saw my indecision as an opportunity for escape, and with a frustrated shake of her head, disappeared behind the bathroom door. A moment later the pipes rattled, the water kicked on and I pictured her nude beneath the spray from the showerhead, wrapped in rising steam, soapy hands gliding along wet skin, cleansing a body I knew every inch of.

I wondered if the woman they'd found had showered the day of her death. Had she tried to wash herself clean, too? Had it been too late? Had she known that day would be her last? Had she moved through her final day on Earth with any knowledge of the horrors awaiting her or had it all come as a big surprise, the grim reaper darting out from behind a papier-mâché rock like some cheesy carnival funhouse prank?

We were all the same, it seemed to me, all of us dented and scratched and damaged, held together with pins and duct tape, the walking wounded making one last stand in the dark before giving in to the inevitable. Sometimes it was easy to see the truth behind the lies, sometimes not. Either way, it didn't really matter. The truth was what I needed, and the truth—however terrible—was exactly what I planned to get.

In response, visions of Bernard coiled in my brain and nested there, a teenage Bernard sitting near train tracks and gazing out at the old animal burial ground, black clouds boiling and churning overhead, carrying with them an incoming storm no mortal could ever hope to stop. *Maybe we got it all backwards, he whispered from our past*, his dead breath cold in my ear. *Maybe none of us really start living...until we're dead.*

"Maybe so," I whispered back. "Maybe so."

CHAPTER 14

For the second time in a week I found myself on Sycamore Way, in the more exclusive section of Potter's Cove, but this time I'd been sitting in my car for nearly an hour, watching the small law offices across the street. A plaque that read *Henderson & MacCovey* was mounted to the wall next to the front door, along with some other information of no use to me. I checked my watch then stepped from the car and moved quickly to the corner so I could time my "accidental" encounter with Brian Henderson.

He had always been more a casual friend of Bernard's than mine, but as youngsters I had hung out with him now and then as well, though always on the fringe and often like a third wheel, of sorts. Brian had gone on to become a successful personal injury attorney and lived in a beautiful waterfront property with a social circle that didn't include people like me. I couldn't remember the last time we'd seen each other, much less spoken, so I knew instigating a conversation with him now—particularly one that might yield pertinent information—was a long shot, but it was all I had.

I had called his office a bit earlier in the day, posing as a telemarketer, and learned he had gone to lunch, so I parked near the usual lunch haunt for local yuppies, a small coffee and sandwich shop around the corner. When Brian finally emerged I noticed he was reading a newspaper as he strolled toward Sycamore. My head down, I walked directly into his path, and just before we bumped into each other I pulled up and met his annoyed gaze. "Excuse me. Sorry, I didn't see you." He glared at me over the newspaper, but his scowl slowly changed as vague familiarity dawned in his eyes. Only then did I pretend I'd recognized him as well. "Hey," I said, "Brian, how's it going?"

He straightened his posture and slowed his stride until he'd come to a full stop, then folded the newspaper and put it under his arm. "Hi there." His smile was dazzling, but I could tell he still couldn't quite place me.

"It's me, *Alan.*"

"Alan, of course," he said, but it was obvious he still had no idea who I was. "Hi."

I didn't know if he was aware that Bernard had died, or even cared, so I decided that unless he brought it up, I'd avoid the topic entirely. "How are you?"

"Can't complain, and yourself?" He casually scratched the side of his neck so I'd be sure to see his manicure and the gold watch on his wrist.

I shrugged. "Doing all right."

He jerked his thumb in the direction of Main Street. "Did you hear about the body over at—"

"Yeah," I said. "Couldn't believe it. Crazy, huh?"

"Imagine that kind of thing happening here? Like *that* won't drive the property values down faster than shit through a goose." He chuckled at his own joke and seemed puzzled that I hadn't done the same.

"I just hope they find whoever did it," I said.

"Yeah, let's hope." Because I was blocking his path, he shuffled about a bit and glanced around, as if to be certain no one could see him talking to me. "So, what are you up to these days?"

"Still working security. Sucks, but it's a living." I smiled. "You're doing well as ever, I see."

"Well, we could all do with more."

While he stood there grinning at me I tried to find some semblance of the little boy I'd once known. But the always jovial and unassuming person he'd been was lost somewhere beneath a perpetual tan, his hand-tailored Italian silk suit, and indifference.

"How are Liza and the kids?" I asked.

"Oh, fine, just fine."

"Still haven't had any of our own yet," I said.

He offered the typical silent look of superiority those who have children often level at those who do not; as if being alive for a certain amount of time without eventually reproducing was a sacrilege simply too depraved to verbalize.

After an awkward silence I asked, "Hey, how's Julie doing?"

Brian's eyes widened almost comically. "Well, Jules is—Jules is Jules."

I smiled innocently. "I haven't seen her in years, she still living in Massachusetts?"

"Cambridge—in one of the worst neighborhoods, of course—for a few years now."

I felt my pulse quicken. "Well give her my best next time you see her."

He looked beyond me, toward his office. "Actually," he said quietly, "I don't see her that often. Sometimes on holidays, but that's about it. Julie still has a lot of problems." He pointed to his ear with his index finger and made a quick circular motion.

He said this as if it were, and had been, common knowledge in town for years—and maybe it was—but I had never involved myself in local gossip. Brian apparently assumed otherwise, so I played along. "What a shame. She's still having those same difficulties?"

"Well, you know, she's just *out there.*" If I hadn't known, I'd have never guessed it was his only sister he was referring to with such disdain. "After a while you pull back and throw up your hands in disgust. We all have our own lives—and I have my standing in town to think of—you know what I mean."

When we'd all been younger, before Julie had developed the *problems* he was so quick to point out, she'd been the main attraction in their family, while Brian, an inconspicuous kid with a buzz cut and bad skin, was relegated to supporting role status. Over time the tables had turned, and he seemed nothing short of ecstatic about it. "The last I heard she was working as a waitress. Imagine Julie still holding down a menial job at her age? *There's* a shocker." His sarcasm approached glee.

"Hey, it's an honest living."

Brian looked like I'd amused him. Perhaps I had. "Yes—well—at any rate, listen, it's great seeing you, Alan." He used my name cautiously, as if to be certain he had it right. Apparently he'd become far too important to remember someone like me. When I said nothing, he offered up a burst of insincere laughter. "We'll have to get together one of these—"

"Yeah, can't wait." I offered an insincere smile of my own. "See you around, Brian."

I walked back to my car without looking back. It felt great to dismiss the bastard, and besides, I'd lucked out. Julie was living a little over thirty minutes away in Cambridge, and my thoughts had already turned to her.

***

Once I got back to the apartment, I called Donald at work and asked him if he could search the Internet for some information. I knew he had Internet access at work and at home, and since I had no idea how to even turn a computer on and didn't have time to go to the public library and dig through microfiche, I figured he was the best person to assign with information gathering. "Do you think you might be able to find anything about homicides in New York City during 1982?" I asked.

"I'm sure there must be some web sites out there with statistical info," he said softly, keeping his voice down so no one else could hear what he was saying.

"Well, that's the year we thought Bernard was in the Marines," I reminded him. "If he told the truth on the tape and was really in New York City for that year then there should be some evidence of the things he claimed he did. Articles, police logs, whatever you can come up with that might somehow tie into all of this."

"I'll do it when I get home. There's no privacy here, such is the life of a lowly corporate word processor. I'm not sure I'll find any specifics but I'll see what I can do."

"Okay, I have to get going but I'll be in touch tonight," I told him. "Depending on what time I get back, I'll either give you a call or swing by the house."

Silence answered me until he said, "Get back from where?"

"Cambridge."

"And do I want to know what's in Cambridge?"

"I don't know yet. We'll talk tonight."

***

I was familiar with Boston but not so much with neighboring Cambridge, so after finding a listing for Julie in an area phonebook, I jotted down the number and address then headed out. I shot up Route 3, the coastal highway that leads to and ends just shy of the outskirts of Boston. Thoughts detonated one after another, blurring my mind as I did my best to focus on the road. The two tallest buildings in the city—the Hancock Tower, a reflecting spire of tinted glass built to appear one-dimensional from certain angles and three-dimensional from others, and the contrasting, more traditionally designed skyscraping Prudential Center, needle nose piercing the clouds—dominated the horizon. A dull sun dangled low in the sky, partially obstructed by the cityscape, as if hiding and mischievously peeking out from behind it.

I had no idea, no plan as to how I might approach Julie—or even if I should—much less broach a conversation about what may or may not have taken place in the forests of Potter's Cove more than twenty years before. Odds were, she'd have no memory of me. In all the times I'd been to Brian's house or played in his yard, Julie and I had probably spoken fewer than twenty words to each other. If I got lucky, she might have a vague memory of me as one of her little brother's friends, but that was the best I could hope for.

I needed a starting point, and trying to find the truth about her and my memories of that day in the forest with Bernard was as good a place to start as any. If Bernard had done something to her all those years before, it didn't necessarily prove he'd later graduated to murder, but it would give me a more objective view of him and hopefully point me in the right direction in terms of solving the rest of what I'd experienced.

Traffic was light, and I made my way into the city quickly. It was a bit warmer here, the air thicker and less typical of spring in Massachusetts. I drove along Washington Street then hopped onto Charles Street, cut through the Boston Common public gardens and headed toward Beacon Hill. The Longfellow Bridge took me into East Cambridge, past Kendall Square and onto Broadway.

I found Demaro Street, a narrow boulevard, a few blocks in and away from the hustle and bustle of the main drag. The phonebook had listed Julie Henderson's address as #12. I slowed the car and noticed many of the addresses were not clearly marked. The neighborhood was rundown, the streets littered and the tenements in various stages of disrepair. The gaps between the buildings were so small the entire street had the confined feeling of an alley. On the corner was a graffiti-decorated and burned out building that had once been a convenience store. A group of guarded-looking young men and one woman stood nearby, watchful eyes locked on my car, lips moving subtly, as if speaking to each other in code. I moved on, their stares still boring through me, and a bit further up I found #12, a two-story apartment building with a flat roof, severely chipped paint and cement front steps. I pulled into the first available space across the street and checked my rearview. The group on the corner was still there but no longer seemed interested in me.

Before I could change my mind I forced myself from the car and jogged across the street to Julie's building. A breeze kicked up but quickly dissipated. Litter and debris blew about at my feet, scraped the pavement then settled quietly.

Not surprisingly, the front door was unlocked. I stepped through into a closet-like entryway. To my right I saw a row of mailboxes, none of which were marked with anything but an apartment number etched directly into their front panels. The interior door before me led to a short foyer and a worn and dusty staircase with a hallway to its left. There was a strong musty smell, like fresh air seldom found its way here, and the industrial tile floor was filthy, the dark tan walls shabby and stained. I looked up at a ceiling beset with watermarks and thick clumps of dust and grime, and released a lengthy sigh.

The address in the phonebook had only listed the building number, not any specific apartment, so I moved past the staircase, into a narrow hallway and followed it to the first door. I hesitated, listened a moment. A man and woman were having a rather heated argument on the other side of the thin wall but were speaking Spanish, so I had no idea what they were saying. I moved to the second and only other apartment on the first floor. A small plastic sign that read *Beware of Dog* had been tacked to the door, and beneath it was a thick piece of masking tape on which the name Barnett had been printed.

I returned to the staircase and slowly climbed it, ignoring the spent paraphernalia and telltale rubbish in the corners along the floor that indicated the foyer was a regular stop for neighborhood junkies when shooting up or smoking crack. The entire stairwell smelled of decay. A bleary shaft of sunlight from a window facing the street cut the second floor landing in two. Dust motes danced in the colorless light, sprinkling the shadows just beyond the reach of the sun. I could hear a television playing somewhere nearby, the sound muffled but loud enough to echo throughout the building. Once I'd reached the top of the stairs I looked in both directions—the hallway was empty—then stepped away from the sunlight, into the dusty shadows and toward the first door.

"Who the fuck are you?"

Startled, I looked to my right and saw the outline of a man standing at the far end of the hallway. "Uh—Hello," I said awkwardly.

"Yeah, howdy-do, motherfucker. You deaf?" He came closer, clad in a soiled t-shirt and grungy jeans. His body was gaunt and his gait clipped, as if walking were something of an effort. I noticed a series of dark purple track marks along his arms. His face emerged from shadow to reveal hollow blue eyes that had probably once been piercing but were now faded and foggy from drug abuse. His hair was mussed and badly in need of a shampoo, and black and gray stubble covered his scruffy face. "I asked you a question—who the fuck are you?"

"I'm looking for Julie Henderson," I said, squaring my shoulders, "*that's* who the fuck I am. Which apartment is hers?"

Realizing he had failed to intimidate me, the man dropped his tough guy routine and shrugged dejectedly. "I don't know nobody, all right?" His eyes darted about as he nervously crossed then uncrossed his arms and shuffled his feet like a child in need of a bathroom. When his eyes finally settled on me again they did so with such intensity it was like being stared at by someone who had never seen another human being and was trying desperately to get his mind around the concept. "I don't know no—nobody."

"Look," I said, relaxing my stance a bit, "I'm an old friend of Julie's. We grew up in the same town. I haven't seen her in years and I—"

"She's at work." His statement seemed to surprise him as much as it had me.

"You live in the building?" I asked.

The man nodded rapidly then stopped the motion just as suddenly.

"Does she work around here?"

"Yeah, she—she should be back any time, okay? Any time now." He pawed at the bruises on his right arm and shivered slightly. "Any time now."

"What apartment does Julie live in?"

"Same one as me," he told me through a hard swallow, cocking his head quickly in the direction from which he'd come but indicating only the darkness behind him.

I was stunned but tried my best to mask it. "You her boyfriend?"

"Something like that."

"I'm Alan," I said, offering a casual wave since I had no intention of touching him. "Alan Chance."

"Cool name. Should be a spy or a movie star or something with that name." The man leaned against the wall and sighed. "You ain't a cop or nothing like that, right?"

"Nope, just an old friend of the family."

"Julie's shift ends at two," he said, wiping some spittle from the corner of his mouth. "She should—she should be home by now, I—I don't know what the fuck's taking her so long."

I looked at my watch: 2:19. The hell with this, I thought. I wanted out of there anyway. "Well look, let her know I stopped by. I'll be back around to see her some other time."

I turned to leave and nearly ran into a woman standing in the sunlight at the top of the stairs, a paper bag stuffed with groceries tucked under one arm and a set of keys dangling from her free hand. Images fired through my mind's eye, a veil of memories slowly lifting to expose the woman now standing before me. Gone was the honey colored hair, the clear brown eyes, the perfect complexion and model body. In their place was a rather disheveled and tired-looking middle-aged woman in a polyester waitress uniform, nylons and dingy white sneakers. "Julie?"

She exchanged a quick glance with the man then returned her focus to me.

"Julie," I said again, my heart racing, "you don't remember me, but—"

"Baby," the man said from behind me, "please can we take care of that other thing first? You got it on the way home, right? You—you got it, right?"

I looked back at him, then at Julie. Eyes trained on mine, she gave a slow nod, reached into her uniform pocket and pulled out a small plastic bag. The man blew by me and rushed to her with speed I wouldn't have guessed he had, snatched the baggy from her hand and shuffled off toward the apartment. "Beautiful, beautiful—I knew—I can always count on you, baby."

Julie approached me. "Who are you and what do you want?"

"My name's Alan Chance. I'm from Potter's Cove. Your brother Brian and I used to play now and then when we were kids."

"Chance," she said, expressionless.

"Yeah, Alan. I was a few years behind you in school," I said. "Like I say, you probably don't remember me, but—"

"What do you want?" she asked, this time softly.

I extended my hand and smiled. She left it hanging there, so I said, "I was hoping maybe you and I could talk for a few minutes."

"About what?"

"Well—look, I—I know this is going to sound strange, but I want to talk to you about someone I think we both knew. Do you remember a kid my age—Brian's age—named Bernard?"

A slight crack appeared in her otherwise vacant expression, but she said nothing.

"Bernard Moore," I pressed. "Do you remember anyone from town with that name?"

"I knew it," she mumbled, as if to herself.

I wasn't sure I'd heard her correctly. "I'm sorry?"

Rather than answering or repeating herself, her eyes dropped the length of my body with the detached air of a formal inspection, finally settling then locking on my chest. I looked down, following her stare, and realized the small gold crucifix I wore had come out of my shirt at some point and was dangling over my collar in full view. I grasped it and carefully dropped it back inside my shirt. When I looked back at her she was still staring quite intently, but now directly into my eyes.

"I don't mean you any harm, Julie," I said gently. "I only want to talk."

"Not here," she said in monotone. "Inside."

CHAPTER 15

Despite having been invited in, I still felt awkward and out of place in Julie's apartment. We entered in single-file and with an unspoken but shared sense of sorrow—livestock to slaughter—Julie in the lead and myself bringing up the rear. She stepped to the side, let me pass, then closed the door and engaged a vast collection of locks.

A tiny parlor opened into a substantial but modestly furnished living room, where an inexpensive circular rug covered most of the worn hardwood floor. The furniture was mismatched and old, and the walls had been painted a light gray, which gave the apartment a gloomy feel even in the light of day. Two windows dressed in faded white curtains stood at the rear of the room overlooking an empty playground and an adjacent avenue beyond. Small silver crucifixes dangled in each window, facing the street like sentinels. I pretended not to notice.

Julie brought me through the living room and into an equally dismal kitchen. A card table, its vinyl top littered with burn marks and small tears, sat in the center of the room surrounded by four folding chairs. A large glass ashtray overflowing with cigarette butts, a deck of cards and various religious books, including an old Bible, lay scattered across it. Suspended from a curtain rod in the window over the sink was another silver crucifix.

The apartment was filled with religious trinkets and small statues, but I couldn't be certain if I'd entered a temple or a bunker. I'd not seen a single photograph of her family, or anything that linked her to anyone for that matter, only an impersonal and joyless space that seemed a shrine to isolation.

Julie motioned to the table so I slid into one of the chairs while she put a kettle of water on to boil and excused herself, vanishing down a hallway off of the kitchen. Though I hadn't seen him since entering the apartment, I caught a whiff of the pungent odor of cooked heroin, and assumed the man was down that hallway somewhere too, filling what was left of his veins. I was still stunned that Julie had let me in at all, and I couldn't lose the disconcerting feeling that she'd somehow been expecting me. That was wildly improbable, of course, but it seemed the only reasonable explanation for her saying, *I knew it*, when I'd first mentioned Bernard, and for allowing a stranger into her home with virtually no questions asked. Coupled with the general feeling of unease the apartment emitted, my nerves were on edge and the back of my neck had begun to tingle. But there was certainly no chill in the stagnant air. In fact, it was then that I noticed all the windows were shut, and I found myself wondering why they would be on such a pleasant spring day.

I could feel the man's eyes on me before he emerged from the hallway and glided over to the table. Much calmer and under control now, but to the point of being just barely conscious, he sat down in slow motion and leaned heavily against the rickety table, a ludicrous drug-induced grin on his face. He seemed incapable of small talk so I looked at the Bible without trying to be too obvious. Like the other books on the table, it was tattered and dog-eared, and an inordinate number of pages had been book-marked with small sticky notes.

But for the man's slow steady breathing, the apartment seemed impossibly quiet.

"You ever ask yourself," he said, slurring the words, "how you got to be here—you know, like—like in *this* place at *this* time?"

I looked into his filmy eyes. "Been asking myself that a lot lately."

"You look...tense."

"It's a tense time for me."

"Well," he said, his eyes closing, rolling slowly back into his head, "I figure worry is like this essentially useless, like, thing, you know? Because—dig it—because it like, it like makes us feel safe because it gives us this illusion, this lying-ass illusion that we have power. More power than we really have, you see what I mean? But in the end, man, in the end, all that leads to is fear, right? And fear leads to confusion." He opened his eyes, smiled at me. "So the way I see it is, we all got to, like, to do whatever we can to clear our heads. You see what I'm saying, man?"

I wanted to get away from him, but continued to hold his gaze. "Yes."

"Questioning where some burned out spike addict gets off tossing around advice, right?" He laughed dreamily.

The creaking floor distracted me, and I turned to see Julie crossing the kitchen to a row of cupboards above the only counter space in the room. "Hush up now, Adrian," she said coolly. She had changed into a pair of old jeans and a lightweight sweater, and had let her hair down, which now hung to just above her shoulders. Tied back, as it had been when I'd first seen her, the gray at the roots was far more evident. "Would you like some tea?" she asked.

"No. Thank you, though."

She took two cups and saucers from the cupboard and placed them on the table along with a bowl of sugar, then went to the refrigerator and returned with a small pitcher of milk. She considered me a moment, as if she planned to speak, but instead moved back to the counter and rummaged through her purse until she'd found a pack of cigarettes and a lighter. She lit the cigarette with her back to us, only turning around once she'd drawn an initial drag and exhaled it with a sigh.

Julie Henderson was not aging gracefully. She wore no makeup and had gained some weight, and that, combined with a look of exhaustion and a clearly intentional effort to mask her natural beauty and appear average—if not outright unattractive—gave her a slovenly look. She took another heavy drag from the cigarette, and I noticed nicotine-stained fingers with nails gnawed down to nearly nothing. She was six years older than I, which still only made her forty-four, but in her current state she looked closer to sixty. An unhealthy, emotionally ravaged and physically debilitated sixty. Somewhere nearby, her magnificence remained, buried beneath lines and crevices and dark rings, as if every instance of pain and fear and sadness and loathing had left a physical mark, a reminding scar. The nineteen-year-old bombshell was long dead, and despite her obvious difficulties, living in her place was an adult, a woman, someone of substance, and someone for whom Madison Avenue-defined beauty was clearly no longer relevant or even of interest.

Julie swept her hair back away from her face. "How did you find me?"

"Your address is in the book, but I didn't know you were in Cambridge until Brian told me. bumped into him in town."

"Brian." She spoke his name as if it left a foul taste in her mouth. "Does he know you're here?"

"No."

She quietly smoked her cigarette for a moment. "Why did you come here?"

It was a good question. What had I been thinking—who the hell did I think I was? Whether my suspicions of what had happened years before were accurate or not, what right did I have to appear from nowhere and disrupt this woman's already difficult life? "It might be better if we spoke privately."

"Whatever you have to discuss with me can be said in front of Adrian, it's all right." Her tone wasn't angry but she had obviously already grown impatient. "I trust him completely."

I saw Adrian grin and wink from the corner of my eye. My palms had begun to perspire so I nonchalantly wiped them on my pants and attempted a coherent sentence. "Look, I know this is beyond odd—my showing up out of the blue like this, someone you never really knew that well and haven't seen in years—but I didn't know where else to turn. It's probably ridiculous, my being here, but I needed to talk to you, Julie." I folded my hands and placed them in my lap in an attempt to hold them steady. "I asked before, but—do you remember someone from town—from Potter's Cove—a boy named Bernard Moore?" This time she gave no reaction, so I described him.

She drew on her cigarette, the smoke slithering about causing her to squint. "What about him?"

"He's dead."

"So, what do you want from me, a sympathy card?"

"He killed himself. Hanged himself."

Julie crushed her cigarette in the already overflowing ashtray on the table between us and expelled a final burst of smoke from her nostrils. "What was he to you?"

"He was my friend."

She backed away, folded her arms over her chest and leaned back against the counter. "Is that a fact?"

I looked to Adrian almost reflexively, but he was staring at the table as if it were the most miraculous thing he'd ever seen, so I turned back to Julie. "But I think maybe Bernard wasn't who I thought he was. Some things have come to light since his death that—"

"What things?"

I stood up. "Look, I've made a mistake. I'm sorry, I shouldn't have bothered you like this."

"I saw the news this morning," she announced abruptly. "A body was found in Potter's Cove."

"Yes. The body of a young woman."

"That kind of thing happens around here quite a bit. Bet it's big-time news in that little shit-burgh though." The kettle began to whistle. Julie strode to the stove, retrieved it and filled the two cups on the table. It occurred to me how easily she could have scorched me by removing the top of the kettle and flinging the scalding water in my direction, and although she had given no indication of violence, there was a troubled expression on her face that concerned me. "Sit down, Alan. You came here for answers, didn't you? Why run off now that you're so close to getting some?"

Adrian dunked his tea bag and suppressed a giggle.

I felt myself sink back into the chair, and once Julie had returned the kettle to a cool burner and rejoined us at the table, I said, "You knew Bernard then, I mean—you do remember him?"

Julie clutched her cup with both hands, brought the tea to her lips and sipped quietly. "I remember he raped me."

At that point her answer should not have surprised me. But it did.

"God, I…I'm sorry, I—"

"That's what you wanted to know, wasn't it? That's what you came here to ask me about. There's nothing else, no other reason to link him to me that you'd know about. You already knew the answer. You would've had to."

"I suspected. He hinted before his suicide that he'd done some things, some horrible things." propped my elbows on the table and rested my face in my hands. "God almighty, this can't be happening."

"I never told anyone," she said.

They never tell.

"I'm sorry, but I need to know what happened, Julie. It's important."

"Oh, I *know* it is." She took another sip of tea, her hands shaking, and before I could respond she said, "It was near the end of summer, 1975. It happened in Potter's Cove Woods."

"I don't mean to be insensitive or—"

"Just ask your questions."

"Bernard wore those thick glasses and was physically small—a weak little runt in those days—how was he able to—"

"The element of surprise. A knife. And help."

My heart was ready to explode. "He had help?"

She nodded, reached again for her cigarettes. "I was doing my usual run, and there was a section of woods I always cut through." She pushed a cigarette into her mouth with a distant gaze, like the memories were just over some horizon only she could see. "Do you remember the stone fireplace out there, the one near the old campgrounds?"

"Yes."

"He was sitting next to that when I first saw him," she said, her voice sliding into monotone. "I stopped, I—I thought he was hurt. He was small, like you said, and he looked younger than he was, I guess. He was just sitting there rocking back and forth and moaning and rubbing his leg. I stopped and asked him if he was all right and he said he'd fallen and twisted his ankle. He said if I helped him he thought he could walk, so I gave him a hand. Why wouldn't I have? He looked like this defenseless and injured little kid. Why—why wouldn't I have helped him? Was I supposed to just ignore him and keep running?"

"No," I said, the word catching in my throat. "I understand."

"When I got him to his feet he pushed me—hard and suddenly—and I lost my balance and fell backwards and..." She drew an angry drag from her cigarette, leaving the filter crushed. "I hit the ground hard, hit the back of my head. I just missed that fireplace. If I'd hit that with the back of my head I wouldn't be sitting here right now, I can tell you that much. I would've died in those woods that day. I still...I still thought I would. I wasn't unconscious exactly but everything was blurry and swirling and...and the next thing

I knew the kid was on top of me. He had a knife, a switchblade he opened right near my face, and he was laughing but it wasn't like any laughter I'd ever heard before, it—it didn't even sound human. He held the knife to my throat and he was talking but I don't remember what he said, only...I only remember the sensation of being undressed, my shorts being pulled down and my legs being forced open."

Adrian slowly rose to his feet. "I need to go lay down for a while."

As he hobbled off down the hallway, I saw Julie wipe a tear from the corner of her eye then take another angry stab at her cigarette.

"I'm sorry to bring all this back up, but...but can you tell me who was with—"

"I couldn't believe what was happening," she continued, as if she hadn't heard me. "I couldn't believe what this little kid, this—this *child* was doing to me. Even the way he'd tricked me seemed like some playground prank or something, it—it just seemed so impossible, like a dream where nothing makes sense—you know those kind? The kind where nothing looks right or makes sense?"

I felt myself nod.

"None of it ever felt real. He was physically so small too, like this little person crawling on top of me, it—even when he was raping me it—I couldn't believe what was happening."

I held closed my eyes until the visions her descriptions had created left me.

"When he'd finished—I don't know exactly when that was because I came in and out of consciousness a couple times during it—I felt him rolling me over. I was on my stomach and he pushed my face down and there was dirt and pine needles in my mouth." With the back of her hand she pawed away tears. Tears of rage, a rage in bondage finally set free, escaping her now like a departing soul. "I don't...I *can't* remember how long I was out there. I had a concussion from hitting my head so hard, and I remember it being light, being able to see the sun through the tops of the trees, the blue sky up there looking down on us and...and then the next thing I knew it had gotten dark. Not total darkness like late at night, the kind of darkness there is right after dusk or right before dawn, you know how I mean?"

"Julie," I whispered, "you said Bernard had help. I need you to tell me who was with him that day."

She wiped away the remaining tears and seemed to regain total control of her emotions. "You do, huh?"

"If you can tell me, yes."

"You sure about that?"

"Yes."

"And you think you'll understand?" she asked, her tone even more sarcastic. "You think you'll have the capacity to understand? Even if I did tell you, you wouldn't have the vaguest fucking clue as to what I'm talking about." She slammed her lighter against the table. "You wanted to know if your *friend* was guilty of raping me. Now you know. Go home to Potter's Cove and get on with your insignificant little life and leave the rest of this alone."

"I wish I could," I said.

"Leave it alone. Walk away."

"I can't. It's not that easy. And I think you know that, don't you, Julie?"

"People think I'm fucked up," she said. "Fucked in the head—and I am, I admit it. Since that day I've had problems, but—but I'm not crazy. I wasn't then and I'm not now. I'm *not*."

"Right about now a lot of people think I'm crazy too." I managed a halfhearted smile. "Whatever you're willing to tell me, I'm prepared to believe."

She sipped her tea, smoked her cigarette; said nothing.

"Julie," I pushed, "who was with Bernard in the woods that day?"

"There weren't any other *people* with him—not really," she said blankly. "But he wasn't alone."

CHAPTER 16

With Julie's words still hanging in the air, I tried to convince myself that her statement had been made metaphorically. But even then I knew it hadn't been. I pushed the fear back like the bile that it was, did my best to keep it under control and contained beneath the surface.

"When it was over, he left me out in the woods," she said, splitting the silence. "Like I told you, I had a concussion from hitting my head and I was dirty, had leaves and twigs and things in my hair and all over my clothes from being pushed down into the earth. It was like for a few seconds he had contemplated killing me, suffocating me there in the clearing, forcing me to breathe in all that loose dirt. I realized later that it was probably just his way of letting me know he *could* have killed me had he really wanted to. In some ways it would've been more merciful if he had."

As Bernard's friend, as an intruder in this shattered woman's life, I couldn't help but somehow feel a sense of responsibility, a need to assume the fault in his absence and to apologize for what he'd done, for what he'd become. "I'm sorry," I said pathetically.

"I told my parents I tripped while I was on my run," she said, her mind still far away and trapped in that horrible forest. "I told them I hit my head and knocked myself out and came to a while later. I never talked about the rest of it. I couldn't, I mean—even if I had they all would've thought I was crazy. Most ended up thinking so anyway."

"I'm not passing judgment with this question," I said carefully, "but why didn't you tell, Julie? Why did you let him get away with doing that to you?"

She let out a burst of pessimistic laughter that was brief and violent and possessed the cadence of rapid automatic gunfire. "My parents kept taking me to doctors. They were sure the bump on my head had caused the changes in me. The nightmares I had, the screaming in the middle of the night, the inability to focus or concentrate anymore because it always felt like I was being watched, the depression and the suicide attempt not even a year later. That little trick landed me in a special hospital in Boston." She sat back a bit in her chair and assumed a more defiant posture. "And that was my *first* stop. Been in and out of nuthouses for years. Ever been on the inside of an asylum, Alan?"

I shook my head in the negative.

"Well, let me tell you, there are some crazy motherfuckers in those places. Full throttle, out of control nuts—I'm talking *crazy*. Only I wasn't one of them. And you know what? I wasn't the only one. There were other people in there just like me, people who knew, people who'd seen. Only they talked about it. They talked about it until their medications stopped them from talking or thinking or being anything with an intellect higher than that of a fucking coffee table. But I knew the truth about things too, and all I wanted was to die, to snuff myself out and hopefully put an end to the chaos. Of course no one could understand why. Just months before I'd been this perfect little Barbie doll with perfect grades and perfect friends and everyone loved me and just knew I was going to go to college and meet the perfect Ken doll man and have the perfect Ken and Barbie life. I was Julie-fucking-Henderson. How could Julie go crazy?" Tears again filled her eyes, but she somehow managed to prevent them from spilling free. "And I wanted to tell them, believe me I did. I wanted to tell my friends, I wanted to tell those doctors and nurses and the other lost souls in that awful place, I wanted to tell my parents and anyone else who'd listen that I wasn't crazy, that there was an evil in this world I'd never known existed, but I'd seen it, I'd witnessed it, experienced it firsthand. It was real. That's what that day in the woods taught me. That evil isn't just a concept or a theory. It's real. It destroyed my life. Destroyed it. You live in Potter's Cove; I'm sure you heard all the whispering and talk about how I'd gone off the deep-end. Everyone knows everyone else's business there. Can't fart in that town without someone hearing it."

"If it'll make you feel any better," I said, "I had no idea until your brother told me you'd had some problems. I always just assumed you'd gone on to college and moved off somewhere else."

She gauged the candor of my reply before she spoke again. "Will you answer a question I have?"

"Of course."

"Do you expect me to believe that you were his friend—his close friend—and never suspected, never knew what Bernard had done?"

"I had suspicions, but—no—I never knew for sure that he'd done this to you."

"You never knew what he really was?" She slowly shook her head, as if she pitied me. "Jesus, you really don't."

I leaned forward over the table and slowly brought myself closer to her in as non-threatening a manner as I could. "I need your help. Please tell me what you know."

Without breaking eye contact, Julie reached for her cigarettes. "Careful, I just might."

"What really happened in those woods that day?" I asked. "What was it you saw?"

"The dark," she said softly. "I saw the dark."

I waited for her to continue. When she didn't, I grabbed her lighter from the table, produced a flame and held it out toward the cigarette resting between her fingers. The ignition sound, or perhaps the flame itself, caught her attention and broke the trance that had fallen over her, and with a startled jump, she rolled the cigarette into the corner of her mouth and leaned into the flame. I placed the lighter back on the table and watched as she ran a hand through her hair, stopping to rub the skin along her hairline before continuing on toward the back of her head. She'd left the cigarette in her mouth, and it dangled there like a tiny smoking limb.

I wondered if she always smoked so heavily.

"Do you have any idea what it's like to have your life become one continuous nightmare? I guess we all do on one level or another, huh?" She raised her head, plucked the cigarette free after a deep drag and exhaled a cloud at me. "But how do you describe evil, what it looks like, what it feels like? How do you describe darkness, how do you describe oxygen? I felt…I felt things watching us, watching me." Her eyes narrowed. "And they were pleased."

I wanted out of that apartment more than ever, but gripped the edge of the table and held myself in place. What if Julie Henderson really was insane? What if we both were?

"He had a stick," she continued, staring at the wall over my shoulder now. "He was saying things but I couldn't make out the words. They were strange words that I later learned were an obscure, ancient form of Latin. But he spoke them quickly and under his breath, and I was dazed and sound seemed to filter in and out—everything came and went like that while I was on the ground—sight, sound, and sensation—all of it. But he had this stick and he made drawings in the dirt next to me while he chanted those strange words and phrases. Urgent drawings in the dirt, he kept scratching them into the ground like he only had a certain amount of time, like he had to do this fast or it might not work. I couldn't see what they were because I couldn't lift my head, I—I tried to lift my head but I couldn't, all I could do was let my eyes fall in that direction. All I could make out were glimpses but I started to feel…I felt something welling up all around us, and then inside me like—like the way a yawn starts in the back of your head and then that tingling slowly spreads out across your body, you—you know how I mean? It was like that sort of sensation, only instead of feeling good, instead of feeling like a release or relaxing, it was just the opposite. It gave me that feeling in the pit of my stomach, deep in my gut, the kind like you get right before you're sick or…or have you ever heard the brakes on a car screech at night? In the dark, you lay there listening for that awful sound of impact, and when it comes, you get that twisting feeling in your stomach—it was like that. Only worse. Much worse.

"Then I heard voices," she continued. "His at first, when he got on top of me. His breath, I—I could feel his breath on me and it made me want to vomit, I wanted him off of me and away from me but I couldn't stop him. He kept saying these odd things and his voice was distorted, like in a dream, only…only then there were other voices too. Voices of torment, of people screaming and wailing in agony and all of it swirling around us like a whirlwind, it…" A tremor coursed through her and she took another greedy drag on the cigarette. "And then I saw things no human being should ever have to see. Things I can never erase from my mind. Things beyond comprehension, beyond description."

Like I had seen when the woman had grabbed my arm in the abandoned factory, I thought, the visions of depravity and gore that had surged through me, as if summoned directly from Hell then injected into me through her.

"I can tell from your expression that you think I'm out of my mind," she said.

"No, Julie, I don't." One of her hands was resting on the table. I reached out tentatively and let my hand touch hers. "I don't think that at all."

She slowly slid her hand free from beneath mine but seemed to understand it had only been an attempt at comforting her and nothing more. "You don't just go on with your life after something like that. You don't just pick up and move forward as if nothing ever happened, as if you never saw or experienced those things. Oh, you try, but it doesn't work, the denial doesn't take. It lingers like a foul odor. It clings to you the way perspiration clings to your skin. And slowly, eventually, like the slow drip of water torture, it drives you insane."

I believed her, fearful that in looking at her I was glimpsing my own future.

"One of the strangest things about everything that happened that day," she mumbled, that distant look returned to her face, "was that in a way, he seemed afraid too, kind of like he wasn't sure of it yet, of what he had, of what he could do. It was like he had this genie in a bottle, and he'd let him loose, only he didn't have total control, he didn't have complete command yet."

"So he was experimenting with—what—Satanism, or something?"

"Or something," she said. "It's not as simplistic as people think."

"*What* isn't?"

"Good, evil—all of it." Julie pushed her chair away from the table, stood up and motioned first to the books between us and then to the crucifixes hanging in the windows. "Those are my reality, my beliefs, so they protect me. I've read and studied as much as I can since that day and all I know is that there's a force in this world we can't just dismiss as a bad dream. It crosses all boundaries: age, race, religion, gender, culture—all of it. But there's also a force of positive energy—of good—you just have to seek it out. Evil is always there, like a loyal companion; see what I mean? It's always available to us, always there, waiting, tempting. The only thing evil requires is consent. You don't have to sacrifice, you don't have to deprive yourself of anything, you just do; you just take it. Good's there too, but you have to search a little harder, dig a little deeper to find it. Good requires that you look beyond yourself, it does require sacrifice, thought, awareness of something greater, better than all of us." She wandered to the sink, fired her cigarette into the basin then ran the water. The butt extinguished, she turned and leaned back against the counter, facing me again with those sad, telling eyes. "And hanging on to it is a whole other story."

"Did you ever see him again?" I asked.

"Every day. Every night. Every time I closed my eyes. Every time my mind wandered, it led me back to him. To that frail little boy, to those woods." She shook her head and seemed to snap out of the trancelike fog that had enveloped her earlier. "It was only a matter of time before he took it to the next level. I knew what he did to me wouldn't be enough later on, the more consumed he became. Before me, there were probably other steps—maybe he tortured animals or molested children in the neighborhood or God knows what else before he was able to do what he did to me. From there, killing was the next step. I knew sooner or later the bodies would start piling up, and the more I researched, the more I read and tried to learn about all that Bernard was and what he was still becoming and would eventually become, the more it all made sense. Read the papers, watch the news—there's a commonality in the crimes happening—and it's existed since the dawn of humanity. Do you think that's an accident?"

"I don't know," I said. "But even if it isn't...isn't it just human beings being..."

"Themselves?"

"Yes."

"You think I'm one of those do-gooders who believes no one is responsible for the shit they do? Do I strike you as that sort, Alan? You think I went through the torture of my life—and continue to—because I believe everyone's innocent, everyone's just a puppet to some grand evil no one can help themselves against? The Devil made me do it, right? The *Devil* made me do it."

I stood up, wiped a single trickle of sweat from my eyebrow with the back of my hand and asked, "Then what are you saying?"

"If you take the Devil's hand, it's still your fault, it's still your choice, and you're still to blame for whatever happens, for whatever you do, for whatever that evil causes in you." Julie moved closer, as if she wanted to be certain I heard what she was going to say next. "But just because you're to blame doesn't mean the Devil was never there."

"He once told me the Devil spoke to him," I said.

"Maybe you should've believed him."

An odd moaning sound echoed from the hallway. Adrian's slurred, distant, indecipherable voice seemed to beckon.

"Is he all right?" I asked.

Julie nodded. "We all chase away bad dreams in our own way. He's trying to kick it. I did more than two years ago now. I met Adrian in rehab, ironically enough. We don't have much, just each other, but that's more than a lot of people have."

"I'm sorry." The words were out before I had a chance to stop them.

"Don't be sorry for us, Alan. Feel sorry for yourself. You're the one in the dark now. We're the meek, just waiting on our inheritance. Burn the days and survive the nights."

"Honey?" Adrian called, his voice breaking and on the verge of tears.

"He needs me."

Time was short, and I knew it. "I don't think Bernard killed for several years after he attacked you. He claimed to have joined the Marines, but he admitted before his death that he went to New York City instead."

"And you think that's where he learned to kill?"

"Yes." I swallowed. Hard. "Or maybe where he perfected it."

"Look for ritual crimes," she said with a nearly casual air. "Ritual murder, do you understand? Once he embraced evil, rituals would've been important—everything he did, every act he committed, would have had purpose. His murders wouldn't be simple killings. They'd be sacrifices. I've spent years studying these things, reading everything I can get my hands on, trying to make sense of something that makes no sense, trying to protect myself from something most people will tell you doesn't even exist." She nervously nibbled at one of her fingers. "I may be crazy, Alan, but I know what I'm talking about."

Adrian called from the bedroom again.

"What about the time between his coming home from New York City and the last couple of years?" I asked quickly. "Could he have stopped for several years and then started again just before he took his life?"

"No, I don't believe he would've stopped."

"But—"

"Look, all I know is what happened that day—and I'm sorry if it's not the answer you want. I didn't see devils with yellow eyes and red horns prancing, or cheesy monsters or some Hollywood version of evil in the woods that day—I told you—you feel it. You feel them, because they're everywhere, and nowhere at all. Never there, but always with us."

"Who, exactly?" I asked.

"Demons."

"Demons," I said, tossing the word back at her.

"You experience evil but...you can't describe it. Describe wind," she said defiantly. "Tell me what it looks like."

"I understand."

"You understand nothing." An odd smile grew along her face. "But you will."

CHAPTER 17

Once outside I realized late afternoon was bordering on early evening, and though the sun had shifted a bit, darkness was still a few hours off. Just the same, I felt a strong need to get off the street and out of Julie's neighborhood well before nightfall. I walked to my car quickly, then hesitated and looked around. The group that had been on the corner when I'd arrived was gone, leaving the street empty and jarringly quiet. Yet I felt anything but alone.

Maybe Julie Henderson was right. Maybe we were never really alone. Maybe demons watched from everywhere, and nowhere at all.

***

By the time I got back to town and pulled up to Donald's cottage, the beginnings of dusk had settled in. On the drive back I'd replayed my conversation with Julie at least a dozen times in my mind, but still wasn't certain I'd be able to relay any of it in anything even approaching a coherent manner. As I sat in the car gathering my thoughts for a moment, I noticed Rick's Jeep Cherokee parked on the street. I hadn't expected him to be there but was glad he was.

Donald answered the door with his usual bleak look. "We were getting worried about you," he said as I stepped into the living room. "I gave Rick a call, told him you were coming over. I thought it might be a good idea if we were all together for this."

Rick was standing in front of the television watching a baseball game with a level of intensity most people reserve for serious news footage. He jerked a thumb at the screen. "Fucking Red Sox. Season's only a few weeks old and they already suck."

Donald flashed me an unexpected grin and held up a glass of vodka. "Drink?"

"Yeah, definitely."

He went to the kitchen and a moment later I heard ice slap glass. He returned with Jack Daniels on the rocks. I thanked him and he slid over to the coffee table, snatched the remote and switched off the television.

Rick turned from the set. "Okay, it's not like I was watching that or anything."

"What are you, a fucking clown?" I said. "Who gives a shit about baseball at a time like this?"

He leveled a severe look at me. "Who are you talking to, Alan?"

I sipped my drink. "I'm talking to you."

Before he could respond Donald thrust a folded section of newspaper into my free hand. "Have you seen tonight's paper?" A black and white photograph of a young woman stared back at me, beneath the headline: MURDER VICTIM REMEMBERED.

"No," I said quietly, "I knew they'd identified her by name but I—I hadn't seen this."

Before that moment she'd been a single mother from New Bedford, a name, a vague casualty—like anyone you heard or read about but had never met, or even seen—but the photograph transformed her into a real person, a young, vibrant woman smiling from beyond the grave. I looked into her eyes, studied her features and tried to imagine what she had been thinking about when the photo had been snapped. She looked so happy and carefree. I wondered what her voice sounded like, what her laugh was like, if she was a good mother, a nice person. I tried to read the article but couldn't tear my eyes from the photograph. I tossed it onto the coffee table and this time took a gulp of whiskey.

"You know Jimmy McCarty," Rick said suddenly, all apparently forgiven.

"Yeah," I said. Jimmy was a cop, a townie we had gone to school with and known since we were kids. While none of us were particularly close to him, he had played high school football with Rick, and over the years they had retained a friendship of sorts, albeit a casual one. "What about him?"

"I was telling Donny before you got here. I ran into him downtown today, and we got talking. He said the state cops are all over this one and the guys on the local force are pissed, but there isn't much they can do. They're in over their heads and they know it. Anyway, we got talking, you know, off the record, and he said there was a lot of shit they weren't telling the press. Shit only the killer knows."

"That's standard procedure, isn't it?"

"I guess." Rick shrugged. "He couldn't go into it but he said they found some crazy shit. That chick was tortured bad before whoever did it killed her. He said it's not your usual homicide, jealous boyfriend or whatever. He said whoever did this was a major league psycho. His exact words were: *We got a for real fucking nutcase on our hands.*"

Donald rolled his eyes. "Such the wordsmith, that Jimmy."

"Did he say anything about the murder having a religious or spiritual angle?" I asked.

"We didn't talk about religion."

"That wasn't the question."

Rick held his hands out at his sides in an exaggerated motion. "Jesus, man, what the hell is your problem tonight?"

"Just answer the question. Did he—"

"No, he didn't. I just told you what he fucking said."

"Enough. Both of you just calm down." Donald stepped between us and put a hand on my shoulder. "What happened today?"

I walked away and sat on the couch. "You first. What'd you find out?"

Donald disappeared into his bedroom, where his computer was set up, and came back carrying a small manila folder. He sat next to me on the couch and flipped it open to reveal several sheets of paper he'd printed out earlier. "I did some searches for homicides in New York City in 1982, like you suggested. Most of the web sites I was able to find didn't have information that went back that far. Remember, 1982 is almost twenty years ago now. The ones that still list '82 provided general statistical information but virtually no specific case-by-case detail." He slowly ran a finger down the center of one sheet until he found what he was looking for. "For example, in 1982, there were a total of sixteen hundred and sixty-eight murders in New York City. Now, I found a couple sites that list the neighborhoods where they were committed and some other details of no use to us, but that's about it."

"Sixteen hundred murders in one year?" I asked.

"I know," he said. "When you see hard numbers like that it's disturbing, isn't it?" He shuffled the papers, settled on a new sheet. "Okay, so I tried a few more searches and I stumbled across a cold case site, one that showcases particularly nasty or sensational homicides from all over the world that have never been solved. I was able to search New York State specifically, and then by year, all those that had taken place in New York City in 1982. You said to look for anything unusual, so I found a couple that investigators believe were linked. This site had a lot of info, much of it surprisingly specific. They even have a link where you can contact officials if you have any information pertaining to the cases. But just so you know, a lot of what I came across is disturbing. I went through it a couple times before you guys got here. It's brutal stuff."

Rick began pacing near the television but I knew he was listening.

"Go on," I said softly.

"Again, this is '82, so this was only five years after the Son of Sam killings," Donald said through a sigh. "Whether everyone in the city was still looking for serial killers behind every car or not is impossible to say, but there were two cases—both homicides—that, according to these reports, police believed were committed by the same person. The first took place near the end of January. Bernard left here in late '81, a few months after we graduated high school, so assuming he told the truth about going to New York rather than joining the Marines, he would've been in the city at this time."

"He'd have been there for a few months already," I said.

Donald looked up from the stack of papers. "In other words, he'd been there long enough to get situated, to come to know the city better, maybe to prepare himself for what he had planned, or to convince himself to actually go through with it." He returned his attention to the paperwork. "At any rate, the first victim was an eighteen-year-old girl, a prostitute. Her body was found in an alley in the Bronx. According to the reports, she was stabbed more than a hundred times. Her throat was also slit. Police described it as a 'rage' killing, one where they initially suspected the killer may have known the victim, because there was clearly such frenzied anger associated with it. *Overkill*, they call it, where the killer just goes berserk and tries to obliterate the victim. Early on the prime suspect was her pimp, but the fact that the woman had been mutilated as well concerned investigators, apparently. Between the incredible number of stab wounds and the slitting of her throat, the killer had not only purposely bled the victim out, he took the time to...Christ, sorry." Donald reached for his drink, took a long swallow then returned it to the coffee table. "He took the time to remove certain body parts."

Rick stopped his pacing and whispered, "Jesus."

"Her tongue had been cut out." Donald's voice splintered. "And her eyelids were gone, sliced off and removed entirely from her face. None of what was removed was ever recovered."

"What the hell's the point of that?" Rick asked.

Julie Henderson had told me to look for ritual crimes, murders that had meaning, purpose. Evil purpose. I remained quiet and listened.

"I don't know," Donald said, "but due to this, and due to the fact that there was a decided lack of blood where the body was found, police believed the killing had happened elsewhere and the girl's body had later been dumped in the alley. A subsequent autopsy revealed the body had sustained damage consistent with torture and abuse prior to and even after death, which confirmed their beliefs that this had all taken place in some other location."

"New York City's expensive," Rick said. "Even with the money he saved, how much could Bernard have had? He probably lived in a cramped room in some shitty-ass neighborhood with people all around him. How the hell could he do something like that to a woman without anybody hearing it?"

"Look what Dahmer got away with in the middle of an apartment building," I said.

"At any rate," Donald continued, "the case remains open to this day. The next killing that investigators say was perpetrated by the same individual took place not quite two full months later, in March. Because the specifics surrounding both killings were identical, the police have no doubt the same person was responsible for them. The second victim was another woman, this one twenty-two-years-old."

Rick started pacing again. "Another hooker?"

"No, an aspiring actress working in retail clothing sales originally from Nebraska. She'd only moved to New York a few weeks before her death. And according to the rundown on the case, the police believe it wasn't a random or impulse killing, but rather one that was planned. They believe both women were probably targeted, followed and marked, as it were, for death." Donald focused his grim expression first on Rick, then on me. "And what's worse is that this murder made the first look like child's play."

More rituals, I thought. *More madness.*

"To begin with, the woman's throat was slashed and she was bled the same as the first. Very little blood was found at the scene itself, and the physical evidence of mutilation and torture prior to death was consistent with the previous murder. Again, the eyelids had been removed and the tongue cut out." Donald paused for another quick shot of vodka. "But this time, rather than dumping the body in an alley it was left on a bench in Central Park. Several occult symbols were found carved into the body. They believe this was done prior to the woman's actual death."

"Fucking wonderful," Rick said. "This is nuts, what does any of this have to do—"

"The body was left sitting up, the head turned completely around to the point where the neck was broken," Donald went on. "The police felt it was more than likely tied to one of the satanic cults known to be operating in the area at that time. Apparently some were very violent. This was never proved, but no other murders took place with these same specifics. According to the info on the site regarding both cases, police believe the killer was either apprehended for some other crime and was sent to prison, moved elsewhere and continued his killing in another location, or died."

"They had two of the three right," I said.

"We have no way of knowing if those murders were committed by Bernard," Donald said, "but let's face it: the similarities between those murders and what little we know about the murder here in town is disturbing to say the least. While they're holding out on some of the specifics, we do know that the woman killed here suffered a very violent death and that her body was bled out in another location, a location where she was probably killed before being dumped in the field. The papers have reported that much. And they don't end there. There's another consistent aspect to all three killings that's absolutely chilling. All three women were single mothers with young male children."

Rick froze. "Are you serious?"

"Just like Bernard and his mother," I said.

"Knowing what we know now, and after listening to Bernard's tape, I don't know what to think anymore."

"Yes you do, Donald. We all do." I shut out the sudden memory of the woman in the warehouse.

Her eyes had begun to bleed after she'd grabbed hold of me and filled me with those hellish hallucinations. They had also seemed unnaturally wide. The way a pair of eyes would if the lids were removed from the face. "Bernard did it. He's guilty as sin."

"You're talking almost twenty years ago," Rick reminded me. "Come on, this is crazy. You're telling me Bernard was killing people for that long and never got caught, never fucked up? Bernard? Yeah, fucking maybe. Even if he was capable of doing some of this stuff, he couldn't get out of his own way half the time."

"He's got a point." Donald put the folder aside. "Bernard was hardly criminal mastermind material."

"He didn't even have his shit together enough to be psycho material," Rick said. "None of this adds up. None of it."

"It does once you realize that Bernard was more than a criminal, more than a psychopath." They looked at me in unison. "He was evil."

"Here we go again with this shit," Rick sighed.

"You've changed your tune since the talk we had at Brannigan's," I said. "You were convinced Bernard did this."

"Yeah, the murder here in town. Bernard had problems, and maybe we didn't have any idea how bad they really were. Maybe he couldn't take it anymore and one day he snapped and killed this chick. I can believe that, Alan, but that doesn't mean I'm ready to believe he was some fucking serial killer." Rick stomped around the room like a spoiled child, then stopped suddenly and glared at me as if another thought had just then occurred to him. "And I'm sure as hell not ready to believe all this boogieman horseshit. Bernard was our friend, but he was a huge fucking loser, and we all know it. He couldn't do anything right. He—"

"Remember Julie Henderson?"

His face turned pale as a corpse in winter. "Yeah, sure, I remember Julie—Brian's sister. What about her?"

I killed my drink and let the glass rest in my lap. "I went to go see her today."

***

By the time I was finished telling them all I had learned from Julie, Rick had stopped his incessant pacing and taken up position in the recliner. Donald remained on the couch next to me throughout, listening quietly, and now stared down into his empty glass with his usual look of isolated sorrow. I let the silence hold us a while as memories of crucifixes dangling in windows flickered through my mind.

After a while, Donald slowly rose from the couch. "Well," he said softly, "who needs another drink?"

I handed him my glass and he headed for the kitchen, moving as if sleepwalking. Rick hadn't moved since I finished talking, and was looking everywhere but at me.

Neither of us said a word until Donald returned with my drink. He remained standing. It was his turn to pace. "You believe her, don't you?" he said.

"Yes," I said. "I do."

The recliner squeaked as Rick pushed himself to his feet. "Look, maybe you didn't hear, but Julie Henderson has some serious problems herself."

I nodded. "And now we know why."

"But you're—you're putting all your faith in some broad that's out of her fucking mind, Alan." Rick looked like he might burst into millions of tiny pieces at any moment. "The bitch is crazy. She's been in and out of nuthouses for years. Ask anybody in town, they'll tell you. Julie Henderson's a loon. She had some kind of breakdown or something and—"

"Have you heard a word I just said?" I stood up. We were all standing now, three grown men trying to figure out what in the hell to do with ourselves. I looked to Donald, but he was staring into space as if in a trance.

"Yeah, I heard you," Rick growled, "I just don't believe any of this shit."

"Why not?"

He moved closer to me in a manner that would have felt threatening had he not been so obviously nervous. "You're awful quick to sell a lifelong friend down the river, aren't you? You believe what some girl with mental problems says about ghosts and goblins and demons and whatever the hell else she was babbling about without even stopping to think that it's probably all in her demented head. She's nuts, Alan, you understand? She's fucking insane."

"You knew, didn't you." There was no doubt I had made a statement, not asked a question.

A spasm-smile wrestled with his face. "What?"

"You knew."

"What are you, serious?"

"He told you he raped Julie Henderson, didn't he? You two talked about it, fantasized about it like typical hormone-crazed teenage boys, maybe even plotted and planned out how you'd do it. But you never expected him to actually go through with it, and when he did and he told you, then it was too late to—"

"You know what, Alan? Fuck you."

I took a sip from my drink then placed it on the coffee table. "No, Rick. Fuck you."

He was on me so quickly I didn't have time to react. Before I knew it he had grabbed hold of my shirt and pushed me clear across the room. As he slammed me against the wall I grabbed his forearms and tried to loosen his grip, but there was no chance. I could have hit him, but I didn't want to escalate it into anything more violent than it already was. He slammed me a second time and I heard Donald screaming for him to stop as my head snapped back and slapped the wall. Pain fired from behind my eyes and blossomed across my face. "Who the fuck are you to accuse me? I don't have to take this shit!"

As my vision cleared I saw Donald trying to push himself between us. Rick let go of me then, pushed his way by Donald and headed for the door.

I regained my balance and stepped away from the wall.

"Are you all right?" Donald looked into my eyes then spun back toward Rick. "Are you out of your mind? What the hell is the matter with you?"

Rick stood near the door looking as if he couldn't decide whether to leave or stay. Finally he turned back toward us, his anger apparently softened. "How did...how did you know he told me?"

"I didn't," I said. "I guessed."

He dropped his head like a reprimanded schoolboy. "Bernard said a lot of things, you guys know that. He lied all the time—exaggerated about everything—made himself out to be more than he was. I never believed half the shit he said and neither did anybody else." He raised his eyes to meet mine. "He told me he made it with Julie Henderson. He told me that he did it but I didn't believe him. Why would I? Why would I believe him? I thought it was just more Bernard bullshit. I blew it off, never thought about it again, you see what I'm saying?"

"This is real, Rick," I told him. "It's all real."

"I didn't know," he said, the last word catching in his throat. "I swear to Christ, I didn't know."

I had never seen such emotion from him, and wasn't sure what to do.

"Of course you didn't," Donald said for me. "Alan only meant—"

"I shouldn't have..." Rick reached out as if to touch me, but he was too far away. "Look, man, I...I'm sorry. Are you okay?"

I rubbed the back of my neck. "Yeah, don't worry about it."

"I'm sorry," he said again.

"This'll destroy us if we let it."

"Then we won't let it," Donald said quickly. "We'll get through this. We'll stick together and we'll get through this."

"I'm as scared as you guys are, but we can't deny what's happening here."

Rick shook his head. "But Jesus Christ, dude, *demons*?"

"It's just like Julie said. You can't see evil, but you know it's there. Maybe I'm the only one who had visions, but we all had the nightmare. We all experienced it. We all felt it. You gonna stand there and tell me we're *all* crazy, Rick?" I grabbed my drink and powered it down in one swig. "I'm telling you right now, there'll be more bodies, more death, and more darkness. Bernard may be gone, but the evil he used isn't."

Donald lit a cigarette. "Let's go with the fantastic then and assume it's true, that this evil is real. What's the solution?"

"We find it," I said, surprised at how calm my voice had become. "We root it out, get it out of the shadows, into the open and into the light where we can see for ourselves just what in the hell it is we're dealing with."

"And then?"

"We kill it."

CHAPTER 18

In an instant, life can change. Sometimes it is reduced to fragments, disjointed shards of a once larger and intact whole, strewn about like pieces from a shattered vase. And those things once striking and beautiful are suddenly rubble, as without warning, existence changes, sometimes irrevocably, sometimes not. If we're wise, or even just lucky, these experiences remind us of who we are, and why. If we're unlucky, we fade to black. No explanations, no condolences.

When I got home, Toni was packing, transferring neatly folded items from her bureau to the suitcase without looking at me, without saying a word. I stood in the doorway to our bedroom and watched, helpless. "What's all this supposed to be?" I said. She shot me a quick, oddly neutral glance, and continued her duties with motions so repetitive and studied they seemed more robotic than human. "Great timing. This is the last thing I need right now."

"The last thing *you* need."

"Come on, Toni." She stopped then, a tan silk blouse I'd bought her as a birthday present a few years before dangling from her fingers. "I remember when I got you that," I said. "The clerk wanted to know if it was a gift, and I said it was, so she offered to wrap it for me. I told her—"

"No. You told her no."

I nodded. "Even though I can't wrap for shit. Never have gotten the hang of it. I told the clerk I always wrapped your presents myself anyway."

Toni pursed her lips to prevent them from trembling. "And what did she say?"

"She said that was very sweet, that most men would jump at the chance to have a gift wrapped for them, especially men with no talent for doing it themselves." I wanted to reach out and pull the blouse from her grasp, or maybe to just hold it with her. "I told her I wasn't most men."

A glint in her eye told me that despite it all, she still believed the same thing. She turned away, folded the blouse as neatly as her shaking hands would allow and slipped it into the suitcase. "When I got home from work today, instead of coming right in I went over to one of the benches by the water and watched the ducks and swans for a while." She pushed some hair from her face and even smiled a little, though not at me. "I sat there and smoked a cigarette, and for a little while everything—all the noise and the bullshit—seemed to soften a little, like somebody had lowered the volume. It was so nice. There was that feeling in the air—you know the one—when you can actually feel the change in season, you can feel spring slowly becoming summer. The air changes, the light, everything. It's new, but it's familiar, and I started to think about how spring used to last so much longer when I was a little girl. Remember when it was more than just a couple weeks? Nothing stays the same—not even the seasons—yet nothing really changes. Maybe that's the whole point. I watched this one swan gliding along the water and I thought, I could stand up, get into my car right now and drive away. Just...drive away. No one would kill me or put me in jail. I could just slip away and no one could stop me. If I wanted to do it, I could. I could, and the world wouldn't even notice."

"The world never does," I said.

"It made me wonder why we do what we do, you know? Why we stay. Do we do it because it's the right thing to do, or because we're afraid of the consequences?"

I found it interesting that she hadn't included love as a possible reason—on either side of the argument. "Regardless, you're leaving town, is that it?"

She shook her head, disappointed. "You're such a literalist."

"Oh, sorry about that. I figured packing your bags was pretty fucking literal." I'd mustered as much sarcasm as I could, and it hardly seemed enough. "So you're not leaving town then. Just me."

She looked genuinely surprised. "Do you want me to?"

"No."

"Then what do we do?"

"Am *I* supposed to leave? I mean, is that what I'm supposed to do? I'm not sure how this kind of thing works."

She gave a little shrug. "Me either." She looked so beautiful I could've killed her.

"I can't believe you think this is the way to—"

"You know the little cottage Martha has down by the beach, the one her parents left her? She said if I needed it for a while I could use it, which is nice of her since she could easily rent it for the entire summer."

"Yeah, how thoughtful." I needed another drink but stayed where I was for fear she wouldn't follow me if I slipped back into the kitchen, and the conversation, such as it was, would end right then, right there. "So I guess you need it."

"Yes, just for a while. I need some time away, some time to think."

"Oh, but after your time at the think-tank you'll be back? Well, there's some good news after all."

Toni closed the suitcase. The sound of the zipper sealing went right through me. "You're obsessed with this Bernard business, and you're getting in over your head. You're becoming involved in things you're not equipped to handle."

"Thanks for the vote of confidence."

"You need to get some help, Alan."

"Is that what your boyfriend suggests?"

"You're such a child sometimes."

"You're right. The mature move is to go fuck someone else." I saw her wilt, as if the words had physically injured her, and for a brief instant, I felt a rush of satisfaction. I wanted to share the pain. "I never had any idea you hated me so much."

She dropped the suitcase to the floor with a deliberate thud, and I pictured the patrons in the pizza parlor downstairs all gazing up at the ceiling. "I don't hate you, Alan. The only thing I feel right now is sorrow. There's no room left for hatred or anything else."

I steadied myself against the doorway, maybe because I'd had too much to drink at Donald's, maybe not. "Have I really failed so horribly?"

"We need some time apart right now. I need—"

"You know I think I could handle this if you just let me have it, both barrels," I said. "If you just called me an asshole or a lousy husband or a fucking loser. But this 'I need some time apart' bullshit just makes me want to puke. Don't make this out to be anything other than what it is, Toni. You're having an affair and you're leaving to lessen your own fucking guilt about it, to make yourself feel better, because if you leave, then we aren't together anymore and then it isn't really cheating is it? At that point you aren't betraying me, and that just feels so much better than feeling like a spineless conniving whore."

She folded her arms over her chest. "Finished?"

"No. Fuck you for doing this. Now I'm finished."

"Feel better?"

"Not particularly."

"Well maybe this'll help. Fuck you right back, Alan." She picked up her suitcase and started to leave the room, but hesitated once alongside me. "Has it ever occurred to you that maybe there is no affair? You believe what you should question, but never question what you should believe."

"Yeah, okay, who are you, Confucius now?" I laughed lightly, but it was merely a defense, an attempt to prevent myself from imploding, from crumbling and collapsing into myself. "If you leave, don't come back. You leave tonight and that's it, you hear me? It's done."

"You don't want to play it that way."

"Oh no?"

"No."

"Then what the hell do you want me to do? You want me to ask you not to go? You want me to beg—what? What do you want from me? Tell me and I'll do it."

"I'm tired, Alan. I'm tired and sad and even a little frightened, but I need to do this."

"Do you love me?"

"Of course I love you."

"Then why do you need to get away from me so desperately?"

"Because right now love alone isn't enough. It seldom is."

"You're wrong," I said. "Love is enough. If it's real, it's enough."

"I want—"

"Yes, by all means let's make sure we attend to what *you* want. The world is in fucking flames, everything is going to shit and right in the middle of it, right when I need you the most, you bolt. That's your solution, to go run and hide. Fine. Go."

"You may not want to admit it," she said, speaking in a loud whisper, "but right now this is best for you too. It's something we both need."

"So that's where we are then? Just like that."

"For now."

"What the hell does that mean?"

"We need some time apart." She approached me slowly, and until she raised herself up on the tips of her toes so her lips could reach my forehead, I hadn't been certain if she'd planned to kiss me or strangle me. Her mouth lingered, warm and soft against my skin, then she dropped down to her natural height. "That's what it means. And that's all it means."

***

I heard her descending the staircase, struggling with the suitcase, bouncing it against each step as she went, and felt guilty for not offering to carry it down for her. The guilt vanished the minute I heard her car start. Until that moment, when I heard the car pull out of the space and saw the headlights glide past the windows, the engine sound slowly absorbed into the night, the authenticity of the situation hadn't quite hit me. But she'd done it. She'd really left.

I had the conversation again, this time alone of course, and I caught myself mumbling my lines aloud as I stood in the newfound silence of the kitchen, numb and unsure of exactly what to do with myself. I wondered if we'd ever be all right again, if we'd ever be whole again. The two of us. All of us. Any of us.

I found an unopened bottle of whiskey in the liquor cabinet, stared at the label a minute, then grabbed the phone and dialed Donald's number. I figured if I could catch him before he finished the vodka at his house I could convince him to drive to mine. "Hey, it's me," I said. "I'm going to get really shit-faced, you want to join me?"

"What's wrong now?"

"What isn't? Come on over, let's get trashed."

"Call me psychic, but I don't think Toni would be too thrilled with that idea."

"Yeah, well she's not here." I held the phone with my chin, broke the seal on the bottle and poured a glass. I could hear Donald breathing through the line.

"Where is she, Alan?"

"She moved out for a while."

"Oh, God, I'm—I'm sorry."

"Come on over and get drunk with me. Bring ice."

"I'm already too drunk to drive," he said guiltily.

"Okay," I sighed. "I'll catch you tomorrow then."

"Are you going to be all right?"

Our roles had switched, it seemed, even if only for a night. "Too early to tell."

"Can I ask you something?"

"Shoot."

"Do you ever think about him? About what he might do if he was still here?"

"Bernard?"

"Tommy." He said it like it should have been evident, like I should have realized he couldn't have been referring to anyone else. "I've been thinking about him a lot lately."

"I miss him too."

"Sometimes it seems like we lost him only yesterday, but other times it seems like it's been a hundred years, doesn't it? Sometimes it seems like it couldn't be possible he's been gone for so long." Ice cubes clinking glass echoed through the phone. "But he would've known what to do, don't you think? Tommy would've known what to do."

Donald was right, of course. Somehow Tommy—or at least our memory of him, the teenage version, the version that remained forever young, forever frozen in perfection even when I remembered him dying along the side of the road—that Tommy would've known what to do, would've gathered us all together like the natural leader he was and made everything all right with a cool, collected sentence or two.

I started drinking. If Donald wasn't coming over there seemed no reason to delay the inevitable. "Yeah, Tommy would've known what to do."

"Maybe he's guiding us."

A comment so lacking cynicism sounded peculiar coming from him. "Let's hope so."

"Do you ever...do you ever feel him around you?"

"Right after he died," I admitted. "But not for a long time now."

"Sometimes I do. Or—well, at least I think I do. Probably just wishful thinking."

I heard him swallow, crunch some ice. "Everything's changed," I said. "Anything's possible now."

"You're right. If we're expected to believe demons exist then why not angels too?" His voice cracked. "I loved him, you know."

"Me too, man."

"No...I *loved* him, Alan."

I poured another drink. "I know."

"And I don't know if I've ever quite recovered from his death." Although when he spoke again he had done his best to collect himself, I could tell by the cadence of his breath he'd been battling sobs only seconds before. "Christ, maybe Bernard was right when he said we're all a bunch of clichés and don't even realize it."

"Bernard was wrong."

"Yes, well Bernard may very well have been the Devil."

"No, just *a* devil."

"Maybe he was right about me. I'm a lonely, pining, overemotional, self-loathing, alcoholic gay man—gee, there's a new twist—never seen that characterization before. Could I be a little more '70s formula, please? Lip-synching to Diana Ross records in a bad wig until the wee hours of the morning can't be far behind."

Even under the circumstances, his sense of humor was contagious. "Far behind?"

"Okay, I've done that too. Apparently my political incorrectness is terminal."

"And I'm a huge loser with no job. And my wife just left me. What's your point?"

"You've lost enough people you loved to know there aren't any second chances," he said softly, his tone serious again. "You and Toni were made for each other, Alan. Don't let her go. Do whatever you have to do, but get her back, because it's a terrible thing when someone's gone—really gone—and you're left wishing you could say all the things you feel, all those things you need so desperately to say. And you do say them, trust me, you do. Only by then, no one's there to hear it." The sound of a hissing match was followed by a slow, deliberate intake of breath. "Get her back, Alan." Then release. "Just get her back. You need her. Hell, we all do. Toni's our den mother."

I laughed lightly. Toni would have loved that description. "I'll see what I can do."

"Don't get too drunk."

"I'll see you tomorrow," I said, though I could no longer be sure of anything.

I hung up the phone and turned back to the bottle.

Let the demons come, I thought. And I knew damn well they would.

But this time, they'd come on my terms.

CHAPTER 19

A while later I found myself sitting in the den, a Robert Johnson CD playing on the stereo as I worked at finishing off the whiskey. The glass no longer necessary, I had taken to occasional swigs directly from the bottle while rummaging once again through Bernard's planner. I studied the photograph of the mystery woman for a while then slipped it behind the lip of a pocket on the inside cover. I wondered if she could be another victim, but that seemed unlikely. Still, he'd known her—he didn't have her photograph for no reason or by coincidence—I was certain of it. There had to be some connection.

I flipped through the remaining pages of the planner, and just like the times before, found nothing unusual. In one of the plastic storage pockets I noticed a few business cards. All were people I didn't know, and I assumed they were most likely customers he had met while at work. The only other card belonged to one of the salesmen Bernard had worked with. *Chris Bentley, Sales Representative*, it read. The dealership name was emblazoned above his name, and a telephone number was listed beneath it, followed by the italicized phrase, *Nobody Beats Our Deals!* I pulled the card free and stared at it. I remembered Bernard mentioning Chris Bentley now and then. He was one of the few people he worked with he ever talked about, and from everything I could recall, if Bernard's side of it was to be believed, they had a decent working relationship. It was a long shot, but I didn't have much else to lose, so I figured I'd pay Mr. Bentley a visit in the morning and see if he could shed any light on anything.

I closed the planner and put it aside, pictured Toni sleeping in Martha's cottage—maybe somewhere else—then thought of the woman in the newspaper. Her face faded, replaced by Tommy's. "Here's to you, man." I raised the bottle, took a long pull.

The room tilted and distorted as Robert Johnson's mighty blues riffs echoed and slurred; his haunting voice singing of hellhounds on his trail and the Devil's relentless pursuit sounding like it was coming to me from the far end of a tunnel.

As my drunken stupor gave way to something resembling sleep the ghosts ended their silence, slipping memories to me piecemeal like a demonic slideshow from the past.

Behind the curtain separating then from now, I saw Tommy sitting on a big boulder out in Potter's Cove woods. The same boulder we'd all congregated around now and then in years past. Tommy, with that knowing smirk and...I had to think for a moment what color his eyes were. Why couldn't I remember something so basic about him? Gray. I remembered them as a kind of light gray. He sat atop that old boulder, smiling down at me, sunlight breaking through the trees and shining against his blond hair and fair complexion, casting him with an angelic aura. Like some wise forest prince, he looked down at me from that boulder and smiled. But now, unlike when he was alive, there was nothing to it, nothing behind it. Blood dripped slowly from his hairline, trickled along his cheek. He seemed disinterested.

And while he sat bleeding, Toni and I leaned against the base of the boulder, our arms around each other the way young lovers constantly cling together so desperately, sharing a beer while Donald stood a few feet away with a can of his own, laughing and talking with Bernard. Bernard—much younger than I remembered him—dressed in fatigues as counterfeit as he was, spinning tales about the Marines and his ill-fated early return, drinking his beer and laughing with the rest of us. We'd all gone to that spot in the woods to celebrate Bernard's homecoming, taking along a couple six-packs as we'd done for years, knowing this could be the last time now that adulthood had caught up to us, now that spending Saturday nights out in the woods drinking like a bunch of high school kids would no longer do.

Rick, still serving his prison sentence, was absent. Bernard raised his beer to toast him, his hand clutching the can, the same hand that just months before had slaughtered two young women in New York City, hands that had stabbed and mutilated, that had held heads steady while cutting, slicing away pieces of flesh, hands that had mingled, played with the dead.

And now he was playing with us, pretending to be the same old harmless and unexceptional Bernard he'd always been, chugging a beer and contemplating his future just like the rest of us. No longer merely a torturer or a rapist, he had by then become a killer—savage, unremorseful, performing rituals and making sacrifices to whatever dark gods he served. Surely there was some sign, some clue we'd missed.

Even in the realm of dreams and whispers, it all seemed so absurd.

Tommy, long dead himself by then, watched us from the top of the boulder, his hair tinted red; the blood from his cracked skull leaking faster, dribbling down the front of him in a steady, sticky stream. His eyes shifted, gazed off toward another section of woods not so far from there, where an even younger Bernard had brutalized Julie Henderson.

Julie, all these years later, existing in that dark apartment, silver crucifixes hanging in the windows, Bibles and used syringes scattered about, the putrid stench of cooked heroin lingering in the air while she struggled so desperately to hang on to whatever slivers of sanity and well-being remained. Working a job slinging diner food, one eye always on the door, hurrying through the neighborhood with head bowed, making drug buys in filthy alleys and on desolate street corners, waiting for the demons to come looking for her again, hoping to make it to the safety of her apartment, her sanctuary, her fortress and tomb, where Adrian waited, scratching at bruised arms.

She emerged from the shadows gradually, rocking gently, her nightgown pulled up around her waist as she rode Adrian's emaciated form. Lying beneath her on the bed, his eyes rolled back in a heroin daze and little eruptions of intoxicated laughter escaped him between slurred words of encouragement.

As she bucked harder, increased speed and ground deeper, tears fell from her eyes like the initial slow and steady raindrops that precede a heavier storm. She wrapped her arms around herself and twisted at the waist as if suddenly forced into an invisible straight jacket. The tears grew worse, flooding eyes crazy and wild and stained with madness wrought by unclean spirits, eyes that had seen Hell, and not from a distance.

Teardrops became the ticks of a clock, and I knew then that the recurring dream had begun again. I had joined Julie in the gulch between that which was real and that which was better left imagined.

The ticking clock began to irritate me right on cue, and from my position on the bed, I heard the floor creak, felt it shift. The headache tingled behind my eyes, same as always, but I ignored it and sat up. I knew Bernard would be standing in the room staring at me, so I wasn't surprised to see him there, pale and dead, smiling his sad smile. This time, I knew why I was afraid. I looked to the doorway. The others would be coming for him soon. He stepped closer, gleeful in the madness, and reached for me with dirt-caked fingers, his nails cracked and brittle and looking as if he'd been burrowing through earth and stone and scraping at casket lids for hours. He leaned closer, touching me now, leering at me the way a butcher leers at a prize hog, rubbing my legs and squeezing my thighs, running his hands over me as I sat paralyzed.

His hand slid between my legs, stroked me roughly before cupping my scrotum. Vomit burned the back of my throat. He laughed soundlessly, his fingers pulling at me, prodding; his breath rancid and warm against my face.

In his free hand something flashed, reflecting what little light existed in the room. Small razor blades moved quickly, individually between his fingers, from one to the next in rhythmic motion, turning and rolling and flipping the way a gambler manipulates a deck of cards with a single hand.

"Stop—Bernard, for God's sake—stop."

He smiled at me, his lips cracking and crumbling like all the times before, dripping blood and spittle. The ticking of the clock became instead a steady buzzing sound. Something moved down by his feet. Flies. They gathered on the walls, along the ceiling, crawled across the window casings, their number steadily growing as they converged on the room, swarming forth from unseen portals.

As they covered the room in a living blanket, Bernard opened the ragged bloody hole that had been his mouth and held it in a silent screech. Over his shoulder shadows appeared, crossing the doorway and signaling the approach—*their* approach. The others.

His cold dead eyes looked directly into mine, and his hand knifed across my lap. I felt quick, dragging, savage pressure, then the gradual and increasingly agonizing burn razors leave in the wake of slashed flesh.

When the others came for him I was still screaming, kicking and flailing and trying to press both hands over my groin in a frenzied attempt to stop the spray of blood that even then was painting the wall.

Splashed with crimson, the glut of flies rippled and heaved like a single disturbed mass, surging higher along the wall.

Then it was all gone, and I realized I was alone. Rick, Donald and I were on our own, alone with Bernard, alone with all he had done.

And with all that remained.

SUMMER

CHAPTER 20

The sun was going down but still bright, still hanging on and struggling against the horizon as if it had waited for us, the shafts a beautiful collage, varied hues of orange and red cutting the sky and reflecting off the gentle waves of the Atlantic.

Rick had been released a few hours earlier, set free after serving his time. He'd emerged from the gates, and upon seeing us, trotted down the steps the way the gangsters in old movies used to do it, sideways and graceful—like a dancer—as if to show that all was well, and the hop in his step proved it. While he was still in good shape physically, his football-player-build had suffered somewhat. Because he had lost a lot of weight his body looked thin and tight as opposed to thick and powerful, and it showed the most in his face, which at first glance appeared drawn. Having been deprived of sound sleep for a long period, large dark circles had taken residence beneath both eyes, and since his time spent outside had been severely limited, his complexion was paler than it had been in the past.

He'd made it very clear in the days leading up to his release that he wanted us there to pick him up and not his family. He'd need a few hours out before he could face them, he'd told me. But even we were nervous, lifelong friends or not, all of us uncertain of what to say or how to say it, of what to do or how to do it. He came to me first, and we hugged. Despite his attempt at a composed demeanor, his body felt rigid and tense.

"How you guys been?" he said, leaving me to hug Donald, and finally Bernard, who had hung back closer to the car like a shy younger sibling. Yet it was Bernard who had embraced him the longest that day, clinging to him until Rick finally wrestled himself free in a rather awkward and embarrassing maneuver, whispering, "It's okay, man, it's okay, take it easy."

Rick looked at the sky like he'd never seen it before. He smiled but it came off as meaningless. Our leader had returned. Locked away the head Sultan—our warlord—only time would tell what had emerged in his place. "Let's go to the beach," he said.

It was the first time I'd heard his voice without having a sheet of thick plastic between us in months, and it sounded rich and full, but not exactly as I'd remembered it. Like his smile, it lacked the conviction it once had. He'd been broken in there, and despite his best effort it showed.

"The beach," I said. "You got it. Whatever you want."

The ride there was quiet. Initially Bernard had tried to make small talk, but no one responded, so he let it drop. Rick sat in the front passenger seat, looking out the window but not focused on anything specific until we hit the beach parking lot. It was early fall, the tourists had all gone home and the beach was deserted. Before I had a chance to park he rolled the window down and drew a deep breath of ocean air. He smiled, and this time it seemed closer to genuine, like he was working his way toward it. "You miss the weirdest shit. All kinds of stuff you never really think about."

We held back, allowed Rick to take the lead and get out of the car first. As he crossed the sand, trudging along toward the waterline, we slowly emerged from the car and trailed him, giving him a wide berth. Once he'd reached the water he crouched down and touched it, then looked out at the waves and the sky and the slowly setting kaleidoscope sun.

After a moment we slowly converged on him and formed a half circle behind him. The temperature was dropping, and the wind off the water was growing stronger. No one said a word—even Bernard knew enough to keep quiet—while Rick bonded with the sand and sky and air and water and whatever else he needed to see and feel and think and know. He ran his hands through the sand, let it fall between his fingers, then grabbed a handful and tossed it out at the water.

He turned back to us, cheeks flushed. "So what do you guys want to do?"

"It's your night, dude," Bernard said. He stepped forward and lit a cigarette. In an attempt at cool that was even less genuine than Rick's earlier efforts, he cupped the flame from his lighter with both hands, cocked his head and did his best James Dean. "How about we go to Brannigan's and get some steaks? We can throw back a few then hit a titty-bar or something like that."

Bernard had begun to prematurely bald his senior year of high school, and since Rick had gone, Bernard had taken to wearing a rather silly looking wig that would eventually become one of his defining characteristics. Between that and his thick glasses, Donald often joked that he looked like he was wearing a bad disguise, but it apparently made Bernard feel better about himself.

"Check this guy out," Rick said, doing his best to appear amused. He had clearly been shocked by Bernard's appearance, but never said a word about it. "You a big titty-bar guy now, Bernard?"

Bernard grinned. "A lot's changed."

"Yes," Donald said quickly, "Bernard's become a wild stud while you were away. *King of the Titty Bars* is what we call him now. It beats *Moronic Dipshit* and looks better on a t-shirt."

"At least I like titties," Bernard said, laughing now too.

"Yes, but do titties like you?" Donald plucked the cigarette from Bernard's lips, took a drag then stuffed it back into his mouth. "That is the question."

"You know better than to ever get into it with Donny." Rick put an arm around Bernard, looked at me and winked as they headed back toward the car. "Sorry that whole thing with the Marines didn't work out."

"Fucking training platform," Bernard grunted. "I was kicking ass and taking names until I fell off that goddamn thing. Wrecked my knee. It's better now though."

"Still, that took a lot of balls, joining up like that. I'm proud of you, man."

Bernard looked back at Donald and me and beamed.

"Like a kid with a cookie," I mumbled.

"True," Donald agreed. "But which one's the cookie?"

As we followed behind them I heard Bernard say, "I told you, Rick, a lot's changed."

And while I had no idea just how right he was, things had changed for each of us in our own way. Tommy was a few years dead, Rick was already fighting to find an old self he'd never quite fully recover, Donald had begun to lose the battle against depression and the alcoholism that accompanied it, I was within months of being engaged to Toni—so certain marrying her would somehow salvage us both, make us complete—and Bernard...Bernard, like Tommy, while not yet buried, was already a couple years dead too, slowly rotting from the inside out. Only no one knew it. Or maybe no one wanted to know it. No one wanted to know anything. Not about Bernard, not even about ourselves.

Later that same night, while Donald and Bernard walked along the beach, Rick and I managed a quiet moment. We had taken up position at a small gazebo set back from the tall grass and overlooking the sand and ocean. After sitting quietly for several minutes, listening to the waves and the wind, I finally said, "It's getting cold."

"Yeah, I like it though." Sensing my discomfort he said, "Alan, it is what is. We just got to keep moving. Like sharks, right? We stop, we die."

"I just want to be sure you're okay. I mean really okay."

"Eventually we'll all be okay."

So many years later, we were still waiting.

***

A pounding on the front door brought me back. I hadn't really been sleeping, but wasn't totally awake either, so it took me a few seconds to realize I was on the floor, next to the couch, having apparently rolled off at some point during the night. Bright sunshine powered through the windows. I was stiff and sore, my muscles and joints ached and my head was throbbing. I struggled to my knees, and using the edge of the couch for leverage, hoisted myself to my feet. The knocking on the door resumed, harder this time. "Yeah, I'm coming," I called. "Hold on, for Christ's sake." I rubbed my eyes, stretched, and staggered to the door.

I found Rick and Donald standing there when I pulled it open, along with a blinding shaft of sunshine that felt like it had gone directly through my skull. I vaguely remembered making plans with them, telling them to be here because I had wanted to pursue the

Chris Bentley angle. But I'd had so much to drink I wasn't even sure how long I'd been passed out, or what day it was. The inside of my mouth felt like it had been lined with cotton. "What are you guys doing here so early?"

"We called four times and never got an answer," Donald scolded. "It's almost three o'clock in the afternoon."

I shielded my eyes and squinted at my watch. He was right. "Shouldn't you be at work then, Donald?"

Rick shook his head. "It's Saturday, you daffy fuck."

Donald launched a disapproving glance. After what had happened with Toni apparently he felt name-calling—even in fun—qualified as piling on at that point. Even in the midst of madness, Donald retained his flair for fair play and a sense of decorum, as if etiquette might tame an otherwise untenable situation. He meant well, but it reminded me of the way characters in those old British novels would stop to change into freshly pressed shirts in the middle of a war zone. "Alan," he said patiently, "it's the weekend."

"You been on a couple day drunk there, paisan," Rick said, as if he truly believed this would be news to me. "Now, we supposed to stand out here like two dicks swinging in the breeze or you gonna let us in?"

I motioned them in and they shuffled into the kitchen. Donald was dressed in a short-sleeved striped oxford, khaki pants and a pair of loafers. In typical contrast, Rick was wearing black lightweight sweatpants and a tight t-back muscle shirt with no sleeves at all, his powerful chest and sculpted arms displayed like the trophies he considered them. I, on the other hand, looked and felt like I'd been run over by a fleet of oil trucks.

I went to the refrigerator, found the orange juice and chugged some right out of the carton. "Aren't you two looking summery," I said. "JC Penney have a sale?"

"You been out cold since last night?" Rick asked.

"Yeah, why?"

"Then you didn't hear the news?"

I leaned against the counter; my legs didn't feel sturdy. "No."

Rick looked to Donald and gave him the signal to tell me what they already knew. "They found another one, Alan. Buried in the sand down at the public beach in the tall grass between the beach house and the water. They found another body."

"Jesus." A wave of nausea and darkness swept through me. "Another woman?"

Rick, with the nervous energy of a child, and equally uncertain of how to dispense it, gave a quirky nod. "What was left of her."

"They haven't released a lot of details yet," Donald said, "but like the first, she's been dead for quite a while."

"Give me ten minutes." I started for the bedroom. "I need a quick shower and a change of clothes before we head out."

Rick struck one of his heroic poses. "Where we going this time?"

"One step closer to the truth, hopefully."

"Or another step closer to Hell," Donald mumbled.

As it turned out, we were both right.

CHAPTER 21

The heat was rising. Spring had become summer with little transition time, as it had become prone to do in recent years. The handful of aspirin I'd popped before we left was finally kicking in and had begun to ease my headache, but the humidity wasn't helping any. The dealership where Bernard had worked was in the south end of New Bedford, just blocks from the warehouse and the job site I'd been fired from, and less than a mile from the cellar where he'd taken his life. As we drove deeper into the city I wondered if I'd ever again be able to go there without those ghosts tagging along for the ride.

Rick parked across the street from the car lot. We'd all been there before at one point or another in the past, to pick Bernard up or drop him off or meet him, but as with everything else since his death, it didn't feel the same. What should have been familiar—even vaguely—seemed distant and alien. I slid a hand into my pocket, touched the photograph of the mystery woman but pulled out the business card instead. I told Donald and Rick I was going alone and wanted to keep it low-key with Bentley. Neither objected.

I put a pair of dark sunglasses on, hopped out of the Cherokee and crossed the street. The lot was large and filled with rows of used cars—many of them quite nice—and a small office building was set at the rear of the property. I had just hit the lot when a heavyset, moon-faced man emerged from the office and made his way toward me, waving and grinning as if we were old friends.

"Hey there!" He offered a pudgy hand. "Great gosh all-mighty—hot enough for you? Phew! Welcome to summer! But what a great day to buy a car!"

I reluctantly shook his hand. It was damp and made a squishing sound when he tightened his grip. He pumped my arm with the enthusiasm of someone hoping to draw water. I smiled, pulled free and flashed the business card. "Is Chris Bentley around?"

The jolly routine vanished. "Sure, pal. I'll get him, he'll be right with you."

I nonchalantly checked out a couple cars while waiting. Within a minute or two a man younger than I'd expected—late twenties at most—strolled out of the office wearing mirrored sunglasses and made his way over to me. "Can I help you, sir?"

I held up his business card. "Chris Bentley?"

"That's right." We shook hands.

"I'm Alan Chance, was hoping I could talk to you for a couple minutes."

"Absolutely." He pointed to the card. "Have we talked before? You look vaguely familiar for some reason."

"I got your name from a mutual friend."

"Terrific. Have you heard about the special financing packages we—"

"I'm not looking to buy a car."

He removed his sunglasses and looked me over. "Then what can I do for you?"

"I'm sorry to bother you at work, but I wanted to talk to you about Bernard Moore."

The veil of defensive hostility he had erected fell away with recognition. "That's where I've heard your name, from Bernard. You're one of his buddies from Potter's Cove, right?"

"Right," I said.

"Man, some crazy stuff happening over there these days, huh?" he laughed lightly. "Bodies turning up in a town like that can't be good. Hell, if you're not safe in Potter's Cove you're not safe anywhere."

"True enough."

"Hope they catch the psycho."

"Me too."

Bentley slid the sunglasses back on, folded his arms over his chest and leaned back against one of the cars. "Anyway, I was really sorry to hear about Bernard's passing. I know he had a hard time after he lost his mom and all, and then when they let him go here he was in rough shape. I didn't even know he'd died, felt bad. After he left here I'd call him now and then, sometimes we'd hook up and have lunch. I hadn't heard from him in a while and I knew he was having a hard time, so I called and talked to his—what was it, his cousin's place he was staying at, right?—and he told me that Bernard…well, you know."

"Committed suicide."

"Yeah." He sighed long and hard. "Bernard was—well I don't have to tell you, being his bud and all—he was kind of out there in some ways, but he was a good guy. He was always cool to me. He was in the biz longer and helped me out when I started, taught me a lot about sales. Most guys won't do that. They feel threatened by younger salesmen. There's only so much of the pie to go around, you know? But Bernard was always cool. He talked about you and his friends from Potter's Cove all the time. Said you guys were all pretty tight."

I watched my reflection in the mirrors covering his eyes. "Yeah, we were close."

"Well, I'm sorry for your loss, man, truly. Real shame."

There was something inherently insincere about Chris Bentley. Like many people, he wore a mask of concern but was apathetic to anything that didn't affect him directly. His controlled smile promised his indifference was nothing personal.

Since I'd been thinking rather than speaking, Bentley said, "So… is there something I can do for you, Alan?"

My mind hadn't been clear enough to strategize prior to talking with him so I decided to wing it. "Bernard's cousin Sammy gave us his duffel bag. Toward the end it was the only thing he had, and it had a bunch of his stuff in it—nothing of any real value—just sentimental. We went through it and we found a photograph." I pulled it from my pocket but kept it down against my thigh while the rest of the lie formed in my mind. "There was a sealed envelope attached to it and a little sticky note saying to forward it to the person in the photograph. The only problem is, none of us know who the person is. I saw your card in his day planner and I remembered Bernard talking about you a lot—you were basically the only guy he worked with he liked—and I thought since you were friends with Bernard too, maybe you'd know who she is." I displayed the photograph for him.

He leaned forward and looked at it for what seemed an inordinate amount of time.

"I'd really like to fulfill his wishes and get that letter to her," I said, "but we don't have any idea who she is."

"Okay, this must be an old picture, but you can still tell it's her." Bentley removed his sunglasses and stared at the photograph again. "You don't know who this is?"

"Should I?"

He chuckled, shrugged and put his glasses back on. "Well if you guys were as close as Bernard always said you were, it's a little weird you don't recognize his girlfriend."

Although I found nothing humorous in his answer I nearly laughed. All nerves. "His girlfriend?" I turned the photograph back to me and glanced at it. "*This* is Bernard's girlfriend?"

"Used to be, I guess. I only met her a couple times but if I remember right they were together for at least a couple years. I didn't see her the last few months before Bernard died and I don't remember him mentioning her. I figured they'd split up or something. He was having such a bad run, it would've just figured, you know? Her name's Claudia something—never got the last name. He used to bring her by now and then, usually just on quick stops, you know, like when he was getting his check or something like that. I really didn't know her or anything, but that's how he introduced her, as his girlfriend. He talked about her a lot too, but never really said much about her specifically, if you know what I mean, he'd just mention shit they did or if they went somewhere or something. '*Went to the movies last night with Claudia*,' '*hung out at Claudia's house yesterday*,' that kind of thing."

It was probably too late to appear anything but shocked. "Just seems strange that he never mentioned her to any of us," I said.

"That it do." Bentley nodded. "But to tell the truth, I always got the impression that Bernard had a lot going on people didn't know about. I don't mean that in a bad way, just saying, I think he kept a lot of things separate. His work life and his personal life, both sides—the side he had with you guys, his older friends, and the side he had with guys like me, guys he worked with. I think he kept them separate—hey, lots of people do, no big thing."

I could tell he was holding back. He knew more but was treading carefully. I ignored the beads of sweat collecting in my hairline and did my best to put him at ease. "Yeah, I know exactly what you mean, but seriously, I can't remember Bernard ever having a girlfriend. Ever. And I'm having a real hard time believing that if she were his girlfriend he wouldn't have told me about her. Knowing Bernard he would've been bragging night and day about it. Seems strange even for him." He laughed lightly, and I joined him. Awkwardness hung in the air like the heat engulfing us. "Either way, I feel like I should get that letter to her. You don't have any idea where I can find her or how I can get a hold of her, do you?"

The discomfort he was feeling revealed itself in his posture. "Look, man, I don't want to get into stuff that maybe you don't want to hear, okay?"

I played it cool, wondering if the smile he wore ever completely faded. "We're both adults here, Chris, whatever you can tell me I'd appreciate. Between you and me, makes no difference who this chick is, I'm just trying to do what Bernard wanted and get her the letter."

"New Bedford isn't a small town," he said, relaxing somewhat, his chin held a bit higher as if he were looking beyond me to something more important in the distance. The mirrors reflected the street behind me, and though I could see the Cherokee parked against the far curb, the glare from the slowly setting sun made it impossible to see Rick and Donald waiting inside. "But it is a small city, if you know what I mean. It's not like everybody knows everybody else, but for natives everybody knows *somebody* who knows everybody else. In other words, the circles are small here. A couple of the guys here knew who Claudia was from being around the city for so long. One of them remembered her from school but couldn't remember her name or anything, and the other one sort of knew who she was through a friend of a friend kind of thing. It's not like they were friends with her or anything, but they basically knew who she was. And they knew what she was. She had drug problems even before high school the way I heard it, and she started hooking not long after that, was into it for years. I don't know if she still is, or still was when she was seeing Bernard, but it's probably a safe bet. Those kind don't usually ever change."

I looked at the photograph again before returning it to my pocket. "At least the whole dating Bernard thing is starting to make sense though."

"That's what I'm saying. I mean Bernard wore those glasses and that stupid-ass wig and all—it was kind of sad. He was always talking about how she was his girl and all this, and the guys would laugh at him behind his back about it because they knew she was a prostitute. Bernard worked in the city but he wasn't from here, and he never really figured out how small a community this city still is."

I finally wiped the sweat from my brow with the back of my hand. "You wouldn't have any idea where I might be able to find her, do you?"

"Try Weld Square," he said with a short, sardonic laugh.

Weld Square was an infamous corner of the city littered with dilapidated apartment buildings, deserted businesses, and vacant, garbage-strewn lots. It was easily accessible from the state highway, and was known in the city and beyond for drug dealing, prostitution and violent crime. In my early days with the company, when I'd been given some of the worst details, I'd worked night security in a few of the businesses still operating in the area at that time. I was in no hurry to return.

Despite the probable accuracy, Bentley knew the humor in his comment had been wasted on me. "You ever heard of The Captain's Hook? It's a bar down by the waterfront. Real shithole. Tough crowd. Bernard told me Claudia worked part-time there as a waitress. I don't know if he was telling the truth, but he probably was, because a lot of hookers hang out there too. You could try checking out that place, but be careful. Cops are forever dragging people out of there, real jewel of a joint. This huge fat chick runs it; she's owned the place for years. She's supposed to be a psychic or a witch or something—probably just a gimmick to rip off a bunch of drunks and druggies, but that's what people say. Supposedly some weird shit goes on in there. Wouldn't put anything past that dump." He hesitated a moment then said, "Anyway, other than that, I don't really know what to tell you. Claudia lived in the city, but I don't know where."

I shook Chris Bentley's hand again, and thanked him for his help.

"Wish I could tell you more, help you find this broad, but Bernard never really dealt much in specifics—you know what I mean? That's just the way he was, at least around me. I worked with him for a couple years, spent hours talking with the guy, and most days even now I feel like I never really knew him at all."

"I know what you mean."

"Yeah," he said, "I get the feeling you do."

"Thanks again for your help." I offered him his business card. "You want this back?"

"You hang onto it." He selected the sincerest smile in his arsenal and pasted it on for me. "The next time you're in the market for a quality used car or truck, you come see me, okay?"

***

Given Bernard's consistent lack of success with women, and the problems he clearly had—many of which we were still uncovering—none of us were particularly surprised to learn he had sought out prostitutes. At a minimum, he had sought out one, and a sense of sadness more than anything else permeated the Jeep as we headed away from the car lot and Chris Bentley's eternal smile. Like so much else with Bernard, it seemed impossible for us to have missed it previously, yet once out in the open, it made perfect sense. Had I assumed him to be a monk? Where else would he have gone for sex? Had I ever really given it any thought at all—and if not, then why not—hadn't it even once occurred to me what he might be doing when out of my sight? I couldn't help but feel as though I had let him down as a friend. Here he was, a rapist, a butcher and killer of young women, and I was the one feeling remorse. Memories of him at our apartment flashed through my mind, memories of how he'd sometimes come for dinner and never know enough to go home, lingering and making excuses and small talk until Toni finally had enough and I was left with no choice but to tell him we needed to go to bed and work the next day and it was time for him to leave. I knew then how lonely he was. We all did. Had he gone home after those nights at our apartment, or had he cruised these same streets in that rundown old car, searching for prostitutes—maybe victims—to sate his needs, however twisted and dark? Had I gone to bed and snuggled into the warm and loving arms of my wife while one of my best friends snuggled into the underbelly of the city? *Had* I known? Deep down, had I? And would it have mattered even if I had?

Ten minutes after leaving the lot we were cruising along the waterfront looking for The Captain's Hook. Rick had heard of it but wasn't precisely sure where it was, so we had to cover a few different avenues until we finally found it on a desolate side street across from a fish processing plant. A small building sandwiched between a vacant commercial property on the corner and an insurance office, it was set back a bit from the sidewalk, receded farther than the buildings on either side of it. A large door that had been painted black but that was nicked and gouged rather badly marked the entrance, and two narrow windows on either side of it housed neon beer signs. Cheap curtains had been slapped up in each window to block what little might be seen through them rather than to serve any cosmetic purpose, and above the door a sign shaped like the bow of a pirate ship protruded from the face of the building. Painted in chipped blood-red letters across the faux bow was the name of the establishment.

The neighborhood was one of great history, home to some of the literal "dreary streets" Melville had written about. A few blocks over, near the famous (or infamous) whaling museum, where renovations and several nice retail and dining establishments had moved in, several years earlier the city had converted a few streets to their original cobblestone in an attempt to lend a sense of quaint historical authenticity to the area. But even now, under the haze of imminent darkness, this lesser-traveled street still radiated the same ominous level Melville had discovered more than a century before.

A few older cars were parked on the street, including one rundown Chevy that occupied the space directly in front of the bar, but otherwise, the area was deserted.

Rick slowed the Cherokee, and from the backseat Donald said, "Have I mentioned what a bad idea I think this is?"

"About twelve times now."

"You walk in there asking questions," Rick said, "you better be a cop."

I motioned to an empty space a bit farther up the street. "Park it."

He mumbled an objection but pulled over anyway. "Fine," he said, slamming the shift into Park, "but I'm going with you."

"I'm just gonna go in and have a quick look around, relax." I knew

Rick meant well, and I knew I'd be safer with him by my side, but I also knew that outside a controlled setting like the club his temper would more than likely get the better of him. "Let me go scope the place out a little, see what I can see."

He stared at me, his jaw clenching then releasing then clenching again. "You got five minutes," he said. "Then I'm coming in looking for you. Donny, go with him."

With a sigh, Donald rolled a cigarette between his lips. "I was so hoping I could."

"Hey," Rick said, "no smoking in the vehicle, ass-wipe."

Donald ignored him and slipped out onto the street with an irritable grunt.

I really didn't want him with me either but the sun had almost set and night was slowly closing in around us; there wasn't time for arguments.

I pulled my sunglasses free, tossed them on the dashboard then turned back to Rick. "Keep this fucking thing running."

CHAPTER 22

The door was heavy and scraped the base of the frame as I pulled it open, making a subtle entrance all but impossible. As we moved into the bar I said, "Let me do the talking," but I wasn't sure Donald heard me because he didn't respond. The only answer was metal grinding metal as he closed the door behind us, the grating sound still resonating as I focused on the saloon. The lighting was sparse, and the place could've used a fan or two. The air hung stagnant and sour, and a colossal cloud of cigarette smoke filled the room like a dense fog. I smelled stale booze and sweat, cigarettes, a trace of marijuana, and the faint aroma of urine. To make matters worse, the lack of air circulation made the already high humidity nearly unbearable within the confined space, and I wondered how anyone stood it in here for any length of time.

The room was narrow and deep, and the building seemed to go back farther than the exterior had suggested it might. The ceiling, low and stained with years of abuse, gave off a claustrophobic feel, and an oak bar—large, long and battle-scarred—dominated the left-hand wall. Opposite the bar were a few small tables bolted to the filthy tile floor, rickety chairs scattered about, and an aged, silent jukebox.

Neither the tables nor any of the stools at the bar were occupied.

The bartender was tall, lanky, decked out in jeans and a leather vest with no shirt, and sported thinning but frizzy hair he had grown nearly to his waist. He turned and glanced at us with disinterest, undersized, rodent-like eyes blinking behind a pair of blue-tinted granny glasses. Without a word he returned his attention to a television over the bar.

The unfinished wood walls were decorated with an array of nautical effects—buoys, lobster pots, harpoons, fishing nets and the like—a couple dart boards, various neon beer signs and posters of scantily clad women draped over motorcycles, racing cars, or posing suggestively with various name brand beers or alcoholic beverages. Perched over the center of the bar, a wall clock that advertised Harley Davidson motorcycles blinked on and off in timed intervals.

Through the smoke and haze I noticed an open doorway beyond the tables that led to a back room of sorts. I was able to make out the corner of a pool table and could hear an old Zeppelin tune playing, distorted and tinny, like it was coming from an inexpensive boom box that had been turned up too loud. Some dark forms were moving around back there too, and a burst of laughter spilled out into the bar area, though I was relatively sure it hadn't been directed at us. From where we stood, I couldn't be sure they even knew we were there.

Donald remained close to the exit, leaned against the jukebox and pretended to read the song list. The bartender had his back to me, so I slid onto a stool closest to the door and said, "Can we get a couple beers over here?"

He finally looked at me. "All out of beer," he mumbled.

I keyed on a full bottle of Jack Daniels displayed among a bevy of others behind him. "How about a couple shots of J.D. then?"

"All out of that, too."

I refused to break eye contact, and so did he. "Well, then what do you recommend?"

He put his hands on the bar between us. "That you and your boyfriend go find someplace else to drink."

I could feel Donald behind me, but he remained quiet. "Is Claudia around?" I asked.

"Who?"

"She waitresses here, or at least she used to."

"This look like the kind of place that has *waitresses*?"

Donald was suddenly by my side. He put out his cigarette in an ashtray on the bar then lightly touched my arm. "Come on, Alan, let's just go."

I pulled the photograph from my pocket and held it up for the bartender. "This is Claudia. She and I had a mutual friend. He died. He left something to her and wanted me to get it to her, only I don't know how to find her. All I know is she used to work here or hang out here or whatever. I really don't give a shit, I only need to find her to—"

"Dude, I don't know what the fuck you're talking about, okay? Why you coming around here hassling me? I don't know you and I don't know nobody named Claudia."

"I'm not looking to hassle you." I waved the photo at him. "I just need to talk to this girl, figured you might be able to help me out."

"Well, I can't." He leaned closer for emphasis. "So fuck off."

This time Donald gave my arm a tug. "Now."

"Thanks, appreciate all your help," I quipped.

The bartender smirked, and as I turned to leave I realized the three of us were no longer alone.

A man from the backroom had filtered out into the bar and now stood staring at us. Another person had remained behind him in back, but was almost entirely concealed in shadow and smoke. It wasn't until I casually slid the photograph back into my pocket and dropped from the stool that I saw there was a third man who had circled behind us and was now leaning against the exit. Donald was a few feet to my right, pale and nervous.

The one close to us, a stocky man with a beard and greasy hair dangling from beneath an equally greasy red bandana, stepped closer. In his hands he held a pool stick. He seemed roughly our age, maybe a few years younger, but there was a lot of mileage on him so it was difficult to tell for sure. His jaw was set at an odd angle, his lips thrust forward to indicate that he was no longer in possession of a full set of teeth. "Everything okay, Mick?" Though his question had been directed at the bartender he never took his eyes from me. It was clear these guys had been ingesting more than alcohol in that backroom.

"They were just leaving, Tooley," the bartender told him.

"Yes," Donald blurted, "we were just—just leaving, actually."

The man continued to stare at me as if I'd spoken instead of

Donald. "They giving you a hard time, Mick?"

"Look," I said, "I—"

"I wasn't talking to you, boy." The man came closer still.

I held my ground but said nothing.

An awkward silence fell over the room and I realized then that even the music from the back had stopped. Images blinked across the TV over the bar, but it too was silent. Donald's discomfort was palpable, and he seemed unable to determine exactly what he should do with his hands. I was as nervous as he was, but knew if I showed it, we'd be in even worse trouble. The one called Tooley held my equally intense stare for what seemed like forever, then slowly nodded and allowed a slight smile to tickle his upper lip. "What are you doing in here, boy?"

Call me boy one more fucking time, I thought.

The man by the door—who was considerably younger, taller, and had his hair pulled back into a ponytail—chuckled as if he'd read my mind. Although he was in his late twenties, from the look on his face I guessed he probably possessed the intellect of a dimwitted teenager. He wore jeans and a grimy Ozzy Osbourne t-shirt that was sleeveless and showcased an array of tattoos that stretched from his shoulders to his wrists. On his feet he wore jackboots. When he smiled I noticed a tiny black tattoo in the shape of an upside down cross just below his left eye. Among the coiled serpents, grim reapers, death masks and other odd symbols painted across his arms, I saw the words *Hell Bound.*

"I'm looking for someone," I said finally.

"He was asking questions about some whore used to come in here," the bartender said.

"Which one?"

The men laughed.

"Claudia," I said.

"But obviously this was a mistake," Donald added suddenly, "and now we're leaving."

I wanted to tell Donald to shut his mouth, to just be quiet and let me handle it, but I maintained my composure.

"I know Claudia." The tall one with the tattoos looked me over. He was flying on something and having a hard time keeping his eyes in one spot.

"You know where I can find her?" I asked.

"What you want with her?"

"I need to talk to her about a mutual friend who—"

"You got any money?" He shuffled his feet, his movements jerky and spasm-like.

"That depends," I said. "You got any information?"

Tooley stepped forward. "You even know where the fuck you are?"

I gave a smart-ass smile right back to him. "A toilet?" If we were going to make a move for the door, I figured this was as good a time as any. "Whatever—forget it."

I turned to leave and Donald did the same, but the man at the door didn't move.

Donald raised his hands. "Look, what—what's all this about?"

"Shit," the man said, "you just got here."

"There's no reason to get into all this, it's completely unnecessary, we—you don't understand, we're not—there's no reason to make more of this than we need to. We're not children here."

Donald looked from one man to the next, the words tumbling from him like he had lost all control of them. "This is absurd. We don't want any trouble, we—"

"Then what the fuck you doing here? This place is all about trouble, ain't you heard?"

His friends laughed.

Donald looked as frustrated as he was frightened. "Fine, you want—your friend asked if we had any money." Donald reached for his back pocket and smiled, like doing so would somehow set everything right. "If it's just a matter of cash then—"

"If we want your money we'll fucking take it." The man motioned to the backroom with his pool stick. "Usually a couple pussies like you cause trouble and we lock the door, take them out back and have a little talk. You see what I'm saying?"

Donald looked to me, his face screaming, *Do something*. But I wasn't exactly sure what there was *to* do. The only thing I knew for sure was that eventually Rick was bound to become impatient, worried, or both, and when he joined us we'd have the definite upper hand, but there was no telling how long that might be or what might happen between now and then.

"Just throw them out, Tooley." The bartender sighed. "Fuck it." Tooley and the other man narrowed their distance from us, book-ending us slowly but brazenly. "Tell you what. Since Mick wants us to give you a break, if you say you're sorry and ask my permission, you can go."

I kept my hands down at my sides but clenched them into fists. Ignoring the tight feeling in my stomach, I looked at the curtains and blinking beer signs in the small windows on the front wall, then back into his dark depraved eyes. "Fuck you."

"This is insane." Donald turned toward the door. "This testosterone-fest has gone far enough, we're leaving."

The taller man blocked his path.

With disturbing casualness Tooley reached out and brushed his fingers along Donald's cheek in a gesture that seemed almost tender. Donald reared back as if the fingers had been flames. "Get your goddamn hands off of me."

I waited, knowing that if the man moved just a bit closer to Donald I'd have a clean shot at him. In my mind I saw my fist crash into his face and knock him to the floor. Rick, I thought, where are you?

"Last time I was in prison I had a little faggot bitch looked a lot like you," Tooley chuckled. "Used to give it to him every night. Fucking queer loved it."

"Well, isn't that the pot calling the kettle black," Donald said.

Both men looked at him quizzically. "What the fuck he say?" the tall one asked.

The main door screeched as it was pushed open.

I had never heard a more welcome sound.

Through the smoke and dim lighting, someone hesitated just inside the main entrance, glanced casually in my direction then walked toward the bar. The others saw him too. Only difference was, I knew who it was.

The three men seemed unsure of what to make of this latest development, and stood silent and staring. Rick strolled into the bar, a slight grin on his face. "Well now," he said smoothly, hands on hips, "what's all this then?"

I was certain I would never again laugh at one of his heroic poses.

"We're closed for a few minutes, bud," the bartender snapped. "Take off."

"No problem, *bud*." Rick gestured in my direction, then in Donald's. "But these guys are with me."

"So?"

"So the three of us are gonna walk out of here. You guys got no problem with that, right?"

Tooley gripped his pool stick with both hands, swung it slowly down by his feet like a pendulum. "What if we do? Then what?"

Rick's grin slowly faded. "Then I kick your ass."

"*That's enough of all that.*"

The voice distracted everyone. It was a deep, raspy voice belonging to someone who smoked too much. It had come from the back, and we all turned toward it in unison.

In the smoky doorway to the back area was an enormous woman in a bright flowery muumuu. Her considerable feet were forced into a pair of flimsy flip-flops, puffy skin and toes strained to the near exploding point beneath her weight. The woman's hair, styled into a sort of bouffant-gone-wild, was dyed jet-black, though several renegade strands of gray survived along her temples. She wore heavy, powdery makeup, gobs of eyeliner and mascara, and her plump lips were painted a brilliant red. When she parted them with a smile they revealed stained brown teeth too small for her otherwise huge face. She leaned on a thick walking stick that appeared to have been carved from gnarled wood, and waved a chubby hand at us. "You come on back here and have a talk with Mama Toots." Waddling around with great effort, the woman started back into the area from which she'd come, but before disappearing into the smoke and darkness, she looked back over her shoulder at the other three men. "Leave them be."

The bartender immediately returned to his duties, wiping down the bar as if nothing had happened, and Tooley and the tattooed man drifted away from us and joined their friend at the bar.

"What the fuck was that?" Rick asked under his breath.

"You got here just in time," Donald said. "Let's get the hell out of—"

"Watch my back," I said, already moving across the room. I could hear Donald scolding me but I kept moving. I hesitated in the doorway; saw a pool table, a boom box sitting on a small counter area against one wall and a row of booths along another. The lighting was worse here, the air just as stagnant and smoke-filled. The woman had somehow managed to cram herself into the last booth and now sat watching me.

Rick remained in the doorway like a guard, arms folded over his chest and one eye on the bar. Donald accompanied me a bit deeper into the room, if for no reason other than to convince me to leave, but by the time I reached the last booth he had fallen silent.

At close quarters the woman was even larger than she'd first appeared. She had to be at least six feet tall and well over four hundred pounds. "Who are you?" I asked.

"Who am I?" A burst of roaring laughter bellowed forth, jiggling the mammoth breasts beneath her muumuu. "Who am I, he says. Maria Tootrachelli, that's who I am, but don't nobody call me that. I'm Mama. Mama Toots." She flashed her brown teeth again. "This is my place."

"We didn't come in here to cause trouble, lady, we just—"

"I heard all that," she said in a gravelly baritone. "Have a seat."

Donald stayed a few feet back as I slid onto the vacant bench across from her. I noticed a deck of cards, a shot glass and a bottle of whiskey in the center of the table between us. Next to her was a smoldering cigar stub teetering on the lip of an ashtray.

"This ain't a good place to come poking around uninvited." She scooped up the bottle and poured herself a shot. "Few months ago a couple college boys came in here acting the fool." The shot glass vanished in her fleshy paw as she drank it down then slapped it back on the table. "They had a bad time."

"Well I appreciate you calling off your dogs," I said.

She looked beyond me to Donald, and then to Rick. "It's okay, Muscles. They won't do nothing."

Rick nodded. "That'd be better for them."

"Do you know Claudia?" I asked.

The fat woman's eyes returned to me. "You must want to talk to her something awful to go through all this."

"I take it you already heard my explanation out there. Do you know her or not?"

"Of course. Mama Toots knows everybody, darlin'."

"Where can I find her?"

She touched the deck of cards, stroked it slowly with chubby fingers. "She lived down off Milner Avenue, an old industrial road not far from the airport, you know the one? Only a couple old houses down in there. I don't know the exact address, it was a little shack all off by itself. Little shithole about a mile in, on the left—can't miss it."

"She still live there?"

"Ain't heard nothing about her moving. Haven't seen her in a long while, though."

"What's her last name?"

"Brewster or Brewer, something like that. Don't use last names much around here."

"How do you know her?"

"From here, where else?" She shuffled the cards. "She used to hook in here on Fridays and Saturdays. A few girls do. It's a break from the street, safer, and it's a regular clientele, you know? They work the customers then kick back a percentage to me. That keeps Mama happy, and when Mama Toots is happy, everybody's happy."

"When did she stop working here?" I asked.

"About a year ago."

"Why?"

"I don't know exactly. She stopped coming around. Girls in that biz come and go."

I cocked my head toward the bar area. "The guy with the tattoos out there said he knew her too. You think he'd know—"

"They used to hang around a lot of the same people."

"Used to."

"That's what I said, darlin'."

"Claudia...is she into that shit too?"

"What shit would that be?"

"From his tattoos I think it's safe to assume he's into some dark shit."

"Aren't we all?" Another brown grin. "Some wear it on the outside is all. He likes to scare people, thinks it's fun, but he's just a punk and a drug addict. Nothing more."

"Why did you help us?"

"Didn't. Helped me. Blood on the floor ain't nothing new here, but I like to avoid all that stuff if we can. Especially with outsiders."

Donald stepped forward. "Thank you for the information, madam. Alan, let's go."

"I know you got troubles," she said to me, ignoring Donald and holding up the deck of cards instead. "You wanna know what the future holds?"

"Not particularly." It was so hot in the backroom I had broken into a heavy sweat. I wiped some perspiration from above my eyes.

"I'm more concerned with the past."

"Too late to do anything about the past."

"Can't know the future without knowing the past, though."

"That's true." Mama grabbed the cigar stub from the ashtray and stuffed the already wet and chewed end into the corner of her mouth. "But I got a gift, and my gift helps me see the future, helps me see spirits. Truth is, the spirits brought you here so I could read you. I know that 'cause don't nothing happen by accident. You're here 'cause they brought you to me."

"I don't believe in psychics."

"You think magic gives a shit if you believe in it or not?" She shuffled the cards again. "Don't matter. Magic's like a tree. A tree don't give a shit if you believe in it. It just is what it is, you see? Tree still gonna be a tree, it's still gonna grow, still gonna be there day in and day out whether you believe in trees or not. Belief only matters if you're fighting it."

"I can see a tree," I said. "I can touch a tree."

"Same thing with magic. Just got to know how."

I swallowed hard. "Ever give Claudia a reading?"

Mama chewed the cigar for a while before answering. "Once."

"What'd the cards say?"

"Ask her. What happens between me and a believer is private."

"What are you, a priest?"

"In a way." Mama shuffled the cards yet again, this time without breaking eye contact. "Why, you want me to hear your confession?" When I didn't answer she caught Rick's attention in the doorway. "How about you, Muscles?"

"I'll pass."

"You afraid?"

"I'm not afraid of anything," Rick said.

Mama threw me a conspiratorial wink. "That means he's afraid of everything."

Rick said nothing, and I was grateful he let the comment go. Donald shuffled about just feet from the booth. "Will you light somewhere?"

"We need to leave," he said. "It's Saturday night, this place will be packed in—"

"Relax," Mama Toots told him before returning her attention to me. "Been having dreams for a while now. Strange dreams. The spirits told me strangers were coming, strangers that needed my help. Now them dreams make sense."

I started to stand. "Thank you for your help, but I told you, I don't believe in—"

"Maybe you don't do what the spirit world say." Mama slammed the deck on the table with such force it stopped me. "But I do, even when I don't want to—like now. Shuffle the cards."

I eyed the deck like a child considering candy from a stranger then picked up the cards. They were warm and slightly damp, but otherwise a normal deck. I shuffled them twice then handed them back to her.

Donald lit a cigarette and puffed away apprehensively.

Mama glanced at him, barked out another laugh, adjusted her considerable girth and slowly placed six cards face-up on the table. She arranged them into a large semicircle then placed a seventh in the center. As she focused on the display something changed in her expression, and she immediately gathered the cards, returned them to the deck and offered it to me a second time. "Do it again."

"What was wrong with those?"

"They're just a prop; a tool. Do like I said."

I complied then watched as she laid the cards out a second time in identical fashion. She studied them for what seemed a long time without speaking then plucked the cigar from her mouth with a moist popping sound. "It ain't good."

"Is it ever?"

Her suddenly humorless face lacked the arrogance it had before. "It ain't good."

"Why, what do they say?"

"You don't believe anyway."

"Thought it didn't matter."

"I'm gonna give you some advice, so listen up." Mama folded her arms across her mountainous breasts. "Long time ago, I learned not to stick my nose in where it don't belong, and to never ask questions you shouldn't know the answers to. So I don't know what three nice, neat small-town gentlemen like you are doing in here, or what you want with that tramp girl—don't know and don't care—but you need to understand the world ain't always what you think it is." She rolled the cigar back between her lips and suckled it. "This is a great city, New Bedford, lots of history here, a long past. Compared to where my people come from in Italy—the old country—this city ain't nothing but a baby. But for America, it's old. It's an old city, lots of spirits here, lots of old ghosts. Take the city away and it's ancient, this land. Under all the light and reality is what come before, you see? All that come before, just…there. Waiting, doing, watching, listening. The city's like that, too. It got a dark side, secrets just like anything else. Just like in life, certain neighborhoods you should stay out of. Spirit world got those same places. Dark places. Not everybody got the gift like me, so not everybody sees what I see, and it's better that way. But you should never fuck with the spirit world. Know why?" She smiled coyly. "'Cause it'll fuck back."

"I'm just trying to find a girl."

"Why you want to go messing around with the dark?"

"Maybe the dark's messing around with me," I said.

"Could be." She nodded and gave me a look somewhere between accommodating and challenging.

"You want to see, then I'll show you." She closed her eyes, drew several deep breaths then consulted the cards. After a moment she said, "There's trouble all around you."

"Go on."

She shook her head and the flesh on her neck swayed as she reached again for the deck. "Usually when I do this it's clearer but this don't…it don't really make sense, I…" She counted off a series of cards from the deck then selected one and pulled it free. Carefully, as if afraid the table might collapse beneath it, she very slowly laid the card next to the one in the center. "There's something here, I—Jesus, Lord—I ain't never seen anything like it before. Not like this, not like…" For the first time her face registered more fear and discomfort than confusion. "I seen my share of negative energy and dark spirits before but not—not like this—never like this. It's so strong. This ain't just dark, it's—it's *unclean*—evil." Despite the heat in the room Mama shivered and began to rub her bare arms with her hands. "And there's something else, something… something about the eyes. *Occhi violenti.*"

"Say again?"

"*Occhi violenti,*" she said, her face a mask of sorrow and burgeoning terror. "Violent eyes."

"What's it mean?"

"Death," she said in a loud whisper. "Sacrilege—it's sacrilege, you can't—you can't stop it now, it's all around you."

"I don't—"

"Whole lot of death." She shivered again, her doughy face contorting into one pained and fearful expression after another. "Jesus—sweet—Sweet Jesus, this..."

I felt my earlier anger returning. I'd had my fill of shadows and smoke. What had begun as a routine she'd probably been through thousands of times before was now transformed into something more, something real, and something she had clearly not expected.

"It's like a current it's so—so strong, but...I never seen nothing like this. It's cold." Her hands were shaking with such ferocity she was having difficulty holding the cards. Even as I struggled with the stagnant and engulfing heat in the room, I noticed goose pimples rising along her arms. She was rocked by another shiver. The deck fell from her hands and cards scattered across the table. Again, she shook her head, as if in answer to voices only she could hear. Her face twisted into a grimace and her eyes narrowed as she stared at the clutter of playing cards. "Jesus, God," she whispered, her hands hovering just above the table. "Jesus...Jesus, God."

Donald dropped his cigarette to the floor, stepped on it. "This is nonsense," he said with little conviction. "Absolute—"

Mama's massive body began to tremble, her lips moving rapidly as if in silent prayer. She seemed to be looking beyond the cards to some deeper horror that had opened a portal known only to her. "No, you—you need to go."

"What do you see?" I asked.

She blinked her eyes rapidly. "You don't understand, you—you have to go."

I stood up, leaned on the table. "What do you see?"

"Get out of here," she growled, her clarity of mind returning. "Get out, I—"

"What!" I slammed the table with my hand. "Tell me, goddamn it!"

Mama's body continued to shake. She held her hands up as if to ward me off. "I don't go there, I don't go there, Christ Jesus, I don't go there, I—"

"The natives are getting restless," Rick said, motioning to the bar. "Let's move."

I felt someone grab my arm, realized it was Donald. I pulled free and stepped closer to Mama. "Where don't you go, Mama? Where don't you go?"

Her eyes turned wet, and as she held her hands out for me I saw that her fingertips were somehow raw and bloody about the nails and cuticles. They looked as if she'd been clawing at cement for hours.

I remembered the dream with Bernard, and how his hands had looked much the same.

"Good Lord," Donald said softly.

A chill scampered up the back of my neck. "Where, Mama?" I pressed. "Where don't you go?"

She began to choke. "There's—there's so much blood, it—*rivers* of it."

"Move!" Rick said suddenly. He stood in the doorway, partially blocking my view of the bar, but even through the smoke and haze I could see movement out there. The volume of Mama's voice had signaled something was wrong, and they were coming.

"Mama, *where*?"

A quiet whimper escaped her. "The dark." She looked at her bloody hands and began to weep, though she seemed far off now, unaware. "The dark beneath the dirt. You don't never come back from that dark. You don't—you don't know what's down there, it—it ain't like us. It wants you—it—wants to bring you down there with it, under the dirt." Her lips moved slowly, slightly out of sync with the sound of her voice. "It's got a taste for you. It's been waiting for you down in that dark under the dirt. You don't never come back from that dark. Never."

"Why Mama? Tell me why."

"'Cause you got to be dead to be there."

Before I knew it Donald and Rick were hustling me to the doorway.

"You got to be dead," Mama's voice cried behind us. "You got to be dead to be there."

Tooley and the tall man ran by us into the backroom, hesitating a moment like they weren't sure if they should stop us or attend to their friend first. They opted for the latter and we kept moving, Rick in the lead, Donald between us, and me pulling up the rear.

The bartender scurried out from behind the bar and stepped in front of us, blocking the door. He held a baseball bat, cocked it back in a threatening posture. "What the fuck did you do to her?"

Rick pivoted and threw two rapid kicks, the first into the bartender's midsection and the second into his throat. The man vaulted back and crashed into the bar, scattering two stools. As the bat left his hands it rattled against the floor and rolled toward the corner.

We were nearly to the door when I heard screaming and the sound of heavy footfalls behind me. I turned in time to see the tattooed man closing on me, Tooley lumbering along a few paces back.

I might have been able to make it through the exit had I kept running, but probably not. Either way, I was not destined to find out, because I came to an abrupt halt, and as the tall man tried to stop he practically ran right by me. I swung at him as hard as I could while he was still off balance. My fist connected with the side of his face, and as the impact reverberated through my hand and up into my arm and shoulder, he groggily staggered back and fell to the floor.

In the blur of confusion Tooley rushed past, and seconds later, behind me I heard scrambling and heavy, urgent breathing, some shouting—Donald's voice—then a grunt. I turned toward the scuffle. Donald swung awkwardly at the man but missed, and Tooley knocked him aside with two hard shots to the stomach and head. As Donald fell, Rick came to his aid and fired a three-punch combination that dropped the man.

I moved to help him when someone hit me from behind. The blow landed between my shoulder blades with tremendous force, and I staggered forward. I spun in time to see that the tattooed man had regained his feet and was closing on me quickly. Struggling to maintain my balance, I threw a punch but he ducked away in time, raised a fist and hammered it across the side of my head.

I knew he had connected directly with my temple because my equilibrium was suddenly off, and a tingling feeling spread across my eyes and jaw—like a yawn that wouldn't stop. My vision blurred, cleared then blurred again before I realized I was toppling to the floor face-first. Before my chin slammed the dirty tiles, I broke my fall with my hands and did my best to roll through it.

I scrambled to my feet, head still spinning a bit. The man laughed like a moron, and there was something so inhuman, so sick in his drug-glazed eyes, I hesitated for just a second. From the look on his face, I knew he had sensed my indecision and interpreted it as weakness. As he charged me again, I timed a punch, braced myself then threw it.

He ran right into my fist. His head snapped back and he stumbled. There was no blood, just a puzzled expression, as if he couldn't quite believe what had just happened. While he wobbled about on shaky legs, I stepped in to finish him, but Donald came out of nowhere and hit him with a wild, arcing punch.

This time he went down. I rushed forward, straddled him and hit him again and again. He covered the back of his head with his hands and started to crawl away, mumbling something unintelligible as he went, but I kept punching him until he was no longer moving.

I fell off of him, my hands slick with blood, most of it his. He was moaning and just barely conscious, his arms still folded across his head in a feeble attempt to protect it. On the floor next to him, near his face, a trickling stream of blood was beginning to pool.

Still a bit disoriented, I watched Donald crouch and pick up the baseball bat the bartender had dropped. Over his shoulder, I saw Tooley and Rick circling each other like a pair of jungle cats. Due to the blood both were sporting, I knew neither had gained a clear advantage since Rick's initial knockdown.

Tooley lunged and Rick countered with a combination that put him down a second time. He coughed, spat blood then slowly began to rise, but Rick pounced again, raining fists down on him in rapid combinations that made sickening sounds as they connected with skin and bone. Bloodied about the eyes, nose and mouth, the man fell again.

Rick stood at the ready, chest heaving. "Stay down, asshole."

The man grunted and began to rise yet again.

I scrambled over to Donald and pulled the bat from his hands just as Tooley let out a defiant growl and stormed Rick in a frenzy of rage. "Rick!"

He looked to me as I tossed the bat into the air. In one fluid motion he caught it and swung it down across the man's shins.

Tooley howled and crashed to the floor. Moaning, he rolled back and forth clutching his legs, knees pulled in to his chest.

Rick and I stood staring at each other a moment, out of breath, dazed and oddly satisfied, if not thoroughly surprised.

Donald had sunk to one knee, perhaps due to the blows he had sustained earlier. I reached down and helped him to his feet. "You all right?"

"Oh, spectacular," he groaned.

Rick threw the bat aside and wiped a slow trickle of blood from the corner of his mouth. "Let's get the hell out of here before any more of these cretins show up."

We turned our backs on the fallen bodies, the blood and the muffled cries still coming from the backroom, and together, walked out of the bar.

Still riding an adrenaline rush, I stepped into the street. No remnants of daylight remained. A hot summer day had become a hot summer evening, and everything was heightened, sharpened and more vivid than normal.

It seemed apt that night had fallen. We'd glimpsed the wisdom of the spirits in this old city—however briefly—and after all that had happened, after all that was breathing down our necks, for now, we were better suited to the dark.

CHAPTER 23

It was still early summer. We were a few weeks away from tourist season, so the landscape had not yet changed. Though a handful of early bird summer residents had arrived and opened nearby cottages, most of Donald's neighborhood remained in the tail end of its hibernation. We'd cleaned ourselves up, nursed our minor wounds then taken the short walk through a small section of woods behind Donald's cottage to a bluff overlooking the ocean. The moon had turned burgundy, and was so full and bright that it didn't look real in the otherwise clear sky. Despite its brilliance the powerful pulse of strobe lights swirling from the public beach below overshadowed it, even at this distance.

The three of us stood in the sand and beginnings of tall grass along the dunes, watching the official vehicles that were still parked at haphazard angles along the beach. A tent had been constructed where the body itself had been discovered, and several temporary stadium-like lights had been set up, giving the small area an oddly surreal look, an artificial glowing oasis surrounded by darkness.

Though it was several hundred yards away, we could make out policemen and various authorities still scouring and investigating the area. Beyond the barriers they had put up along the parking lot, a small crowd had gathered to watch the goings on. Since the body had been found hours before and was long gone from the scene, I wondered what the townsfolk were hoping to see. I watched the red and blue beams pan and play about Rick and Donald's faces, and wondered the same thing about us.

"I wonder if he came here," Donald said. "The night he put that body there. I wonder if when he was done, after he'd buried that poor woman's remains down there, beneath the sand, I wonder if he came here to see me. I wonder if he came and sat in my home and talked about nothing at all the way Bernard was so good at doing, the way he could do for hours. I wonder if he laughed to himself about it later. I wonder if he found it amusing."

Rick was holding a six-pack of beer held together by plastic rings. He pulled one can free and ran it against his forehead. "Lot of FBI guys down there. They must be turning over every grain of sand hoping to find something. The local politicians were already bitching on the news about how this is going to hurt the tourist season. You believe that shit? Even the poor folks who can't afford a real Cape Cod vacation won't be showing up here if they think a serial killer's on the loose."

"Or so it would seem." The lights painted Donald's face. He looked so strange with a bit of dried blood along his slightly swollen lip. It didn't suit him, the face of a fighter. "They can bring in the CIA and it won't matter. They're hunting a ghost."

"Bodies popping up out of the fucking ground and all they're worried about are summer businesses being down," Rick said.

My hands were sore, my knuckles covered in several small cuts and gashes, but the bleeding had been minor and stopped on the ride back to Potter's Cove. I looked down at them, flexed my fingers. "Let me get one of those beers."

Rick held the cans out, dangled them from his grip on the vacant ring of plastic. I reached out and plucked one loose. It was cold and felt good in my hand. The heat was still high but a slight ocean wind made it somewhat tolerable. I opened the can and took a long swig. It could have been—should have been—a beautiful night.

"We could've been killed tonight," Donald said, and it was then that I realized we'd been speaking in hushed tones.

"But we weren't," I answered.

"We could have been."

"Yeah, but we weren't."

Donald ran a hand through his hair, eyes trained on the beach below. "The bodies will keep turning up, and once they've reached the end of the road Bernard created, all of this will end. They'll either never know who the killer was, or they'll somehow discover it was Bernard. Regardless, he's dead and gone, and there'll be nothing anyone can do. After the news stories have been reported, the television shows have aired and the books have been written, this whole horrible business will end. It'll just fade away quietly until it's reduced to some vaguely heinous memory, a scar Potter's Cove will always have to endure, but little else. It'll be a Remember When bit, that's all. And in the end, none of it will have meant a goddamn thing. It's a storm, Alan, and I plan to sit and wait it out." He turned to me, his face half concealed in darkness, half illuminated by the moon and alternating swaths of police lights. "And once it passes, I'll get on with this semblance of a fucking life I have. It's not much—God knows—but it's all I've got. I'm out."

I killed the beer. "I'm sorry about tonight, I never should've—"

"I'm out."

"Donald, you heard what that woman said tonight, you saw—you saw her hands."

Rick moved a few feet ahead of us toward the edge of the bluff and sunk down onto the seat of his pants, the beers balanced in his lap.

"Yes," Donald told me, "I heard what she said and I saw her hands."

"And you still want to just walk away?"

"You're flipping over rocks, Alan. Don't be upset with me if I don't want to roll around with the bugs slithering in the mud beneath them." He nervously wiped a bead of sweat from his temple. "I've never been in a brawl in my life, and here I am pushing forty and suddenly I'm in some used tampon of a bar trying to avoid being killed by lowlife thugs who may or may not have known some prostitute Bernard was seeing. I'm listening to a woman either possessed or insane babbling about evil spirits and darkness and grave soil, her skin splitting and bleeding right in front of me like some cheap parlor trick only it's real—it's real because I saw it and felt it. But it's still madness, Alan, and it's only going to get worse. I want nothing more to do with any of it."

I tossed the empty can aside, in Rick's direction, and squared off with Donald. "Sticking your head in the sand and hiding isn't the answer."

"Call it whatever you'd like. I'm out."

"Donald, I—"

"I'm sorry, Alan. I'm out."

I was hoping Rick might back me up but he was watching the beach or the water or the night sky and clearly had no intention of getting involved.

Donald let a hand rest on my shoulder and gave it a gentle squeeze. "I need a cigarette and a drink. Beer's not going to come anywhere near touching what I require this evening. I'll be inside, you guys are welcome to join me."

I watched him turn and walk back along the path toward his cottage. The darkness and trees swallowed him within seconds.

"He's right, man," Rick said from behind me.

I moved over toward him and crouched down. He had opened another beer and was nearly finished with it. "You out too?" I asked.

"It's a miracle one of those assholes wasn't packing, Alan." He glanced at me and smiled, somewhat helplessly. His eyes were red and glassy. "I get into scuffles all the time, shit, it's my fucking job, happens at the club on a regular basis. But it's different there. It's my turf, I'm in control, I know the situation, the score, and in most cases, the players. It's a controlled setting. But in a place like tonight it's different. You never know what you're walking into."

I knelt into the sand, felt it shift and sink under my weight, then sat back on my heels. The faint sounds of a police radio echoed up along the dunes before escaping across the slow steady waves of the Atlantic. "You saved our asses back there."

Rick shrugged. "You're gonna go look for that chick, aren't you?"

"Yes."

"You're playing around with people who aren't like us, man. These people don't live in the same world we do. Shit, they're just barely on the same planet. You go fucking around with that kind of crowd and all the shit they're into and sooner or later you're gonna find yourself in a situation. It'll either get you killed or you'll end up killing somebody else, and either way, Alan, you fucking lose." He chugged some beer, belched. "I can't be in situations like that, man, you understand? What if I'd killed that guy tonight? Oh, sorry, your honor, my dead friend and the motherfucking spirit world made me do it in self-defense. I can bring that fucking whale into court in a wheelbarrow and she can do her bleeding fingers trick. Yeah, that'll work."

"This shit's not funny, man."

"You see me laughing?" Rick shook his head to emphasize the point. "I'm not ever going back to prison. Not for anything. Not for anybody. What if somebody had gotten killed tonight?"

"Rick, what if whatever's out there wants us dead anyway?"

A cooler breeze rustled the tall dune grass as if in answer, but it was chased by a swell of heat and continued on through the trees behind us, making the respite from humidity short-lived.

"Then we're probably gonna die," he said. "Look, I'll always be here if you need me—you know that—but I can't keep chasing—"

"You saw what happened in that backroom tonight."

He turned to me quickly, like he planned to snap at me, but instead looked away and drank his beer. After a while he said, "Let the dead lie, Alan." Rick opened another beer, held it out for me. "Let the Devil have his Hell, and let Bernard and the rest of them rot there. Go find Toni and get her back. Whatever's real or whatever isn't, that's the only world—the only life that matters."

I began to respond but thought better of it. I took the beer he was offering and replaced it with my hand. We shook for what seemed forever. When he finally let go he looked out at the water and quietly continued drinking. I wanted to tell him there wasn't enough beer in the world to make all this go away, but stayed quiet and gazed down on the scene of the crime instead.

Somewhere down there was that darkness beneath the dirt Mama had spoken of. Darkness you didn't come back from because you had to be dead to be there.

And not only was I on my way there, I knew now I'd be going alone.

CHAPTER 24

The prospect of returning to an empty apartment was less than thrilling, but I did it anyway. I checked the answering machine, hopeful to find something from Toni, but there were no messages. The refrigerator was nearly empty and the cupboards weren't doing much better, so I called downstairs and caught the pizza parlor just before they closed. One of the kids who worked there ran me up a couple of plain slices and a Coke. I ate out on the steps and let the sounds of Saturday night in downtown Potter's Cove distract me for a while. The apartment was beyond hot, and everywhere I looked I saw Toni. The place still smelled of her, of her cologne and gels and powders and lotions, and even though she had taken quite a few things with her, traces remained, traces of us.

By the time I'd finished eating and forced myself under a cold shower, it was nearly two in the morning. My back was sore, the side of my head where I'd been punched was throbbing and my hands still ached. Rather than think about how old and out of shape I felt at that moment, I did my best to enjoy the brief break from the humidity the cool water provided.

I emerged to find that things had quieted the way things do in towns—even big towns—after midnight. I stood at the foot of the bed and looked at the rumpled sheets for a while. I'd been unable to sleep in it since Toni left.

I wrapped a towel around my waist, went into the den and settled down onto the couch, certain I'd be unable to sleep. Within minutes, I had slipped off.

I awakened in the morning to the realization that I'd had the dream again. This time, in addition to Bernard and the strange people accompanying him, Mama Toots was there too, wiggling fat bloody fingers at me and grinning demonically with her grimy teeth.

My body was stiff and sore, and although I had slept, I didn't feel rested at all, and wondered if I'd ever be able to totally relax again. I rubbed my eyes, stood up and shuffled to the bathroom.

While I dressed all I could think about was the bar and everything that had happened there. The events continued to replay in my mind despite my attempts to concentrate on other things, and I felt confronted by a strange fusion of satisfaction and anxiety.

I dressed in a pair of jeans, sneakers and t-shirt, then went to the bedroom closet and pulled a large lockbox from the top shelf. It contained several holsters, my 9mm, a box of ammo and two clips. I checked the weapon over, laid it on the bed then turned to the holsters and selected one that attached to my belt. Grabbing a clip of ammo, I shut the box, locked it and returned it to the shelf.

Because of my job I was licensed to carry a concealed firearm, but the only time I ever did was during periodic work details that required me to do so. I felt strange strapping on a gun outside of work, but I had no idea what might be waiting for me out there this time. Wading through the dark alone was bad enough; I didn't intend to do it empty-handed as well.

I secured the holster and gun to the back of my belt and pulled my t-shirt down over it. Studying myself in the mirror, I stretched the shirt out a bit until it hung looser and the bulge was less noticeable. Sweat had already formed across my forehead and down the back of my neck. It was a little after eight o'clock, so I knew if the humidity was already this high we were in for another scorcher. Strange to see a heat wave this early in the season, I thought. But then again, everything else had gone haywire, why not weather patterns too?

On the nearby bureau one of our wedding pictures distracted me. We looked impossibly young, happy and unaware, the two us sitting at the head table, Toni in her gown and me in my tuxedo, arms entwined while sipping champagne from each other's glasses.

Bells from a church about a mile up the street chimed, echoed beautifully in the distance, reminding me today was Sunday.

I reached out and gently laid the photograph face down.

***

Milner Avenue was an old, nearly forgotten stretch of desolate road not far from the airport. At the very end of the road sat the shell of an ancient mill that was slowly crumbling from years of neglect. Most of the outer walls were covered in graffiti, and the grass around the property was badly overgrown and unkempt. Garbage littered the area. Amidst the brush and vacant sand lots an occasional ramshackle cottage emerged, remnants of the inexpensive housing provided decades earlier for some of the workers employed by the then thriving mill. Most of the tenements were condemned and boarded shut.

I drove the four-mile length of Milner so I'd know where it came out, and found that beyond the old mill was a dirt road that eventually led to an intersecting paved boulevard. Less than a mile from there, I came across an onramp back to the state highway.

Comfortable with the way in and out, I circled around and this time paid closer attention to the tachometer from the moment I pulled onto the avenue.

A little more than a mile in, in the middle of a dirt lot horseshoed by an expanse of brush and dead trees, I saw a small cottage off by itself just as Mama had described. It was set atop cinder blocks and in horrible shape, but still looked somewhat livable. There were no cars parked alongside the cottage, but there was an old mailbox at the edge of the lot closest to the road. I checked my watch. It was nearly nine o'clock.

I continued on a ways, then turned around and came back again. Diagonally across from the cottage I pulled over to the side and dropped the car into Park. The far-off rumblings of a slowly awakening city battled with the hum of the engine. The desolation of this empty and forgotten corridor on the outskirts of the city made me uncomfortable. It was the kind of place where you could scream, and even if anyone in the distance was able to hear you, odds are, no one would care. I leaned back against the seat and felt my gun press into the small of my back. Although I had never drawn or fired it except at the range, the reminder of its presence gave me a slight sense of security nonetheless.

After watching the house for a few minutes, I climbed from the car and slowly approached the property.

Dulled by the haze of humidity, just over the span of brush and dead trees, the sun hung low but fierce in the sky. I moved across the dirt lot until the shade of the cottage itself blocked the rays. I gave a quick look around. The building was in rough shape, and the screen door and screens on the front windows were old and battered. A filthy bare bulb sat in a socket above the front door and an ancient welcome mat had been thrown down before it. I knocked and waited. Nothing. I knocked again. More nothing.

After a moment I stepped over to the window to the left of the door and leaned into it, cupping my hands on either side of my head so I might see the interior of the cottage. The screen was hard to see through however, and the window itself was so dirty it blurred all that lay beyond it. I backed away, knocked a third time.

I could hear cars rushing along the highway in the distance. Slowly, I walked around the side of the house and peered into the area behind it. An old picnic table that looked like it hadn't been used in ages was propped against the back of the house and there were two small trash cans parked along the far corner. Another short stretch of dirt led to the beginnings of the brush at the rear of the property, and I noticed a clothesline had been strung from the back left corner of the house to a thin pole several feet away that had been planted there for that specific purpose. The clothesline was bare, and I began to wonder if anyone lived here after all.

Carefully, I walked behind the cottage to the trashcans. Flies buzzed about noisily, and when I pulled the lid free of the first can I realized I still couldn't be sure if someone was residing here because the garbage was mostly frozen dinner boxes and food, and most of it looked anything but fresh. The smell in this heat was gripping, so I replaced the lid and continued back around the corner of the house until I'd again reached the front door. I looked back across the way. But for my car, it was empty.

I went next to the mailbox near the road. There were two pieces of mail inside. I looked around again then reached in and pulled them free. One was a light bill and the other was an advertising flyer for a department store. The postmark on the light bill was less than a week old, so I knew it had been delivered within the last day or two. I slid them back into the box and closed it.

Once back at the car I hesitated before getting behind the wheel. *Maybe this was a mistake*,I thought. *Maybe it's just as well she isn't here.* But just as I slid my sunglasses on to combat the glare of the sun, something near the mangle of dead trees caught my attention.

My legs shook and my stomach clenched. I pulled the glasses off, forced a swallow and heard indecipherable whispers breaking over the trees and across the dirt lot. They swirled around me, and I told myself not to be afraid, that this was all in my head, but the fear refused to subside. My mind told me to run, to get into the car and drive away from there without ever coming back. Instead, I drew a deep breath, closed my eyes and held them shut. After a few seconds I slowly opened them.

The whispers had stopped. Or maybe they'd never really been there at all. Somehow it didn't seem to matter as much now.

I climbed back into the car and headed toward the city proper.

***

After nursing a cup of coffee at a local diner for over an hour, I drove around New Bedford for another thirty-odd minutes until I'd summoned the nerve necessary to return to Milner Avenue.

It was nearly eleven when I pulled over in front of her cottage a second time. Everything looked the same, until I realized the front door was open. There were no other cars around so I assumed she'd either been sleeping when I'd come before or someone had dropped her off in the interim.

I stepped from the car and scanned the trees and brush. Visible waves of heat rose from the dirt to distort the landscape, but nothing else moved.

I removed my sunglasses, tossed them onto the dash then walked toward the house with a purposely-unassuming gait. At the screen door I hesitated and craned my neck in an attempt to see deeper into the cottage, but due to the lack of light within, it was impossible. Both of the front windows were also open and protected only by screens. The house was quiet but for a subtle thudding sound from somewhere nearby. I knocked on the screen door but no one appeared or answered, so I listened more carefully.

The thudding was coming from behind the house.

As I turned the corner I saw a large throw rug draped over the clothesline. Behind it, someone was hitting it, knocking dust free with a broom. The thudding stopped rather suddenly, and from behind the rug a woman emerged.

Her hair was cropped short and spiked in a style that made it difficult to tell if it was meant to look disheveled or if she just hadn't combed it in a while. Hair that had been auburn in the photograph was now jet-black. She looked physically smaller than the photograph suggested, far thinner and considerably older. The woman in the photograph had been no more than early twenties; this person was early thirties. I raised a hand to my eyes to shield the sun so I could get a clearer look at her, but still couldn't be certain it was the same person.

"I'm sorry to bother you," I said, "but are you Claudia?"

She slipped under the clothesline, the broom still in her hands. She wore an old shirt with faint black and white checks she'd only bothered to button to the middle of her chest. The shirt arms had been hacked away with scissors, leaving behind strings and strands dangling awkwardly from sockets where sleeves had been. Heavily worn Levis and a pair of scuffed black boots rounded out the ensemble. Her left ear was pierced several times but her right sported only a single small hoop. Her complexion was pale, her eyes tired, and it looked as if this was the first time she'd seen sunshine in quite a while. She wore heavy eyeliner but no other makeup.

She sized me up a moment without responding.

"I'm looking for Claudia Brewster."

"You a cop?" she asked, her voice whispery and a bit deep for such a petite woman.

"No, I'm—"

"Then you're trespassing. Fuck off."

"Are you Claudia Brewster?"

"Brewer."

"Brewer then."

"What do you want?"

"My name is—"

"What do you want?" She let the broom rest on the ground and leaned on it, crossing her hands over the end of the knob. I noticed small black tattoos just below the first joint of each of her fingers. Each was different—a star, a crescent moon, an ankh, a pentagram—but inked in the same bland, amateurish style.

"I want to talk to you."

"About what?"

I wiped my hand on my jeans and offered it to her. She glanced at it with disinterest. "I'm Alan Chance," I said. She gave no reaction. "Bernard was a friend of mine."

She maintained her distant cool. "Who?"

"Bernard Moore."

"Never heard of him."

"I'm not here to play games, lady. Bernard's dead. He hanged himself."

After a moment she nodded, face expressionless. "I know."

"I found this in with his things after he died." I pulled the photograph from my pocket and held it out for her. "I've been through hell trying to find you."

"You wouldn't know Hell if you were burning in it."

The deadpan tone of her voice gave birth to a tide of discomfort—if not outright fear—that fired through me like electrical current. As it dissipated, I pushed the photograph at her again.

This time she reached out, took the picture and studied it a while. The quiet returned until she said, "That was taken years ago. Another life. Long...long fucking time ago."

"You can keep it if you want," I said.

"I don't know what he was doing with it, that was taken years before I met him. An old... somebody I knew back then took it."

"I figured you gave it to him."

"Maybe I did. Maybe he stole it. Who knows? A lot of life's a blur, know what I mean?" She tucked the photograph into her back pocket. "So is that it, you just came here to give me that?"

"I came here for answers."

"If you got this far you already have them," she said.

"Some. Not all."

We stared at each other a while. Her eyes were disconcerting. They had once been rather beautiful—like in the photo—but now looked dull and old beyond her years, soulless. "I need to know what you know."

"About what?"

"About Bernard. About what he was involved in and about what in the name of Christ is going on."

She ran her tongue slowly along her bottom lip, moistening it. "Christ ain't got nothing to do with it."

"I need to know what you know," I said again.

"No you don't. You *want* to know. There's a difference."

"Strange things have been happening since Bernard's death."

"I bet."

"I need your help."

"With what?"

"With all that's happening. I need to find the truth."

"Truth's overrated." Claudia swung the broom up behind her head until it rested behind her neck, then slung an arm over either end the way James Dean had held a rifle in that famous pose from the film *Giant*. Even in her own space her movements were telling, her body language indicative of someone for whom most of life had been spent in situations where she was unwelcome, made to feel self-conscious or didn't want to be. At once a longtime victim and battle weary survivor, she possessed an inherent toughness and a deliberately honed exterior that left no doubt about the authenticity of either. At close range, it was easy to believe she had likely been victimized in more ways than I could ever imagine, but she was far from a helpless waif. She looked as strong and potentially dangerous as she did pained, just as capable of victimizing someone else, if need be. She seemed to me the kind of person who would kill if cornered, and perhaps already had at some point.

I stood there awkwardly. "Will you help me or not?"

"What do you want from me?" She shook her head. "I don't even know who you are and I'm supposed to just—"

"I told you, my name is Alan Chance. I was a friend of Bernard's."

"So fucking what? You're just a guy in my yard. I don't know you."

I sighed and ran my hands through my hair. They came back damp with perspiration. "I'm sure Bernard mentioned me."

"Yeah," she said, "he did. But you were his friend. Not mine. He kept things—people—separate. If he hadn't we would've met a long time ago, right?"

"I take it you've heard what's been happening in Potter's Cove?"

"I've been away for a while. Just got back yesterday, but yeah, I heard." She nodded. "What's any of that got to do with me?"

"You tell me."

The broom came down from behind her neck and she held it by her side. "You accusing me of something?"

"Are you guilty of something?"

She turned toward the house. "Get the fuck out of here."

I reached out for her arm. "Claudia, wait, I—"

She spun around, bringing the broom with her, and in a split-second the handle was less than an inch from my eye. "You put your hands on me again, asshole, and I'll drive this thing right through your fucking brain, you hear me?"

I believed her. "I'm sorry." I raised my hands but otherwise stood perfectly still. "I'm not looking to hurt you. I only need your help."

Claudia lowered the broom and relaxed her stance a bit. After a beat she said, "I told you, I just got back into town. I'm here a few hours and already I got a call from some old friends downtown—friends who aren't friends anymore, who I don't want to hear from no more—telling me there were people looking for me, causing all kinds of trouble. That crazy old bitch Toots giving me warnings and throwing her hexes around, as if anybody besides greenhorns and marks give a shit, and then I got you sniffing around like some dog with his nose up my butt. I don't want any of this, okay? I just want to be left the fuck alone."

"I didn't ask for any of this, either," I said quietly.

She looked at the sun and drew the back of her hand across her forehead, wiping away some sweat. "I don't expect you to understand this, and I don't give a shit if you do or not, but I want to make a clean break of things this time. I'm starting over. I don't want no part of whatever problems you got. I got enough of my own."

"I'm not expecting you to get involved. All I ask is that you tell me what you know."

She let go a brief, ironic smile. "Oh, is that all?"

"I wouldn't be here if I didn't need your help."

Claudia leaned the broom against the back of the house. "I don't know anything."

"We both know that's not true."

She threw me a defiant shrug.

I sighed. "Like I said, strange things have been going on since Bernard's death."

"Oh yeah?" As she dug a pack of cigarettes from the breast pocket of her shirt, I noticed an oddly benign flash in her otherwise apathetic expression. She slid an unfiltered Lucky Strike between her lips then patted herself down for a lighter, which she eventually found in her jeans. "Like what?"

"You mean besides bodies turning up in Potter's Cove?"

Claudia drew a deep initial drag on her cigarette, held the smoke a bit longer than normal then released it in a slow steady stream from her nostrils. She gave me a stern look that made it apparent my question didn't warrant an answer.

"I know this is going to sound crazy, but—"

"We're all crazy. The world's crazy."

"Since Bernard's death," I began again, "we've all had the same dream, we—"

"*We*?"

"My friends—Bernard's other friends—Rick and Donald."

She waited a moment before responding, as if what I'd said was slowly solidifying in her mind. "He used to talk about you three a lot."

I flicked a bead of sweat from my temple. "We all started having nightmares not long after Bernard's death. Identical nightmares. And I've been–" I forced myself to say it, "I've been having hallucinations or visions or waking dreams, I—I don't know for sure exactly what they are. Then the other night, that woman—Toots—she told me—"

"I know what she told you," she said. "The fat bitch thinks you're possessed, said she saw your demons and they attacked her, drew her blood."

"Do you believe her?" I asked.

"You'd be surprised what I believe."

"I know it's all tied together. I know Bernard was involved in—"

"Why are you so sure I know anything?"

I stared at her without answering.

"Even if I do," she said, "why would I tell you?"

"To help me."

"And why would I want to do that?"

"Oh, I don't know, how about because it's the right thing to do?"

"What the hell universe you living in?"

"Thought you said you wanted a fresh start."

She left the cigarette perched between her lips as tendrils of smoke crept past her face. "That gun on your belt loaded?"

I was stunned, unsure of how she had seen it since she'd been in front of me the entire time. "Yes."

"Planning on shooting somebody?"

"It's strictly for protection."

Apparently she found my answer amusing because her face hinted at a smile, but it left her quickly. Slowly, she turned her attention to the trees behind us, as if searching for something hidden there, watching. "Come on," she said softly, cocking her head toward the house. "Let's get out of the sun."

CHAPTER 25

The interior of the cottage was the disaster area I'd anticipated it to be. There was an undersized kitchen, an equally small living room, and a dark jog of a hallway I assumed led to a bathroom and bedroom. It took a moment for my eyes to adjust after crossing from bright sunshine into this cave of sorts. What little light existed seeped through the two open windows in the living room, but in the kitchen area, which we had walked into through the back door, the windows were closed and covered with cheap green canvas pull-shades. A musty smell hung in the air, and everything was covered in a thin film of dust. I stood awkwardly near the door, watched Claudia cross to an ancient refrigerator. The door opened with a clang and light from within punctured the room. She reached in, pulled out an unlabeled brown bottle and held it up. "Want one?"

"No," I said. "But thanks."

She closed the door, leaned back against it. Her throat was slick with perspiration. "It's only root beer." She twisted off the cap and casually tossed it into the nearby sink, which was brimming with filthy dishes and hundreds of swarming ants.

I moved closer to a table in the center of the room, noticed a suitcase sitting in the doorway to the living room.

Claudia saw me looking at it and said, "I just got back last night, haven't had a chance to unpack. Or clean up, obviously." She drank from the bottle, gulped loudly.

"I came by a little while ago but—"

"Yeah, you woke me up with all that knocking."

"Sorry." I smiled uncomfortably and pulled one of the chairs out from the table. "Mind if I sit down?"

Claudia motioned to the chair with the bottle. "Been in rehab for a while. Had a meth problem. It was fucked up but, man, so is this. No more drugs, no more booze. All I got left is nicotine, sugar and caffeine. Figure one of these days I'll kick butts too, but one step at a time, that's what they say. I beat heroin and coke a few years back—so I figure I can do this. Least that's what I keep telling myself. You got to play these little head games with yourself, it's fucking sick but it works. This one counselor told me I had what's called an addictive personality. I was like: Yeah, no fucking shit, Kreskin." She let slip a genuine, very pretty smile. Her teeth were a bit too large for her mouth, and there was a noticeable gap between the two in front, but like the rest, they were straight and bright and lit up her entire face.

"You don't have to justify yourself to me, Claudia."

The smile crept away. "That what you think I'm doing?"

"I don't know."

She finished the root beer, pushed away from the refrigerator and placed the bottle on the counter. "I've been on my own since I was twelve years old. I've lived most of my life like a fucking animal. Worse. Animals have standards. They're better than us. All that superior species hype's a bunch of bullshit. We're the fucking mistakes, man. We're the deformities, the abominations of evolution. Any fool knows that. But I don't apologize for nothing and I don't explain myself to nobody. Know why? Because I didn't make the fucking rules and I don't owe anybody a goddamn thing, that's why."

The level of natural intelligence she possessed was surprising, and I couldn't help but wonder what she might have accomplished had her life been different. "I didn't mean to infer—"

"'Course not." She walked slowly along the front of the counter, her eyes never leaving me, the heels of her boots clacking on the tile floor. "I've been a junkie and a whore and a whole lot of other things you don't want to know for so long it doesn't seem real for me to be anything else. But I am. I am something else now. It's still a fucking mess but I'm working on it. And I'm leaving soon." She pointed at a tattered and stained poster on the wall advertising Florida, a bathing suit clad couple with their backs to the camera running hand in hand across a beautiful stretch of sand toward the ocean beyond. "Never been, always wanted to go. Now I'm gonna do it. This time I'm really gonna do it." She eyed the poster for a few seconds. "Ever been there?"

"On my honeymoon, a long time ago."

"Does it really look like that?"

"In parts, yeah."

"Gonna get some stupid waitress job or something, and every day off I'm gonna lay on the beach and go swimming and all that shit. It's all about the forgetting now." Claudia snapped out of her dream and leaned back against the counter. "Point is, I ain't gonna be around here much longer. I been where you're going—and like I told you, I don't want nothing to do with it anymore."

"I understand."

"This conversation and the one we're gonna have never happened. You were never even here, got it? And if you go to the cops I'll—"

"I won't."

"You do and—"

"I *won't*. For Christ's sake, I have to trust you too. You could just as easily go to the police after I tell you what I know."

"Yeah, well, you know us junkie whores." She grabbed the front of her shirt, pulled it away from her chest and blew down between her breasts. "We ain't too reliable."

"I'd say you're taking less of a risk in trusting me than I am in trusting you," I told her. "We are what we are, right?"

"Oh, that's fucking deep, Plato." Claudia let her shirt go. I followed it to the curved tops of her breasts. "Only problem is most people don't have clue-one about who they are. They know even less about the world they're living in. All sunshine and picket fences and ice cream and roses, right? Cockeyed motherfuckers. I've seen the shit out there no one ever wants to see. I've been treading water in swill since I was a kid, and I'm still here. I've seen and done things, and had things done to me you couldn't believe even if I proved them. Your mind couldn't get around them. You think you know what hell is? I've fucking lived it, and through it all, I'm still here… what's left of me anyway. You want to put your trust in something? Put it in that." She dug her cigarettes from her pocket. "You want to know what I know? Fine. You first. I ain't saying shit until you tell me what you know." Like a cloud slipping past the moon, a condescending look appeared, rolled across her face and was gone. "What you think you know."

"I knew Bernard from the time we were little kids," I heard myself say with a fondness that made me uncomfortable. "Since he died I've done nothing but think about things, back on things, and none of us ever suspected him of anything because we didn't take him seriously. One thing you never did with Bernard was take him seriously. He was always kind of weird, but—but we were used to it—it's just the way he was, the way he always was, so none of us ever gave it much thought. What might have been red flags for most people didn't mean anything when it came to Bernard. He used to lie a lot. He'd exaggerate everything and always make himself out to be something he wasn't. At least that's what we thought. You never really knew what was true and what wasn't. He'd make so much shit up you never knew for sure, but it—as strange as it sounds—it didn't matter. Bernard was just Bernard. I always thought he told his stories and went on and on because in reality he had nothing. In reality he was alone and hadn't accomplished much of anything with his life. We got good at letting things go, at looking the other way when it came to him. We were all different, Donald and Rick and Bernard and me, but in a lot of ways we were the same, too. None of us were perfect, who the hell were we to judge Bernard or think less of him for being himself, for stretching the truth now and then or making a fantasy world for himself where he wasn't the brunt of jokes, the weak one, a person no one other than his friends would ever give a second look or thought to?"

Claudia nodded. "If you want to sweeten it up while you walk down memory lane, that's your problem. But remember, I knew him too. Maybe the side I saw was different, but it was just as real. He was a lying sack of shit most of the time, but the thing with Bernard was that he'd tell just enough truth to make you think, to make you wonder if what he was saying was real. He'd lie and lie and lie and then throw in a truth, but you never knew which was which. And the few times I questioned him, I was wrong and he *had* been telling the truth. He'd prove it. You want to still make excuses for him, go ahead, but Bernard was a trickster, and he'd been one for years. He was evil."

"He was human," I said softly.

"Partly."

What bothered me most was that she meant it. "Partly?"

She dismissed me with a look. "You were saying?"

I ignored the smells hanging in the stagnant air as I took a deep breath and tried to organize my thoughts. "Not long after he died, I started to think back about things, like I said, and some things from the past I hadn't thought of in years came back to me and took on new meaning. One of those memories led me to a woman who lived in Potter's Cove with us when we were kids. I found out that Bernard raped her while he was still in his teens. It destroyed this woman, and she's been in and out of institutions ever since. She claimed there was more to Bernard than met the eye even then." The look of disgust on Claudia's face made me think there was a response coming, but she remained silent. "God knows what else he did before that. Later, after high school, we thought Bernard had joined the Marines," I continued. "He came back saying he'd torn up his knee in a fall during basic training, and that he'd been discharged, but we found out after he died that the entire thing was a lie. He'd never been a Marine and went to New York City instead. He claimed...he didn't exactly come right out and say it but he claimed he had started killing women there."

"You said you found this out *after* he died?" she asked.

"Yes." Although I had promised Donald and Rick I'd keep the subject of the tape between us, I felt at that point I had no choice but to trust Claudia with the information. If I had any chance of gaining her trust in return, I'd have to put all my cards on the table and risk it. I calmly explained about the tape being sent to Rick, how we had all listened to it together, and the specifics of what had been on it. I then explained how Donald had researched crimes in New York City during that time and how he had found two unsolved homicides that were strikingly similar to the murders in Potter's Cove.

She gave no reaction until I'd finished. "So you know he was a liar and a sick little boy who liked to torture and rape and who knows what else."

"Yes."

"And you think he killed these women?"

"I know he did."

"Then what more do you need? Isn't that enough?"

"It would've been," I said, "if it hadn't been for the dreams."

"Tell me about them."

"Donald, Rick and I all had an identical recurring nightmare. We're still having it." I described the dream for her in detail. "And then I started to experience worse things. Hallucinations—or visions or whatever the hell they are—of this woman and her child. Horrible visions. They started subtly, but they were so real, and eventually I had them while I was on a job. This woman in the vision, she lured me to an old condemned factory down in the south end and I saw…I saw some things down there. If there is a Hell, these things she showed me came straight out of it."

"If," Claudia scoffed quietly.

"I saw other things I can't explain or even fully remember down there. I don't know for sure if I want to remember them. It's the same when I think back to when Bernard and all of us were kids. The memories are scattered, you know? But there are huge pieces I can't remember that come back to me now in scraps and blurs. Maybe it's the same thing and I don't want to remember them more clearly either. Maybe if I do it'll unlock something else, something worse." Everything I was saying sounded absurd to me, like I was completely out of my goddamn mind. "And besides the visions, sometimes I hear things—whispers or—or I just feel something." I explained the experiences with the woman and child in as much detail as I could. "It's like all of this is stalking me somehow, together with my memories and nightmares of Bernard. I lost my job, my wife…maybe my mind. And it still won't stop. I need it to." A rush of emotion suddenly welled in the base of my throat. "I need it to stop."

Claudia finished her cigarette with a succession of repetitive drags then tossed the butt into the sink with the dishes and the ants. It rolled behind a plate, disappearing into the clutter, and I heard a soft hiss as ember hit water. "My childhood lasted about ten minutes," she said through a sigh. "Kids like me grow up quick, you know? But one time, when I was still a kid, before the world got a hold of me, I was talking to this priest. My grandma used to take me to church, dress me up in little dresses and hats, gloves—the whole bit. She died when I was twelve, but before that she was this all-star Catholic, used to go to the rectory and help out the priest with dishes and cleaning and shit like that after mass. One day I was at the rectory waiting for my grandma to finish, and I started talking to the priest. Father Naslette was his name. Old bastard, looked like a bald eagle with glasses. My grandma used to have *National Geographic* magazines at her house, and one time I saw these natives in like New Guinea or some shit, and I started wondering, you know, the way little kids do? Anyway, Father Naslette used to tell me that if you didn't believe in God and obey His laws, you'd go to Hell. So I asked him what about the natives in *National Geographic*? They didn't even know what a Catholic church was, so how come they were going to Hell?" She scowled like she'd suddenly tasted something bitter. "And you know what he told me? He told me that only people who had the knowledge were responsible for it. He said that if you didn't know about God then it was okay and wouldn't nobody blame you for that. Those natives, they didn't know, they were innocent so they wouldn't be punished. Hell was only for those who knew and fucked up or didn't obey. So sometimes it's better to not know, because whether you believe in that shit or not, once you have knowledge, you're responsible for it. Well I got news for you. God ain't the only one who works that angle."

The only emotion I felt now was growing anger. "Look, the woman I told you about, the one Bernard attacked when they were teenagers, she acted the same way you do. Like there's some big fucking secret everyone knows except me, and I'm sick and tired of it. I want to know what's happening. I want to know what all this means. And I don't give a shit what kind of strings are attached to it, you understand me?"

"Oh, *I* understand," she said. "You just better hope you do."

Claudia lingered near the counter and folded her arms across her chest, crushing her breasts together in a swell that revealed a considerable amount of cleavage and created the illusion that she was bustier than she was. The pose, and its result, were executed in a wholly blasé manner and had not been intended as a means of affecting me. She clearly could not have cared less if I took notice or not.

"That's the problem with people like you," she said in her throaty voice. "You want and think everything's out in the open—explained and seen and safe. Things are only like that on the surface. The real world is the one underneath. The one I moved in for years. The one

Bernard moved in. That world's different. It's shadows."

I nodded. "Then show me the shadows, Claudia."

She grimaced but quickly masked it, as if specters of what lived in those shadows had suddenly flashed before her. "I got into drugs real early in life, had a lot of problems," she said. "I lived with my grandma, she always took care of me. She was the only one who ever gave a shit about me. When she died I was only twelve, and I pretty much been on my own ever since. Met my mom a few times when I was a kid, but never really knew her. Wouldn't know my father if I fell over him. My mom died when I was nine. Somebody strangled her and threw her in a dumpster in Fall River. I found out later she was a drug addict and a hooker, my mom. Apple don't fall far from the tree, right? I had nothing, no family, only the system, and when you're a kid going through that—foster homes, shelters and halfway houses—all that bullshit—you can just slip away and let the world take you. And nobody cares. See, unless you kill somebody, try to kill yourself or do something real bad, the system can't be bothered. It's not about helping people, only punishing them, so until you do something the system thinks needs punishing, they got nothing for you. Thing is, there's so many runaways, lost and fucked up kids, and so many real crimes and shit that the cops can't cover it all. Half the time they don't even go through the motions, and kids like me just fade away. We either die or we survive. Period. Either way, it ain't pretty.

"So I'm my mother's daughter, right?" she continued a moment later. "It don't take long. The streets love girls like me, swallow them right up. One fucking gulp and you're gone. And it's like a maze, you know? You go a little ways before you get stuck, only there's always somebody there to take you by the hand…or the hair or the throat…to take you to that next level. And on and on. 'Cause they never tell you the only way out of that maze is death or fucking insanity, and that's only if you get real lucky, because the deeper you get, the meaner and darker those shadows get. And the Devil, he gets closer. So close you can feel him. It's his game, his maze. That's how he works. Devil don't want you to fear him until it's too late to get out from under him. Like a trap, you know? No cheese, no motherfucking mouse." She looked at me with a hard stare. "It's tough to understand if you're a mark. No offense, but—"

"None taken."

"I'll try to put it in a way that'll make sense to you." A thoughtful pause, and then, "You ever watch porn?"

I hadn't expected the question but answered it honestly anyway. "Well, I'm not an aficionado or anything but I've seen it before, sure."

"It's kind of like that," she said. "Works the same way. Pulls you in, but slow. Gradually. It don't want you to fear it at first. It's fun. Be happy. No harm. And for a lot of people that's just how it is, they get whatever it is they get from it and walk away. But some don't. Some can't, and those are the ones the world wants. Starts with a little T&A, then it gets harder. Pretty soon straight sex gets boring, right? Seen it a million times. Been there, done that. So you wonder, what else you got? And the Devil, he's got plenty. He offers it, and you look. A little while in you're watching shit you never would've believed could turn you on. Fantasies you keep pushed way down because they're more powerful than you are. But now they're on the loose and you want more. You want to see what else they can do to that cunt in the pictures or in the movie, in the magazine or on the web site. Cum on her face, piss on her, shit on her, get a dog, let's see the bitch fuck it—how about a horse? Rape the little slut, beat her ass, cut her throat and watch her bleed. And one day—"

"Christ almighty, I get the point."

"*And one day*," she said again, "you realize the person you were is gone, and somebody else is there instead. Somebody as mean and dark as the shadows you're living in. Somebody who forgets and then doesn't care that on the other end there's a person too. And what you don't see is all the shit that person went through to get that far in, to do things so fucked up. Not a picture or a movie but a fucking human being. Or what's left of one. And the Devil, he just smiles. 'Cause by then he's got you both."

I was unsure of what to say. Picturing Bernard with this woman required a healthy dose of imagination. It seemed outside the realm of possibility that he could have manipulated someone as savvy and streetwise as Claudia. But if manipulation hadn't been the culprit, then what was? I hadn't expected her to open up to this extent, to pour out her life history as if she'd been waiting for years to have the opportunity to do so, and I still wasn't sure what any of this had to do with Bernard. What I knew for sure was that her pain was palpable, so hideous and utterly her own that it had become as much a facet of her being as any physical characteristic. Regardless of who or what she had been, was now, or hoped to be, she was demanding respect, and I gave her mine.

"So you drown in it," she said. "You close your eyes and you drown in it, and all of a sudden life's not about survival anymore. You stop giving a shit. You open your veins and slide in whatever gets you through the day or night, and you wonder every time you stick that spike in if that'll be the time you don't ever wake up. Before long you start to pray for it. You don't really want to live anymore, but you're afraid of death. Devil's waiting on the other side of that long sleep, right?"

"Maybe God's waiting there instead," I said.

"Maybe." Her tone was flat. "But when you been throat-deep in evil as long as I was you ain't about to lay money on it any time soon, you see what I'm saying?"

"You keep talking about evil. What—cults or something?"

Claudia waved as if deflecting the words from the air between us. "That's always there, those kind are never far from that world. They're either right in the mix or hanging nearby, Satanists and those types. I ran with people like that for a while, when I had to. But they're no different than the Bible-thumpers when you get right down to it, because both of them are banking on the easy answer, and both are convinced they're right. Maybe they are, maybe they aren't. All I know is that evil is whatever it needs to be. It's not a simple answer like both sides of that old fight want it to be." She leaned back against the counter and crossed her feet out in front of her, at the ankle. A long time ago, she might have looked demure and childlike in such a stance. "The truth is deeper, beyond all that other stuff. The truth is that evil is different for everybody. That's the power, and that's why it preys on Man. It's the perfect predator because it's totally individual. It touches everybody, no matter your religion or belief, and it does it on your terms, whatever they are. So how do you stop something that manifests itself in totally different forms to different people, that can be anything to anyone, that can be whatever you need it to be? It knows who we are, our fears and worries and dreams, our weaknesses and strengths, and it uses it to twist its way through our fucking minds and bodies. And when you get past all the formal crap on both sides and you look closer, you figure out that Evil doesn't give a shit who you are or what church you go to, what you do or what you don't do. None of that matters, because it's coming for you anyway. And you can't stop it. All you can do is learn to deal with it, to keep it caged up more than you don't. Because just like good, it's inside of us, it's a part of us, and you can't just cut it loose. Like they say, personal demons, right? Well that's exactly what they are."

I remembered Julie Henderson, the crucifixes in her windows, and how she'd told me that they were "her reality," and therefore worked for her.

"That's what you see when you get beyond the cults and bullshit and see evil for what it really is. It doesn't give a shit about rules or laws or books written by either side, 'cause that's just the point. There are no fucking sides. There's the light and the dark. They just are what they are, and somewhere along the line somebody or something decided to drop us all right into the middle of it. From there, you draw your lines in the sand and fight your fights, whatever they are. Or you close your eyes and let one or the other take you." Claudia drifted closer to the table. "By the time I was in my mid-twenties I was already too old for the crowd I'd been running with, the crowd that owned me. I'd been through the blood and gore and sex and crazy-ass shit and I was still here. Used up, drugged out. That's when that world tosses you aside and they go looking for the next wave of twelve-year-olds. So I did what I'd been doing for years, I peddled my ass. I stopped running with any crowd, just kept pumping shit into my veins and started working the streets to pay for it, all the while hoping sooner or later my body would give out and the shit would just take me, let me drift off to wherever the fuck I was going.

"Did that for years," she continued. "Ended up doing a lot of time in jail, and one two-year stretch in prison for drug possession and prostitution. Figured out quick that prison makes jail look like a fucking motel. Ain't much to do inside besides fuck with people, get fucked with, eat pussy or read. I learned everything I could while I was inside, read everything. Some people find God in prison. Some find the Devil. I found my brain. Hadn't used it since my grandma died. But it still wasn't enough, 'cause the nightmares never stop. The shit I saw and did, the shit that happened to me again and again, it wouldn't ever go away. And when they finally let me out they just pushed me right back out onto the street. So I ended up where I was before, shooting up and selling my ass to pay for it. Fucking zombie. Still part of the dark. Still a piece of shit on the bottom of somebody's shoe. I'd known some scary motherfuckers, some seriously evil bastards. But they knew how fucked up they were, they got off on it. I figured by then I'd seen it all, wouldn't nothing surprise me or show me any corner of the dark I hadn't seen." She clutched the back of the chair across from me, applying a grip that turned her knuckles white. "And then one night I met Bernard."

CHAPTER 26

A mosaic of memories regarding Bernard unexpectedly appeared in my mind, though this time they were random—his face, a smile, quick flickers of trivial past events—a reflexive parade of flashes and subconscious recollections of no particular import. They grew fainter the moment Claudia continued speaking.

"The first time I saw him it was just after dark. He was cruising Weld Square. A lot of the girls on the street knew him on sight as a regular, he cruised the square three, four times a week. I hadn't worked that area in a long time and I'd only just started working it again, so I had no idea who he was, but a lot of the girls liked him, said he was an easy date, never any hassle, always paid and usually just wanted head or a straight lay. They all saw him as the harmless lonely heart type, you know? The kind who'd take you out to breakfast afterward or try to be your friend. The kind you can string along, work for extra cash or whatever. I was in his car ten seconds and figured him for a pure mark, and let me tell you something, Plato, I'm not wrong very often. I had way too much experience to misread people, especially men, and in that world a fuck-up can cost you your life. But I was wrong about him. Totally wrong." She spun the chair around so that it faced her then straddled it and sat like a rebellious teenager. "Bernard played up the sad sack image, and same as the other girls, I bought it at first. Like I told you, he was a trickster. That's what Bernard did. He deceived. But every now and then he'd let his guard down, the mask would slip a little and you'd see pieces of the demon behind it."

The sun shifted in the sky, betrayed by a fresh beam of light that crept from the front of the cottage and struck a small section of kitchen just over Claudia's shoulder. There must have also been a slight breeze, as ash from an ashtray on the counter momentarily swirled and flew a few inches into the air before gracefully spiraling to the floor like tiny black snowflakes.

"I'm sure you know what I mean," she said.

"Yeah," I answered. "But I guess I just never knew there was anything behind that mask besides an eccentric, sad and lonely guy. A childlike, harmless sort of guy."

"You and everybody else. And that's what he found his power in. Deception." Claudia scowled. "The only thing behind Bernard's mask was evil. I know. I saw it." She reached into her back pocket, pulled out a red bandana and mopped her forehead with it. "Fucking hot," she mumbled. She moved the rag to her neck then slid it across her chest, over the tops of her breasts and between them, soaking up the perspiration as she went. "Bernard got to be one of my regulars. I built up a group of them. They'd call me and we'd meet on neutral ground for dates. It was easier and safer than walking the street, and these were clients I knew I could count on to pay me and not give me a hard fucking time. Bernard was a steady for a couple weeks before we really started to get to know each other. He had this dork side to him but there was something else there too. It was below the surface and it took me a while to see it, but once I did I knew he was more than just some stupid mark like the rest of them. There was shit going on behind those eyes, you know? In that head." Another far off look overtook her as she absently wiped herself with the bandana. "When you're in the life, and especially if you've walked the darker roads out there, you get like this radar almost, this sense where you just know when you come across somebody else who's been there too. Everybody who's been in the dark—the real dark—has a way about them, and we can see it in each other. It don't go away no matter how far from the dark you run. It's always with you, like a brand. Kind of like the way all us jailbirds can pick each other out. I can spot somebody who did hard time in a second, and they can spot me. Same thing. I knew Bernard was moving in the darkness, knew he was more than he pretended to be, and I knew he had some sort of plan, too. People in the dark always got some sort of plan. Most of them never pull it off because the dark has a way of beating you down to where you just don't give a shit anymore, but I could tell Bernard wasn't like that. The dark didn't control him like it did me and all the others I knew. *He* controlled *it*." She dropped the sweat stained bandana on the table. "And that told me something very important about him. It told me he wasn't new to the dark, that he'd been moving in it and mastering it for a long time. Years. Nobody who moves in the dark is ever that confident unless they've been there for years.

"It was all real subtle at first," she went on. "He never really talked about it or anything but we both knew what the other was about. We started to hang out a lot more, not just on dates but other times too. He'd always pay, didn't seem to have anything else to spend his money on, and like I said, he had a plan. Figured I fit into that plan somehow, and he brought me into his world slow and careful. For me, I was still strung out then, still pumping that shit into myself every chance I got, so Bernard was good for me. He'd supply me with the cash I needed to buy it, and sometimes he'd even get it for me. Sometimes he'd fix me himself. Got good at it, actually."

I searched her bare arms. A few old scars; mostly faded. She no longer bore the typical ravaged flesh many addicts did, but glimpses of those same arms bruised and bloodied flashed before my eyes anyway. I pictured Bernard on his knees, administering a syringe of heroin into this woman's veins.

"Couple times near the end I fixed him, too," Claudia said. "He wanted to try it and liked doing it now and then, but he never got deep enough into it to get hooked. He had other addictions."

"Like what?"

As if staged, the shaft of sunlight that had invaded the room earlier slipped away, returning the kitchen to near-darkness. "The other side," she answered. "Torture and death. Destruction. Blood."

A chill swept through me, temporarily defusing the humidity. "The other side," I said, "like an afterlife?"

She nodded. "That was part of his deal, getting shit ready for when he crossed over to the other side. He believed what he did in this life would determine the kind of power he'd hold in the next one. Ain't about Heaven and Hell to those like Bernard. It's all about power. Only power he had here was what the darkness gave him, but on the other side he thought he could be different."

"He was insane."

Claudia raised an eyebrow. "You think?"

"Don't you?"

She watched me a while. I could almost hear her thinking. "We got close, me and Bernard. Wasn't really something I wanted but I was a drug addict, and drug addicts ain't exactly got a lot of options. He kept me fixed, and he made me feel powerful too. Like I told you, I'd been around, seen and knew a lot of things before I met him, but Bernard let me get in close so I knew what he was doing. And it was fucking intense. Besides, I hadn't left the dark yet myself, still thought it was where I belonged, and he was all I had."

"You knew he was killing people?" I asked.

Claudia stood up slowly, gradually, and slid the chair out of her way. She moved around the side of the table with a slinking, feline-like stride, until she was right next to me. I looked up at her, uncertain of her intentions.

She reached down and touched my t-shirt, running her fingers across the collar and onto my throat. Her flesh was damp and slightly warm, as was mine. "Come here," she said in a loud whisper, and in one motion, grabbed hold of my t-shirt and pulled me from the chair. I cooperated and allowed her to stand me up. I was taller than she was, and had to look down to meet her eyes. She stepped closer, so close that her chest touched mine. She smelled of cigarettes, sweat and cheap perfume. Her arms wrapped around me and she smiled as her hands roamed along my back to my waist, past the gun on my belt and onto my ass. One hand slid between my legs. I swallowed nervously as she clutched me—hard—then ran her hands along the insides of both thighs.

"I'm not wearing a wire," I told her.

Without answering me she sunk to her knees, her hands following, moving along my knees and calves. She looked up at me, her face in line with my crotch. I resisted the sudden desire to touch her hair, the side of her face. Claudia rose, nonchalantly spun around and strolled back across the kitchen. "You hear a fucking word I said, Plato? You think that was the first time I was ever around a killer, around violent bastards who did the most depraved and fucked up shit you've ever imagined?" She faced me again once she'd reached the counter. "Difference was, most of the people I knew fell into it one way or another, went looking for the dark and found it or just got dragged in—you see what I'm saying? But not Bernard. Bernard was born into it."

I remained standing. "What are you talking about?"

"Another one of his addictions," she said softly. "His mother."

"What about her?"

"You've heard the stories."

"Before he was born she was in New York City, got mixed up with a bad crowd, mob guys or something, and got pregnant. That was the rumor around town. She never talked about it in specifics and neither did Bernard."

"'Course not." Her eyes nearly sparkled, and I couldn't tell if she was genuinely amused or only making fun of me. "She went off and got mixed up with a bad crowd, that much is true. But they weren't no mafia guys. The people she fell in with make the mob look like choirboys."

"More of these people from this world you keep referring to?"

"Crazy motherfuckers who think their rituals can conjure the Devil himself, can blur the boundaries between this world and the one underneath. People who believe they can manipulate both worlds with rituals and hexes and spells and dark prayers."

"This is what Bernard told you?"

"He didn't know himself until his mother brought him into it. He was in his early teens by then."

The same timeframe in which he had attacked Julie Henderson and begun his descent into madness, evil or whatever the hell it had been. "But his mother left all that and went to Potter's Cove to have Bernard and raise him in a safe environment. She ran from these people, from this world, so how could—"

"She didn't run, she moved back into the world like they all do."

"Like all *who* do?"

"All of us who come up against them, who run with them." Her eyes turned dead. "Demons, Plato. Fucking demons."

In my denial, or inability to fathom what she'd said, I responded with a burst of nervous laughter. Julie Henderson had sworn they were all around us, and just like Julie, Claudia was either completely sincere, or completely out of her mind. Maybe both.

"It ain't like some cult that dances around fires in silk robes and calls themselves Satanists so they can do drugs and fuck and listen to bad rock and roll," she said. "I'm talking about the dark, man. The *real* dark and the *real* things that move in it, that live in it, you understand? This ain't like some movie, it's fucking real. They don't use junkies like me, or street trash or even the innocent little girls who vanish from corner stores or parks or schoolyards or their own beds in the middle of the night—we're just minor league players on the sidelines, around to be used and abused, demonic fucking toys. They scoop up the older ones like his mother, the small-town girls who go wandering into places like New York or L.A. looking for a better life. They show them the dark, show them the way then send them back to the world to give birth to the next wave."

"The next wave of *what*?"

"Killers. Destroyers. The ones who devour."

Be sober, be vigilant; because your adversary the devil, as a roaring lion, walketh about, seeking whom he may devour. Bernard's final words on the taped suicide note.

I suddenly felt confined in the tiny kitchen, like the walls were creeping closer. "This is ridiculous. For Christ's sake, Bernard never even knew who his father was. His mother never told him."

"Why do you think that is?"

"Probably because she had no idea who it was either."

"Maybe it was because she knew *exactly* who it was."

Anger swelled. "Okay, so I'm supposed to believe there are demons walking among us like people and that *they're* the ones responsible for all the evil in the world—not us, not human beings, but *demons.* They're to blame. What's next—garden gnomes? And let me guess, Bernard's father was the Devil himself, right? Bernard's *Rosemary's Baby* now, is that it? Give me a fucking break. This is bullshit. I told you before; I'm not playing games. I need answers, goddamn it, not fucking fairy tales from the dark ages."

"Ooh, big strong man making demands." Claudia gave a mock shiver. "You're the one who came to me, remember? You're the one telling me about your dreams and visions and all that. You're the one who wanted to know the truth, so listen real close, jack-off. I never said it was anything but people who are responsible for all the bad shit in this world. But people make choices—decisions—you understand? There are temptations, and once choices are made there are forces that influence people. Real forces. Some good, some bad, and they're in constant battle with each other. They're inside us, all around us, and you know it. We all know it because we all hear the voices in our heads, the whispers. We just learn to ignore them, to write them off, to label them with words like *conscience*. That's the way of the worlds, Plato. This one, and the next."

I ran my hands through my sweat-dampened hair. "Christ, I'm so confused."

"That's the shit Evil thrives on. Confusion. Deception. Uncertainty. Chaos. And the deeper you go the worse it gets, the more powerful it grows and the less sense it makes, because nothing ever makes sense in the dark." Claudia stabbed another cigarette between her lips. "Welcome to the big leagues, asshole."

"I knew Bernard's mother," I insisted. *Skimpy bikinis and skimpier towels—slipping, shifting and falling—blended to suntanned skin slick with oil.* "I knew Linda." *The bedroom at the top of the stairs—her room—the bed against the back wall, the mismatched nightstands on either side of the headboard, the clutter of overflowing ashtrays and empty liquor bottles.* "She was eccentric but—" *Garments stuffed into plastic clothesbaskets and strewn about the room as if thrown there or dropped there, an ironing board against one wall, a dressing table with mirror and closet against another.* "—she was harmless, completely harmless." *Lipsticks and makeup, small bottles of polish and colognes and body sprays, tins of soap and powder rattling, clicking one against the other.* "I knew her," I said again.

"You knew Bernard too, what's your point?" Claudia obviously sensed I was trying to recall the past without coming completely undone, but I couldn't be sure if she meant to help or only make things worse. "She brought him into it the way you bring an innocent into it. Their little secret, got it? Things you don't talk about, even with your best friends, because nobody would understand. It's slow, a seduction. It's not the truth she had to tell him, only lies and sacrilege masked in love and trust. She didn't have to do anything else, no explanations or definitions of what he was or what he needed to do. She just positioned him, set him on the right course and let him go, knowing from the start that his path was already determined by destiny—or whatever label you want to give it—and that he'd find his own way. And that's exactly what she did." She threw a look my way that might have been pity. "I knew Linda's kind too—dime a dozen. Sex, drugs and rock and roll, little devil stuff thrown in—why not, it's trendy and harmless, right? I've seen the ceremonies, the gangbangs where they break in bitches like her. Father could be anybody—anything—but it don't matter because what's behind it, what's holding their hands is pure fucking evil. Stupid cunts never have a chance; they're in over their heads before they know it. When it's over all that's left is that same smiling Devil. By then Linda wasn't no saint." She plucked the still unlit cigarette from her mouth. "But then, I ain't telling you anything you don't already know."

Knock once and go on in. I closed my eyes, saw that staircase again, the landing at the top and the open doorway just to the right; heard the bottles on the dressing table clicking together, the headboard slapping the wall, rattling everything in the room. I felt sick, like I had that day, a cramping, churning feeling deep in my bowels, as if someone had pushed their fingers through the skin below my navel, worked them deeper until they were inside me up to the wrist, curled around my intestines, twisting, crushing and yanking them free in one slimy, bloody mess. "No," I said softly. "You're not."

"The dark loves denial. Broken memories. Buried memories."

"So that's where it started then?" I asked. "With his mother?"

"Where'd she go when she got pregnant with Bernard?" she asked. "And where did Bernard go when he lied about joining the Marines? New York City. Think that's a coincidence? Think maybe he went there to see the same crowd his mother knew? The same crowd she was running with when she got pregnant with him? Think maybe it was a homecoming? Think maybe that's where he learned to do what he ended up doing so well?" Claudia slid the cigarette behind her ear. "There were lots of killings there, especially back then, lots of activity, lots of history. Destroyers walked there, fed the streets. Fed them with blood. That's what they do; they want blood flowing in the fucking streets. It goes in cycles, and with every wave there's a destroyer, a beast. The rest of them, they're just gone, dead or vanished. Fucking poof, like they were never there."

"But wait," I said. The heat was so thick I was having trouble breathing. "He attacks Julie Henderson when he's thirteen years old, does nothing else for five or six years then goes to New York

City and suddenly becomes a killer?"

"How do you know he did nothing else for five or six years?"

"Even if he did other things we don't know about, he goes to New York and he starts to kill—maybe these, whatever the hell they are, his mother fell in with, taught him or helped him—and he slaughters two young women inside of a year. Then he stops as suddenly as he began, moves back to Potter's Cove with the Marines story and doesn't kill again for nearly two decades? Serial killers can't just stop killing once they start."

Claudia actually chuckled. "Is that what you think Bernard was, a serial killer who killed at random and couldn't stop? His murders were ritual killings, you understand? And besides, he didn't stop after New York and only start up again right before he died. There were others." She rubbed her eyes with her palms and sighed. "We were in his car once, headed up to the Cape for a couple days." She brought her hands down; her eyeliner had smudged. "He told me one day they'd find them scattered along that highway, back in the scrub brush, in the woods. He told me he'd left a lot of them there.

"I was high. I laughed. Crazy motherfucker. Maybe he was telling the truth, maybe not. Didn't know, didn't care. And in the end it didn't mean shit anyway, because it was all practice for those last killings he did in the months before he offed himself. Everything led to that. Those bodies they're finding in Potter's Cove now? He meant for them to be found."

"How many are there?"

"I don't know."

"You don't—"

"I don't fucking know, I said. You think I went with him, watched, helped?" This time when Claudia put the cigarette in her mouth she lit it. "I knew his plan, I was around, I listened—that's it."

I took a step away from the kitchen table and toward the back door. I needed to be closer to the sunshine. "Fine, you knew his plan. What were the rituals?"

Claudia took a drag on her cigarette, exhaled and picked a flake of tobacco from the tip of her tongue. "It's all about the blood."

"The victims in Potter's Cove were bled," I told her. "They were killed somewhere else and dumped. The same was true of the two unsolved homicides Donald came across in New York."

She nodded. "The strongest spells—the darkest—always involve human blood. Blood holds life. Some believe the soul travels through the blood. It's an ancient ritual. Kind of like back in medieval times, if someone was sick or possessed they believed you could bleed disease and evil out of them. And they weren't that far off. You take the blood and you steal the soul, the life. From there, ain't no telling what you can do with it if you're powerful enough. At least that's what a lot of those types believe."

"Do you know where he did it?"

"No." Claudia smoked her cigarette quickly, and after a few hard drags it was reduced to a butt she tossed into the sink along with the last. "You're the one with the visions, man, not me."

"That factory down in the south end," I said.

She slowly shook her head in the negative. "He didn't know the city well enough, it wouldn't have been there. He would've done it where he felt safe, where he knew his way around, in and out."

"Then why did that woman appear to me and lure me there?"

"They say the underworld don't fit together exactly like this one does," she said. "Sometimes it's all representational, know what I mean? What's the word—symbolic?"

I moved closer to the back door. "There's a bunch of old abandoned factories in Potter's Cove, too."

Claudia shrugged.

"And why is this woman coming to me?" I asked. "Why me?"

"All the victims were single mothers."

"I knew that much."

"No." She slid down the counter a bit, closer to me. "You have to do more than know, you have to *understand*."

"But I don't even know who the hell she is."

"The victims were single mothers, all of them with sons. Just like Bernard and his mother. He was lining them up to join him on the other side, no doubt, but what he was doing was symbolic too, see? He wouldn't be what he was without his mother, so in a way, he was killing her, killing the one who provided him with life, again and again and again. Then, near the end, he went one better. That's how the rituals go, he would've taken it another step and not just killed the woman who represented his mother—life—but he'd kill the life itself. The child, the son who represented him."

I was close enough to the doorway now to brace myself against the casing. Sweat trickled into my eyes, across my cheek. I wiped it away with my wrist. "Why?"

"It's one sacrilege on top of another on top of another," she said. "Spitting in the face of God, understand? He thought his rituals made *him* a god. He took life so he could make life. And after he took that step with the mother and child both, there was only one step left. The ultimate in sacrilege: suicide. Literally taking his own life, the one God gave him. It's the final insult. And it ain't like someone sick who does it for different reasons. This was calculated, so that even his own death was a ritual, you see?"

"They're going to find the bodies of that woman and little boy, aren't they," I said softly. She didn't answer so I said, "I just wish I knew why she came to me."

Claudia had followed me to the door, and I hadn't realized how close she was to me until she spoke. "Maybe the riddle isn't about her."

I looked over my shoulder at her. "What do you mean?"

"Deception. Maybe it's more about Bernard, more about you. Could be she's trying to help you."

"And what about Bernard?"

"Maybe he knew you'd listen, maybe he has unfinished business, or he's restless or can't let go yet. Not all spirits cross peacefully. Some hang on." She slipped past me, so close that her hip brushed my leg before she took up position on the other side of the doorframe. A tracer of sunlight formed a thin line across her face. The smudged eyeliner made her look strangely sinister. "Go back to the beginning. Watch. Listen. Keep your mind open to it and follow your instincts, those voices in your head—whatever you want to call them. If the other side's looking for you, it'll find you. That much I *do* know."

The more I searched those sad, liner-smudged eyes, the less sinister they became. "Why do you think he never hurt you?"

"Never said he didn't."

"Didn't *kill* you then?"

"I didn't fit the mold. I was just a stupid junkie fuck-toy." She smiled ever so slightly. "Didn't have to worry none about me, right?"

I could've talked with her for hours, picking her brain and delving deeper and deeper into her time with Bernard, but I had to get out of that cottage. It was closing in around me and there were unsettling vibes passing between us. "Thanks for your help," I said.

"Don't thank me. I ain't sending you anywhere good."

"You aren't sending me anywhere I didn't ask to go." I glanced at the poster across the room. "Hope things work out for you in Florida."

She pressed a hand against the screen door and pushed it open, holding it there as she leaned closer to me. We stood together in the doorway a moment, our faces mere inches apart. I could feel her breath against my neck. "Be careful out there, Plato."

CHAPTER 27

Sunday afternoon. It was hot, and I was exhausted. I paused at the base of the steps to my apartment and gazed at Life a moment, as if I was the only one moving and everything else was standing still.

Couples walked hand-in-hand and children played along the sunny bank of the cove across the street. Bass-heavy car stereos thumped from passing vehicles, and the air was filled with food smells typical of the neighborhood.

I was halfway up the staircase before I realized the door to my apartment was ajar. I froze a moment, then grabbed the railing and pulled myself a step closer in an attempt to see beyond the slight opening. I stole a quick glance back down the stairs at the parking spaces below. The cars blended one into the next like everything else under the rippling heat. Nothing looked distinct or individually defined; the world was all smooth edges and rounded angles, a nebulous blur of colors and shapes distorted by the slow steady burn of a brilliant and scorching sun.

I climbed the remaining stairs cognizant of my weight and the sound of my footfalls against the aged wood. When I reached the landing before the door, I pulled my 9mm free, and holding it down by my thigh, pushed the door open the rest of the way with my free hand.

Toni stood inside, shaded from the sun.

I don't know why I'd suspected it might have been someone else.

My nerves settled and I joined her, closing the door behind me. I slipped the 9mm back into the holster then pulled the entire thing free of my belt.

"Why are you carrying a gun, Alan?"

I hadn't heard her voice in a while, and was troubled by how quickly unfamiliar it had become. Her clothes looked new, small purple shorts with a matching sleeveless top and a pair of white Keds. Sunglasses sat atop her head. She was tan and healthy-looking, which somehow seemed appalling under the circumstances. "I didn't know you were going to be here," I said.

It was then that I noticed the nylon bag dangling from her hand. Perhaps because she swung it rather casually down by her leg. "I came by to pick up a few more things."

I nodded in answer. I'd been hoping for something better. *I'm coming home*, maybe. *I wanted to see you*, even. It didn't seem possible that such a chasm could exist between us so quickly. Good, bad or indifferent, just weeks before I would have spent the day with this woman, cuddling on the couch or going for a walk, maybe catching a movie, ridiculously unaware that even with our problems it would ever change, that anything else might ever have meaning beyond our little cocoon, so certain it would always be her breath on my neck, her head on my chest, her arms around my back, her lips against mine, her dreams and fears and desires intermingled with my own. Didn't she understand I was coming apart at the seams? Didn't she understand that Bernard was a devil and that I was lost, lost in the dark and that he was there with me? Didn't she know how much I needed her just then? Didn't she still need *me* too? Had she ever?

"How are you?" she asked. Before I could answer she said, "You look tired."

"Among other things."

Toni clutched the bag with both hands, as if for comfort, and held it tight against her chest. It crinkled in her grasp, still empty, and for a moment I entertained the notion that I might be capable of convincing her to stay, or at a minimum, to prevent her from taking anything else from the apartment. I wasn't sure how much more could be removed before what remained would become vestiges of a relationship no longer relevant. "Can you believe they found another body?" she asked.

"Yeah, down at the public beach." I emphasized the word public because the cottage her friend Martha was letting her use was located on one of the few private stretches of beach in town.

She sighed and frowned a little. "The whole town's terrified. It's all everyone talks about. It's all over the news, on TV and the radio, in the papers. There's even national media in town some days. People look at each other on the street with such distrust now, and there are FBI agents and strange law enforcement types all over the place, it's like something out of a movie. Have you noticed how at night it's so much quieter than it used to be? Everyone goes home, locks their doors like prisoners, and hides. It's awful."

I shrugged. "It's never been that noisy where you are now."

She continued speaking like she hadn't heard me, the words spilling from her quickly. "The police even released a statement about how the bodies are not recent murder victims. They were killed months ago, and they say it as if that fact should put people at ease, like the killer has moved on or hasn't killed anyone lately. One article even quoted an unnamed source in the police department that said the killer might be a transient, and that there's a good chance he's already left town. Apparently some killers cross the country traveling by rail, like hobos or something, hopping trains and killing people from one end of the country to the next, and since the train runs through town, well…you know. One article said the killer might be targeting low income single mothers." Toni lowered the bag, holding it with both hands against the front of her thighs like a schoolgirl. "Anyway, the selectmen had an announcement in the paper about it too, with tomorrow being the Fourth of July and all, did you see it? About how it's the official kickoff of the tourist season and tourism doesn't need to suffer because of it—blah, blah, blah—can you believe it?"

"Yeah, actually, I can."

"They're still going ahead with the fireworks."

"I've always hated fireworks," I said.

She became very still. "Alan, do you really think Bernard may have been involved in these killings?"

I stood there idiotically, the holstered 9mm in my hands. "I don't know."

"So you're no longer convinced then that—"

"No," I said. I didn't want her involved, didn't want her to know what I knew, and it wasn't until that moment that I realized how much I still loved her, still felt the need to protect her in some antiquated, intrinsically male way. Beneath the older and wiser exterior, beyond all the disappointments and complexities, this was still the girl I had held in my arms as a teenager, still the girl I had whispered silly and melodramatic love snippets to while gently sprinkling her face with kisses. I remembered the taste and texture of her then—her eyes and nose and cheeks and lips and chin, so certain I could prevent pain from ever again reaching her simply by willing it to be so, by holding her in my arms and loving her so desperately. "I don't...I don't know anymore, probably not, I—no, I was wrong, I guess. He probably had nothing to do with it, I was just—I thought he did but not anymore." I smiled self-consciously.

"Are you sure you're all right?"

"Of course I'm not all right." I wanted to scream it but didn't. It came out uncertain and hushed instead. "I just need to work some things out."

"I wish you'd talk to someone, Alan."

"I'm talking to you right now."

"You know what I mean."

"No, I don't think I do." Truth was, we'd talked more since our troubles began than we had in years. Despite the familiarity of our relationship, much of our time together had been spent in silence. Some days that silence was a testament to the potency of our bond—we hadn't required small talk, we were beyond all that and could be together quietly, without the chatter—but it also shone light on that which festered beneath.

Toni held the bag up again. "Well, just wanted to grab a few things."

"You mean I should talk to someone like Gene," I said.

The mention of his name didn't sting her as I'd intended. If anything, her expression softened. "Are you still taking your pills?"

"No."

"They'll help you sleep."

"I don't want to sleep," I said.

"And you think that's a healthy way to feel?" I wondered what the two of them did together, besides the obvious. What did they talk about? Did she settle trustingly against him in the night the way she had with me? Did they laugh like we had? Did she tell him the things she told me? Did any of that even matter anymore? I wondered if she ever thought about me when she was with him. "I just need a little time to get things together," I said. It sounded lame the moment it left my lips, but it was all I had.

She nodded at me, like everything suddenly made perfect sense.

"I miss you," I said, and without thinking, reached for her. She shrunk a bit—a subtle reaction, but an honest one. I dropped my hand to my side.

Her eyes filled. "Do you think we'll ever be all right again?"

"You're the one who left," I said. "You're the one who had to think."

She looked at me with an expression that said: And you're the one who went crazy.

I let her go, watched as she walked into the bedroom with a spring in her step I hadn't seen in years. Her body was out of sync with her emotions, one spry and the other pensive. It seemed a clever deception, like an illusionist's use of misdirection, and I found myself resentful suddenly of her attempt at a healthy, lively veneer. Yet deep down I could hardly blame her, and was glad she'd again be leaving soon, distancing herself from me, if only for now. Bernard was a disease, and he had infected me. I didn't want the same for her, and until I could rid myself of him, she was at risk. I felt particularly contagious of late.

In the kitchen, I put my gun down on the counter and had a quick shot of whiskey. It left a warming path as it slid through my body, and I embraced it, allowing my nerves to calm. By the time I'd had another and put the shot glass in the sink, I heard Toni rummaging about in the bathroom.

I met her near the front door, careful not to get too close.

"All set," she said softly. The bag was now bulging in places with items removed from the medicine cabinet and bathroom shelves. I had also heard her bureau drawers closing earlier, so I knew she'd taken more clothing as well. She smiled, though it was solely for my benefit. "I hope you have a nice Fourth. We'll talk soon, okay?"

I had run out of chitchat. The whiskey was seeping through my pores and mixing with the sheen of perspiration already painted across my skin. The goddamn humidity was swallowing everything whole. I nodded but said nothing.

With head slightly bowed, Toni slipped past me through the door.

From some black corner of Hell, Bernard whispered to me, and as my wife moved down the stairs and blended into the blurred heat below, I couldn't help but wonder if I'd ever see her again.

CHAPTER 28

Go back to the beginning, Claudia had said. And that's exactly what I did.

After Toni left, I drove across town to the neighborhood where I'd grown up, and parked in front of the house Bernard and his mother had called home for years. I experienced the same waves of nostalgia I had the last time I'd revisited these hallowed stomping grounds of my youth, and although most were of the pleasant variety, once I focused on Bernard's old house—still empty and slowly rotting away—all the thoughts and memories turned to black. The house looked about the same as it had in winter, but for a realtor's sign stabbed into the front lawn. Apparently the bank had decided to sell the property after all, but had yet to do anything to dress it up, which led me to believe this was a recent development. A few feet from the realtor sign was a No Trespassing sign with a warning to any who vandalized the property that they would be prosecuted to the full extent of the law.

I checked my rearview mirror. It was late afternoon but the humidity was still lethal. The other houses on the street sported window fans and air-conditioners, and but for two young boys riding their bikes, no one was on the street. With all that was happening in town, with all the police everywhere, the last thing I wanted to do was draw attention to myself as someone sitting in a parked car in a neighborhood where I no longer lived, so I grabbed a pen from my visor and pretended to jot the number on the sign down as the two boys pedaled past, laughing and shouting to each other. I watched them until they disappeared around the bend at the end of the road. Shirtless and in cut-off denim shorts, hair buzzed down for summer, bodies tanned brown from hours spent playing outdoors and at the beach, they might as easily been ghosts of Bernard and me; trouble-free versions of us in less complicated times.

If those times had ever really existed.

Once the boys were out of sight and quiet returned to the street, I climbed out of the car. Just in case anyone was watching, I strolled across the property like a prospective buyer then circled around to the fence that ran along the side yard. As in winter, the lawn was dead again, only now it was burned and matted down from sun and grubs. I opened the gate and stepped through, closing it quietly behind me. I looked up to the circle of trees just beyond the backyard as I had the last time I'd come here, but on this occasion no birds welcomed or warned me. Only silence.

Even more windows had been broken from thrown stones, and additional graffiti had been added, spray-painted along the back wall of the house, including a crude pentagram, a parade of profanity and the scribbled names of a few rock bands I recognized. I could see how in a town like Potter's Cove, where teenagers had little to do, a house like this could quickly become a late night retreat, the neighborhood spooky house, abandoned and easily accessible for hanging out, drinking beer, smoking pot—whatever.

I crossed to the cement patio in back. The chaise lounge, lawn furniture and plastic garbage bags that had been there before were gone. Cigarette butts and a few spent beer and liquor bottles littered the area instead.

It was then that I noticed the sliders off the patio.

A section of glass near the bottom was missing, kicked in from the looks, and while the sliding door was closed, the wooden rod that fit into the track and held it that way was gone.

That same uncompromising feeling that I was being watched returned. I looked back at the yard and trees. Nothing. Not even a breeze. Just heat and sky and silence.

I tried the slider. It quietly slid open, and a waft of musty air met me, a dank, mildew smell that intensified once it mingled with the humid air outside. I fanned the initial blast away with my hands then stepped through the open slider and into the kitchen.

Vivid memories still lived here for me.

I could almost see Bernard's mother flitting around on a hot summer day just like this one, dressed in high-heeled slippers and a terrycloth waist-length cover-up that did little to cover much of anything, especially the bikini beneath. I remembered her pouring us lemonade and dancing her way back to the refrigerator while music played from a radio on the counter, Tommy, Rick, Donald, Bernard and me—just kids—huddled around the table, sweaty and out of breath from playing, gulping our lemonade and laughing, reliving adventures we'd had earlier in the day.

It occurred to me then just how long it had been since I'd set foot in this house. Although Bernard continued to live here as an adult, he had preferred instead to come to our houses or to meet us at some other neutral point—and strangely enough that had been fine with us. The last time I could remember being inside the house was a few weeks before his mother was hospitalized with cancer. A few years now, I thought. Odd.

The memories receded, leaving behind a dirty, dilapidated kitchen and a musty stink. There was an uncomfortable stillness to the house, the walls and those windows still intact providing an unnatural quiet, a buffer to the world outside that seemed different somehow, more intense and final. Though the windows that were not broken were filthy and smudged, I was careful to avoid them anyway.

The floor was dirty and littered with dirt tracked in from outside and what appeared to be small rodent droppings. I crossed the kitchen and slipped through the doorway into a living room. There had once been wall-to-wall carpeting here, but that had been ripped up for some reason to reveal old wooden flooring beneath. Void of furniture, and stripped bare of everything else, the room looked larger than I remembered. The wallpaper was cracked and hanging in places, and more graffiti had been spray-painted across the walls and even on the floor. I stepped around a pile of trash and debris and continued on to the foyer just inside the front door. To my left was the staircase leading to the second floor. Beyond it was a short hallway that led to a bathroom.

I stood at the base of the stairs and looked up. Darkness waited at the top in more ways than one. I wiped sweat from my hands onto my pants and slowly climbed the staircase. The carpeting remained and cushioned my steps, but the banister was gouged and scarred, as if someone had been at it with a knife. The destruction kids had caused in the time the house had been unattended was surprising. All those years before, when we'd been kids ourselves, I could never have imagined this result for a house where I spent so much time, where I had so many memories, good and bad. But here it was, a dead shell, a decaying monument to nothing.

When I reached the top I hesitated, hand still on the banister. It wasn't quite dark but due to the low ceiling and location of the landing in relation to any of the upstairs windows, light was limited. The musty smell wasn't as bad here, but there was another odor I hadn't detected previously. It smelled like sulfur, recently lit matches. I took the final step, and once on the landing at the top of the stairs, saw a bedroom directly ahead. Linda's bedroom. Further down the hallway was Bernard's old room, so I lowered my eyes and fled to it, hoping to escape the other if even for a short while longer.

The light increased as I neared Bernard's room. There had once been a door there but it was now removed and leaned against the wall next to the doorway. It had been kicked and broken in places. The room itself was empty. I walked in as I had so many times over the years, but now it was as impersonal and barren as an open grave. In my mind I could still see his bed, his desk, his record player, and the posters that had once covered his walls. I ventured deeper into the room. His closet stood to my right. I opened it, swinging the door wide. But for a string dangling from a light bulb fixture on the ceiling, it too was empty.

A soft scratching sound stopped me cold. Movement. Scurrying movement within the wall, as if Bernard had been sealed away behind it and was now clawing his way out.

Mice, I told myself. *It's only mice.*

Familiar laughter from the past echoed through the empty hallway, each echo reverberating one atop another until it sounded like a group laughing, the dead amused by the living. But the laughter was Bernard's, duplicated again and again.

Even in death he was abandoned, hidden in shadow and deceit.

My mind calmed a bit, absorbed the laughter and quieted it.

I slowly scoped out the room, found only a rather lethargic wasp slinking across one of the cracked windowpanes facing the street. For now, we were alone.

I forced myself back into the hallway, back toward the other bedroom at the top of the stairs. I felt like that sleepy and disoriented wasp, just another creature that had taken a wrong turn and become lost within these dying walls, destined to spend its final hours sharing space with all the secrets trapped here.

What secrets, Alan? What secrets live here?

Secrets. Memories. Lies. Nervous smiles and downcast eyes replaced all that had existed prior, as comfort turned to dread. Forgotten, pushed down—deep down—pretending that not believing in the Devil was enough, that it would disarm him and protect you from him, when all the while disbelief only made him stronger.

All the good and clear memories were before—before we were teenagers—before the changes in us, in our bodies and minds and in the way we saw the world, the way we experienced it—before Bernard had been introduced and brought into a realm he did not yet know was his legacy. What had been a regular hangout and a safe haven—Bernard's house—ceased to exist as such once those changes happened because it had become too difficult, too strange. The memories turned from good, carefree and innocent to bad, dark and shameful, and we needed to stay away—we all needed to stay away—or we might remember. And we did not want to remember. I did not want to remember.

But now that was no longer an option.

What did you see?

The bedroom was closer now; I could have reached out and touched the doorframe had I wanted to. My throat became dry, my lips pasty, and as I moved into the room I realized my entire body had begun to tremble. I made myself look.

It was empty like the rest of the house, but I saw the past—Linda's bedroom—and all that had been there so long ago. The bedroom at the top of the stairs, the bed against the back wall, the mismatched nightstands on either side of the headboard, the clutter of overflowing ashtrays and empty liquor bottles. Garments stuffed into plastic clothesbaskets and strewn about the room as if thrown or dropped there, an ironing board against one wall, a dressing table with mirror and closet against another. Lipsticks and makeup, small bottles of polish and colognes and body sprays, tins of soap and powder rattling, clicking one against the other.

And what else? What else did you see?

"Jesus, God," I whispered, falling against the doorway for fear I might otherwise collapse.

Candles. The shades all pulled tight and candles scattered throughout the room. Black candles. Who—why black candles? Why—

What else, Alan?

Pain pierced my temples like ice picks, and I brought my hands to either side of my head with the hope that clutching my skull hard enough might ward off the throbbing. Tears filled my eyes and dripped into the back of my throat.

The bed, moving and shaking, the headboard slapping the wall and the box spring wailing in rhythmic squeals as shadowy fingers cast from candlelight skipped along the ceiling. And sounds—words—no, *prayers*, but alien and backward, twisted and mocking.

Linda's eyes, her body nude, slick with sweat and lunging forward then back with each thrust, her head hitting the headboard and her voice still deep and urgent even after her dark prayers had been recited. *Good...good...good boy.*

I shut my eyes but vision remained, refused to let go.

It is night and that makes no sense, because it is not night, not really. Neither was it night then—but here, in this dream place, it is night. I am lying on the floor watching TV, and she is sitting behind me on the couch. She calls me, gets my attention, asks me to come and sit next to her. I do, though hesitantly, unsure of her motives, and my own. Such motives and feelings are still new to me. I am still trying to decipher many of them, to identify them for what they are and why I have them, but I sit beside her anyway.

She turns her back to me, looks over her shoulder and smiles, tossing her hair. She looks like a model in one of those makeup commercials on TV; like a movie star. I'm afraid and angry with myself for feeling so nervous—I should be a man even though I'm not yet a man—I shouldn't be afraid of a woman, a barely dressed beautiful woman who is my friend, who likes me and wants me to like her. Only a few short months before Bernard and I were huddled in the woods giggling over his secret pornography stash, unaware that such childish things were mere tips of the flames inching closer and closer to us even then.

Lust and fear are one as she raises her hands to her breasts and cups them. She asks me to please unhook her bikini top. I laugh. This can't be happening, but it is. She's serious; she means it. Don't worry, she says, I want you to.

While she continues to encourage me, I struggle with the plastic hook, my hands shaking.

When it finally comes free I feel a rush of excitement along with nervousness in my stomach. My face is so warm I know it must be flushed bright red. I worry that I look idiotic even as I stir beneath my shorts, feel it press angrily against my thigh.

She holds her top in place now, her hands the only thing preventing it from falling to reveal that which lies beneath, that which I have seen only in quick flashes and glimpses.

She is the most frightening and beautiful woman I have ever seen. So many times in recent months I have wondered if this would happen, and now that it is I'm unsure of what to do. The confident and skilled lover I am in my teenage fantasies is in reality an awkward and frightened fool—and besides, this is different, this is—I hate myself for being so weak and childlike. I smile, knowing this is wrong but gazing at her tanned skin just the same, a smooth bronze, soft and warm. She knows I'm looking.

Her hands fall to her lap and the top follows, fluttering to her knees, the strings dangling across her shins. Her bare toes, painted light pink, wiggle into the carpet and she turns at the waist so that we face each other. She slides one hand between her legs, rubs at the front panel of her bikini bottoms, and with the other reaches out and touches my face, strokes it gently with her fingers. Her hand slowly pulls my face toward her, toward her chest, and I go, I allow her to draw me there and to push my mouth against her. Her brown nipple brushes my bottom lip, shrivels, tightens and hardens. She moans quietly, her breath escaping in a series of murmurs.

I suckle, my mouth working, pulling, my teeth nipping as she forces me closer, crushing my face into her until I think I might suffocate. All I can smell is her skin and tanning lotion mixed with perspiration and perfumed deodorant.

Why I think of God then, I don't know. I think about my father too, wonder if he can see me, can see what I'm doing from wherever he is. I envision my mother next, sitting at the kitchen table like she so often does, sipping a drink.

I can't breathe—I can no longer breathe.

Her skins seeps sweat, and I slip against the pressure. Her belly is flat and firm—but still soft—and the perspiration forms a puddle in her sunken navel. With a loud popping sound her nipple pulls free of my mouth, and I fall forward, against her, my face sliding along the damp skin between her breasts. She pushes me back—gently—then takes my hands and places them on her. I knead her breasts, squeeze them harder when she arches her back and moans again. They feel almost exactly as I imagined they would. I manipulate them with my fingers, watching her for a sign that this is what I'm supposed to do next.

It's okay to be frightened, she tells me. It's okay.

Then she is suddenly on her feet, her back to me again as she hitches her bikini bottoms with her thumbs and peels them down, revealing the two sculpted halves of her ass, milky and white against her otherwise tanned skin. Even her breasts are not this pale in comparison. As she steps out of the pants and drops them to the floor she smiles at me. I watch her buttocks bounce a bit, and she backs into me so that they're against my face like two small pillows. She reaches around and again takes my hand, this time wrapping it around the front of her, pushing my fingers between her legs. She's so wet and sticky I wonder if there's something wrong, if it's supposed to feel like that, but she pushes me deeper, still standing and grinding against my hand now.

I try to pull away. I want to stop and I'm angry with myself for being such a baby but I don't know what to do or how to express what's happening inside me. I want—I have to stop, I tell her, and it sounds stupid and immature but I just want to stop. I want to run out of there and forget this, I'm not ready, and she's not the one I should be doing this with. I—I want to stop, I say again, shuddering as a wetness of my own explodes into my shorts.

Mortified, I wiggle away from her and collapse to the floor. I'm dizzy and embarrassed and when I look up at her she is so naked, right there in front of me—I've never seen anyone so naked—and this is wrong it's all wrong, all wrong, all wrong.

She kneels next to me on the floor, takes me in her arms and tells me to do as she says and everything will be all right. Trust me, she says. Trust me.

I don't want to do this.

It doesn't matter.

Darkness closes in and she swallows every bit of me, devouring scraps

I can never regain, pieces of me I can never rebuild.

Wandering through the house now in this new darkness, I stumble about, hands reaching for the walls, hoping they might guide me or give me some bearing. None of the light switches work and I can't find any of the windows—where are the windows?

And then I am back in the same living room, and she is there on the couch, smiling at me. Her breasts are bloody, the nipples ringed in crimson and dripping. The sight sickens me, but she wanted me to, demanded that I hurt her like that with my teeth, and so I can taste her too—on my lips—her blood, her life, her soul. All that is inside her is now inside of me, and I'm afraid. I'm afraid.

She reaches out, walks her fingers up my leg like a spider and grabs hold of me. It's okay, she says, no one will know unless you tell. She drops to her knees, whispering her demented prayers again and smiling at me like a mannequin—hollow beyond her exteriors, void of anything real.

I am inside her again, this time between her legs.

She is warm, wet, empty and soulless.

I can feel blood running through my veins; I can hear my heart pumping it.

Something from deep inside her crawls into me, slips beneath my skin, slithers through me like a garden snake, its tiny head and scaled skin slinking up the back of my throat, gagging me as its tongue flicks at the roof of my mouth.

More echoes from the past taunt the present. Someone calls out to the angels, calls them by name. Someone screams in agony.

I'm certain it's me.

When those memories part like dark curtains, I again find myself at the top of the stairs peering into Linda's bedroom, listening to the sounds and watching all that is happening to her there. Her eyes meet mine, though briefly. She knows what I have seen, knows by the grimace on my face that I am terrified and repelled, but she is neither.

She is pleased.

Good...good...good boy, she whispers, though not to me.

I back away and move as quietly as I can down the staircase, my heart racing. I can see the door, am moving toward it, but it seems impossibly far away—painted on a distant backdrop—a light at the end of a tunnel I can never reach.

And then it's quiet, gone from me, buried so deep that maybe it was never there at all.

It wasn't until I came awake that I realized I had either fallen asleep or passed out.

My first thought was that I'd been sealed into a tomb of some sort, because the darkness I opened my eyes to was no longer dreamlike. This was real. The flooring beneath me was cool and damp, and at the farthest reaches of my peripheral vision I could make out only slivers of faint light. Visions of being deep in a grave, of having been buried alive flashed through my mind, and I tried to move as I came awake, gasping and lurching into a sitting position all at once.

What I intended as a screech strangled the base of my throat and came out as a gagging cough instead, and I scrambled around, flailing, slipping on the cement beneath me while trying to gain my bearings.

As the haze cleared and my eyes gradually adjusted to the near dark, I saw that I had somehow ended up in the basement of the house. The light was from a series of squat windows positioned along the foundation. The stale smell was worse down here, but despite the heat wave it was relatively cool.

I leaned against the brick wall and ran a hand through my hair. How the hell had I ended up here? I had no memory whatsoever of having left the upstairs. Slowly, I sank back down into a squat and tried to collect myself.

Across from me was an area that had once housed a washing machine and dryer. A bit further down the wall was the bulkhead, the doors intact but rotted and splintered in places. I followed the light to one of the windows and, on tiptoes, saw the backyard from ground level. There was still daylight but it was burning fast.

Night was on its way.

Behind me was a wooden staircase that led back upstairs. I remembered that on the other side of the door at the top of those stairs was a small pantry off of the kitchen. In my state of sleepwalking, hallucinating or whatever was happening to me, I must have wandered back downstairs, through the kitchen and down these stairs to the basement. "But why?" I asked the walls, the darkness. "Why here? Why here, Bernard?"

Something told me to look back over my shoulder to the section of cellar I had awakened in. Empty space. Brick walls and a cement floor. Nothing.

I walked back across the cellar, glancing at the array of thick cob and spider webs lining the rafters overhead. At the spot where I had awakened, I looked more closely at the rafters, at the wall, and finally the floor. I had either subconsciously put myself here or had been placed here by some external force for a reason, so I crouched down and searched the area for clues or some sign that might explain why.

On hands and knees I swept my hands along the floor. It was damp and a bit grainy from small particles of sand and dirt but I found nothing out of the ordinary.

Until my hand came across a small pile of dirt where the floor met the wall.

I looked closer, and though the light was sparse I managed to see that it was a small mound of some substance, though not dirt. I grabbed a handful and let it slide back to the floor between my fingers. It was gray in color and had a granular feel. Cement.

Cement from an interior wall that had been constructed to separate the washing machine and dryer from the rest of the basement.

Tracing the short jog of brick wall with my finger, I followed a logical path upward to a point where the debris had more than likely originated. The first few rows of bricks were intact, so I followed the narrow avenues of cement between them with a fingertip, running my hand along as if following a maze, and eventually hit a soft spot a bit higher up the wall.

On my knees, I looked at the brick more closely, and saw a small divot. I pushed my finger against it and it gave way, widened and grew as more loose granules fell to the floor and joined the little pile below. I continued working the area with my finger, pushing and scraping until enough had given way for me to get two fingers into the crevice. The brick began to loosen rather easily, and I realized then that it had been fitted back into this section of the wall and made to look intact when in fact it was anything but. I grabbed the face of the brick and wiggled it, and with minimal effort pulled it free of the wall with an eerie scraping sound.

Dust motes flew about from the now open segment of wall like tiny escaping entities.

I placed the brick on the floor and peered into the hole I had created, but I couldn't see a thing, so I tried one of the bricks next to it. To my surprise, it too gave way with little effort, and suddenly, the one beneath it fell out as well.

An odd clicking sound emanated from behind the bricks, like

dice or dominos clacking one against another, and I moved back a bit while still trying to gain a better view of what was happening.

Something emerged, sliding from the opening like the granules before it, but these objects were bigger and shaped in various patterns, and rushed from the open wall like they had been piled and hastily hidden away behind it.

It was the bright white color that gave them away.

I backed away, watched the growing pile of bones accumulate as they continued to pour from the ruptured wall. Little skulls and legs and spines and teeth and pelvises tumbling one atop another, cleaned and so white they appeared bleached, the remains of countless small animals that had been systematically killed, skinned and dismembered, their remains sealed off behind this wall.

Bile gurgled in the back of my throat.

The skeletons just kept coming, spilling onto the floor until the mountain of bones was complete.

I choked back the horror and realized I was seeing Bernard's early work, those things he had killed before human prey became the preferred method of achieving whatever sick and demonic triumphs he had hoped to attain.

Our mutual love of animals had been a common point between Bernard and me.

More fucking lies.

The fact that he had left the brick loose in the wall could only mean that from time to time he had returned to this portion of the cellar to view his little trophies from the past. He had come here and pulled that brick free and watched the bones fall as I had, then—what? What did he do down here? Plunge his hands into them like a pirate rummaging a treasure chest? Relive the moments when he first killed these poor creatures? Compare them to his slaughter of human beings? Was there any difference, or was it all just death, ugly, violent and unnecessary death, killing just to kill?

Regardless, it had begun the same for Bernard as it had ended, in a cellar, alone in the dark with his deeds and demons.

I wanted nothing more than to get the hell out of there, but crouched down and made myself study the bones instead. They were glossy and white. The sonofabitch had cleaned and polished each one.

I took a closer look at the opening in the wall and noticed something protruding from it. A piece of lightweight metal, the corner of a larger piece, was clearly visible. I reached in and pulled it out from under what I thought were the few bones that hadn't yet fallen out. But the items lying across the metal sheet were not bones. It was jewelry.

"Oh, Jesus," I whispered.

Several women's watches, rings, necklaces and earrings rained across the pile of bones. None of them looked to have any significant value, and one was even a medical alert bracelet. But they were scraps, belongings of human beings who were surely as dead and gone as the animals who had once inhabited those bones.

And Bernard had killed every last fucking one of them.

The bile was back. A shiver grabbed me by the neck and throttled me a moment, so I turned my attention to the piece of metal I had pulled free. To my surprise it was fairly large, at least two feet in height and perhaps one foot in width. The corners were worn with age and the entire thing was caked with dirt, but overall it was in relatively decent condition, and most of the colors were still distinguishable. The cartoon face of a man smiled at me, waving a hand as if we were old friends. I wiped at the dirt caked across it with my thumb and more shapes beneath began to form. Letters. I stood up and moved closer to one of the windows, holding it up to the slowly dying light.

It looked like something out of the 1950s. It was a poster of sorts, with an illustration of a man waving, complete with pompadour, big bright smile and a jumpsuit reminiscent of factory workers at that time. Across the top of the poster were the words: *Employees! Please be sure to wash your hands!* Each corner of the discolored and aged metal had a hole where it had been fixed to a wall, and along the bottom, in small but still legible print it read: *Buchanan Textile Corporation.*

Another evil souvenir, a clue, an inside joke—what? Had he laughed when he tore it from the wall? Had there been a dead body within reach?

Buchanan Textile was one of the old mills that had once operated in Potter's Cove years before. For decades now, like the string of other dinosaurs that had once constituted the town's industrial area, it was an old, immense, condemned and forgotten husk of a building on the edge of town.

Now I knew where he killed them, where he bled them.

I dropped the poster, left it there with the bones and jewelry of the dead, with the memories and nightmares and secrets, and slowly made my way back across the cellar, up the stairs and out of the house.

As I slipped through the side yard gate, I froze.

Rick was across the street, watching me.

CHAPTER 29

His Jeep Cherokee was parked in front of my car. Rick was leaned against it, arms folded. I crossed the street, approached him. "What the hell are you doing here?"

"I was gonna ask you the same thing," he said.

"You tailing me?"

"Yeah, since you went to see that chick in the shack in New Bedford."

"Thought you wanted out."

"I do."

"Then why are you following me?"

"Somebody's got to watch out for your stupid ass. Besides, I can't let you do this shit by yourself while I hang on the sidelines, ain't my style." Rick's gaze alternated between the house and me. "What's the matter?" he asked. "Don't know who to trust?"

"Do you?"

"Not any more than you do. But I'm hoping."

"Well that's not exactly the same thing, is it?"

Above us, the sky was turning bleak and gray. Storm clouds were creeping in off the ocean, promising much needed rain and a respite from the heat wave.

Rick sighed. "I figure it's like shooting craps, you know? Even if it's not your turn to throw, you take a long hard look at the guy rolling the dice, at his history and your history with him, then you decide. You place your bet and you watch him throw, and in a way, you're throwing too. You *think* you know, you even go so far as to bet on it, but until the numbers come up all you really know for sure is that you hope you're right."

"Maybe it's all in the history."

"That and the throw."

We were quiet a while, recognizing and remembering that history in each other's eyes.

"We good then?" I asked.

"You tell me."

I held my fist out to him, and after a moment he tapped it with his own.

I motioned to the house. "Have you been in there too?"

He nodded slowly, as if not certain he should, and from the look on his face I knew he had found the same things I had. Despite his efforts to mask it, the dread Rick was feeling was apparent. "Me and Donny checked it out. I was gonna tell you, man, but then when you headed here I knew you'd—"

"Tomorrow night," I said. "That's when we make our move."

"Tomorrow's the Fourth."

"Exactly, the whole town's going to be distracted with the fireworks, parties and all that shit. The cops will be tied up with traffic and crowd control. Nobody's gonna be watching the edge of town, and that's where we're going."

"Okay, I'll grab Donny and—"

"No, leave him out of it."

"Why?"

"Let him know what we're doing, but he stays home. We need somebody on the outside of all this in case something goes wrong. In case—"

"I say we stick together and—"

"*Rick*," I said, grasping his arm, "in case we don't come back."

He thought about what I'd said for a while before reluctantly agreeing. "Okay."

A moment later I said, "The old Buchanan Mill."

"You think that's where Bernard is?"

"The evil he left behind."

"What if it *is* there, what do we do then?"

I looked back at the house, at the past. "We end it."

CHAPTER 30

The plan was set, but still twenty-four hours away. Rick went to work and I decided to kill some time at Harry's, a quiet lounge I sometimes went to a few blocks from my apartment. I'd been drinking a lot more heavily than I normally did, but it took the edge off my constantly wired nerves, and although the results were only temporary, I needed the reprieve from anxiety liquor provided.

I recognized some regulars huddled at the bar, and since I wasn't in the mood for conversation, I ordered a drink and sat instead at one of the tables along the opposite wall. The bartender was a summer-hire I didn't recognize. He brought my drink along with a little white napkin, placed it before me and hung his hands on his fleshy waist. "Hot enough for ya?"

I was certain if one more person asked me that I'd snap. "Rain's coming."

"Yeah, any minute. About time, huh?" He scratched at the stubble along his chin. "You believe the shit going on?" He lowered his voice. "Scary, huh?"

I nodded, sipped my whiskey. "Sure is."

"You hear the shit he did to them poor girls? Christ. Sick mental fucking bastard."

I gave an obligatory smile and wondered if this was the way Bernard had felt when he was alive, knowing something no one else did, carrying around knowledge of things others could only speculate about and all the while pretending he was as clueless as the next guy.

"Anyway," he said, motioning to my drink, "you need another one gimme a holler."

I thanked him and he went back behind the bar. I sipped my drink and tried to clear my mind, but everything was piling up, streaming through me as if a floodgate had burst. Even stronger than what had happened in the house were the things Claudia had told me. I could hear her voice in my head. I could see her face, her body, her feline-like movements and dark eyes. We could not have been more different as people, and yet, I felt an undeniable bond between us. We were both isolated, in pain and afraid in our own ways. Truth was, I hadn't stopped thinking about her and all she'd said since we'd met, and wasn't certain I ever would.

A thunderclap shook the bar.

The rain had finally arrived, but all I could think about was Claudia, and whether she'd left town yet.

I finished my drink and signaled the bartender for another.

***

By the time I reached my car I was soaked to the bone.

The rain was falling in torrents, bringing with it the darkness of night and pouring from the heavens with a steady ferocity that made driving more of a challenge than it should have been. The downpour had begun to cool things down almost immediately, but the heat was still high.

With three whiskey and sodas under my belt, I took the highway to New Bedford.

Visibility was low, and by the time I reached the city limits the rain had become even heavier. Occasional forks of lightning split the black horizon, and thunder exploded every few seconds, as if in timed intervals. No one was on the street, and even the normally busy interstate was eerily empty.

I pulled onto Milner Avenue, which was deserted as ever, and followed it to Claudia's cottage. The entire area was pitch black. I remembered there had been a light bulb above the front door, but it too was dark. Between the rain and darkness I couldn't even make out the building until I turned toward it and crept closer with my headlights on high beam. The dirt lot was flooded, a mass of puddles and rivers as the rain continued its assault. I checked my watch, holding the face close to the lighted dash. It was only a little after nine. Claudia was a night person, so it seemed doubtful she'd be in bed at this hour. Odds were she had already left town.

Still unsure of exactly what the hell I was doing there, I wiped some rainwater from my face and neck and sat watching the cottage, as if for some sudden revelation.

It came to me in the form of a slight flicker of light.

I sat forward and squinted through the rain and swinging of the windshield wipers. A tiny patch of light wavered in the darkness.

I dropped the headlights down to low beam and waited. After a moment the front door opened a few inches. I leaned out of the car, into the rain. "Claudia?"

"Who's there?" she called from behind the door, her voice barely audible above the storm.

"It's Alan."

"Who?"

I shut the car off but left the headlights on. "Plato," I said. "It's Plato."

The door opened a bit wider, and I could see her eyes reflecting the light. "What are you doing here?"

I stepped out of the car. Thick raindrops pelted me like water-bullets. "I was hoping maybe we could talk."

"Didn't we already do this?" She raised a hand to shield her eyes from the headlights, so I reached in and shut them off. As my eyes adjusted to the darkness, I saw that Claudia was holding a candle. She opened the door wider still, but I couldn't see much of anything beyond her face. "What do you want?" she asked.

"Getting out of the rain would be nice."

"So go home, you got a roof there, right?"

"I need to talk to you."

"Again?"

"Yes, for Christ's sake—obviously."

She may have smiled a bit, but I couldn't tell for sure. She watched me a few seconds then motioned with her head for me to come inside. I tramped through puddles and mud to her front door. Rain dripped from my hair to my eyes and across my face. My clothes were drenched and pasted to me like a second skin. Claudia held the candle higher for a better look at me.

"I wasn't sure I'd still find you here," I said.

"Well I wasn't sure I'd still be here." She swung the door enough for me to pass and stepped back out of the way. Once I was through the threshold the door closed behind me and she was at my side, the candle providing enough light to reveal pieces of the front room and bits of us. Claudia was wrapped in a large white towel and nothing else. Her hair was nearly as wet as mine. "What do you want? What are you doing back here?"

I stood dripping on her floor. Rain spattered against the windows and gushed from gutters along the roof, splashing into puddles in the mud. "I just—I was hoping maybe we could talk for a while."

"You've been drinking, I can smell it on you."

"Yeah, a little."

"You one of those guys who grows a set once he's had a few?"

"I'm not sure what kind of guy I am right at the moment."

She shook her head, both annoyed and amused from the looks. "Look, I thought I made this clear before. I'm not in the business anymore."

"I understand that."

She spun away, walked over to a battered couch and sat down. Darkness closed around me, the light encircling her as she placed the candle on a rickety coffee table in front of her. "I was soaking in the tub, chilling out and trying to groove with the rain, and I'd like to get back to it if you don't mind. In case you haven't fucking noticed, it's nighttime, this is my place and you're here uninvited *again*. So I'll ask one more time. What do you want?"

I moved closer to her, closer to the flame. "Why don't you have any lights on?"

"They turned the electric off. I'm leaving tomorrow, so who cares?"

Lightning blinked, washing the room in blue for an instant.

"We're going in different directions," she said. "You're running into the dark and I'm running away from it. I tried to be cool with you before, I was honest, I told you what you wanted to know, so why are you fucking with me now?"

"I'm not fucking with you, Claudia. I..."

She glanced at my wedding ring. "Go home to your wife, Plato."

"My wife's not at home."

Her dark eyes blinked at me through the candlelight. "What do you think I'm running here, a lonely hearts club?"

"I'm sorry to just show up like this," I said. "I just..."

"You just *what*? Jesus H., you got any complete sentences going on tonight?" Claudia stood up, holding the towel tight against her chest. "You think you can just come strolling in here like Joe Stud and fuck me, is that it? Or you just slumming tonight, out for some cheap thrills? Wife's gone and you're all fucked up, so what the hell, me being a used up old junkie whore and all I'd have nothing better to do than to put my legs in the air for you, right? Man, what a lifesaver, thanks for coming by."

"It's not like that, I—"

"Get out." She moved out from behind the coffee table. "Just get out."

"I only want to talk."

"No you don't."

I stood staring at her, still dripping like some pitiful lost puppy wandered in from the storm. I had never felt so ridiculous, and never quite so alone. "Did Bernard ever come here?" I asked.

She left the candle behind on the coffee table and joined me outside the light. "Yeah, a few times. So what? Why?"

We were standing so close I could hear her breathing. "Do you ever still feel him?"

She closed her eyes as if hopeful that not seeing me might mean I was really no longer there. "I don't feel much of anything anymore."

"Claudia—"

"Just get out and leave me alone."

"Drop that wall a minute and let me talk to—"

"It's a good wall, a sturdy wall. Been building it for years. It keeps me safe."

"It keeps you numb," I told her. "I know because I've been behind one for years too."

"Better to be numb than in pain."

"At least if you're in pain you know you're alive."

"You don't have to be alive to feel pain." Her eyes glistened. "The dead feel it too." She walked away and mumbled, "Get out." But as she slipped into the hallway she allowed her towel to loosen, and it fell open to reveal her bare back and the curve of her buttocks in the faint candlelight.

I followed her. The hallway was short and narrow and led first to a bathroom that was filled with lit candles placed around the tub and on the sink and counter. I hesitated in the doorway, but she was not there, so I continued on to the bedroom at the end of the hall. A handful of candles burned here as well but did little to combat the darkness. The only furniture was a bureau and an old unmade bed, the sheets in a heap near the foot. Over the bed was a framed but faded black and white poster of Billie Holiday. The floor was bare. I stood just inside the room, watching the flames play in the night, illuminating what they chose to show me, including Claudia, standing beside the bed and still holding the towel in place in front of her.

Our eyes locked for what felt like hours, and though neither of us made a sound, countless words passed between us.

The towel fell to the floor in a twisting motion and lay at her feet.

An enormous black tattoo began at her left calf, wound upward, wrapped along her thigh and encircled her waist. It ended just below her navel, where it split in two. The forked tongue of a serpent, coiled around her, marking her.

Her pale skin contrasted with the dark hair on her head and between her legs, but the tattoo was so dominant it was difficult to look at anything else. She seemed smaller out of clothes, more petite and delicate, at ease and not nearly so tough. But the essence of her—the physically weathered essence—remained even in candlelight. The majority of scars Claudia had collected over the years were internal, but a handful lived in plain sight, material evidence of a brutal past sprinkled across her body.

She radiated a primordial animalism in her movements and stances, and even in her nakedness she possessed a raw and dangerous edge, a kind of unpredictability one might encounter in a tiger just released from its cage. I imagined her as sexually aggressive and wild, if not outright violent. Heart thudding, my eyes skulked across her body. When my eyes finally returned to hers, her face bore a look as alluring as it was defiant. "This is what you came here for, isn't it?" she asked quietly.

I nodded.

"Do you even know why?"

"No," I said.

"I can feel what you think."

As could I, and it sickened me. I wanted to take her, to fuck her. Hard. I wanted to hurt and abuse her in every way the darkest corridors of my mind could conjure. I wanted to hear her scream. And

I didn't know why. My anger and fear was frothing, bubbling to the surface, and I wanted to take it out on her. Maybe because others had, maybe because I could, maybe because I imagined it was all she knew.

"I've never had thoughts like this," I stammered.

"Yes you have. You just keep them bound like all good devils."

"They're not me. They're not who I want to be."

"They're not who any of us wants to be."

There is instinct, and there is judgment.

I crossed the room in two long strides. My hands were suddenly in her hair, pulling her into me. Our lips met, and as I held her against me our tongues entangled and her hands slid up my chest and onto my shoulders, grasping me there with surprising strength before she broke the kiss and pushed me away. Nearly out of breath, I kissed her again. She tasted of cigarettes and rainwater. She cupped my face and looked up at me in a manner I had not until then thought her capable of. Deep inside her shreds of innocence still remained, vulnerability and need. "Not so rough," she whispered.

"Slower...gently. Like this, it's better like this." Her lips brushed mine, and her tongue softly traced my bottom lip before slipping into my mouth.

Still locked in our embrace, I lifted her from the floor, and the violence and madness left me like blood flowing from a fresh wound. In its wake lay the simple beauty of passion, of two scared and lonely people pooling their sorrow, trading it in for tenderness, for a chance to be safe and wanted and loved and needed unconditionally and totally, even if only for a short while.

At that very moment, I thought of Toni. But as Claudia wrapped her legs and arms around me, the thought retreated, leaving us alone.

There, in the dark.

CHAPTER 31

I met Toni in high school and immediately thought she was the sweetest, most beautiful girl I had ever seen. Cynical even for a teen, the instant and often overwhelming love we felt for each other surprised me, but like most couples that meet and commit in high school, our relationship was very intense. The highs were amazingly high, the lows amazingly low—a typical stormy romance—and not long after graduation we were forced to make a decision. Either we stayed together and got married, or went our separate ways as a test of our relationship, and ultimately, ourselves. If our love was real and meant to be, our theory concluded, then we'd end up together eventually anyway. Although it was painful for us, we decided the best move was to split up and see other people for a while. Little did we realize three years later we'd be back together and engaged, and that a year after that we'd be married. In the time we were apart both of us dated and slept with other people, but since our engagement I hadn't been with anyone other than Toni.

When I found Claudia I had no idea we would eventually wind up in bed together. It hadn't been something I'd thought about or even wanted until that night, and I was certain she had felt the same. But here we were. And while I struggled with feelings of guilt and regret, there was also exquisiteness to it, a raw sensuality and honest affection existing for a time amidst a dreamscape of devils and nightmares, an oasis in a desert of shadow.

It ended with silent intensity while rain sprayed the windows. The candles had burned down to nearly nothing, but lightning still blinked, illuminating the room every few seconds. Exhausted, we drifted off to sleep, her body draped over mine, head on my chest, breasts crushed against my stomach, our nude forms slick with sweat, warm and wet, entangled from head to toe.

In the night I lost my way, wandered from our sanctuary to the murky borderlands of sleep, where all that was ghastly and unclean waited for me.

I groggily opened my eyes. Claudia was still wrapped around me, her breath hot and steady on my chest. The storm clouds had dissipated and the rain had softened, giving way to the moon. Shadows moved along the walls. The floor creaked. I sensed movement before I saw it sweep past the corner of my eye.

Blended with darkness, new moonlight revealed several figures shrouded in black silently circling the bed, dancing around it like part of some ancient ritual. My muscles constricted in terror. I tried to sit up but my body remained paralyzed, stuck to the mattress and pinned beneath Claudia. I tried to call out to her but the words stuck in my throat, and the harder I tried to speak the worse it became. The figures continued their dance, increased their speed and began to violently convulse.

Claudia's head suddenly jerked up, her chin in my chest and her eyes alive and wild. "Ever wonder what happens when you close your eyes?" she giggled. "What comes awake once you go to sleep?"

I struggled to get her off me but my arms and legs wouldn't respond, and the more I attempted to thrash about the harder Claudia laughed.

"Get...*off*," I finally managed to choke out.

"Ever wonder what that odd feeling is you sometimes get in the night?" she whispered, looking over her shoulder only long enough to grin at the beings still circling the bed. "The feeling that you're not alone, that there's something in the room with you once the lights go down and it's quiet? We all feel it sometimes. Like maybe somebody or something is standing right next to your bed? We all open our eyes and look even though we know we won't see anything. But deep down you know you felt something, and it scares you. Know why? Because something really is there."

Suddenly I was able to move, and my arms pushed her away with such force that she became momentarily airborne before crashing back onto the mattress beside me. I scrambled from the bed, swinging punches at the darkness and releasing a primal scream. But the shadows were gone.

I staggered across the room, still off-balance, and crashed against the wall.

Claudia remained on the bed, sprawled out on her back. Snarling whispers filled the room as smoke rose from her body and it began to convulse. The cottage followed suit, shaking as if from an earthquake. Terrified, I scanned the room and ceiling, half expecting things to fall on me from above. I clutched the gold crucifix hanging around my neck. It had been a gift from my mother just months before her death. I held it tight as tears filled my eyes. Do you still believe? My mother's voice, from so long ago...

"Are you all right?"

The sound of Claudia's voice stopped it all as quickly as it had begun. I traced her voice to the bed. She was sitting up, watching me with a confused look on her face. "Are you dreaming?"

"I don't know," I said, voice breaking.

"It's okay." She crawled to the edge of the bed and sat back on her knees. Her body was still damp. "Keep the evil in your dreams and nightmares, whether you're asleep or awake, it makes no difference. As long as it's there its bound and you can control it. If it gets in here," she said, pointing to her temple, "*it's* in control. Once you let it in your head, or it fools its way in, once it's there for real, it can do whatever it wants."

Slowly, I moved back toward the bed, still uncertain of who or what I was dealing with. "Am I awake?"

"Remember what I told you." Claudia opened her arms. "It's all deception."

As I leaned in to accept her embrace I heard a strange cracking sound, like small bones or pencils being broken, snapped in half, cracked and splintered.

Before I could process any of it an appendage burst through her abdomen. Warm blood sprayed my face, and I threw myself backward to the floor as more jointed and furry appendages burst from her stomach and chest. Coated with blood and bodily fluids, her body glistened. With more cracking sounds her back arched and the spider-like legs clicked into position to support the weight of her torso.

I scuttled across the floor to the door, but it slammed shut before I could get to it. Behind it I could hear growling and scratching. On the other side of the room Claudia's destroyed body had transformed into some bloody, writhing and macabre hybrid of human being and arachnid.

Flames appeared, encircled the bed and rose nearly to the ceiling. The thing that Claudia had become was gone. Her normal form had been restored, but impossibly, she began to climb the wall like an insect might, scaling it slowly, as if crawling across the floor. When she reached the ceiling she stopped and looked down at me.

Her eyelids were gone.

From the darkness behind me two bloody hands grabbed either side of my face and pulled me back.

I fell against whoever was there, and their clutch tightened, the blood from their fingers sliding across my cheeks. In a voice that sounded like he had just gargled cut glass, he said, "Don't you know who I am?"

I struggled to break free but couldn't. The hands shook me, gave my head one quick but savage jerk, and I went limp. "*Bernard*," I gasped.

"Wrong," the voice whispered in my ear. Something wet touched the side of my neck. A tongue. Gliding upward. Hot. Moist. Fetid. "His father."

***

It was no longer night, but not quite morning either. Dawn was moments away, and the rain had stopped. Though the sun had not yet broken through the darkness, in the distance I could hear birds singing, welcoming its approach. I was still covered in sweat and had come awake not with a sudden jolt, but gradually, the way one might emerge from a peaceful sleep. I slung a hand out for Claudia but found only mattress and pillow next to me. My heart still racing, I rolled over. She was sitting near the window in a small wooden chair, smoking a cigarette and watching the sky. Nude, with her tattoos and dark eyes, she reminded me of a vampire anticipating sunrise and contemplating her escape.

Without looking at me she said, "You were having a nightmare."

"Yes," I said quietly.

"You were thrashing around." She drew on her cigarette. The orange tip glowed bright in the fading darkness. "Couple times you called out."

"Why didn't you wake me?"

"It's better to let these things run their course."

My body was sore and despite the nightmare I could have easily gone back to sleep. "Been a long time since I've woken up anywhere but next to my wife," I said.

She looked at me. "Is she coming back?"

"I don't know."

"Do you want her if she does?"

"We've been together a long time."

"Do you love her?"

I nodded.

"Does she love you?"

"Used to."

"But she doesn't anymore?"

"I don't know."

She turned back to the window. The sun had just begun to break over the horizon. "What's it like?"

"Being married?"

"Being loved."

I went quiet, unsure of how to answer. Had she still been beside me I would have pulled her in close to me and held her a while.

Eventually she said, "Did you dream about the dark?"

I sat up, swung my legs around until my feet touched the floor. "Claudia, remember before when we talked about Bernard's father? Do you know who it was?"

"No."

"Bernard never told you?"

"He made claims, but Bernard was a liar."

"Who did he claim his father was?"

She smoked her cigarette a while before answering. "The Devil himself."

Fear scraped my spine. "Did you believe him?"

"Of course not." She crushed her cigarette on the windowsill and tossed the butt to the floor. "But it doesn't matter if I believe it or not."

"Why?"

"Because it's all a mind-fuck, Plato." She crossed her legs, folded her arms across her breasts and sat forward a bit. "I think his mother got gangbanged like all the rest of them. Lots of guys, probably an animal or two—those types are into that stuff—could've been any number of people or things. All that matters is what she believed. And what he believed. That's what evil lives on—belief. You either believe it or you don't, can't change it either way. It just is what it is. That's where people fuck up. They think they can control what they believe. They can't. They can pretend they do, convince themselves they know what's real and what isn't, but they're just blowing smoke up their own ass. I told you before, the dark knows us better than we know ourselves."

I sighed and rubbed my eyes. "This evil, Claudia…can I kill it?"

"It's already dead."

"Can I stop it? Destroy it somehow?"

She smiled, but it was a helpless gesture. "Believe."

"Is it still Bernard I'm dealing with? Was it ever?"

"It's more about you at this point than you realize," she said. "In ritual black magic, human body parts are powerful ingredients, all with different uses. The first thing Bernard did to his victims was to take their eyelids. He made his prey look into the afterlife for him. Whatever he is now, he was once a man, so his struggles and obsessions are still those of Man. He's more powerful now, but he's not without weakness. He's faithless, and the faithless are weak."

"Why the hell is this happening to me?" I asked.

She shrugged. "It's the way of the world, his world."

I held my hand out. After a moment she stood up and accepted it. "If I asked you not to leave town," I said, "if I asked you to stay, would you?"

Claudia ran her fingers through my hair with her free hand then sat next to me on the edge of the bed. "If I asked you to come with me, would you?"

I managed a cowardly smile. "I feel a closeness to you I can't explain."

"I'm part of your nightmare, Plato. And you're part of mine."

She was right. More had existed between us from the very start than we'd realized, and even on this night more had transpired than just sex. Pieces of us had passed from one to the other, body and soul, kindred spirits clawing their way out of a shared hell. And wherever we were going, both of us knew then that regardless of final destination, we'd never be coming back. I touched her tattoo, ran my fingers along the bend in her thigh then kissed her on the forehead. She leaned into me and we fell back onto the bed together, quiet and holding each other as the sun continued its slow climb over the city.

For the first time in recent memory I slept peacefully, and for hours, through the morning and into the afternoon. When I finally awakened, Claudia was gone.

CHAPTER 32

As Rick's Cherokee pulled away I watched Donald grow smaller and smaller in the side mirror, receding into the distance the further we got from his cottage. Standing in the driveway, watching after us, the look on his face was a mixture of disapproval and guarded relief. None of us knew what Rick and I were walking into, and while Donald felt reticent about speculating, he had made it perfectly clear earlier that he wanted out. This time around I didn't blame him, but I could tell he felt guilty staying behind, so I didn't offer it as an option, which spared him having to reconsider while also providing a graceful way out.

The plan was simple. While the town was distracted with the evening festivities, Rick and I would check out the remains of the Buchanan Mill on the outskirts of Potter's Cove. Donald would stay by the phone and wait to hear from us. If there was no word by nine o'clock the following morning, the decision was his from there on out, either follow us to the mill and take his chances, or notify the police and tell them everything.

We took a corner and I quickly inspected my 9mm before returning it to the holster on the back of my belt. Rick brought along a large scuba knife he strapped to his calf whenever he went on one of his diving excursions. The weapon was double-edged, one side smooth and the other serrated, both razor-sharp. It lay in its scabbard on the console between the seats. In a sullen tone he asked, "You think we'll need any of this shit?"

"I don't know. Let's hope not." In truth, I felt like an ass. Two grown men with knives and guns on their way to a rumble with demons or ghosts or God knew what, going to war with the past, with some dark demented corner of ourselves. Straightjackets all around, please.

It was already growing dark. The sky had taken on a strange fiery glaze, streaks of red and orange mixed with rolling black along the horizon like brushstrokes from an ethereal painter-gone-mad hidden in the outlying clouds.

The fireworks were set to begin soon after nightfall, so the streets leading to and near the public beach, where tourists and residents alike gathered to watch the display, were already packed with bumper-to-bumper traffic and a bevy of pushcart vendors selling everything from flags to inflatable animals to food to glow-sticks. Luckily we were headed in the opposite direction, farther down the coast, and skirted the congestion easily.

We rode in silence for several minutes, the neighborhoods becoming more and more desolate the further we went. "When you hit the woods, pull over."

"We can drive right up to the gate," Rick said. "Hop the fence and—"

"I got a plan." I turned and looked out the window, wrestling the tension, the fear. "Just do it, okay?"

"Sure." Rick gave an awkward nod. "Okay."

The old mills had all been built inland along a series of bluffs overlooking the Atlantic. They'd been constructed in a cleared out section of state forest, one after another, to form a line of enormous old structures on huge plots of paved land. The Buchanan Mill was first in line. Prior to the property was a fairly dense but minor section of state forest, and behind the mill was a short stretch of land followed by the cliffs then the ocean below and beyond. The next mill was nearly a full mile away, separated by an enormous expanse of parking lot and another small patch of forest.

We pulled onto an old service road, the pavement cracked and littered with potholes. "So what happened with you and that chick?"

"Claudia?" Before leaving Donald's I had gone over our conversations and all the things she'd explained to me. "I already told you everything she said."

"You believe her?"

"Aren't we beyond all that by now?" I asked. "Yeah, I do." I remembered waking up in her cottage to find nearly all trace of her gone. The candles were burned down and extinguished, and even the poster of Florida had been removed from the wall. The rain had stopped but puddles littered the area and water still dripped slowly from the gutters and dead tree branches. The sun was blanketed in a hazy glow as the heat again began to rise and burn away the remnants of the storm the night before. I wondered if Claudia had sat on the bed and watched me a while before she did it, contemplating the evening prior, or had she quietly slipped away while I slept, already thinking of other things, other places?

Visions of her flashed before my eyes, accompanied by images of Toni, and eventually, Bernard. We were all tied together now—forever—and I could no longer separate the three, could no longer think of one without also thinking of the others. When I'd been inside Claudia, her past—and those who had been there before me—didn't matter. It wasn't until I thought of Bernard having been there too that for one brief but brutal moment I'd been sickened, and from that point forward I knew that even if Toni and I ended up back together, I'd never be able to look at her again without also experiencing these spectral memories.

"So she's gone now, huh?"

I saw her in a blink, the towel pressed against her chest, her face washed in candlelight. *You're running into the dark and I'm running away from it.*

"Yeah," I said. "She's gone. She wanted to go someplace else and start over. She believed she could, anyway."

"Must be nice."

"Starting over?"

"Yeah."

I nodded. "Guess it all depends on how you do it."

"Think we'll ever get the chance?"

"Think we'll take it even if we do?"

"Probably not." He laughed lightly, ironically. "This fucking town's all we know, all we've ever known and probably all we ever will know."

"Kind of sad," I mumbled.

"It's not so bad. This is our home. Where the hell else are we supposed to go?"

The road had grown a bit more uneven and rugged. The Cherokee jostled us about and Rick slowed his speed. The beginnings of forest awaited us in the distance. "Pull over," I said. "We'll walk in from here."

We locked up the Jeep and stood near the edge of the woods. Just over the treetops, the highest points of the Buchanan building were visible in the distance, an unnatural glitch in the otherwise pristine skyline. The sun, all but swallowed by the horizon, continued to sink, a final hurrah of red glowing radiance filtering through the trees as it gradually slipped from sight. We watched the sky without speaking. Before we reached the end of the forest and crossed onto the Buchanan Mill parking lot, it would be completely dark.

Rick clutched his scuba knife in one hand, a large flashlight in the other. He held them both up, as if to remind me that he had them. In a sleeveless, skintight black shirt, black jeans and black hiking boots, hair slicked back and skin tan and muscular, he looked like some special ops commando on a night raid. But the usual expressions that colored his face, those of confidence bordering on arrogance, enthusiasm and an ease with himself and his surroundings, the premeditated satisfaction he had always drawn from being in control and self-assured, had gone missing. The last thing I needed at this point was a paper tiger.

"You all right?" I asked.

"I'm good." He slid the scabbard into his belt. "Let's just get this done, okay?"

I turned my head toward the distant sea. We weren't quite close enough to hear it yet, but I could smell it. I could feel it.

I could also feel faded vestiges of Bernard here. He had driven these roads, walked these woods, breathed this air and watched night close in over the tops of these trees the same as us. Had he done things here, *right* here? Had his victims looked at this same sky, all the while wondering if it might be the last thing they'd ever see? Did they know, as they stood on this very ground we now walked on, that death was inescapable? Did they cry here? Fight and plead for their lives?

Did they bleed here?

We trudged into the forest, moving toward glimpses of the distant mill through the trees. Rick took the lead with long, powerful strides, forcing me to hurry to keep up with him. The cool air the storm had brought with it the night before was already gone, replaced again with stifling humidity, but within moments we encountered a welcome and steady breeze bounding in off the ocean.

Unexpectedly, Rick came to an abrupt halt and looked around. "Why'd we have to come through here?" he asked quietly.

And then I knew he felt it too. Bernard had used this stretch of forest, I was certain of it. He had brought them here first. It made perfect sense. His earliest prey had been victimized in the woods, and for some reason it had a connection to the hideous acts he committed. This particular stretch was the perfect area for his demented games. Isolated but accessible, there was nowhere to go, nowhere to run other than to the rocky coast and ocean beyond, or the old mill. And once there, he would have even more privacy. No one could hear them. No one could help them. Cries and shrieks of terror and agony would go unanswered, echoing through the bowels of a forgotten and decaying relic.

"He brought them here, Rick."

He nodded but said nothing. The ghosts were back, and they spoke to me instead.

***

Bernard held her tight, one hand on the small of her back, the other cradling her neck. Her hair, wet and matted, streaked and stuck together in clumps from rain and dirt and sweat lay pasted against her cheek. He drew a deep breath, inhaled her scent, detecting earth—soil—mixed with perspiration and some uniquely feminine smells. He tightened his grip, held her closer still and leaned back his head. His eyes struggled to focus through the darkness and rain falling through the treetops overhead, tickling his face and reminding him just how alive he was. His lips parted, allowed the drops to trickle into his mouth. As it accumulated and sloshed free, running over his chin, across his throat and over his neck like the blood of Earth it was, he looked into what was left of her eyes. "Can you see God?" he whispered, so only she might hear.

Her clothes, strewn across nearby branches, billowed in the wind. He kissed her forehead and squeezed her tight. Her bones, so close to the skin, brought him back. And then it was just the two of them—for now—there in the forest, Earth and sky, night and day, good and evil, blood and dirt, all exploding into one.

As he released her frail form, she slumped over into a bed of wet leaves, arms flopping out, legs bent and pinned beneath her. He rose slowly to his feet, his legs shaking and unsteady, chest frantically rising and falling as cold rain gushed from a night sky. He staggered to a nearby tree, found the knife he had plunged into it earlier, and yanked it free. Turning in a slow pirouette, he threw back his head, arms outstretched to worship the rain. His dance led him back to her, and he dropped to his knees, draping himself across her upper body, his cheek against hers, one hand clutching the knife and the other gently stroking her throat. Cracked and battered lips moved as the woman's chest heaved. He pressed his ear to her mouth. "Kill me," she whispered.

He touched her face tenderly, stunned she still had the strength to speak. "What do you see?" he asked, gazing into her mangled eyes. "Tell me what you see."

The wind answered, as did the rain, but she could not.

"Tell me," he insisted. "I need…I need to know for sure."

Thunder rumbled in the distance, breaking his concentration. He stood up, slipped the knife between his teeth and grabbed her by the feet. Trudging through the leaves and mud, he dragged her to the designated tree, found the rope and used the dangling end to bind her legs at the ankle. With three strong pulls of the rope she was raised upward, her limp nude body swaying, arms and hair hanging, reaching for the ground.

Once the rope was secured, he pulled the knife from his mouth and squatted so his face was in line with hers. He pawed at his eyes, wiped away the rain and gently brushed his lips against her.

"It's all right to be afraid." He looked to the section of forest from which he'd come. Interspersed with flashes of lightning, visions of him skipping and tossing her clothes as he went flickered through his mind. And like a child who had peeked under his bed to find that a monster did, in fact, reside there, he struggled back into a standing position, feet slipping and sliding beneath him.

He placed the blade against her pubic bone with a disturbingly steady hand and found himself wondering if his suspicions were correct. Maybe Hell was here on Earth. Maybe he'd already found it. And as the master had tempted the one he despised—the one from Nazareth—all those years before, perhaps this too was little more than a final temptation, a test of his conviction.

Bernard turned back to the woman. "You're supposed to die screaming."

And as he thrust the blade forward, gripped the handle with both hands and dropped to his knees, gutting and tearing her open from pelvis to throat in a single ripping motion, she did her best to comply...

***

I was sure whatever evidence these woods had held was long gone. No one ever came out here, and animals and the elements would have destroyed remains within days. Months later, besides the ghosts and the stories they felt compelled to tell me, there might be a bone here or there, but not much else.

Silence followed the breeze, whispered through the forest. It hadn't become completely dark yet, but night was close.

Rick snapped his flashlight on. Through a loud swallow he asked, "You think there's bodies here?"

"Not here." I motioned over his shoulder. "*There.*"

We were mere feet from the edge of the woods. Beyond the last line of trees stood a chain link fence separating the beginnings of parking lot from the wooded area. Perhaps one hundred yards away sat the phantomlike silhouette of an enormous structure, the decomposed remains of a behemoth from earlier times staring down at us through rapidly darkening skies.

Without a word, we headed for the fence.

CHAPTER 33

Thankfully the fence was only about five feet high. We scaled it and dropped down into the parking lot, and I suddenly felt like I was twelve years old again, hopping fences and climbing trees, going on adventures like the world was still new and innocence still meant something.

Waves crashed the beach beyond as darkness closed in around us.

"My grandparents worked here," Rick said.

I'd driven by a few times but had never set foot on the property before. I vaguely remembered walking miles of beach or riding our bikes along the sandy coastline when we were kids, watching the huge old buildings ominously perched atop the cliffs, rundown and neglected even then. In those days they had represented intrigue and menace, dinosaurs at the edge of town only the elderly could speak of with firsthand knowledge. To us, as kids, they were oddities, the topic of endless imaginary possibilities.

"No unions then, fucking sweatshops," Rick continued. "In those days there was nowhere else to work in this town besides the mills. Broke their fucking backs in this place. A lot of people did. Made them old before their time."

"Life has a way of doing that," I mumbled. "Come on."

With Rick leading the way, his flashlight aimed at the cracked and uneven pavement before us, we started across the parking lot.

"I wonder if the cops checked out these buildings?" he asked a moment later. In the dark, and in this strange place, the sound of our voices was somehow comforting.

"Probably."

"I mean, they already said they know the killer tortured and murdered his victims somewhere besides where they found the bodies, right? These buildings make sense. They're about the only places in town where you could do something like that and no one would know. Problem is they've all been condemned and abandoned for so long they say they're unsafe to the point where you can't even walk around in most of them. If they checked them out, I bet they did it half-assed. That's if they even got this far yet. If you read the papers or listen to the news, they're all stuck on the drifter bit and the killer already being long gone."

The killer. Even now, he couldn't bring himself to use Bernard's name.

The smell of sea air grew stronger, and the wind off the ocean was a bit steadier, which helped to lessen the humidity some.

"I think even if the cops did check these places out they only found what it allowed them to find, what it wants them to see."

"*It*?"

We stopped, looked at each other. "Those other bodies were found because Bernard wanted them to be found and eventually revealed to the authorities. The rest of it, I'm not so sure about." He motioned to the mill. "I think whatever's in there is for us to find. Things he wants revealed to you and me. Maybe *only* you and me."

Rick puffed his chest out like he hoped to intimidate his own fear. "Something's either there or it's not, Alan."

"Maybe," I said. "Unless it all depends on who's looking."

Neither of us spoke for several seconds, but as we turned and continued toward the mill, I said, "I wonder why the town still leaves these beasts standing in the first place?"

"It'd cost a fortune to demolish the fuckers," he said. "Plus, it's Potter's Cove history. About all this shit town has for history, anyway."

Until now, I thought. Now town history would forever hold hands with violent and bloody death, with torture and mayhem and madness.

We were within one hundred yards of the main building when

a loud boom stopped us. The sky lit up over the mill, brilliant blues and reds bursting and streaming in various directions before trailing slowly toward the ground. The fireworks had begun, and against the night sky, in this old and forgotten hellhole, they offered a beautiful contrast, a magical presence of the surreal against an otherwise decidedly conventional setting.

Forgetting it all for a moment, we stood looking up at the sky like starstruck kids.

Every few seconds a new display briefly painted the sky, washing our faces in colorful hues that slipped past like headlights along the walls of a dark room.

The spell finally broken, we approached the front of the building. Rick slowly raised the flashlight, moved it gradually up the face of the mill. Most of the long vertical windows were broken or completely gone, and the few panes still intact were blurred with years of grime. The doors and windows on the first floor were boarded up, covered in graffiti and filth.

"Getting inside might be a problem," Rick said. "They got it boarded up pretty good."

And then, as I studied the mammoth before us, it hit me.

"I've seen all this before," I said quietly. "That night in New Bedford. The old factory across from the car lot, I—it was the same. It wasn't this building, but—but it was. It looks the same. I was in a completely different place, but what I saw was the same. What I saw was this."

Rick swung the flashlight around, pointed it at my chest so that there was just enough light illuminating my face. "Say again?"

"I've been here before."

I snatched the flashlight from him, aimed it at the front of the building and swept the beam across the first floor until I located a doorway. The large doors that had once constituted the main entrance had rotted and mostly fallen away, and a partially decayed wooden plank that looked like it had fallen from above and landed there ages ago was wedged diagonally across the doorway. It was all exactly as I had seen it before.

"There," I said, stabbing with the light. "That's the way in."

Squatting at one end of the plank was an enormously plump rat. Making odd grunting noises, it sat back on its hind legs, reared up and bared its teeth.

Everything was the same, the same as that night.

"Shit, dude," Rick whispered, "that is one bulbous motherfucking rat."

I trained the beam on the animal, and it reflected off its eyes, causing them to glow fire-red. As before, the standoff continued until, after a few contemplative sniffs, the rat turned, waddled to the end of the plank and dropped from sight.

"Let's go," I said.

We carefully climbed over the plank and through the doorway, and immediately slammed into a host of nauseating smells. I stepped over a pile of rubble and garbage and panned the light slowly in front of us. The nearest wall was covered with graffiti, and the floors were thick with debris.

"All this trash and shit, I bet some homeless dudes squatted here," Rick said, his voice echoing through the empty bowels of the building. "You think there's still any around?"

"There's nothing alive in this place anymore," I said. "Except them."

A group of rats a few feet ahead of us scattered, escaping into darker corners as the pyrotechnics resumed. Fireworks exploded and roared overhead like thunder, and multicolored shafts of light spilled through various holes and wounds in the building, shooting through the open spaces and puncturing the darkness. As one round faded, another followed seconds later.

I could hear the nervous cadence of Rick's breath beside me. "Now what?" he asked.

I looked up. The ceiling was so high I couldn't make it out. I turned to my right, brought the flashlight around and followed the beam to the far end of the large room. "This way." We walked through the debris and clutter, the ray of light bouncing with each step, and as the fireworks subsided for a moment, I focused on a hallway I knew would be there. My heart began to race as memories of the night in that factory—this factory—beckoned me. A clammy sweat broke out across my forehead. "Down here," I said.

Moving through the hallway, the building seemed to close in around us and become much smaller, and although once the fireworks started up again we could still hear them, we were no longer able to see them. The confined space rapidly became overwhelming, the walls narrow and the ceiling low. I swept the light up and down repeatedly as we continued on, trying to reveal as much of the hallway as possible.

The stench grew worse here.

We reached a smaller room off of the hallway. An old plaque to the right of where the door had once been caught my attention, and I focused the flashlight on it. "Looks like this was some sort of office." I wiped at the filthy plaque until I could make out a few letters. "Personnel, I think."

I slipped through the doorway. The room was the same one the woman had lured me to that night. There was garbage strewn from one corner to the next, and as I moved the light about the room, I saw the familiar symbols painted in red paint or blood smeared across the walls. What was once the door to the office had been suspended between two small stacks of cinderblocks to form the same makeshift altar I had seen that night.

The same as before, something lay beneath it in a heap on the floor, dark and unmoving, but I couldn't make out what it was.

"What the fuck's that shit all over the walls?" Rick asked from behind me.

"Hexes or spells—God knows." I sighed. "I have no idea."

"Is it blood?"

"I think so."

"Jesus."

"I think it's some sort of announcement, or a marking, something like that."

"Maybe it's a warning."

A chill of fear reminded me I hadn't thought of that. I nodded, swung the light over to the door across the cinderblocks. "That's supposed to be an altar, I think."

"What's that on the floor?"

I swallowed so hard I nearly gagged. "Not sure."

"I got a bad feeling about all this, man."

"Yeah, no fucking shit, do you really?" I shot him an annoyed look, crouched a bit and crept deeper into the room, toward the altar. When I was within a few feet of it, I realized that whatever was beneath it had been covered with an old wool blanket. I waved Rick over and handed him the flashlight. "Shine it here," I said, pointing.

He did, and I noticed it trembling slightly, along with my hand, as I reached for the blanket and yanked it free.

"Oh, Christ." I dropped the blanket and backed away. "No."

Rick kept staring, the flashlight pointed at it. "It doesn't look real."

I ran a hand through my sweaty hair. "It's destroyed."

He shook his head, his lips moving rapidly but soundlessly.

"That night in the factory," I said, "the woman lured me to this room and showed me her little boy. He was dead. They were—they were both dead." Memories of that night flooded my mind, but I no longer needed them, they had become truth right before my eyes. "Bernard's victims were all single mothers with sons. The killings were rituals, and Claudia told me the final victims, the final ritual sacrifices before he committed suicide would include not only the mother, but also the son."

"Why would he do that to a…a little kid?" Rick mumbled. "Why would he do that?"

"Goddamn bloodbath," I said. "He slaughtered him and painted the walls with his blood. He butchered a helpless little boy." I forced myself to look back at the small body crumpled beneath the altar, tossed there like the rest of the garbage littering the floor. That which Bernard hadn't savaged, the rats had. What remained was mutilated and battered to the point that when I had first seen it I wasn't entirely certain of what it was. I could only imagine the terror the child had suffered, the abject terror. Anger joined the fear coursing through my veins. "You motherfucker!" I screamed at the darkness, my voice echoing eerily in the empty space. "Motherfucker!"

Rick grabbed my shoulder, hard. "We need to get the fuck out of here."

I shook free of him, reached down and threw the blanket back over the body. "We're not going anywhere until this is finished." I faced him. "This ends here, tonight."

Just then, Rick noticed something in the darkness. His eyes slowly lifted, and I could tell from the look on his face that there was something above us. "Jesus—Jesus Christ," he babbled. "Sweet Jesus Christ in Heaven."

Following his stare, and then the flashlight beam to the low ceiling overhead, I saw the woman—the boy's mother—floating in midair.

CHAPTER 34

I was either in shock or frightened to the point where I was incapable of running. Instead, I stood gawking, struggling to prevent my mind from splintering, and a moment later realized the woman was not floating after all.

She had been crucified to the ceiling.

I heard Rick vomit as I moved closer and gazed up at the carnage. The woman had been gutted, and her emaciated torso lay open and empty. Nails roughly the size of railway spikes had been driven through her hands and feet. Her eyelids had been sliced away, and her eyes were sunken and covered in gray mucus, forever forced to look down upon her maimed child. Her face was drawn and sallow, just as I remembered it.

You here about the plumbing?

"No," I whispered, "and neither was he."

In those few seconds it seemed all sanity deserted us. We were in Hell, and I was so terrified, so overcome with fear, I could barely prevent myself from completely breaking down. Emotion was raw now, and all the rules of life and death had changed. Lies and truth, fantasy and reality, good and evil—they had all become one.

"He's here." I took the flashlight back. "I can feel him."

Rick wiped his mouth clean and gave a resolute nod.

I pushed past him and left the room. There were two small offices and a large metal staircase at the end of the hallway. We inspected the offices quickly. They were filled with broken furniture and garbage but nothing else, so I shone the light toward the staircase. Most of the steps were cluttered with debris. Two large windows at the head of the stairs were smeared with filth, but as more fireworks exploded, the colorful lights bled through the old panes and offered a glimpse of the top of the stairs.

In the flash of light, something on the landing moved.

"Fuck!" I backed away and nearly tripped. I swept the flashlight around but the beam wasn't strong enough, and darkness again swallowed the top of the stairs.

"What? What is it?"

"There's something up there," I whispered. "I just saw it move."

"More rats?"

I shook my head in the negative. "Too big."

"There must still be homeless living in here then," he said hopefully.

Rather than answering, I held my hand up for him to be quiet. We stood still a moment and waited for lapses between the fireworks to listen more carefully, but each time, all we heard was wind and ocean.

I climbed the first two stairs, distributing my weight carefully to make certain they could still safely accommodate us. Rick followed close behind. Once we'd covered three stairs, the flashlight was finally able to reveal the landing. I leaned against the railing and aimed the light, but from our vantage point all I could see beyond it was more darkness. We had no way of knowing if the second floor was safe to walk on, but something was up there, and one way or another, I was going after it.

We crept onto the landing and saw that the second floor was entirely gutted, an enormous open space with high ceilings. Again, the floor was cluttered and the same horrible smells pervaded the area, but the darkness here seemed different.

It was nearly alive.

I slowly swept the pool of light across the vast room.

"Who's there?" Rick yelled suddenly. "Come out, we just want to talk to you."

I glared at him but he didn't notice, his eyes staring straight ahead. There was no answer, no sounds of movement.

"You're sure you saw something?" he whispered.

As I slid the light along the wall closest to us, it illuminated a nearby open doorway. Shadows darted away, and this time I knew Rick had seen them too. "Positive."

My heart and mind were racing so fast I wasn't sure how much more I could endure. I wrestled with a tremor of fear, fought it off and stepped closer to the doorway. The light reflected off something within the room. Tiles. A wall covered in old filthy tiles.

"It's a bathroom," Rick said.

The sign buried in the cellar wall of Bernard's house had been taken from a bathroom, a bathroom in this mill.

With my free hand, I reached behind me, pulled my 9mm free of its holster and glanced nervously at Rick. He dropped a hand to the grip of his knife but left it in the scabbard. His face and neck were slick with sweat.

Another round of fireworks burst across the sky, and on this floor, with all the windows and open space, it lighted the area far more intensely than it had below. I pictured countless people gathered on the public beach several miles down the coast, watching the displays and enjoying their Fourth of July. I pictured Donald pacing near his telephone. I pictured Toni dressed in dark clothes, standing at my gravesite with another man and grinning at me from behind black lace. I pictured Claudia in her dark and dirty cottage, straddled atop me, rocking slowly, hands pressed flat against my chest, pushing me deeper into the worn, stained mattress, her breasts full, wet and dripping sweat as I tell her, "I'm closing in on him." And her shaking her head and whispering, "He's closing in on you." I pictured the families and loved ones of the victims crying and mourning, walking alongside caskets leaking blood. I pictured Bernard painting walls with the same blood, with body fluids and excrement, and from somewhere deep inside, heard the shrieks of the dead mingled with his laughter.

The fireworks faded to black, returned us to darkness.

We followed the shadows into the bathroom. The stench wafting from within was gut-wrenching, and as the flashlight crawled along ahead of us, we saw that the tiled walls were awash in a caked crimson so dark it was nearly black. I moved the beam around the room. The entire area was covered in blood. Even the floors were smeared with it. With the smell, in limited light and enclosed space,

I imagined it was similar to being trapped within the bloody carcass of some enormous, brutally slain animal.

"Over there," Rick said, his voice flat, void.

I swung the light in the direction he indicated.

A large industrial-sized sink ran nearly the full length of the back wall, above which had once been a mirror, though only shards and small sections of glass panels remained intact, fracturing our dark reflections back at us as if through some demented prism.

There was a line of urinals to our right, but only a few were still attached to the wall; the rest had fallen or been torn free and lay in pieces on the floor. On the opposite wall were the devastated remnants of stalls and toilets. Blood spatters were everywhere, like a painter had taken a very wide and wet brush and flicked it repeatedly about the room for hours, only to finish by taking up the paint bucket and dousing the area with whatever remained.

We inched closer to the sink. It had overflowed long before with what could only be a sickening combination of various body fluids and blood. Whatever the concoction had once been, it was now reduced to a dark gelatinous slop.

And within this demonic fluid lay a bevy of body parts protruding from the mess like dinosaurs stuck in tar pits. I moved the light along the sink, past a human head, to a portion where what appeared to be a torso floated on its side. Maggots writhed along the surface. Rick turned away and vomited again, and though my body wanted to join him, I was hit with violent dry heaves instead.

"Fucking slaughterhouse," Rick gasped.

I holstered the 9mm, bent over, put my hands on my knees and took several deep breaths. The pool of light fell between us. On the floor, facing the sink, an upside down cross was painted in blood. Other strange symbols had been drawn around it, along with a word that had been smudged and neither of us could make out.

"I can't even tell how many are in there," I managed a moment later.

Rick spat on the floor. "Have you ever—ever—felt anything like this before?"

I knew exactly what he meant. There was a pervasive sense of evil here, a tangible essence of it hanging in the air like dense fog, and it was so strong that I could feel it being absorbed into my pores, mixing with the moisture in my eyes, inhaled up and into my nose and clinging to the roof of my mouth. "No."

"We're leaving right-fucking-now." He staggered away and headed for the door.

I followed, trying my best to keep the light aimed in front of him, but he was at a full run before I reached the main room, and once there, it took me a few seconds to locate him. Firing the flashlight in various directions and calling his name, I finally found him running through the room, stumbling through piles of garbage and debris as he went, the knife free of the scabbard and clutched in his hand, blade down.

A glow of various colors lit the sky and a greater portion of the room, which gave me my bearings. Instead of making for the staircase, Rick had become disoriented and was running the wrong way, deeper into the darkness. "Rick, no! Wrong way! Wrong way!"

He looked back over his shoulder, nearly fell, quickly regained his balance and spun around in an attempt to change directions. But as he did so a loud cracking sound echoed across the room, and with a frantic and helpless shout, he fell straight down and out of sight.

The floor had given way and swallowed him whole.

I ran toward the spot where I'd last seen him, doing my best to keep the light level and all the while fearful the floor might also give out on me at any moment. I arrived at the hole quickly, crouched next to it carefully and shined the light through. A large section of flooring had collapsed and now lay in a heap on the floor below, along with Rick, who was sprawled out and covered in filth, but conscious.

"Are you all right?" I called down. He didn't answer, but moved groggily and shielded his eyes from the light. His arms and legs were moving, albeit slowly and with some effort, but it didn't look like he had sustained any serious injuries. "Stay there," I told him. "I'm coming down."

I noticed his knife near the edge of the hole. He had apparently dropped it when he fell. I scooped it up with my free hand and aimed the light back in the direction of the staircase. But before I had taken a step I heard a strange squishing sound, and from behind me came a deep gurgling voice.

"*Welcome to my Eden.*"

CHAPTER 35

A stream of fireworks shot through the sky, firing sparks into the air and releasing shrill wails as they fell to the ground in slow spirals. A rapid-fire series of red and blue bursts followed. The finale had begun.

Against the rear wall of the mill, draped in shadow, a huddled figure watched me from the darkness. Its head was shiny—slick and wet—and it wasn't until I stepped a bit closer that I realized it was covered in blood. His head was bald, like it had been completely shaved—the wig gone—but I recognized the face even before the eyes opened, two white orbs emerging from crimson. They looked at me as if I were some sort of anomaly, as if I were the one out of place in the universe. And maybe I was.

My emotions became too great, and even attempting to control them seemed inane. Laughing, crying and choking all at once, I was certain I had slipped off the precipice into complete madness, because that which stood before me was not possible, could not be possible, and yet, there it was. But with this awareness also came an odd clarity, a release and an acceptance of the inevitable—whatever it might be—and at the moment of this epiphany my fear tapered off, my tears stopped and I became surprisingly composed. I had come to this house of horrors to find the evil, to stop it or to die trying. And now, I had found it.

He cocked his head as if he had heard my thoughts. For a fleeting moment something in his eyes spoke to me, and I glimpsed who he had once been so very long ago.

"Bernard," I said.

"Come closer, Alan." His voice was a bit deeper than normal, and gurgled and reverberated like his lungs were full of fluid, or like he was gargling while attempting to speak.

I did as he asked, and the closer I got the wider and more intense the flashlight beam became. He was nude and covered in shining blood to his shoulders so thick and bright it looked almost like paint. The fireworks finale continued, one explosion on top of the next as colors rained through the mill and slinked across our faces and bodies. I followed one moving shaft of blue light to his lower extremities. He was crouched there in the dark like a suddenly discovered and cornered animal. Around his feet the floor was covered in a kind of jellylike mass of quivering flesh, blood and bone, a great deal of which was also on the wall behind him, as if violently thrown there. It looked to be gradually passing through the floor and wall to somewhere else, like little by little, it was being absorbed.

Not all spirits cross peacefully, Claudia had said. *Some hang on.*

He seemed to have a normal range of motion but moved groggily, and at a snail's pace. He reached a blood-soaked hand to his face, wiped a space clear around his eyes then looked away to indicate brooding, contemplative thought. As he exhaled each breath through his nose, more blood ran free of his nostrils and joined the sheen already coating him. Eventually he began to breathe loudly through his mouth.

Movement to my left distracted me. The shadowy figures from our nightmare stood several feet away, barely visible in the dark corner and just beyond the reach of both my flashlight and the illumination of the now constant barrage of fireworks.

But I knew who they were. I had seen them before.

"And you know why they're here," Bernard gurgled.

"You're not real," I told him. "None of you are real."

"Are your dreams real? Your nightmares?"

"You're ghosts in my mind."

"Close." He exhaled through his mouth with a loud hiss that sounded like air escaping a pipe, and his bloody lips peeled back into a grin. He no longer had teeth, only slick pink gums. "There are no ghosts, Alan. Only memories...echoes...residue."

"Why did you do this?"

The eyes shifted, and a black tongue slowly traced his lips. "It's my nature."

"No," I said, shaking my head. "You were my friend."

"A friend, a relative," he gurgled. "Someone you trust, someone you believe in. I have no unique characteristics; there are no give-aways. Don't you realize that by now? I'm everywhere, Alan. I'm everyone. *Anyone.*" His mouth opened wide as a gush of dark blood spilled from his mouth and poured over his chin. "The inconsolable, the weak, the lonely and the lost, the faithless and the unclean. The damned. The lovely damned."

The fireworks stopped, and both silence and darkness returned to the mill. Only my flashlight remained, along with the sounds of the nearby ocean. I tightened my grip on the scuba knife.

"You came here to kill me, is that it?" The wet white eyes dropped to my hands. "With your ridiculous toys?"

I stared at the monstrosity before me, my chest heaving.

"Well, I have *darker* toys," he said.

"Why are you tormenting us?"

Wet crimson fingers caressed his bloody chin. After a moment, those fingers reached out for me, the tips dripping. "Come together, Alan. I'll show you the beauty of torment." He grinned as I stepped a bit closer. "Did I mention your mother's down here with us?"

"My mother's nowhere near you."

"Can you be sure of anything anymore? Ever again?"

I forced a swallow. "I'm sure of that."

"You had such nightmares then," he said, using my mother's voice now. "When you were a little boy. Do you remember, sweetheart?"

***

I'm afraid—so frightened I can barely breath. I'm crying violently, choking, and my entire body trembles. But then I realize my mother is there—so loving and patient, with the most beautiful deep brown eyes I have ever seen. She is holding me, sitting with me there on my bed, rocking me in her arms and whispering to me. She smells fresh and clean and warm, and I feel safe. "It's okay," she tells me. "Just bad dreams, little one, only bad dreams." She gently wipes away my tears with her fingers, and the blur I had seen her through previously vanishes. "What were you dreaming about that frightened you so?"

"Something in the dark was chasing me," I tell her. "I was running and it was behind me and it was growling and biting me, biting me on my feet and on my legs."

She kisses my forehead. "There's nothing in the dark but the dark."

"There's monsters in the dark," I tell her.

"No such things as monsters, kiddo."

Even though I know different, I also know she will never fully understand, so I focus on her face, and the perpetual sadness in her eyes. I am afraid and she is sad. These are our markings, burned into our flesh and mind and as much a part of us as spots to a leopard.

"Why are you always so sad?" I ask. "Is it because Daddy died?"

"I'm not always sad, my love." She's lying, but smiles and kisses me again. "Think you can try to go back to sleep now like a big boy?"

I look over her shoulder at the darkness from the hallway leaking in under the door...or maybe escaping beneath it. There is nothing to see, nothing hiding behind the curtains or beneath my bed. But we're not alone. I can feel it. Inside me, I can feel it.

"Sweetie, it was only a dream," she says, sensing my uncertainty. "Are you still afraid?"

I shake my head. This time it is my turn to lie. "No."

***

"Leave her out of this," I said. "Leave her alone."

"But I gave her to you, Alan. I gave you your perfect mother."

"You don't frighten me."

"Everything frightens you," it replied, again using Bernard's distorted, gargling voice. "You're still a terrified little boy whistling in the dark, Alan. And I see you. I've always seen you. Now, you see me."

"And what do I see?"

He hunched over a bit, turned, looked down at the floor and back at the wall as if he too were dissolving into it. "The beginning. The end. The old. The new. The past. The future. Different faces, different names, different lives, but you're always with me and I'm always with you, feeding on you, on your fears and weaknesses."

"A parasite," I said. "A bleeder of innocent women and children."

"No one is innocent." More blood poured from his nose and mouth but he seemed not to notice. "I set those silly cunts free. I let them see their useless gods." The thing grinned again with its gums. "I'm on the threshold of something wonderful, Alan. You're the lost one, lost in your own self-righteousness just like the rest of them. The world doesn't want to stop me, not really, it gave birth to me—created me—and made me whole. The truth is in the dark, Alan. Here, with me."

"You're a disease."

"No, only a symptom. I'm the open sore festering and blistering across their flesh, eating them from the inside out and laughing at their arrogant attempts to ignore me. They don't try to stop me, they only pretend I'm not there. Nero fiddled, Alan." He sighed, ran a bloody hand across his equally bloody dome. "And Rome burned." He looked around like he had momentarily forgotten where he was. "I set those women free of their hypocrisy and meaningless lives. I gave them purpose. No one cares about some low-rent single mothers and their bastard children. No one cares if they live or die, if they suffer or bleed. The world won't miss them. The world misses nothing, no one. But I made them immortal. I brought importance to their useless existences. In death, they matter, don't you see? They have purpose. And now, like all of you, they belong to me. In my darkness, they belong to me. *I'm* their God. *I'm* their messiah."

The figures in the corner stepped forward, their forms crossing into the pool of light, their eyes black as a shark's, just like in the dream.

I squared off between them, doing my best to keep both in my line of sight. The bloody atrocity against the wall straightened, and a cage of ribs rose then fell within its slimy skin. Unseen things scurried beneath its flesh, scuttling about like spasmodically stirring insects. He caught my eye and grinned at me again, slurping blood from his gums.

It was no longer possible to find any semblance of Bernard in this creature. Gone were any traces of the little boy I had grown up with, played baseball with, rode bikes with, laughed with and experienced so much with. Gone was the young man I had become a teenager with, experienced the loss of our friend with and graduated high school with. Gone was the grown man who attended my wedding, who had been my lifelong friend. Yet even in the midst of this madness I couldn't help but remember him as a young boy, as it was perhaps the only time he had truly been who and what I believed him to be. For that little boy, for what happened to him, my heart broke, because the innocent small town boy Bernard had once been was long dead. And simple death had apparently not been sufficient. He'd been completely annihilated.

Bernard nodded. He had heard me thinking again. "You and I, we know quiet little towns are never what people think they are," he said. "Quiet little towns hide quiet little secrets … quiet little screams. Listen to the screams, the whispers in your mind. Obey them. The voices are mine, don't you see? In this world, and the next."

"You're no prophet, no dark messiah," I said, spitting the words at him. "You're no sorcerer. It's all lies. Fucking *lies* meant to frighten and intimidate. You're a lie."

"Not me, Alan—you. You're only real because I made you real. I fucking made you, all of you. My rituals made you real, and they made me a god."

The world is not always what you think it is.

"You're just a sad and pathetic little man," I said. "A loser full of rage and violence with delusions of grandeur. A deeply disturbed man, nothing more."

He smiled at those awaiting us in shadow, then at me. "There's no need to be anything else. Our capacity for evil, mindless brutality and destruction is unequalled. We're never free of it, Alan. We pretend to be, but we're never free of it. Those black places in our souls never let us go. Never."

The real world is the one underneath, and that world is different. It's shadows.

I ignored the ringing in my ears and motioned to the others. "I know why they're here. Just like in the dream, they're here for you."

"They're not here to take me to Hell, Alan." He blinked blood drops from his eyes. "They're here to take you."

My blood turned cold. "No."

"Come together, Alan," he said. "Wash with me in their blood, feel it running over you while it pumps free of their slowly dying bodies. Let it run in their filthy fucking streets. Bleed them with me, Alan. We're gods."

I held the knife down by my thigh, gripping it tightly. "I'm sorry for what happened to you as a child, Bernard. I'm sorry for what your mother did to you—to all of us. For that little boy, I'm sorry. But for what that little boy became, I'm not sorry. For that sorry excuse of a human being I feel no compassion whatsoever. You're the same now as you were then, the same as you allowed yourself to become. You're nothing. Powerless. Alone. And you need to die."

Bernard laughed, his voice bellowing and echoing through the empty space. Blood again gushed from his lips. "What happened to me as a child made you possible, you fucking fool. My rituals allowed you to stay behind, made you real. You should have paid more attention to what the whore told you. I'm already dead and buried. It isn't me you're dreaming of. It isn't me you see. It's you. It's yourselves you see, the part of me that lives in you, in all of you."

Screams cut the night, screams of unimaginable terror. Rick's screams.

"We're all one. We're all the same. Come home to me, Alan."

Rick's screams grew worse. "Stop it." I said.

"Everything you have, I gave you. It all started with me."

"Stop it!"

"Such beauty," he hissed. "Such beauty."

I pitched forward and lumbered toward him. Bernard rose from his crouch but made no attempt to defend himself. With a primal scream of my own, I slashed the blade down across his face then back across his throat. Swinging my arm in a violent repeating arc, I slashed again and again across the crimson mass, spraying us both with blood and bile. Bernard staggered back, still grinning, and finally fell back against the wall.

Winded, I slammed the knife into Bernard's belly, fell back and dropped to my knees. I reached beneath my shirt, fingered the crucifix my mother had given me.

Do you still believe?

I slowly regained my feet. Spattered with blood, I watched the creature watching me, slashed and punctured but still standing and still staring me down, still grinning.

Do you still believe what it stands for?

Blood pulsed from the thing steadily, and he slowly sank to the floor, sliding along the wall until he was sitting in the mixture of flesh and bone.

I stepped closer. "Do you believe in Hell?"

"Hell is on Earth," it gurgled. "See what's right in front of your eyes. The whole planet, they're all damned and don't even realize it. They're already in Hell. I'm just closer to the core, and now, so are you. You're all fucked. All of you, fucked."

Are you still afraid of the dark?

With a quick tug I snapped the chain holding the crucifix around my neck, pulled it out from under my shirt and held it tightly in my free hand. The flashlight had become surprisingly steady.

Do you still believe He can protect you?

"Do you believe in a God who never punishes?" I asked.

That He loves you?

"A forgiving God?"

That He has never forgotten you?

"Rather than a vengeful God?"

Are you still afraid of the dark?

I saw the crucifixes dangling in Julie Henderson's windows, her reality protecting her, remembered the day my mother had pressed this crucifix into my hand and told me she loved me. I remembered how not long afterward, she was dead, and all I had left of her was what I now held in my grasp.

Do you still believe?

"Tell me...do you believe in that kind of God?"

Blood ran from its mouth. "I don't believe in God at all."

"No," I said. "But I do."

I slammed my fist down into its mouth, past its slimy gums to the sticky wetness of its tongue, and as it tightened its jaws around my wrist, I pushed my hand deeper and stabbed the crucifix into the back of its throat.

It vomited up my arm with such force that I toppled backwards and crashed to the floor. I dropped the flashlight and it rolled away, sweeping circular light across the walls as it went with a strobe-like effect.

I saw my arm, slick with its blood up to my elbow. I saw the nightmare forms watching from the shadows.

"I *gave* you your beliefs." The thing that had once been Bernard stared at me with its wet white eyes then began to convulse and writhe. Faster and faster still, it became an impossibly rapid blur of frantic, hideously violent movement.

Growls and whispers circled me like a pack of wolves, and the old mill began to tremble and quake.

The building was coming down all around us.

CHAPTER 36

As the building shook, pieces of ceiling began to fall, the walls crumbled and the floor split. I got to my feet, stumbled through a pile of debris and saw a thick piece of old wooden beam within reach.

I snatched up the board and closed in on Bernard. His bloody form sat collapsed against the wall, still a blur, still writhing and shuddering with inhuman force. I raised the board over my head.

He stopped, suddenly still, the violence now around him, transferred to the collapsing building. The wet eyes opened, looked up at me with something akin to innocence. "Alan?" His voice was high-pitched, like when we were kids. "Alan? Help me, it's—it's so dark here, I can't find my way out."

I held the weapon suspended above me.

"I'm afraid! Alan, I'm—I'm afraid!"

"You're a lie. You're not real."

"But I'm you, Alan," he said. "I'm *you*."

I swung the board as hard as I could. It connected with the side of his face, splitting it open. He slumped over onto his side, spasms wracking his body, and with the mill imploding around us, I raised the board like a bat and smashed it down again and again, disturbingly calm and collected—cold—while I pummeled his head to a thick soupy pulp. I stood staring down at what I had done, oblivious to all else.

Maybe he was right.

I heard commotion in the distance followed by labored breathing, and somewhere through the numbness I heard Rick screaming my name. Everything came back into focus and suddenly he was standing behind me. His clothes were dirty, he was scraped and disheveled and had a small cut on the side of his face but otherwise looked unharmed. He was shaking from what appeared to be equal doses of fear and anger. "I saw him down there," he said. "I fucking saw him."

I looked back over my shoulder, but darkness had swallowed the creature.

"This way!" Rick called.

I dropped the two-by-four and dodged a chunk of ceiling as it hurtled past me and exploded against the floor. Shielding my face with a forearm, I ducked and ran toward the sound of his voice. The floor tilted and shook, and I lost my balance but kept running, rubble falling all around me.

Rick had found a pair of large vertical windows against the back wall of the building that reached to the floor and had been boarded over. By the time I got to him he had begun smashing the wood with his fists. It splintered and we both began peeling and tearing the pieces free. Ignoring his bloodied hands, Rick kicked and punched at the breaks until he'd made an opening large enough for us to squeeze through.

He grabbed my shoulder and pulled me toward it. "Go! Go!"

I pushed through, the jagged edges tearing at my shoulders and legs, and was met by a burst of fresh sea air. I tumbled to the ground, found myself lying on sand and surrounded by the tall grass that signaled the beginning of the cliffs along the rear of the property. The fireworks had ended but the sky was clear, and a three-quarter moon perched high above provided enough light for me to find my bearings.

I knew even then that if we took the time to negotiate the steep slant of the cliffs we'd never make it. The building would topple and crush us before we could reach the cover of overhang on the beach below. We'd have to run and jump and hope to do so with enough velocity to clear the beach and reach the water. From there, it was a matter of pure luck. The drop was not enormous but considerable—at least ninety to one hundred yards. Even if the water was deep enough at our point of entry, we'd have to pray the tide would bring us back to the beach in enough time to find safety against the base of the cliff. Otherwise we'd have to swim to deeper water and hope to get far enough to avoid the falling rubble.

Rick climbed through the opening and fell next to me in the sand. "The whole goddamn thing's coming down right on top of us," he gasped. "Keep moving!"

"There's nowhere to go but down!"

Rick and I exchanged a quick, frantic glance. We were out of options.

With the sounds of destruction exploding around us, we ran as hard and fast as we could, right off the edge of the cliff.

I leapt, my fear of the ocean screeching in my ears as I clawed and kicked at the air in an attempt to straighten my body for the fall. I knew I had to hit feet-first or I'd be in trouble, but the moment I left the cliff I couldn't be sure of anything. I closed my eyes, and all the air in my lungs left me in a single frenzied rush.

I remembered plummeting as if in a void. Time stopped, all sound ceased.

Until I felt the crash of impact on the bottoms of my feet and the rush of water as I plunged into the ocean.

***

I kicked reflexively and rose to the surface, but initially had no idea where I was or in which direction I was facing. I was swallowing a lot of water and knew I needed to fight the panic and relax to the extent that I was able. Once I had accomplished this I felt the waves carrying me, drawing me toward the beach.

I turned over, spinning toward shore. It came into view through the darkness then vanished beneath my line of sight as I bobbed along the surface. Still stunned and disoriented, I kicked my feet and swept my arms through the water, this time deliberately and to make sure they were still intact and functioning properly.

My legs brushed something solid, and I realized I was no longer floating but bouncing along the ocean floor with the balls of my feet. I climbed from the surf and flopped belly-down into a foamy pool of shallow water and moist sand breaking against the shore. I coughed out more water, wiped my eyes and face and forced myself up into a half-pushup. I could hear things crashing into the ocean, and saw debris raining down around me. Calling out for Rick, I jerked my head to the left then right, searching for him hysterically.

Across the narrow stretch of sand was the base of the cliffs. Safety. I rolled onto my knees and saw Rick tumble out of the ocean behind me, rolling lifelessly with the tide onto the beach.

Still gasping for breath, I crawled to him, put him on his back and dragged him away from the reach of waves. He came awake with a sudden, agonizing scream, and I noticed the sickening position of his lower body. His left leg was bent at an obviously unnatural angle, and a nub of thick bone with chunks of flesh dangling from it protruded through the torn pants on his right thigh. I had never seen a fracture so horrific but tried to downplay my reaction for Rick's sake.

I pulled him the rest of the way and collapsed against the base of the cliff with his head and shoulders in my lap. I tried to find my breath as his screams subsided and became muffled sobs. "My legs," he moaned. "Christ Almighty, my fucking legs."

I held him tight, his wet hair against my chin and my arms wrapped around his chest. "Hang on, man. Hang on. I'm gonna get us out of here."

He went limp, and for a moment I thought he'd died. But I felt his chest rise and fall. Though he'd only passed out I knew he had to get to a hospital, and fast. Police and fire personnel were more than likely already rushing to the scene, as the collapse of the building had surely rattled everything as far as downtown, and the disturbance in the ocean could easily be seen further down the coast, where the fireworks display had originated. But it would take them a while to locate us, and I wasn't certain Rick could hold on that long. I'd have to get him out on my own. It would mean carrying him on my back along the water's edge for nearly a mile. Once I reached the forest I could make the lesser climb then cross back to where we had left the Jeep. If I got lucky, someone might see us as I trudged along the waterline.

I looked out at the ocean. The ground had stopped shaking and although numerous small particles of debris still flickered about like swarms of flying insects, the massive portions of the mill that had fallen into the sea had now come to rest.

Exhausted, I allowed my eyes to close a moment.

As they opened, the moonlight revealed dark figures slowly breaking the surface of the waves, creeping toward shore, emerging from the surf and walking toward us like zombies, black eyes sparkling.

CHAPTER 37

I came awake with a start to find a young nurse gently shaking me by the shoulder. "Mr. Chance?"

"Yeah—yes." My body was sore from head to toe, and the hard plastic chair I had fallen asleep in wasn't helping. My clothes were filthy and still damp in places, and mud from my shoes had marred the waiting room floor.

"I'm sorry I startled you," she said warmly. "Are you all right?"

A daytime talk show was playing silently on a small television in the corner, and in a chair across from me a middle-aged Hispanic woman sat nervously leafing through an old magazine. "Yes, sorry," I said to the nurse. "I was just—I fell asleep."

She smiled. "Mr. Brisco is out of surgery and awake."

I struggled to my feet and followed her down a quiet hallway. "How is he?"

"He's got a long road ahead of him in terms of physical therapy before he'll walk again, and he may need further surgery at some point, but he's doing miraculously well." She stopped at an open doorway, motioned for me to enter then left us as I slipped into the room.

Rick lay in a bed against the wall. It didn't seem possible he could be so seriously damaged.

I sat in a chair next to the bed. "Hey, man. How you feeling?"

He opened his eyes. He was pale, drawn and groggy, but his face brightened a bit when he saw me. "Well, there goes my fucking ballet career."

I wanted to laugh but couldn't quite summon one. "You're going to be all right."

"So they tell me. You okay?"

"Little banged up, but yeah."

Without raising his head from the pillow he tried to take in as much of the room as he could. "Is it still night?"

"No, morning." I checked my watch, still uncertain of how long I'd slept in the waiting room. "I called Donald. He's on his way."

His arm flopped onto the edge of the bed. He opened his hand, offering it to me. "You saved my life."

I put my hand in his. He gripped it weakly.

"I must've hit shallow water, I don't know what the hell happened."

"We got lucky," I said. "When the mill let go, police and rescue responded to check it out. By the time they got there I had us a ways up the beach. They saw us, thank God."

He sighed faintly. "I'm all doped up, man. Can't think straight yet."

"It's okay, just try to rest."

His glassy eyes searched mine. "What'd you tell the cops?"

I checked behind me. The doorway was clear; we were still alone. "That we were up on the cliffs watching the fireworks," I said quietly. "I told them we were a bit farther down the coast than we actually were, and when the mill collapsed it shook the cliffs. We were closer to the edge than we should've been, lost our balance and fell."

"They buy it?"

"Yeah, no reason not to. Chalked it up as an accident and our own stupidity for being up there in the first place. They said they'd be by to talk to you about it. It's no big deal, just a formality. Tell them the same thing and we'll be all right."

His thoughts seemed to wander elsewhere, and I saw fear rise in him then gradually recede. I was sure he'd sensed the same in me. "I saw him, you know. When I fell. Down in that hole, I saw him." He motioned for me to come closer, so I leaned in. "He was biting me," he whispered. His eyes filled with tears. "He was down there waiting for me and he—he—"

"Easy," I said softly. I tightened my grip on his hand. I understood his tears all too well, but it was still difficult to believe he was actually crying. "I saw him too."

He looked deep into my eyes then, like he was praying I had told the truth. "How could we both—"

"I don't know."

"I killed him," he said. "I think I—I'm pretty sure I killed him."

I nodded. "Me too."

He sniffled, fought off the tears. "You think they'll find what's up there?"

"I don't know. I don't think so."

"But they're bound to find—"

"What if it wasn't really there?"

"We both know what we fucking saw, Alan."

"Like I said before, maybe it's all in who's looking."

"Well, when I look, I...I don't want to see this anymore."

"Hopefully there's nothing more to see."

His fear now in check, he turned to anger. "Why us?"

"Maybe he knew we'd listen. Maybe he knew we had to."

The devils in our heads grew quiet, slowly faded. Shadows moved along the walls.

"Always figured something was either real or it wasn't. But it's not that simple, is it?" When I didn't answer, he said, "I don't remember anything anyway. If I did I...I think my mind might come apart, you know? So I don't. I don't remember anything. Okay?"

"Okay, man." I gave him a look that let him know I understood. "Okay."

"Had some horrible dreams while I was out, though. Horrible dreams." He pulled his hand free of mine and wearily rubbed his temple. "But I can sleep now. They're over."

"Yeah," I said. "They're over."

***

Just outside the emergency room exit I found Donald smoking a cigarette in his typical manic fashion beneath a sign on the side of the building that read: No Smoking On Hospital Grounds. He looked tired and hungover but otherwise all right.

The sky stretched above us like a giant cloud-filled canopy, the sun a dull sphere veiled in haze. It wasn't yet noon and humidity had already thickened the air.

Donald noticed me standing there like the disheveled survivor I was. He looked guarded, uncertain. "I hate hospitals," he said. "I've been standing out here for at least ten minutes trying to convince myself to go inside."

I could think of nothing to say.

Smoke leaked from his nostrils. "Quite a Fourth in old Potter's Cove this year. First the Buchanan Mill collapses and a good portion of it falls into the ocean, then very late last night—the wee hours of the morning, actually—a terrible fire broke out over on Bridge Street. Seems Bernard's old house burned to the ground. Completely gutted and destroyed. The authorities are convinced it was arson. Isn't that scandalous?" Donald smiled ever so slightly. "Damn kids."

"Shame," I muttered.

"Mmm, pity."

I was glad Donald had torched the place, and was only sorry I hadn't been there to watch it burn.

"I saw him." His face cracked into an overwrought smirk. "In that house. In the flames, I saw him, Alan. I watched him watching me through the windows. I watched him burn." He studied me a while, taking stock. "As I was leaving something drew me to the backyard, to the trees. I saw Tommy standing there, but I wasn't afraid. I felt safe, protected, and completely out of my mind. And then they were gone and so was I."

I knew what it felt like to be gone, to feel like the world had devoured you from the inside out and left behind only a husk. We all did. We always had.

"What happened up on those cliffs last night?" I could tell Donald sensed my apprehension the moment he asked, but he gave no indication of letting me off the hook.

"We put a stop to it. In our own ways, we all did."

"It's over then?"

"As much as it ever can be."

"Why did he do this?" he asked angrily.

"I think Bernard came apart when Tommy died. Then when his mother...Donald, the same evil touched us. All those years ago Bernard drowned in it and the rest of us pretended none of it ever happened. He knew what frightened us because it frightened him too.

It consumed him and wanted more. It wanted us."

His lips became a thin tight line. "But what did it—he—want?"

"I don't know. Maybe he wanted all of us to be together again. Maybe he woke up alone and afraid in the dark. Not a god, just a scared little kid. He knew us, knew our lives, our pasts. He knew what was inside us, what was lacking in us." I ran my hands through my hair and sighed. "But he was just out of reach. And to him, so were we. Kind of like knights chasing dragons, you know? They never caught one because in the end all they were really chasing was some dark, fire-breathing piece of themselves."

"How do you know they never caught one?" He exhaled some smoke for emphasis, perhaps in a desperate effort to lighten the mood and salvage our sanity. A moment later he said, "Nothing's ever going to be the same again."

"Would you want it to be?"

Donald pulled his sunglasses from his shirt pocket and slid them on. Our childhoods seemed so very long ago. "What did you find in that mill, Alan?"

"Hell."

"I'm not sure I believe in Hell."

I moved closer to him and lowered my voice. "They say you can't see evil, but you can feel it. We saw it, Donald. We all did. For Rick and me it was up in that mill, for you it was in that old house. We all saw what we needed to see—whatever versions we needed to confront and kill off. Whether they were a real entity, a part of our own souls, or both, I don't know. Is he really out there somewhere, watching us? Or is he only in our heads? Does it even matter? The only thing I know for sure is that sometimes you have to believe certain things to make it through the night. And sometimes you have to not believe them. It doesn't matter if they're real or not. Either way, it's all we've got."

"What about Bernard then?" he asked. "Do you still believe in him?"

I plucked the cigarette from his lips and tossed it away. "Bernard's dead."

CHAPTER 38

Toni was waiting for me on the apartment steps. I was too tired to be anything but happy to see her, but she was tense and looked worried to death. We said hello with our now customary awkwardness and went inside. I walked directly into the kitchen to pour myself a drink. She followed without being invited. I dropped into one of the kitchen chairs and said, "There was an accident."

"I know." She nodded so furiously a sprig of hair fell across her face. She hooked it back behind her ear without missing a beat. "Donald called me. He said Rick was hurt."

"He filled you in then?" I asked, hopeful I wouldn't have to.

"Yes." I could tell she wasn't having any of it. "Is he going to be okay?"

"He was sleeping peacefully when I left him."

Toni stepped from the doorway into the kitchen as if for the first time, looking around like I'd redecorated in her absence. "And how are you?"

"I feel like somebody worked me over with a crowbar, but I'm not hurt."

"I'm glad you're okay."

"Never said I was okay."

We were quiet for a long time, and in our self-imposed silence I thought of her alone in that cottage by the beach, and me alone here. Maybe being alone together had been worse, but even now I wasn't so sure. I thought of her smiling, pleased I was still able to recall it. I thought of how deeply I loved this woman. How I loved the lines in her face and the depth in her eyes. I thought of her body, familiar even as it changed—evolved and improved with age—the way living things do, even though they're also slowly dying.

"I'm sorry, Toni," I said. "For everything I've ever done or didn't do, I'm sorry."

She let me touch her, and instead of wincing or recoiling, she fell into me the same as she had years ago, before we knew the future.

"Me too." She kissed my cheek.

"Come home."

"I can't," she said faintly. "And you know it."

I sat back, away from her, only then aware that for her, our embrace had been a goodbye. She was already there, already living a different life, a life apart from me.

As Donald had said, nothing would ever be the same again.

She began to cry, though silently, one hand pressed flat against her forehead and the other gripping her side, her delicate frame bucking subtly. "I love you, Alan," she finally said, her voice shaking. "But we can't do this anymore."

"I always meant to protect you, Toni. Not to drive you away or to hurt you, never to hurt you."

She wiped the tears from her cheeks, and I envied her. I wanted to do it, to be the one to dry her tears like I once had. "I'm not having an affair." She said it in a way so void of emotion it startled me to silence. "I didn't leave you for someone else. I just left."

Despite the ghosts, we had once found safety in our love; it had protected us. But now our very presence tied us to a past we both wanted to forget enormous pieces of, and no matter how much we loved each other we could never undo that which was already done. Our pain had always outweighed our joy, but in these recent seasons of violence and blood, memory and nightmares, death and rebirth, it had become impossible to segregate one from the other.

"Gene's just a friend," she said. "He helps me sometimes. He'd help you too, if only you'd let him."

"If I did…would you stay?"

"I'm sorry," she whispered. "I'm sorry."

Like a drowning man still clinging to a life preserver he knows he'll eventually lose the strength to hold onto, at first I refused to let go. In my mind I fell into bed, asleep in her arms while we nursed each other back to health. I was whole and she was happy loving me. But then I let the life preserver go, felt myself slip beneath the surface and slowly sink, deeper and deeper, further and further away from her.

Although the finality was frightening, there was also something peaceful about it.

Our secrets were safe with each other, even if we no longer were.

I pictured Claudia as I sat there stupidly, not for reasons of guilt or anger or even revenge, but because despite her very brief but real influence on my life—on my still being alive—she seemed make-believe, in a sense. And Toni did not.

I stood, wrapped my arms around her and kissed her forehead. She held on tight, but only for a while, and when she left, all I could think of was the escape sleep might once again provide. I wanted to sleep away the rest of this awful summer. I wanted to sleep until it all went away. I wanted to sleep until I learned how to live again without this madness creeping through my brain.

I'd already seen what was behind the curtain, and I didn't want to look anymore. I didn't want to look ever again.

I only wanted to sleep.

CHAPTER 39

Summer eventually left us but it refused to go without a fight. Though nothing of significance was ever found in the ruins of the mill itself, after its dramatic collapse the town selectmen ordered the remains bulldozed and immediately set out to have the rest of the old mills either destroyed or inspected for structural damage.

In late July, while crews were still working onsite, a worker accidentally came upon a shallow grave when he wandered into the neighboring forest to urinate. The skeletal remains of two more bodies were uncovered, and dental records identified them as a woman and her young son. They had lived in a low income section of a nearby city, and though both had been reported missing months prior, because the woman had a minor criminal record and drug problems police assumed she and her son had moved away in order to skip out on their rent. From the location described in the newspapers and on television, Rick and I must have walked right by it. Another of Bernard's slight¬of-hand tricks, perhaps.

The bodies brought the total number of victims found in town to four. The fact that one was a child caused even more press and greater anger and fear from residents and local politicians alike.

No one was safe now, they said. Imagine that.

But summer became fall and still the police had no answers or even any decent leads. Little did they know, they never would. A few people were paraded about as possible suspects in the press but all were quickly exonerated, and the violent transient theory remained the favorite of the day with both Potter's Cove residents and the media. By the time September rolled around the town and the "unsolved" murders had been featured on numerous national media programs, written about in scores of newspapers, and even two books were authored on the subject and quickly released. But nothing came of any of it.

Oddly, by October the murders were becoming a thing of the past, and people had gone back behind their picket fences and into their tidy homes, content with the knowledge that whoever perpetrated these hideous crimes was gone. Like someone who wakes up terrified but just as quickly slips back once they realize it was only a nightmare, the people of Potter's Cove closed their eyes and went back to sleep. The same quiet secrets, the same quiet screams still resided here, but townsfolk were no longer listening. A few well-meaning law enforcement people vowed to solve the murders, but no one ever did. News reports became fewer and further between, and the police and FBI presence in town dwindled. Interest waned, and I fell into line with everyone else, just another sleepwalker pretending all was well.

Of course the knowledge I had left me with tremendous guilt, and every time I'd see a family member of one of the murder victims in the newspaper, their faces so full of dread and anguish, I wanted desperately to tell them what I knew. But who would believe it? Even months later I wasn't sure I believed it myself. Anything I might have done would only make things worse for them, would only complicate matters. Their loved ones were gone and they weren't coming back whether I told them ghost stories or not. Bernard would never be found out, and even I had no proof that he had done anything other than kill himself. So I lived with the knowledge and stopped reading the articles, stopped looking at the pictures of mourning and confused family members hoping for explanations.

The leaves turned and the air became crisper—especially in the evenings. I tried my best to occupy my mind with things more pleasant. I even tried to write again, but every time I sat down with paper and pen, all I could see was Toni or Rick or Donald or Bernard, or those faces in the newspaper and all the sorrow and screams and blood that came with them.

The decision to leave town was surprisingly easy. Though Potter's

Cove was all I had ever known, it was time to go somewhere else and hopefully start again. Within a few days I'd be in Florida, and just as Toni had once wondered aloud, I couldn't be sure anyone would even notice, much less care or try to stop me. In fact, in my mind, I had already left, and spent my time posturing like some strange hybrid creature suspended at a mysterious point between life and death, filled with perpetual uneasiness now rather than terror, forever destined to watch the windows for anything out of the ordinary, to feel that queasy and uncertain chill when strange headlights swept a darkened room, a telephone rang in the night, or a knock came on the door, forever bound to the knowledge that I was not alone and forced to survive on select memories and the reassurances I whispered to myself each sunset.

I still had bad dreams—and probably always would—but I was no longer having the bad dream. Like Bernard, it had returned to shadow, consumed by the lightless passages in my mind. But just the same, it left behind a residue, a slick trail like the moist wake of a slug, and those things within its wake would remain with me—with all of us—and bind us, one to the other, forever.

Pieces of the whole, as Tommy, Bernard's wise and patient best friend, had said. I'd never quite understood how right-on his description had been until all these years after his death. But it had been his death that started it all. Bernard was devastated, damaged, his young mind shattered into fragments at the sight of his only friend so violently taken right before what were then his eyes, and that's when we became like different sides to the same person, the whole split into several distinct and individual sections. Rick, our fearless and indestructible protector; Donald, our witty and urbane intellectual; Toni, our mother, sister, wife and lover, our consistent feminine presence, our voice of reason; Bernard, our evil and angry dark side. And me, a little bit of all of them, and whatever else was left.

Once fractured, Bernard was introduced to the darkness by his mother, and so we all were, and from that point forward we were reduced to confused and frightened children jockeying for position, doing our best to protect one another and trying to find our way through a world none of us understood or felt particularly comfortable in.

Much like our skin.

And whenever I thought of us together, I didn't see the tormented and devastated adults we had become, but the children I still wanted to believe we'd once been. Riding our bikes in the sunshine, chasing clouds and the dreams that lived behind them, coming more and more alive with each breath, with each new day. I preferred to remember us that way, healthy and happy—together—the way it was meant to be.

***

On my way out of state, I found the courage to return to Claudia's cottage. It was a particularly cold afternoon, which seemed fitting. I got out of my car and stood in the road, watching. With winter ready to descend upon us, it looked even more desolate, more detached from the rest of the world than usual, and maybe that wasn't such a bad thing.

I studied the clouds for several minutes that day. They were rolling, gliding across the sky—dark and full—graceful even in their impending violence, perhaps because of it, and it occurred to me, while gazing up at the top of the world, how truly insignificant we were.

But when I remembered Claudia—when I missed her—I'd think of this cottage.

I'd remember the cheap ceiling fan slowly rotating above us like a helicopter blade, the way it split the light and dark and formed zebra stripes across her nude body, her head on the pillow next to mine and her eyes opening as she whispered, "You can't outrun it."

I'd remember saying, "I want to wake up. I want to wake up now."

And her saying, "You're not asleep."

And I'd remember her dead in the blood-filled bathtub, eyelids cut away, wrists ripped open, the straight razor smeared and bloody on the floor just beyond the reach of her dangling hand, the poster advertising Florida—a destination not quite far enough—crumpled in the corner, candles all around, Heaven and Hell and everything in between watching us.

I'd remember touching Lucifer's tail as it flicked past in the night. And only then, with the Devil rising, could I begin to imagine what Bernard had felt, what he had done in my absence. Only then could I begin to understand his rituals and who he was.

Who we all were.

He had left behind more than evil and that which he destroyed. He also left behind that which his rituals had made possible: His creations, all of us living on borrowed time, on false memories and histories he had created—but alive nonetheless. A young man fractured beyond repair, gone but for those other personalities he procured to protect him, befriend him, allow him to be things he was not, and to make him whole.

Shadowy forms mistaken for demons and fulfilling his demented prayers, we cast him down into the Hell where he belonged, unaware that by doing so, we could never be completely free ourselves. His rituals had transformed us, but in the end, Bernard was only human and I hated him for it. I hated us all for it. Because without Bernard, there can be no us; there can be no me. And yet, without evil, there can be no deliverance.

Those horrible specters rode the autumn winds, carried off like pollen on the breeze and replaced now with absolution and a dark vision of Julie Henderson watching me through crucifix-adorned windows. "I know who you are."

I nodded to her, because now I did too.

Those gathered among the skeletal trees beyond Claudia's cottage called to me across the barren landscape, reached for me with leper-hands and gawked at me with dead eyes.

We're here, Toni whispered, her voice echoing in my ears.

"Sleep," I told her. The same as I'd told Donald, the same as I'd told Rick, and the same as Bernard had once told us all. But we were no longer one, we were gone from his nest and he was no more. "He can't hurt us now. It's all right to sleep."

I felt them leave me for the peace they had earned. I turned my back on those taunting me, on those bound and writhing in the unending darkness of the damned, and looked toward the future instead.

My wounds remained. They always would.

But at least for now they had stopped bleeding.

I closed my eyes and smiled, glad to know I still could. Like Claudia had said—for me, for us, and from now on, here in our world of shadows—it was all about the forgetting.

AFTERWORD
Eric Shapiro

Strangely, I'm finding I can't go into *The Bleeding Season* and its author, Greg F. Gifune, without first commenting on a philosophy book called *The Society of the Spectacle* (1967), written by Guy Debord.

Though by all outward appearances, *Spectacle* is indeed a book, it's actually more like a lengthy, sustained dictionary definition. It attempts to define what the author calls the Spectacle. The Spectacle is not what we at first might think in this day and age; it has nothing to do with fireworks, special effects, or professional wrestlers.

No, the Spectacle is (to the best of my understanding) more like a sheen that's layered over contemporary reality. The Spectacle is an ongoing, multifaceted force of reassurance, a saturating illusion that this reality is knowable and under control.

When you're at the ATM, and you see those crisp colors and compact fonts, that's the Spectacle. When you're watching the news on TV, and witnessing those fine production values and crystalline graphics, receiving information by way of confident, official-sounding voices, that's the Spectacle. The Spectacle is everywhere. It's in the very structure of our economy. It's in the packaging of our bills, the design of our computers and phones, the fabrics and dyes of our clothing, the language of our laws and stereo instructions.

It's hard to explain, which is why Debord had to lay it out across something resembling a book.

But the point is: the Spectacle's unreal. It's a lie we tell ourselves. It's mass hypnosis accumulating in the penetrating illusion that everything around us is navigable, comprehensible, and okay.

In other words, it's bullshit.

Greg F. Gifune does not exist in the Spectacle. He's opted out. That's why I love the guy and all his work.

The Bleeding Season does not exist there, either.

This is a novel that insists upon the deeper, more troubling nuances of reality. Some would, with good reason, place it in the horror genre. But I'd take a different tack, and propose it's one of those novels that, regardless of genre placement, simply makes the case that to exist in this reality is, on some fundamental level, horrific...

***

That's what Gifune gives you in *The Bleeding Season* and elsewhere: the horror of uncertainty. He doesn't have to take you to far-off places to get you there. He points out that this horror is right there, all the time, in the basics of not only your day-to-day activity, but your every waking (and sleeping) thought.

For example, how well do you know your spouse? Alan thought he knew Toni better than anyone, and her departure from him was—for him and for us—a departure from the stable, clean comforts of our everyday expectations.

Moreover, how well do you know your friends? Everybody in Alan's clique thought they had Bernard pegged, and look how that turned out.

It goes beyond trust in our fellow humans, though...

How much can we trust our own sanity? How stable is the borderline between what's real and what's not? How reliable are the memories we prefer to go to, as opposed to the ones that pay us sudden visits?

Gifune makes a strong case against the solidity of our reality. He punctures the Spectacle, and he doesn't even need monsters or evil to do so, although he uses them brilliantly. He'll make you think twice about what's really in the next room, the one you just walked out of. He'll make you think twice (and more) about who's really residing behind your own eyes.

***

I had my own clique growing up, as did so many of us. I also—though I still can't believe it—had an experience not unlike the hypnotic, tour de force scene in *The Bleeding Season* when Alan, Rick, and Donald listen to Bernard's tape-recorded suicide "note."

I won't name names, but suffice to say, my high school clique's equivalent of Bernard sent the rest of us, four of us, an email. In that email was a poem, as this guy had been the group's poet. I was the writer-filmmaker, we had a couple of painter-illustrators, and we even had a politician in the making who became a lawyer. I daresay we'd done better in life than the gang from Potter's Cove, but then again, we'd never had to endure the loss of a Tommy.

In any case, that wasn't the way our poet saw it.

He ripped into us, by way of poetry. It came out of nowhere. He damned us against our own past aspirations. He painted a present tense marked by despair.

As with Bernard, though, that was his world, not ours.

And fortunately, unlike Bernard, he was alive, which gave me the opportunity to respond.

But anyway, what if he'd been gone? What happens when the past speaks and you can't talk back? What happens when what you thought to be true is revealed to be false, and you're left in the maddening position of having to play catch-up and make spontaneous revisions?

Such is the nature of Alan's journey—he isn't Frodo going after a ring. Gifune's far too nuanced and realistic for that, despite his close companionship with the supernatural.

No, *The Bleeding Season* is a book about retracing.

Anyone who's ever gone through a detox knows what a healing crisis is: It's when the old symptoms flare up in an attempt to rid the body of disease. You can't bury disease, or else it'll just stay there. It has to be brought up.

That's *The Bleeding Season.*

It's also, in many ways, the social media age. Since the dawn of Facebook, Twitter, Instagram, and so on, world culture has swerved into a nauseating U-turn. Here we are, logging on each day and keeping tabs on people we haven't seen in three dimensions in 20 years. Here we are getting depressed 'cause our old crush gained weight and seems addicted to painkillers.

Talk about the Spectacle.

What's past is present. We're digging up the old graves. We've strapped on permanent memory helmets and don't go anywhere without taking everyone we've ever known along with us.

Which is why, sad and haunting as it is, *The Bleeding Season*'s final note has a ring of healing to it.

Gifune wrote the novel before social media opened its world-sized jaws and devoured us all, but his wisdom resonates just the same—perhaps more now than when the book first came out.

It's all about the forgetting.

We must, eventually, move on. To heal, to grow, to live in the world.

We can't carry the backpack everywhere we go, otherwise it'll weigh us down, and perhaps, as in Alan's case, drag us into Hell.

By forgetting, we gain a shot at innocence. I have two little kids; they're both so innocent. It's because they don't remember as much as I do. As memory grows, innocence goes.

So, forget. Move on. The sunshine awaits.

But remember, always, the stories of the masters, and all the things they taught us.

Eric Shapiro
Milpitas, California
March 20, 2018

Greg F. Gifune is a best-selling, internationally-published author of several acclaimed novels, novellas, and two short story collections. Working predominantly in the horror and crime genres, Greg has been called "the best writer of horror and thrillers at work today" by *New York Times* best-selling author Christopher Rice, "one of the best writers of his generation" by both *The Roswell Literary Review* and horror grandmaster Brian Keene, and "among the finest dark suspense writers of our time" by legendary best-selling author Ed Gorman. Greg's work has been published all over the world, translated into several languages, received starred reviews from *Publishers Weekly*, *Library Journal*, *Kirkus* and others, is consistently praised by readers and critics alike, and has garnered attention from Hollywood. Two of his short stories, "Hoax" and "First Impressions," have been adapted to film. His novel, *Children of Chaos*, is currently under a development deal to be made into a television series.

His novel, *The Bleeding Season*, originally published in 2003, has been hailed as a classic in the horror genre and is considered to be one of the best horror/thriller novels of the decade.

Greg resides in Massachusetts with his wife, Carol, a few cats, and a dog named Dozer. He can be reached online at gfgauthor@verizon.net or on Facebook and Twitter.

www.ingramcontent.com/pod-product-compliance
Lightning Source LLC
LaVergne TN
LVHW050920080826
845145LV00001B/151